Contemp                    tastic

*Also by Lucie Armitt*

THEORISING THE FANTASTIC

WHERE NO MAN HAS GONE BEFORE: Women and Science Fiction

# Contemporary Women's Fiction and the Fantastic

Lucie Armitt
*Lecturer in English*
*University of Wales, Bangor*

Published by PALGRAVE
Houndmills, Basingstoke, Hampshire RG21 6XS and
175 Fifth Avenue, New York, N.Y. 10010
Companies and representatives throughout the world

PALGRAVE is the new global academic imprint of
St. Martin's Press LLC Scholarly and Reference Division and
Palgrave Publishers Ltd (formerly Macmillan Press Ltd).

*Outside North America*
ISBN 0–333–69452–X hardcover
ISBN 0–333–69453–8 paperback

*In North America*
ISBN 0–312–22666–7

This book is printed on paper suitable for recycling and
made from fully managed and sustained forest sources.

A catalogue record for this book is available from the British Library.

Library of Congress Cataloging-in-Publication Data
Armitt, Lucie, 1962–
Contemporary women's fiction and the fantastic / Lucie Armitt.
p.   cm.
Includes bibliographical references and index.
ISBN 0–312–22666–7 (cloth)
1. Fantasy fiction—Women authors—History and criticism.   2. Fiction–
–Women authors—History and criticism.   3. Fiction—20th century–
–History and criticism.   4. Women and literature—History—20th
century.   5. Fantastic, The, in literature.   I. Title.
PN3435.A76   1999
809.3'876'082—dc21                                        99–36163
                                                            CIP

Printed and bound by Antony Rowe Ltd, Eastbourne
Transferred to digital print on demand, 2003

*For Judith, Jennifer and Rosemary*

# Contents

# Acknowledgements

Thanks are due to many people who have helped and supported me in this project. To Charmian Hearne for her editorial support. To Tom Corns and the University of Wales, Bangor, for granting me the study leave which helped me finish it. To departmental colleagues, in particular Ian Gregson and Peter Kitson, Ceri Sullivan for her remarks on my discussion of the grotesque utopia and Tony Brown for information on the Tylwyth Teg. To Linda Jones for her ongoing technological advice and internet skills.

In the wider academic community particular gratitude goes to Susan Bassnett, David Punter, Paulina Palmer and Barbara White for supportive criticism about aspects of this work at an earlier stage. Lynne Pearce, a trusted and valued friend and colleague, features centrally in this book. Her ideas on both the chronotope and the ghostly reader have proved immeasurably influential upon my own, even where we differ in our precise interpretation of them. Sarah Gamble, another valued friend, must take the credit for introducing me to Donna J. Haraway's *Modest Witness*. Avril Horner was an early supporter of this project and, along with Sue Zlosnik, was kind enough to send me an advance copy of their paper, "Daphne du Maurier and Gothic Signatures", which helped my ideas on the connection between ghosts and vampires to cohere. Most importantly of all, unending gratitude and admiration go to Scott Brewster, for his kindness, support, and generosity of time.

# Copyright Permissions

# Introduction

There is an obvious paradox inherent in writing on the "contemporary" on the threshold of a new millennium, particularly when the original publication dates of the 23 novels upon which the study is primarily based span the last 35 years of the "old" millennium. That we recognize the existence of the paradox also reminds us that the contemporary is not a synchronic "pausing for breath" which implies that a novel written in 1967 somehow shares the same politics or poetics as one written in 1996. Particularly in relation to feminism, the three decades in question have been both revolutionary and disappointing: so much has been achieved, and yet so much remains uncharted, or even lost.

It is fitting, therefore, that this book is Janus-faced in approach, looking forward (in both senses of the phrase) through futurist projection, while being repeatedly revisited by the past. Equally dualistic is its position regarding optimism and pessimism. Some chapters take a positive, celebratory tone while others (most noticeably Chapter 1, on the grotesque utopia) qualify or complicate such positivity in order to effect a collectively feminist self-interrogation. Boundaries, borders and thresholds are always key concepts for any reading of the fantastic, linking together concepts of nation and the otherworldly, bodies and the grotesque, housing and hauntings; but these metaphors are doubly applicable here. Poised on the threshold of the (imminent) future, we are located on what Louis Marin calls "Today, the separating gap . . . the interval structure".[1] As this reference to "the interval" reminds us, in an auditorium we reflect on what has gone before while anticipating what will come next. That moment of conjecture is the temporal hinge upon which *Contemporary Women's Fiction and the Fantastic* swings.

## Literary Antecedents

In the early decades of the twentieth century, Virginia Woolf's *A Room of One's Own*, first published in 1929, took as its theme the subject of women and fiction. Though Woolf's is not in any immediately recognizable way a text of the fantastic, several flashes of fantasy are to be found in it. One such is the "little fish" into which her insignificant thought metamorphoses once confronted by the face of the hostile Beadle. Another involves the fantasy scenario on the beach in which Phoebe becomes first "quenched in the flood of [Alan's] views" and then by his "passions" as "It" is done "very openly" and "very vigorously" on the sand. The third and most resonant is, of course, the ghost of Judith Shakespeare, who, though having "killed herself one night and [lying] buried at some cross-roads where the omnibuses now stop outside the Elephant and Castle", resurrects herself at the end of Woolf's text to "put on the body which she has so often laid down".[2]

It is not these disruptive moments alone that make Woolf's text the obvious starting-point for this book on contemporary women's fiction and the fantastic, but the major legacy two of the tropes she explores in that text have had upon contemporary women's fiction, namely the room (which she sets out as the crucial space for female creativity) and the problematic relationship between the narrative "I" and textual authority and the unified subject, a problem much deliberated upon by female writers (fictional and non-fictional) since. The room is, of course, a microcosm of the domestic interior, purportedly women's place and space. This is the rationale behind Woolf's choice of it, for if the domestic interior is a familiar space for women it has the supreme advantage of being an environment within which they feel sufficiently secure to embark on the risky process of putting pen to paper. Ironically, however, as woman's social relationship with the home has become increasingly alienated as the century has worn on, this apparently positive space has become a site of anger and tension. Domesticity as it features in the novels discussed in this book is almost always suffocating, claustrophobic and even, as we will see in the context of Octavia Butler's novel *Kindred* (1979), mutilating.

Gaston Bachelard helps to open up the domestic interior as a site of fantasy and the fantastic when, in the *Poetics of Space*, he attributes houses and rooms with a psychology seemingly of their own yet, in reality, projected upon them by their inhabitants. As his own title suggests, like Woolf, he finds in these spaces innate creativity: "The space we love is unwilling to remain permanently enclosed. It deploys and appears to move elsewhere without difficulty; into other times, and on different planes of dream and memory."[3] But Bachelard's relationship to the home is one in which gender identity is taken for granted. His house is a metonymy, the place of the good mother, who welcomes one home with tea on the table. In the novels under discussion in this book, while domesticity maintains these psychological characteristics, they are more in keeping with the tyrannies typical of the gothic. Mark Madoff notes, "The Gothic is full of locked rooms ... locked rooms of the mind; locked rooms of history; locked rooms of secret sexual expression".[4] Perhaps, then, we should note that even Woolf's eponymous room, which begins simply as "a room of her own", ends up being "a room with a lock on the door".[5] How significant that she omits to mention on which side of the door the lock is fixed, or who holds the key. But a lock does not have to be literal to imprison. Melanie, in Angela Carter's *The Magic Toyshop* (1967), is not *literally* locked in the toyshop (although the presence of keyholes infers its possibility); nor is Offred, in Margaret Atwood's *The Handmaid's Tale* (1985), *literally* locked in what she gradually learns to identify as a room of her own in the Commander's house. The lack of the literalism in the image does not prevent either protagonist from feeling imprisoned by their respective domestic interiors, hostile manifestations of the law of the father being the affective principle, rather than Bachelard's endlessly welcoming space of the good mother. In novels as culturally diverse as Bessie Head's *A Question of Power* (1974), Pat Barker's *Blow Your House Down* (1984), Isabel Allende's *The House of the Spirits* (1985) and Alice Thomas Ellis's *Fairy Tale* (1996), we find domesticity oppressing, disturbing, haunting and defying in potentially gothic ways.

Returning to the issue of narrative subjectivity in *A Room of One's Own*, in the passage immediately preceding that in which Woolf relates the story of Alan and Phoebe, Woolf's fictional protagonist "(call me Mary Beton, Mary Seton, Mary Carmichael or by any name you please – it is not a matter of any importance)" takes from the library shelf "a new novel by Mr A" and continues:

> ... after reading a chapter or two a shadow seemed to lie across the page. It was a straight dark bar, a shadow shaped something like the letter "I" ... Back one was always hailed to the letter "I". One began to be tired of "I". Not but what this "I" was a very respectable "I" ... I respect and admire that "I" from the bottom of my heart. But – here I turned a page or two ... the worst of it is that in the shadow of the letter "I" all is shapeless as mist.[6]

The obvious phallic resonances of the "I" here, from the "straight dark bar" which shadows the page to the unspecified "It" which takes place on the beach, sets up a long-standing discussion about the gendering of the affirmative speaking subject taken up subsequently by many critics. Adalaide Morris shares my conviction that Woolf's approach to subjectivity in *A Room of One's Own* is crucial to a full understanding of contemporary women's fiction. She notes that Woolf's character adopts, instead, the non-specific "one" as "a clear refusal to put her mouth to Mr A's megaphone".[7] But although Woolf does employ "One", both here and, in its possessive form, as the litany that names and reverberates through her text, we should not miss the fact that the phallic "I" of Mr A is not the only one (or 1) present. Ghosting it is Woolf's own signifier, the I which lacks *scare* quotes as it fearlessly shadows that "straight dark bar", seemingly "respect[ing] and admir[ing]" while "turn[ing] a page or two". It is this subversive ghostly presence, fractured between three clones (Mary Beton/Seton/Carmichael) of that "One", which renders this female protagonist "shapeless as mist" in a positive, possessive sense. Here we find the apparition of Judith Shakespeare: Woolf, it seems, has written us a ghost story after all.

## Contemporary Phantoms and Other Monsters

A similar ghosting strategy finds resonance here in two works of criticism that have proved highly influential to my own reading and insights. The first is Lynne Pearce's *Feminism and the Politics of Reading*, in which she adopts the strategy of the "ghostly romance" to document her changing interpretation of a variety of cinematic, visual art and literary texts.[8] The ghostly romance is, she reveals, a relationship set up between two "I" personae, both readers and both "the self that is Lynne Pearce", yet one past and one present, set up in a dialogic relationship with each other. Textually she differentiates between these two reading positions by means of differing fonts, ghosting one text upon another or, more accurately (as it is the earlier position that is documented in *sans serif*), allowing the phantom to erupt from within the main body of the text, articulating its subversions (like Woolf's) from within an apparently orthodox structure (the academic text). This disruptive eruption is not dissimilar to the cultural role played by the ghost in Terry Castle's *The Apparitional Lesbian*: "The lesbian is never with us, it seems, but always somewhere else: in the shadows, in the margins, hidden from history." Like Pearce, Castle bases her study on cinematic, visual art and literary texts, but where, for Pearce, the ghost emerges as presence, the visible trace underscoring the surface text, for Castle the lesbian's real "flesh and blood" existence is "ghosted" by a patriarchy that wills her to disappear. So she fills the point of erasure in a text, that place where "The kiss . . . doesn't happen . . . can't happen . . . Even when 'there' . . . it is 'not there'".[9]

Daphne du Maurier's *Rebecca* takes over from Woolf at this point, becoming a mid-century ancestor to the contemporary female gothic with a key intertextual influence upon those strategies of ghosts and ghosting which connect women with women during the contemporary period.[10] *Rebecca* may seem an unlikely antecedent, being traditionally read as a popular gothic romance in which a young girl marries an older, richer aristocratic widower called Maxim de Winter. Rejected as inferior to her forebear, Rebecca, by servants, herself and, she believes, her own husband, a substantial part of the novel traces the unnamed replacement's sense of perceived inferiority until Maxim's hatred and murder of this first wife gradually emerges. The rest of the novel concerns the couple's successful attempt to save Maxim from prosecution (through false testimony) and ends with Manderley, the family home, being burnt to the ground, presumably by the vengeful housekeeper, Mrs Danvers. This last section of the novel raises more questions than it answers, not least why this unnamed narrator is so determined to become the next wife of a man who might well prove to be a modern-day Bluebeard. It is this apparent schism between the surface and sub-text that enables the interrogative layer of the narrative to come to the fore.

Although one might expect *Rebecca* to fall into the type of formula set up by fairy-tales like "Cinderella", in fact its gothic elements render it closer to a reworking of "Snow White". The same triadic interconnections are set up between female characters and, as in the fairy-tale, they cross generations. In this context Rebecca begins the text as the first Queen, who is "good at everything . . . clever and beautiful and fond of sport" (*R*, 131), the dead, perfect ideal who "had beauty that endured, and a smile that was not forgotten" (*R*, 47). Only later does she metamorphose into the wicked Queen, as Maxim de Winter describes her as "vicious, damnable, rotten through and through" (*R*, 283). Remaining in its central place, however, is the central signifier of the magic mirror, which speaks with the voice of "the King" (here Maxim), convincing the unnamed protagonist of her own inadequacy as a rival for Rebecca, with her "lanky" hair (*R*, 105) and "tan-coloured stockinette frock" (*R*, 66). It is this crucial dynamic of "women almost inevitably turn[ing] against women because the voice of the looking glass sets them against each other"[11] that is reversed through my own use of ghosts and ghosting as an established reading position for this text. Once in place, Rebecca becomes a powerful influence on my reading of the phantom in avowedly feminist, contemporary novels, such as Jeanette Winterson's *Written on the Body* (1992) and Margaret Atwood's *The Robber Bride* (1993).

As my use of Pearce's and Castle's books implies, the fantastic is starting to play an increasingly powerful metaphorical role in the development of feminist criticism and theory in general, quite aside from its interpretation of the motifs of fiction. At the forefront of that development is the work of Donna J. Haraway. In *Simians and Cyborgs* she gives us "a cybernetic organism, a hybrid of machine and organicism, a creature of social reality as well as a creature of fiction" the hybridity of which, she claims, enables it to deconstruct "the mundane fiction of Man and Woman" while continuing to serve the specifically feminist concerns of contemporary women's writing.[12] In Chapter 3 I place this claim under scrutiny in conjunction with Cyndy Hendershot's concept of "The One Sex Body",[13] a combination that proves particularly productive as a strategy for reading the romantic relationship between Shira and Yod in Marge Piercy's science fiction novel, *Body of Glass* (1991). In Haraway's more recent work, *Modest_Witness@Second_Millennium*, she explores a variety of further, contentiously metamorphic female forms, looking in detail at two cultural hybrids, OncoMouse™, a patented product of the interface of transglobal capitalism and genetic engineering, and the FemaleMan©, offspring of Russ's novel of the same name, transformed in Haraway's terms, through the erasure of the intervening space between the two words "Female" and "Man", into "a spliced hybrid that signals a subject that looks suspiciously like an object".[14] But at the centre of Haraway's work lies a further "body of glass", Robert Boyle's experimental air chamber, a contraption which configures Haraway's reading of masculinity as objectivity, as discussed in full in Chapter 2. It is the cumulative complexity of a variety of glass surfaces – magic mirrors, Lacanian origin stories, Snow White's glass coffin, the winged hourglasses of Margaret Atwood's *The Handmaid's Tale* (1985) – that gives the latest contribution by Haraway such resonance in this study.

## Echoes and Exorcisms: Nineteenth-Century Reflections

In this reference to the looking-glass we find two further important intertextual comparisons in this book, both the product of the nineteenth century. The first is Mary Shelley's *Frankenstein* (1818), the second Alfred Lord Tennyson's "The Lady of Shalott" (1831–2). In *Frankenstein* we recall the moment at which the monster stares into a reflective pool of water, finding reflected back at him a hideous form he wishes not to own as his. Feminist critics in particular have made much of the obvious intertextual allusion to Eve staring into the pool in John Milton's *Paradise Lost*, Book IV (1667, 1674), but of course where God has to reprimand Eve for falling in love with her own image, the monster is appalled by his. Jenijoy La Belle refers to this moment as a "Shock of Nonrecognition", demonstrating the monster's own "feminine, exterior notion of self in which mirroring can play a key role". Anne K. Mellor qualifies this feminization by saying that this point signals the moment at which the monster is self-defined as "a unique being, an original . . . the sign of the unfamiliar, the unknown . . . without diachronic or synchronic context, without precursor or progeny".[15] Haraway demonstrates the falsity of Mellor's remark, providing another "hideous progeny", offspring to the monster in the form of hybrids such as OncoMouse™ and the FemaleMan©. In that sense, then, Haraway's work is as much that of reconceiving originary genealogies, writing new creation myths as it is an exploration of postmodern femininity. Indeed, in essence she demonstrates the interconnectedness of the two, as we will also find reflected in Joanna Russ's *The Female Man* (1975) and Fay Weldon's *The Cloning of Joanna May* (1989).

The second issue raised by the monster's encounter with the mirror is that he engages with what will come to be known as Lacan's Mirror Stage of subjective development, the child gazing at his/her reflected image in the glass and simultaneously perceiving within its surface the other who is and is not the self (the I and the not-I). But while Lacan shows us that we are all split subjects, a combination of the subject of the enunciating and that of enunciation, post-Lacanians such as Irigaray gender the paradigm to claim that women are doubly alienated from the self by the mirror.[16] But this need not be a negative phenomenon. As Morris asserts, we need a "first person plural in which the words 'first', 'person' and 'plural' would keep both their separate meanings and their collective force". Rosemary Jackson's view of the mirror dovetails perfectly with this stance:

A mirror produces distance. It establishes a different space, where our notions of self undergo radical change . . . By presenting images of the self in another space (both familiar and unfamiliar), the mirror provides versions of self transformed into another, become something or someone else. It . . . [suggests] the instability of the "real" on this side of the looking-glass . . . [17]

This brings us on to "the fairy/ Lady of Shalott", the key intertextual allusion for Chapter 5. Tennyson's poem is, of course, part of a larger intertextual chain of texts relating the mythology of King Arthur and his Kingdom of Camelot, sometimes read as fairyland by folklore scholars. It is, however, the dynamics of the room and its relationship to female artistry and the gaze that proves so important here. Imprisoned in "Four gray walls, and four gray towers" [l. 15], this lady conducts her artistry unseen, banished from gazing upon the world by her denial of the world of the window, substituted by that of the looking-glass, a space that underlines her relationship with the world of fantasy rather than mimesis, but that also enables her to express that fantasy for herself as she weaves it onto the tapestry held by her loom. She is thus a spinster in both senses of the word, a solitary woman and a woman who spins, although as Mary Daly reminds us, this identity can be positive. While patriarchy reads spinsterhood inseparably from the frustration of desire, Daly might well wish to reconceive this Lady as "She who has chosen her Self, who defines her Self, by choice".[18] After all, there is once again no lock which forces this woman to stay and she chooses to leave of her own accord, as the emphatic reiteration of the personal pronoun conveys: "*She* left the web, *she* left the loom,/ *She* made three paces through the room,/ *She* saw the water lily bloom,/ *She* saw the helmet and the plume,/ *She* looked down to Camelot" (ll. 109–13, my emphasis). This Lady does not make one choice here, she makes a whole string of them, hence emphasizing this is no momentary lapse in concentration, rather a self-willed, premeditated decision.

Of course, in typical fairy-tale tradition, it is the arrival of a handsome suitor who acts as the catalyst for the transformation that can never be reversed. But what makes Tennyson's poem so interesting is, as we have seen, the manner in which ideology is fractured, just like her cracked mirror, deflecting us away from any one reading. Though the poem purports to sanction female conformity, not focusing on the Lady's banishment but upon her apparent "punishment" and death resulting from rebellion, a clear critique of that ideology is woven through it like the warp to its weft. The Lady begins the text an artist and ends it as a work of art: "Lancelot mused a little space;/ He said, 'She has a lovely face;/ God in his mercy lend her grace,/ The Lady of Shalott'" (ll. 168–71). Following on from the suspicion of the villagers, who "crossed themselves for fear" (l. 166) at the sight of her corpse, we might read Lancelot's words as a consolation prize: she may be dead, but at long last she has won her heart's desire. But notice that from beginning to end, Tennyson makes it clear that the Lady has simply exchanged a living death for a literal one, a point highlighted in the poem itself when Lancelot's arrival, the catalyst for the transition, is immediately preceded by a reference to a funeral procession "with plumes and lights/And music" (ll. 67–8) (presumably the same type of plume she sees in Lancelot's helmet). Gilbert and Gubar's reading of this character is strangely unsympathetic. She is, for them, a manic depressive, a "mad, alienated artist",[19] but there is a far more intriguing duality here for me, and not just in the interface between two glass surfaces, the window and the mirror, those same surfaces that frame so many women, in this text and others, and that takes its obvious point of antecedence from Snow White's glass coffin. Tennyson's Lady is not the passively adored other Lancelot wishes to make of her. Her fascination lies in the active gaze she projects onto the world. She is a visionary, not a vision, a point that severs her relationship with the "wooden frame" (the boat) by which she appears to be encased in the final lines. Like Rebecca's signature, this Lady's name writes itself across both the boat and the page beyond her death. She is, in that sense, a sister of Scheherazade.

## Dora Meets Scheherazade

Scheherazade is *the* archetypal female storyteller, the frame narrator of *The Thousand and One Nights*, a collection of fantasy tales seeming to date from the tenth century. King Shariyar, disenchanted with all women since the proven infidelity of his own wife, selects a new virgin with whom to sleep every night, only to command her execution in the morning. Soon Scheherazade is the only virgin left in the land, but as she goes to King Shariyar's chamber she determines to outwit him by ravelling him up in the spell of her tale, spinning an elaborate tapestry of interconnecting narratives, each one embedding itself in the next as the last is closed off so that at least some of the threads of the tapestry always remain hanging and the Sultan remains gripped by the (narrative) possibilities of the next night. As the tapestry analogy demonstrates, this persona immediately signals a gendered dynamic of storytelling very much in evidence in this book, whereby fabric and fabrications come together. This is an ancient connection in fable and fairy story, but also manifests itself in more complex narrative works such as, here, Margaret Atwood's *Alias Grace* (1996), in which Grace tells her story to Dr Jordan while engaged in her own needlework or, more explicitly, stitching her own story into a Tree of Paradise quilt. These types of analogies are also found, in a theoretical sense, in texts such as Louis Marin's essay "The Frontiers of Utopia". Here, documenting the onward movement of the fantasy narrative as one in continual engagement with a quest to reach an ever-diminishing horizon, Marin sees the progression of that movement as one defined by the *"lisière"*, which he understands as "the fringe of an edge", "the space of a gap, but uncertain of its limits". More specifically, in the context of Scheherazade's elaborate interweaving, we find "a fringe-structure which has on the one side a well-determined edge, and on the other side an edge fraying"[20] as one narrative is fastened off and another opens up.

But this storytelling figure, who takes up the Sultan's time while outwitting him, never allowing him to reach the end of her elaborate fabrications, has a sister-self in Freud's famous patient "Dora". The similarities are particularly clear in Claire Kahane's description of Dora's voice as that of "the ostensible speaking subject, [who] told a piecemeal story to a privileged ear...[as] her voice issued from a body that was under scrutiny",[21] these dynamics being shared in *Alias Grace*. We return to the subject of Dora on several occasions in this text, including in the interface between Fevvers and Walser in Angela Carter's *Nights at the Circus* (1984) and, with regard to her Second Dream, the story of Melanie in *The Magic Toyshop*. Freud's Dora's story could be summarized in the following terms. Her parents become intimate friends with Herr and Frau K., with whom they stay while Dora's father recuperates from a long illness. The woman nurses him through ill health and the two of them become close, while the man becomes a particular favourite of Dora herself, accompanying her on long walks and buying her presents. Dora, in return, sometimes looks after their children. One day, however, Dora becomes distressed and informs her mother that Herr K. has made her an indecent proposal. Confronted by Dora's father, Herr K. denies any knowledge of the incident and suggests that Dora has fabricated the story. Dora having already manifested a variety of depressive symptoms prior to their sojourn with Herr and Frau K., her father chooses to believe Herr K. rather than his own daughter, a choice Dora attributes to her father's unwillingness to leave Frau K. with whom, by now, he is having an affair. Her astute belief is that she has become the commodity of exchange offered to Herr K. by her father in recompense.

Unlike King Shariyar, however, Freud refuses to settle for the role of spellbound addressee; instead he takes Dora's tale and spins a few circumlocutory yarns of his own. Refusing to accept Dora's interpretation of herself as an object of barter, he replaces it with a variety of salacious details, including his insistence that her refusal of Herr K. and the development of a nervous cough demonstrates that she is haunted by the threat of fellatio, a fear ironically inflicted upon her by Freud himself, who insists on soliciting from Dora graphic and detailed knowledge about her own sexual experience which, in their verbal exchanges, becomes another form of "oral" sex. Later, for a variety of rather tenuous and unconvincing reasons, he accuses Dora of bearing her own father ill will, not because he has betrayed her over Herr K., but because she desires Frau K. and is jealous of him. Finally, and inevitably, Freud also believes her to be in love with himself.[22]

Like Scheherazade's, therefore, Dora's story becomes a multi-faceted interweaving of embedded and interlocking narratives involving multiple members of her own family, two family friends, their children, and (for reasons not pertinent enough to worry about here) their governess. But while Scheherazade refuses to finish her story, Freud refuses to allow Dora to close hers. Having abandoned analysis for fifteen months Dora reappears "to finish her story". Freud insists, "One glance at her face…was enough to tell me that she was not in earnest",[23] but of course it is Freud who cannot shut (it) up. Instead, in this last page and a half he opens up an entire Pandora's box of tricks: the death of one of Herr K.'s children; the near death of Herr K. as he is run over by a carriage having encountered Dora unexpectedly in the street; the development of a new facial neuralgia by Dora, which Freud again manages to read as proof of her fascination for him; and finally her marriage – presumably the only way she can finally "give Freud the flick". The narrative does not end, it just stops, and at a point at which it can so easily be opened up again. This message is clear: Dora may have evaded his grasp for now, but she will be back – after all, the husband is set up as a mere poor substitute in this endless merry-go-round of Oedipal displacements.

Oedipal relations brings us to our final literary ancestor, E.T.A. Hoffmann's short story "The Sandman" (1816).[24] Most famously, for readers familiar with Freud's own works, Hoffmann's story is the centrepiece of Freud's essay "The 'Uncanny'", and it is both within and beyond Freud's text that "The Sandman" is shown to open up productive territory for explorations of the interface between the gothic and the magical real and the mannequin and the market-place in the context of the work of Isabel Allende, Angela Carter and Margaret Atwood. Hoffmann's story is first evoked in conjunction with Carter's *The Infernal Desire Machines of Dr Hoffman*, in which the explicit intertextual connection flagged up by the title is developed further in relation to their shared concern with the precarious relation between subjectivity and objectivity as embodied by the automaton. Subsequently we return to Hoffmann's text, but in this case in relation to a comparative treatment of the libidinal economy as depicted in "The Sandman" and Carter's *The Magic Toyshop*.

It is not just that the contemporary owes a profound debt to the past as it teeters on the brink of the new millennium, but that several of these novels explicitly juxtapose past, present and future within the core of their concerns. *Sexing the Cherry, Body of Glass, Kindred, Alias Grace*, as well as Angela Carter's *Nights at the Circus* (1984), Toni Morrison's *Beloved* (1987) and Jane Palmer's *The Watcher* (1986) all rework historical material relating to previous centuries from a late twentieth-century standpoint, while sometimes simultaneously projecting forward into the future. Others, such as *The Female Man, The Handmaid's Tale, The Cloning of Joanna May, Les Guérillères* and *Across the Acheron*, super-impose present and future possibilities, often by challenging our inherent will to believe the goal of feminism has been achieved. This superim-position will bring us to the subject of the chronotope, a concept fully analysed in another of Pearce's books, *Reading Dialogics*, in which she sets out to gender what she terms the polychronotopic text.[25] This dis-cussion forms the bridging point between Chapters 1 and 2 and is one of the keystones of my own argument for the political significance of fantasy and the fantastic.

I concluded my last book, *Theorising the Fantastic*, by posing the ques-tion "But What of Utopia?" a question in which is ravelled up issues of melancholia, the postmodern, loss and desire.[26] The first chapter of this book tries to answer that question by arguing that feminist utopias have moved on, and for the better, from their supposed heyday of the idealis-ing 1970s. In this chapter I look to develop a new, riskier reading of the utopia that focuses upon novels which ask questions rather than give pat answers, recognize problems even/especially if they cannot fully solve them, but remain firmly committed to the ongoing search for new horizons while recognizing that utopia will always, by definition, be elsewhere. Some readers may be surprised that this is not a chapter built entirely around sf (speculative/space/science fiction/fantasy). Such fic-tion features readily in parts of this book, but never in a manner that seals it off from the uncanny, the ghost story, the grotesque or fairy tales. Even *The Female Man* is read in a manner that refuses to prioritize its final peroration, so like Woolf's own, in which Russ signals the pos-sibility of an 'end' to her project:

> Go, little book . . . bob a curtsey at the shrines of Friedan, Millet, Greer, Firestone . . . behave yourself in people's living rooms . . . Do not scream when you are ignored . . . and fume when you are heisted by persons

who will not pay ... [D]o not mutter angrily to yourself when young persons read you to hrooch and hrch and guffaw ... Do not get glum when you are no longer understood ... For on that day, we will be free.[27]

My argument has always been, and remains, that carving up fantasy and the fantastic and jamming its literature into a series of discrete, neatly labelled boxes kills literature dead. So much ground has been lost in comparison with other fields of literary criticism while critics of fantasy have been futilely squabbling over whether a text is marvellous or fabulous, or how to subdivide science fiction into space opera or sword and sorcery. Although it could be argued, by any reader wishing to do so, that the skeletal structure of this book moves, chapter by chapter, from utopia, to science fiction, to vampires, to ghosts, to fairy-tales, to magic realism, to the uncanny, that is as far as the genre identification can be stretched. In essence, these terms are simply nodal features around which the central argument of each chapter clusters, while harnessing together novels which, left to their own devices, could not always fall into the type of "genre categories" such themes might infer, not least because, in some cases, they are discussed in different contexts in more than one chapter. So, to reiterate, this book blows genre categories wide open, as do the vast majority of the novelists whose work is discussed here. My use of key terminology reflects this concern. The term "fantastic" is employed, throughout, in line with its usage by Tzvetan Todorov, namely as a disruptive presence which oscillates around a narrative site of uncertainty regarding the boundary-points surrounding the real and the imaginary.[28] It is a term always differentiated from the term "fantasy", which is used less frequently, but equally specifically, either to denote genre labelling, a formulaic structure, or wish-fulfilment fantasy of the day-dreaming variety. Occasionally the reader will encounter the word "phantasy", a psychoanalytic term signalling the source of our unconscious fears and desires.[29]

Ethnicity is a primary point of identification for explorations of the fantastic in Chapters 3 and 5. In Chapter 3 it takes as its manifestation two related fantastic tropes: the vampire as a metaphor for anti-semitic cultural propaganda, read in connection with *Body of Glass* and *The Robber Bride*, and the succubus, Afro-American near-relation of the vampire, a figure manifest in Toni Morrison's depiction of the mother/daughter bond in *Beloved* (1987). In Chapter 5 we look at a late twentieth-century rereading of ancient fairy mythology as it centres on issues of Welsh national identity in relation to incomers, rooted in the folk tradition of the Tylwyth Teg and discussed in relation to *Fairy Tale*. In Chapter 6 a less culturally specific reading of the fantastic as "foreignness" is explored in my analysis of magic realism as a literary trend which, though emanating from South America, has emerged in British writing as a particularly displaced form of contemporary gothicism. This discussion centres on a comparative reading of Isabel Allende's *The House of the Spirits* and *Eva Luna* (1988) and Angela Carter's *The Infernal Desire Machines of Dr Hoffman* (1972), *Nights at the Circus* (1984) and *Wise Children* (1991). In the book as a whole, however, a fertile cross-pollination of British (including Anglo-Welsh), Black and White American, Canadian, French, Chilean and Botswanan writings takes place. Within the limited scope available in a study of this kind I have tried to do justice to those elements of cultural difference that directly define their relationship to the fantastic, while remembering that *all* aspects of the foreign, not just its national or cultural aspects, form the terrain of the fantastic.

In turning now to a discussion of women who are "larger than life", we find ourselves immediately face to face with an iconic embodiment of the grotesque utopia told from a feminist perspective. The figure of the giant is one we carry with us from the fearful fantasies of childhood, when all around were giants and ourselves little dwarves. Leslie Fiedler argues that neither children nor the adults who read to them think to identify with the giant of the nursery tale, eagerly awaiting *his* downfall "since in our deepest consciousness we remain forever little Jacks".[30] Perhaps this is true, even for female readers, for the extent to which girls learn early on to translate themselves into male personae if they are to have any active adventures of the imagination at all is, by now, well-known and documented. But Fiedler goes further, assuming that just as the reader is always the terrified and oppressed little boy, so this fantasy figure is simply a textual version of the immense and at times brooding father. If this is the case then giants must be consistently male even when not consistently malevolent. What if this is not the full story? Far more powerful than a recognition of ourselves as "little Jacks", women know all too well that we live in a society that continually tries to treat us as "little girls". From this perspective, the woman who is "larger than life" becomes, not a terrifying Gorgon, but an empowering utopian possibility, a being not simply physically larger than *the norm*, but in reputation legendary and thus fabulous. In Chapter 1 we find Angela Carter, Joanna Russ, Jeanette Winterson, Jane Palmer and Monique Wittig all getting in on this act in their various fictional contributions to what I have called the "grotesque utopia" in contemporary women's fiction.

# 1
## The Grotesque Utopia: Joanna Russ, Jeanette Winterson, Angela Carter, Jane Palmer and Monique Wittig

And once the old world has turned on its axle so that the new dawn can dawn, then, ah, then! all the women will have wings...[1]

Fictional utopias can be deceptively unsatisfactory. Elsewhere I have even claimed they may be threatened by redundancy, being "among the most rigid (and rigidly reductive) of generically bound forms".[2] Literary fantasy in general has always had to negotiate the establishment's determination to trivialize it as mere narrative formula. While increasingly successful challenges to these attitudes are mounted by such magic realist writers as Allende, Carter, Márquez and Rushdie, utopia still tends to carry a reductive stigma. Nevertheless, readers and writers of fantastic fiction continue to return to that space with an almost melancholic constancy, always looking to find a "shared identification with the trajectory of the 'beyond'".[3] One might adopt, as a definition of that impulse, Susan Stewart's term "longing", for, as she affirms, the word not only refers to an exaggeration or unnatural overstepping (the elongation) of the limits and limitations of the real, but also a sense of ongoing, "yearning desire",[4] this surely being the presiding motivation behind these texts. In a conventional utopia we are confronted by a closed text and reduced parameters. But, as Stewart's definition implies, "longing" has a more sustained dynamic that requires the ongoing textual interrogation of boundaries. In narratives that employ utopia as a destabilizing series of glimpses, or as a means of opening up a chink of light onto the unknown and unknowable beyond, we often find more interesting textual gaps, absences, lacunae: invitations that forbid as much as they instill desire.

During the 1970s and '80s, a noticeable increase in the publication of feminist utopias accompanied the more general expansion in the availability of women's writing. The reason for this disproportionate interest in the utopic seems predominantly political rather than literary, as feminism's strength has always relied on a sustained belief that the "not-yet" can and must become the here and now. Angelika Bammer's in-depth study of 1970's feminism sets utopianism at its core: "to the extent that feminism was – and is – based on the principle of women's liberation . . . it was – and is – not only revolutionary but radically utopian".[5] But the strength of Bammer's work is that she refuses to restrict this utopian impulse to that set of texts which satisfy themselves with closed narrative visions. Instead she defines utopia as "partial vision", a concept in process. This is an important shift in understanding for, however radical the political vision of the "closed" feminist utopia, women's writing is often at its most transformative (read influential) when looking to transform its own narrative structures similarly. In the process such texts take on a "riskier" dynamic, in that they positively invite disruption rather than close off dissenting voices. In refusing to shut up, they invite readers in, desiring us to enter into the discursive spaces they leave. Such texts will never be guilty of putting words in our mouths; on the contrary, they leave us to do that to them.

These lacunae embody the crux of my title: the oxymoron which couples utopianism with the grotesque. Like the gaping mouth defined as one of its central images, the grotesque body has collective as much as individual significance, being an anti-establishment carnival force which, in its excesses, forms the epitome of all that most threatens order. According to Mary Russo the grotesque is therefore a crucial asset to contemporary feminism. As "nice" women, she warns, we have no voice at all; instead we must look to construct a female body politic which is "heterogeneous, strange, polychromatic, ragged, conflictual, incomplete, in motion and at risk".[6] The same might be said for the structures and preoccupations of a new, more radical, literary utopia which likewise eschews squeaky-clean lines and accommodates more thoroughly that which "revolts". Silvia Bovenschen has noted that the movement towards a new feminist aesthetics requires a dynamic relationship between " . . . conquering and reclaiming, appropriating and formulating, as well as forgetting and subverting" established forms.[7] This seems a useful strategy to adopt in rethinking feminist utopia.

## Female Grotesques: The Female Man, Dogwoman and Fevvers

If oxymoron is the defining term of the grotesque utopia then it is rarely more clearly marked out in political terms than in Joanna Russ's novel

*The Female Man* (1975). Russ shows us four main protagonists: Jeannine, Joanna, Janet and (Alice) Jael all linked by a single subjectivity at the same time as having autonomous existence. Their relationship to each other is akin to that of identical twins, except for the small fact that they are not identical. In that sense they operate as a collectively grotesque being. It is Joanna who is attributed with the contentiously defining label "female man". Far from being hermaphrodite, Joanna is totally womanly, but a woman who refuses to be defined as:

> ...mirror and honeypot, servant and judge...the vagina dentata and the stuffed teddy-bear... This until you're forty-five, ladies, after which you vanish into thin air...leaving behind only a disgusting grossness and a subtle poison that automatically infects every man under twenty-one.[8]

What Joanna articulates here is a loss of faith in society rethinking its view of women. Instead she rethinks her own identity in what we recognize to be *grotesquely* utopian terms, the grotesque element being the fee paid for the (social) transformation:

> I'll tell you how I turned into a man.
> First I had to turn into a woman.
> For a long time I had been neuter, not a woman at all but One of the Boys... Of course there's a certain disembodiment involved... But it's necessary to my job and I like my job... I'm not a woman; I'm a man. I'm a man with a woman's face. Everybody says so. [*FM*, 133–4]

Alarm bells ring as Joanna articulates a state of transformation that takes her from honorary male status to pseudo-male status, all in the name of learning how to become a woman! At best Joanna's identity is self-contradictory at worst it seems self-defeating, but as Donna J. Haraway observes, Russ's model of the female man "is not an unmarked feminist utopian solution"; like the innovative narrative form of the text out of which "she" emerges, it is one which "fracture[s] ...figural expectations"[9] and, in the process, opens up new interrogations of formerly closed modes of writing.

A different and more appealing dynamic is at work in Carter's *Nights at the Circus* (1984) and Winterson's *Sexing the Cherry* (1989), although a similar mode of hybridity is established and, in the case of Winterson's novel, becomes so via a similarly deconstructive narrative framework. For both central protagonists, Fevvers and Dogwoman respectively, a precarious balance is effected between living legend and sordid freak, the fantastic and its relationship to the real being the pivot upon which this balance swings. Both characters, in their different ways, interrogate pro- and anti-feminist readings of the female body and its inevitable relationship with the body politic, an interrogative strategy which, as in Russ's novel, is inherent in their very names. On a purely mimetic level Dogwoman gains her name because she keeps dogs, but this does not account for the name's textual significance. Instead the term "Dog-woman" situates her, again like Russ's Joanna, as a grotesque hybrid challenging the accepted parameters of "normal" womanhood while, in this case, simultaneously playing with the pejorative sexual connotations of the word "dog". Fevvers's name works similarly, prioritizing her wings (the very element that detracts from her "womanly"/human status) over all other aspects of her body, while reminding us that, to men, she is still a "bird". Both characters are "larger than life", a feature in itself synonymous with challenging patriarchal norms. Both, like Joanna, find that this legendary status involves an element of unwomanly identification. As Jordan notices, "If you're a hero you can be an idiot, behave badly, ruin your personal life, have any number of mistresses and talk about yourself all the time".[10] If you are a heroine such behaviour is not heroic but monstrous, heroism not being the domain of the heroine. Her role is to be passively desir*ed* and ador*ed*, in other words perfect*ed*: dead even when saved. Ironically, it is not Dogwoman herself who articulates the full significance of her own huge dimensions, but her twentieth-century double who, referring to her own childhood fat, explains:

> . . . I wasn't fat because I was greedy; I hardly ate at all. I was fat because I wanted to be bigger than all the things that were bigger than me . . . It seems obvious, doesn't it, that someone who is ignored and overlooked will expand to the point where they have to be noticed, even if the noticing is fear and disgust. [*SC*, 141]

Though this character is living proof that "It's one of the mysteries of matter, that fat appears and then disappears again, and all you have to say it ever was are a few stretchmarks and some outsize clothes" [*SC*, 142], patriarchal society takes a very dim view of this type of female visibility. As Naomi Wolf observes, "female fat is the subject of public passion . . . A cultural fixation on female thinness is not an obsession with female beauty but an obsession with female obedience".[11]

Ironically, even when obedient (or at least obliging), patriarchy never succeeds in getting the upper hand over Dogwoman, as the following amusing anecdote demonstrates:

> A man accosted me on [the] way to Wimbledon and asked me if I should like to see him.
> "I see you well enough, sir," I replied.
> "Not all of me," said he, and unbuttoned himself to show a thing much like a pea-pod.
> "Touch it and it will grow," he assured me ... "Put it in your mouth ... as you would a delicious thing to eat."
> I like to broaden my mind when I can and I did as he suggested, swallowing it up entirely and biting it off with a snap.
> As I did so my eager fellow increased his swooning to the point of fainting away, and I, feeling both astonished by his rapture and disgusted by the leathery thing filling up my mouth, spat out what I had not eated and gave it to one of my dogs. [*SC*, 40–1]

It is the endearing combination of sexual naivety and outrageous comedy that makes *Sexing the Cherry* a totally delightful, even inspirational text. Set in the seventeenth century, in the period dealing with the English Civil War and Interregnum, Dogwoman is an early-modern urban guerilla, who fights for the Royalists in opposition to Cromwell. And yet it is this political affiliation that Lynne Pearce finds distasteful, denying that Dogwoman is a carnivalesque, excessive, womanly hero, instead sticking at the point of her counter-revolutionary identification, a point which, in Pearce's opinion, prevents her from taking on any benefit for feminists. If, she claims, Dogwoman is "associated with the preservation of the constitutional status quo", then ultimately she must fight for, not against, patriarchy.[12] Politically, Pearce is correct in her reading of Dogwoman's relationship with the State, but wrong, in my opinion, to see Dogwoman as an upholder of patriarchy. She is also, of course, refusing to enter into the spirit of the joke, a joke that is very much anti-patriarchal, as scenes like the following show:

> ... Firebrace set up such a farting and laughing that I feared he would explode before I had time to dismember him.
> I ran straight at the guards, broke the arms of the first, ruptured the second and gave the third a kick in the head that knocked him out at once ... another took his musket and fired me straight in the chest.
> I fell over, killing the man who was poised behind me, and plucked

the musket ball out of my cleavage. I was in a rage then. "You are no gentleman to spoil a poor woman's dress, and my best dress at that." [*SC*, 69]

What we are given here, in effect, is a wonderful parody of all those masculinist wish-fulfilment narratives in which the central male character, surrounded, shot at and attacked from all sides, emerges unscathed without even having to pass a comb through his hair. Apparently emulating such ridiculous heroics, in effect she subverts them by "sending herself up". Yes, Dogwoman fights for the King against the puritans, yes she is outrageous, dangerous, volatile and excessive, but she is a woman fully aware of being a woman, taking men on at their own vile and offensive games and beating them to a pulp in the process. Of course there is nothing "nice" or politically correct about it, but why would that change if she fought for the other side? Dogwoman, though purportedly fighting for the King, actually fights for herself, and for those readers sympathetic to her she seems to be fighting for us too, bearing in mind that the enemy is patriarchy, in either guise. Nor does her problematic political affiliation prevent her from being defined in carnivalesque terms, unless we take an extremely idealising reading of the politicization of carnival. As Allon White, among others, warns critics too keen to stress the supposedly liberating view of such forces of rebellion:

> ...there is a mechanism in traditional carnival which may be identified as 'displaced abjection'...[and which] occurs when an oppressed group uses carnival to invert its own low position with respect to another even weaker group, often women or ethnic minorities. The people who celebrated carnival tended to displace their own abjection onto those other groups...[13]

The paradox is that if Dogwoman was "worthy" she would not be grotesque, and if she was not grotesque she could not be fantastic. Dogwoman victimizes others in a horrifying and ruthless manner, but does so in a way that makes us laugh and, in the process, question why we laugh. The humour is, in that sense, ideologically interrogative:

> ...I have the Clap and my flesh is rotting beneath me. If I were to stand up, sir, you would see a river of pus run across these flags. The Rule of Saints cannot begin in pus...It is the stench of a three days' dead dog and not for the noses of the tender. [*SC*, 72–3][14]

In essence, though a scapegoater of other people, it is Dogwoman who takes on definition as the *a priori* site of abjection, within which "looms ... one of those violent, dark revolts of being ... ejected beyond the scope of the possible, the tolerable, the thinkable"[15]. This is one of the key qualities she shares with Carter's protagonist Fevvers in *Nights at the Circus*, as illustrated when Fevvers, pouring a glass of champagne, is described as "topp[ing] *herself* up with such a lavish hand that foam spilled into her pot of dry rouge, there to hiss and splutter in a bloody froth" [*NC*, 12 – my emphasis]. It is as if, confronted by Walser's fearful but fascinated gaze, Fevvers's own juices bubble over, unable to withstand containment by her skin. "Queen of ambiguities, goddess of in-between states" [*NC*, 81], Fevvers is repeatedly equated with abject processes, not least because her major point of definition is through her wings: that part of her body which is neither inside nor outside, neither self nor Other: "On the edge of non-existence and hallucination, of a reality that, if I acknowledge it, annihilates me".[16]

While Dogwoman offers us swashbuckling excess, Fevvers treats us to a series of music-hall routines, regaling Walser with her outlandish tall tales, not afraid to use her body as both butt-end of the joke and its *pièce-de-résistance*. By the end of the text, still telling her tale in the first-person but now aimed at an unspecified "anyone who will listen", Fevvers delivers the story of her long-awaited delight at finding Walser alive with all the camp shamelessness of the stand-up comedienne:

> I spread. In the emotion of the moment I spread. I spread hard enough, fast enough to bust the stitching of my bearskin jacket. I spread; bust my jacket; and out shot my you-know-whats.
> The Escapee's mouth dropped open, which is a risky thing to happen in this climate, your lungs can freeze. The old man fell on his knees and crossed himself, curiously ... I forgot my wing was broken ... with the aid of the other, I fluttered lopsidedly a few yards more, until I could no longer sustain myself aloft upon it and crash-landed on my face in a snowdrift as the woodsmen kicked up their mounts and fled ... [*NC*, 251].

Inevitably, what augments the humorous tones of this passage is not just the indecorous crash-landing, but also the smutty humour of the phrase "my you-know-whats". In the act of a "normal" comedienne this would be a joke related to breasts and sexual display, and Fevvers carries the *double entendre* along for good measure. But this returns us to Russ's grotesque "female man", because the voice Carter uses here, ventriloquized through this larger than life woman, is less evocative of a Victoria Wood or a Julie Walters than it is resonant of a female impersonator such as Lily Savage. No wonder Walser contemplates "Is she really a man?" [*NC*, 35].

It is perhaps this implied yet ultimately rejected gender ambiguity that explains Walser's simultaneous intoxication and repulsion:

> ...she stretched herself suddenly and hugely...As she raised her arms, Walser, confronted by stubbled, thickly powdered armpits, felt faint ...A seismic erotic disturbance convulsed him – unless it was their damn' champagne...If he got out of her room...away from her presence...if he could fill his lungs just the one time with air that was not choking with "essence of Fevvers", then he might recover his sense of proportion. [*NC*, 52]

It is significant that the physical effect Fevvers has upon him is so closely linked to whether or not he perceives her as a fantasy or everyday being. Left alone with her while Lizzie goes out for some food, Walser sees her as a "giantess" [*NC*, 51] who might devour him sexually, yawning "not as a tired girl yawns...[but] with prodigious energy, opening up a crimson maw the size of that of a basking shark" [*NC*, 52]. Two chapters further on, however, she has retreated back into her "everyday" guise, this time yawning "not like a whale, not like a lioness, but like a girl who has stayed up too long" [*NC*, 87]. Much has been made of Fevvers's utopian potential, not least by Ricarda Schmidt, who reads Fevvers at face value in her claim to be the epitome of "the New Woman" so prevalent in the 1890s, the temporal setting for Carter's text. Certainly Fevvers's social significance as representative of the female grotesque is one which links her to this contemporaneous figure. As Elaine Showalter observes:

> As women sought opportunities...[beyond] marriage, medicine and science warned that such ambitions would lead to sickness, freakishness, sterility and racial degeneration. In France, the *femme nouvelle* was often caricatured as a *cerveline*, a dried-up pedant with an oversized head...or a masculine *hommesse*.[17]

Paradoxically, it may actually be this trend which explains why Fevvers, though anatomically deviant, proves disappointingly conformist in social terms in the end. This proves the validity of Anne Fernihough's astute observation, that "With a body that is always the centre of attention, prominent yet at the same time elusive and enigmatical, Fevvers is an exaggerated version of woman as posited by late-nineteenth-century doctors, sexologists and psychoanalysts."[18] Linda Ruth Williams goes further still, discussing Fevvers as an embodiment of woman as (Freud's) enigma, not least in the fact that she perceives, in her narrative relationship with Walser, Freud's own story of the castration complex. Rehearsing one of Fevvers's slogans, "Seeing is believing", Williams places Walser in the same category as Freud, "writ[ing] of men who see the impossible",[19] namely that which cannot be seen because there is no-thing to see. Fevvers, then, confronts Walser with his own emasculation, a point Mary Russo also seems to accept in reminding us of his observation, at one point, that "Fevvers really needs a tail".[20] But I wish to add a further ironic twist to this argument, in that Walser's detective-style analysis is actually far less interested in the phallus and its absence than he is in the presence or absence of the omphalos (navel), that site in which Walser believes Fevvers's truth will cohere, for "The oviparous species are not, by definition, nourished by the placenta" [*NC*, 18]. In her folds of fleshly excess lies the secret to such originary mythologies, beginnings and endings being the crux of the larger global concerns, centring on the dawning of a new century. It is with this proviso that I embrace Paulina Palmer's more cagey reading of *Nights at the Circus*, which likewise acknowledges and welcomes its utopian potential, but recognises along with it a healthy dose of antithesis in the form of what she calls "the analytic and the 'demythologising'".[21] Fevvers's increasing normalisation during the course of *Nights at the Circus* matches what Mary Russo sees as Anglo-American feminism's own normalizing tendencies towards the end of the twentieth century, in contrast to the activism by which it has been characterized in other decades. Still, for all that, just like Fevvers we cling to the *possibility* of utopia, "fl[ying] in the face of much evidence to the contrary".[22] As we have seen, none of the authors discussed in this chapter write utopias in their static, *perfect*ed sense, instead they scan the sky-line for what Louis Marin claims to be the epitome of the utopian trajectory, namely the dialectic set up between "frontier", "limit" and "horizon" and their respective relationships to "travel", "Utopia" and "infinity".[23]

## Horizons and Hybridity: Jeanette Winterson and Monique Wittig

According to Marin global exploration holds the key to this etymological shift, and he points out that whereas, in the thirteenth century, the term "horizon" implied a finite end, by the eighteenth it had taken on a type of topographical significance in which it had become just another part of the landscape. Linking it later with the Romantic fascination for mountains and the sublime, Marin concludes that "higher and higher view-points" allowed the final step of the transformation in the term "horizon" away from a marker of limits towards "infinity". *Sexing the Cherry* intersects with Marin's historicist reading at the point at which the horizon is taking on the realizable dimension of a landmark and, in the process:

> ... as edge of the world, joins on to another edge, that of the other world, and on this limit between the two, a space, a gap is opened up, which belongs neither to the one nor the other, a gap between the interior space which is enclosed by the routes of travels, the *terrae cognitae*, and the unknown outer space: this is the indiscernible gap which is the imaginary site of the voyage.[24]

It is the utopian aspects of this text that enable characters like Winterson's Fortunata to anticipate the next historical move in the chain leading endlessly upwards into infinity. Inhabiting an unspecified location known only as "a remote place" [*SC*, 76], it is there she teaches pupils that "Through the body, the body is conquered" [*SC*, 76]. Jordan's inability to take possession of her in the manner that Walser does Fevvers means that his compulsive desires always drive him on further towards an end that has no end:

> Curiously, the further I have pursued my voyages the more distant they have become ... I begin, and straight away a hundred alternative routes present themselves ... Every time I try to narrow down my intent I expand it ... The Buddhists say there are 149 ways to God. I'm not looking for God, only for myself ... Perhaps I'm missing the point – perhaps whilst looking for someone else you might come across yourself unexpectedly, in a garden somewhere ... [*SC*, 115–6]

Jordan's search for Fortunata epitomizes what Stewart sees as the definition of longing: "Nostalgia is a sadness without an object ... it remains behind ... the past it seeks has never existed except as a narrative ... [It] continually threatens to reproduce itself as a felt lack".[25] That Fortunata is simultaneously autonomous and a reproduction of his desires is clear from the manner in which they double up in the text. The narrative opens with the words "My name is Jordan. This is the first thing I saw", before opening out onto an apparition of the self as a ghosted double image: "I began to walk with my hands stretched out in front of me, as do those troubled in sleep, and in this way, for the first time, I traced the lineaments of my own face opposite me" [*SC*, 1–2]. It is much later that Fortunata reveals herself in the guise of Jordan's echo: "My name is Fortunata . . . This is the first thing I saw" [*SC*, 104]. Only gradually do we realize that Fortunata also has another double in the text in the form of the equally fleeting glimpse we are given of Dogwoman's own mother, described as both short-lived and "so light that she dared not go out in a wind, [but] could swing me on her back and carry me for miles" [*SC*, 21]. As so often in contemporary women's fiction, the mother is a space of longing and loss. Jordan is a foundling, adopted by Dogwoman, a characteristic that also impels his insatiable search for the lost woman who is also his other self. Instead of the birth canal, therefore, Jordan conceives his own origins as "The shining water and the size of the world" and the goal of his journeys to be "always the same place I return to, and that one place not the most beautiful . . . " [*SC*, 11]. This re-encoded reading of the mother's genitalia is entirely in keeping with Hélène Cixous's own utopian reading of The Voice of the Mother, the source, as she sees it, of *écriture féminine*: "There is almost nothing left of the sea but a word without water . . . But a clarice voice only has to say: the sea, the sea, for my keel to split open, the sea is calling me, sea! calling me, waters!"[26] Similarly, when Jordan compares his life to a secret letter " . . . written in milk . . . squashed between the facts . . . [*SC*, 2], he again forges an image of Cixous's Medusa who, writing " . . . in white ink",[27] laughs in a similarly Medusan style to Dogwoman.

In the work of Monique Wittig, we find a similar preoccupation with the nature of origins and their relationship to self-definition. Here, though, as the title of her second novel *Les Guérillères* (1969) makes clear, such originary identities are always seen as collective in nature and can again be specifically related to Russo's grotesque female body-politic. The journeys undertaken in this text function as metaphors for the development of the women's movement, in the literal, mobile sense of the word, but in psychoanalytic terms, we might see in this recurrent patterning Lacan's infantile and extra-uterine Imaginary Realm, defined by and bounded by the outer limits of the anatomy, but experienced as a boundless but unattainable space of originary bliss. Where Jordan's search for origins begins on the bank of the Thames, here Wittig's characters peer into another reflective surface:

What was the beginning? they say. They say that in the beginning . . . [t]hey open their mouths to bleat or to say something but no sound

emerges... They move over the smooth shining surface. Their movements are translation, gliding. They are dazed by the reflections over
which they pass... Vertically and horizontally, it is the same mirror...
the same brilliance that nowhere holds them fast. They advance,
there is no front, there is no rear. They move on, there is no future,
there is no past... They are prisoners of the mirror.[28]

Here we find these questing travellers acting out our own passage from
the Lacanian Imaginary Realm into the Symbolic Order, pausing here at
the precise moment of engagement with the Mirror Stage. This is that
transitional point of our subjective development that first brings us face
to face with the self in the guise of the reflected other, a moment that
again brings us into an awareness of presentness as lack and the past as
a utopian but unrealizable world.[29] The use of tenses in this passage is
particularly worthy of attention. Starting with the past (which implies a
"post-lapsarian" location in the Symbolic Order, futilely trying to reac-
cess the Imaginary Realm), we quickly shift into the present. The passage therefore functions as a physical revisiting, not a cognitive reflection.
We, as readers, seem to feel the "smooth shining surface" of the mirrored sheet in contact with our skin, imagine the language of the body
in movement as a "translation" between surfaces, and accept that the
boundaries of time and space have lost their delimiting definitions.
Existing in a state prior to what Luce Irigaray perceives as the one-to-
one relationship between subjectivity and the unified phallic "I" of patriarchy (which, as we saw in the Introduction, is how she conceives of
the Symbolic Order in gendered terms), this is a vision of collective utopia for the female body politic.

   Again, *Les Guérillères* does not fall into the trap of an unproblematic
progression into a limited utopic horizon. Its allegorical structure is deeply
complex, explicitly polemic, and prophetically details the ongoing but
determined struggle in which feminism will remain engaged during the
1980s and 1990s. Later in the text the women, standing in huge num-
bers alongside the lake shores, peer into watery depths which are rip-
pled, rather than smooth, finding their multiple reproductions "all
identical, [but] all distorted" [*LG*, 69]. What is anticipated here is Russo's
metaphor of "fun-house mirrors" which, in challenging the clean lines
of passive female beauty, offers up a fantastic and destabilized vision
of positive resistance to what we have seen to be patriarchy's neutral-
izing and normalizing codes. The result for Russo is access to a series
of unfixed subject positions which, as a collective "mutant anatomy",
offers "an extra exit, a different way out", potentially enabling women

to break free from the shackles inherent in Wittig's term "prisoners of the mirror".[30]

Throughout Wittig's work, both fictional and non-fictional, the greatest concern is with how to employ utopia as a means of freeing women from the biological shackles of maternity. To that extent her use of narrative journeys often forces women to cross and re-cross a variety of waters, confronting them with the abject excesses of birthing, but only so that they might be empowered to move on beyond them. This sense of opening out or crossing limits is how Cixous perceives a fully-fledged female sexuality in general: "the adventure of such and such a drive... trips, crossings, trudges...";[31] but Wittig takes a differing perspective, emphasizing the need to separate female sexuality away from the mother in order to give her autonomous definition. Hence, in her fourth novel *Across the Acheron* (1987), her protagonist, also called Wittig, underlines her horror for "anything to do with grottoes, cellars, subterranean passages, trenches".[32] Wittig's sustained exploration of how to reconceive the female genitalia in ways that disconnect them from their status as reproductive apparatus anticipates the work of another feminist thinker, Luce Irigaray, whose work has much in common with Wittig's, not least in her superimposition of a type of crosscurrents metaphor upon the female anatomy. Women's lips, she claims,

> ...adopt a cross-like shape that is the prototype of the crossroads, thus representing both *inter* and *enter*, for the lips of the mouth and the lips of the female sex do not point in the same direction... those "down below" are vertical.[33]

Wittig's situation of feminism upon a number of similar crossing-points is inferred by the title *Across the Acheron*. These crossroads provide positive opportunites for change as much as they do problematic dilemmas, as is made clear from the nature of the character Wittig's quest. Beginning in confusion, "what crossing? There's no river here. There's no sea" [*AA*, 8], this protagonist has to learn that the crossing in question refers, in utopian terms, to a movement set up between two figurative planes which, like the double-face of a sheet of paper, one side filled, one side blank, reveals a palimpsest of possibility underlying the here and now. As her guide, Manastabal, informs her, "There's nothing where we are going, Wittig, at least nothing you don't know already... I'm taking you to see what can be seen anywhere in broad daylight." [*AA*, 8]

We may be forgiven for dismissing Manastabal's words, for many of the magical creatures Wittig meets on her way are anything but "what can be seen anywhere" – at least from a realist perspective. These creatures reflect the author Wittig's belief (a belief we have found already embodied by Russ's female man, Winterson's Dogwoman and Carter's Fevvers) that, under patriarchy, "woman" can only exist as a hybridized construct unfamiliar, perhaps grotesque, by Anglo-American feminist standards. As she claims in her essay, "One Is Not Born a Woman", women's socially perceived status is either that of "a group of men considered as materially specific in their bodies", or a "creature, intermediate between male and eunuch, which is described as feminine".[34] Therefore, as if to epitomize this state Wittig confronts us with a series of transitional grotesque creatures such as the bicephalics, who are, at first, as seemingly resistant to the laws of physics as Fortunata, the protagonist Wittig finding them distorting her own gaze as her "vision [becomes] confused and multiplies every object I see" [*AA*, 71]. Janus-faced, these creatures seem to epitomize the sense of possibility that a grotesque utopia offers, looking simultaneously:

> ... forward and backward, their bodies following a direction sometimes dorsal, sometimes frontal ... their arms and legs [being] bent at will either forward or backward, since their elbows and knees are reversible ... [and their heads being] two in one, one turned towards the past, the other towards the future. [*AA*, 71]

More positive, nevertheless, are the implications inherent in this peripherally transgressive stance. Teetering on limits, inhabiting "the tangent Hell/Limbo", though their chances of reaching Paradise, at least under patriarchy, are slim their bodies act out the real, expansionist possibilities of reversing this trend and taking possession of their own futures. Living already under a spectrum of natural light which "lin[es] fragments of sky with silvery flashes" [*AA*, 71], the potential for a utopian reawakening is there. The issue, for Wittig, always resides in collectivity.

In contrast to the oscillations and multiple axes of the bicephalics are the "two-dimensional" women encountered earlier on in the text who, as a result of physical, social and economic limitations, "look as flat as boards, passing and walking sideways, pivoting in order to present only a flat surface ... They make use of everything to avoid a collision: walls, wide entrances, sewer openings" [*AA*, 51]. Analogous to playing cards, these figures are invisible to those whom Wittig refers to as inhabiting "the third dimension" [*AA*, 50] and who are described by using masculine pronouns. Rapidly effacing themselves by diving flat on the floor or "crush[ing] themselves against the first available doorpost" [*AA*, 50], these creatures are unlike the bicephalics in being all too recognisable and in expending what little energy or motivation they have by "jostl[ing] only among themselves" [*AA*, 50]. These are women whose invisibility is social rather than literal and who bow before the face of patriarchy in their midst. They are also perhaps reminiscent of those women whom Kim Chernin has seen to be:

> ... practicing genocide against themselves, waging a violent war against their female body precisely because there are no indications that the female body has been invited to enter culture ... instead [we find] a sustained social coercion to reduce the body, to make it smaller than nature intended it to be and perhaps to destroy it altogether as we move out of the home and into the world.[35]

Of course female invisibility need not always be the friend of patriarchy, sometimes it operates as subversive stealth. Dogwoman, despite her mighty form, delights in the fact that, under cover of darkness, she becomes "invisible ... I, who must turn sideways through any door" [*SC*, 8]; the difference, as always, resides in the context. As Patricia Parker argues, "Changes in the semiotics of body size are subtly tied to other economies and exigencies of representation, including those linked to the shifting figure of the body politic ... ".[36] This brings us to the ideology of a generically enclosed utopia such as Jane Palmer's novel *The Watcher*.

## Women in Flight: *The Watcher* (1986) and *Across the Acheron* (1987)

Palmer's novel is a work of speculative fiction which makes as much use of grotesque female creatures as does *Across the Acheron* and demonstrates the innately transformative power of female subjectivity by giving us a character called Gabrielle who, though appearing in the realist sections of the novel as a young, assertively inquisitive woman, is also, in the futurist elements of the text, a metamorphic creature known as the Star Dancer, "a ghostly butterfly ... sucking power from the [energy] pool like nectar from a blossom".[37] According to Russo, metaphors of aerialism and flight are key metaphors of female possibility, operating as resistance to being tied down. In her terms such imagery can even reverse reductive *put*-downs of women, operating as a fantastic prosthetic application which, if "put on ... with a vengeance suggests the power of taking it off" (and presumably, in aerial terms, of take-off).[38] In

*The Watcher*, prior to our first encounter with Gabrielle/the Star Dancer, the opening of the text introduces us to a species called the Ojalie, represented by three creatures in dialogue with one another: Opu, Annac and Anaru. Feminine in gender, what is particularly notable about them, placing them in a very different category from Wittig's creatures, is their fascination with themselves as the culmination of the evolutionary chain, a chain that infers that utopia (at least in its anatomical guise) has been attained. But what at first seems a reductively closed text is opened up to dissent by Palmer's use of wry humour. The Ojalie are parodic in their narcissism, and hence continually undermined in their belief in the attainment of perfection. Again these are creatures capable of flight, being more bird-like than Fevvers in having not only "long wings", but also a "blunt beak" [*TW*, 1]. Lacking bowels, however, the Ojalie have simply "a small mouth leading to a narrow tract and bladder designed to deal only with liquid" [*TW*, 1–2] and "Their pelvic girdles [are] so wide they [are] unable to walk very well, but their wings more than compensated for this" [*TW*, 2]. They are, in other words, ugly and ungainly creatures whose aerialism has lost its status as superlative mobility and become a reductive loss of the legs. More disturbingly still, with their wide pelvis and incompetent legs they actually seem more of an extreme form of passive femininity than a (r)evolutionary new form of the female grotesque.

Challenging the common identification of the grotesque with the "low", Russo speaks of aerialism introducing a "principle of turbulence" into the equation, which will not only shake up patriarchy but also continue to stir up the female body politic.[39] Take, for example, *The Female Man*, in which references to women in flight occur repeatedly, if fleetingly, as in the case of Etsuko Belin, a superior of Janet's, who is depicted piloting a glider, "stretched cruciform . . . seeing fifteen hundred feet below her the rising sun of Whileaway reflected in the glacial-scaur lakes of Mount Strom" [*FM*, 17]; or the first moment of teleportation, when the police officer who swops chronotopes with Janet perceives her only as "a flying machine with no wings but a skirt of dust and air" [*FM*, 5]. Later, we see this ability to transcend the laws of gravity and temporality forms a clear foundation for characters' own fantasies: "At this point Joanna the Grate swoops down on bat's wings, lays He low with one mighty swatt, and elevates She and Dog to the constellation of Victoria Femina, where they sparkle forever" [*FM*, 118].

We have seen that, in *Sexing the Cherry*, aerialism is largely associated with Fortunata, who "flew from the altar like a bird from a snare and walked a tightrope between the steeple of the church and the mast of a ship weighing anchor in the bay" [*SC*, 61] and who, like Wittig's free-dom fighters, then teaches others to succeed in taking flight, before "releas[ing them] like butterflies over a flowering world" [*SC*, 76]. In Wittig's work butterflies are also connected with fighting, taking shape as gigantic warriors, each of whose

> ... suctorial proboscis ... though rolled up on itself, seems able to transform itself into a redoubtable weapon if needs be. As it unfolds its wings ... they beat in silken fashion ... At a given moment it descends ... Its proboscis is unwound like a lasso and, without poun-cing down ... without arresting its flight, it encircles the waist of a swordswoman and lifts her fully armed into the air. [*AA*, 60–1]

Such aerial forms also appear in *Les Guérillères*, the labial analogy pro-vided by the silken wings obviously rendering this image appropriate as an analogy for the various crossing-points these writers associate with female identity and its connections with fantastic possibility. In this novel she further develops the auspices of the grotesque, creating a new spe-cies of woman who amalgamates aerialism with spinsterhood, as if to show just how threatening anti-conventional feminine forms can be:

> Spinning-glands are at work on each of their limbs. From their many orifices there emerge thick barely visible filaments that meet and fuse together ... giv[ing] the women a sort of wing on either side of their body. When they resemble giant bats with transparent wings, one of them comes up and, taking a kind of scissors from her belt, hastily divides the two great flaps of silk. [*LG*, 132]

It is at this point that we come to the crucial aerial form in *Across the Acheron*, a reconceived reading of the angel motif. Here Wittig exorcizes the oppressive associations the angel takes on in nineteenth-century lit-erature, or in Russ's vision of Jeannine, the docile character whose per-ceptions of utopia are always linked to genre romance. In both of these cases femininity has been associated with the "angel of the house", the idealized wife and mother who turns out to be little more than a passive tool of patriarchy.[40] Wittig's use of the angel once again links up with the theories of Irigaray, who steps into the realm of fantasy herself in utilizing the angel as one of the primary signifiers by which we might rethink sexual difference. As an icon whose flight plays fast and loose with a variety of cross-currents ("horizontal and vertical, terrestrial and celestial") and whose form transcends traditional gender identities (angels traditionally being read as androgynous), the angel is a perfect symbol for the construction of a new, utopic reading of woman. Its full potential, she claims, is harnessed by means of an "envelope" which, in locking away secrets within a series of folds and, more actively, embracing the other from within the boundaries of the self, gives coherence to the feminine on its own terms. Being, for Irigaray, a "figurative version of a sexual being not yet incarnate", in Wittig's work the angel opens up a space-between, a zone of fantasy perfect for expressing this search for a utopian reconception of fantastic femininity.[41]

In contrast to their sexless nineteenth-century "sisters", Wittig's angels are defined by the "low" vulvic parts of the woman's anatomy [*AA*, 18]. But Wittig is not the first contemporary feminist to make these connections, or pick up on their age-old resistance to spatio-temporal limits and the accompanying defiance of all mimetic constraints. Russo refers us as far back in time as St Thomas Aquinas (1225–74), whose philosophy claimed that the motion of angels "can be as continuous or as discontinuous as it wishes. And thus an angel can be in one instant in one place and at another instant in another place, not existing at any intermediate time".[42] Again we find the angels' fantastic space of oscillation Irigaray circumscribes through the term "envelope". Simultaneously hybridizing the static nominal and active verb forms of this term, she produces a metonymic reference to labial folds which pleasurably embrace/envelope the self while also more threateningly engulfing the other. As much messengers as freedom fighters, this angelic presence opens up the afore-mentioned space-between, a zone of fantasy turbulent to patriarchy and its interactions with women. This may even open up the way for a more positive reading of Palmer's unappealing Ojalie; after all they are winged and transcendent and forced into a confrontation with a creature angelically named "Gabrielle". Irrespective of the form all these grotesque manifestations take, these writers advocate a new, sublime vision of the grotesque which, in replacing the discredited fairy of flighty femininity, gives rise to "the figurative version of a sexual being not yet incarnate". In the process Wittig manages to reverse what Bown sees as the usual aerial pattern of "representing something difficult or unbearable [feminine sexuality] as something small, sweet, and harmless".[43] Her work also anticipates the cautionary note Russo adopts in her reading of contemporary Anglo-American feminism. Never, Russo asserts, will we overcome the tyrannies of a patriarchy hell-bent on reading us as monstrous simply by appealing to its better nature.

In *Literary Fat Ladies*, Parker takes a similar political stance to Russo, also focusing upon the grotesque as a mode of deconstructive femininity but here looking in detail at the imagery of the mouth as a displaced gendered metaphor for female sexual assertiveness. For both Irigaray and Cixous, it is the oral aspect of writing that is most crucial, allowing woman to visually "speak" herself. Parker takes a similar line, seeing in the dilated form of the woman's grotesque voice/text, the manifestation of what patriarchy most fears: "uncontrollable female sexuality, a woman speaking in public, and a woman usurping her proper place...". She continues:

> One of the chief concerns of the tradition that portrays women as unflappable talkers is how to master or contain such feminine mouthing... [which] is not only in this misogynist tradition the representative of the infuriating opposite of silence but... inseparable from the vice opposed to the corresponding virtue of Chastity, as both are ranged against Obedience.[44]

Reminding ourselves of Wolf's recognition that the passion evoked by the expansive woman's body is tantamount to "an obsession with female obedience", we recognize that just as the dangerous harridan is prevented from expressing herself through her unrestrained body, so the dangerous female fantasist must be prevented from expressing herself through the unrestrained body of her text: "The supposed copiousness of the female tongue... has its textual counterpart in the danger of losing the thread of a discourse and never being able to finish what was begun... "[45] In articulating this strength, Parker illuminates a difficulty faced by the character Wittig in *Across the Acheron* as she is accompanied on her travels by her guide, Manastabal. Faced by the hostility of a gale-force wind, Manastabal turns to face Wittig, who "can see from her lips that she is making a whistling sound, but I can't hear it" [*AA*, 7]. This sets a tone for the treatment of female articulations throughout the text, dialogue becoming parenthetical as brackets replace speech-marks, woman's language becoming as muted as her body as serial mutilation takes its eventual toll. Not surprisingly, for most of the text orality becomes a central signifier both of absolute pain and absolute pleasure, finally culminating in "The Great Gorge" section. This section, as the title suggests, simultaneously describes the chasm that exists between the status of men and women in this novel and a description of the men's orgiastic, bulimic feasting which leaves starving women to stand and watch:

> ... unsteady on their feet, tears running down their cheeks and saliva dripping imperceptibly from mouth to chin... A long, low, hoarse

wailing rises from the crowd of them as they are made to leave the Gorge Palace, some choking with hunger. [*AA*, 112]

What Wittig offers us here is an allegorical reading of the many ways in which patriarchy robs women of oral pleasure, not just in shutting us up by threats of monstrosity, but in denying so many women that basic pleasure that comes from food. As Chernin rightly observes, "The food obsessions of contemporary women are a deadly serious affair precisely because of the imperative need for female transformation expressed through them".[46] Not surprisingly, then, having withstood the "Great Gorge", utopia fulfils all those denials in the form of "baskets and bowls of fruit . . . cherries, strawberries, raspberries, apricots, peaches, plums, tomatoes, avocados, green melons, cantaloups, water-melons, lemons, pawpaws, pineapples and coconuts" [*AA*, 119]. Much is made of the fact that *Across the Acheron* adopts a shocking and at times dystopian vision even though it searches out utopia in the end. But, to reiterate, the route to utopia is neither easy nor clear-cut and, like Russo, Wittig recognises the need to jolt us out of our complacent willingness to accept what some may see as the "good enough" point 1980s and 1990s feminism has reached.

Intriguingly, Eden is a space that haunts several of these texts even though, with the exception of Winterson's, Judeo-Christian mythology is anathema to all. Even in *The Female Man*, Jael's own questing past, described as a series of metamorphic transformations across time and space, includes her own Dogwoman-style contest with a serpent, as she dresses herself up as a heraldic knight, "sav[ing] the King's life once by pinning to the festive Kingly board a pretty little hamadryad somebody had imported . . . to kill His Majesty" [*FM*, 189] and, a couple of pages later, revealing to her most loyal retainer the "marks of Eve" [*FM*, 191] in her body that differentiate her from him. Feminist theorists are also among those writers whom Eden continues to haunt, even in these cynical postmodern times. Cixous, for example, maps Eden as the eternal source, space and place of *écriture féminine*, "from which [women] have been driven away as violently as from their bodies".[47]

More recently Nicole Ward Jouve has returned to this space, seeing the "Female Genesis" in terms not dissimilar to Cixous's own. Reconceiving the Biblical phrase "Male and Female Made (S)He Them", Ward Jouve notes that since the cultural adoption of the Genesis myth, "Man has been the universal category. Woman the endless problem." In a sense this is the dilemma the female grotesque addresses as it begins its search for new and outlandish configurations of the woman's body as the space and place from which a new, renewing utopia will emerge. It is, Ward Jouve claims, with the simple insertion of the "(S)" in her own essay's title that disruption is effected from within the hegemony, being the site not just of the banished, deviant Eve, but also the "female knower, the female creator ... [who] mutates as contexts and civilizations mutate".[48]

The importance of the grotesque utopia is that it always resists its own easy options. We rebel against the characters and creatures of this chapter even as we are invigorated, delighted and appalled by their appeal. If our journey is to move forward rather than backwards into the unknown territory of a new millennium, we must not lose sight of the fact that the struggle against patriarchy may sometimes get ugly. All of these novels reach out towards a new understanding of utopia which *envelopes* the grotesque. In the process they collectively carve out a fictive zone which reaches out into the beyond, including the *unknowable* beyond, while engaging with the unsatisfactory here and now of perceived liberation.

## Gendering the Chronotope: *Sexing the Cherry* (1989)

The utopian novel in its paradigmatic sense might be said to take a single chronotope and sever it cleanly from all others, permitting no two-way traffic with competing or overlapping chronotopes to provide an hermetically sealed society. The chronotope is, in its simplest terms, a fictive spatio-temporal framework. At its most formulaic it might, say in the context of the gothic, crime fiction, the classical quest narrative, be summed up as a nineteenth-century haunted castle, a contemporary metropolis and an ancient Greek citadel respectively. In the context of the traditional utopia what, precisely, it would comprise cannot be stated, but its mono-dimensionality would be structurally assured. Except, of course in the context of the grotesque utopia, set out above. Here, in the ragged lacunae and discursive spaces erupting from within the body of the text one expects the simultaneous existence of multiple, competing, even contradictory chronotopes. Mikhail Bakhtin broke new ground in arguing that all works of literature contain not one but many intermeshing chronotopes and that these minor chronotopes can often either be related to an individual character who may carry a particular chronotope with her/him (the chronotope of the villain/ess, the adventurer, the lover), or expected scenarios, among the most significant of which Bakhtin lists the "chronotope of the road" and its closely related motif of "meeting" in which, he affirms, "the unity of time and space markers is exhibited with exceptional precision and clarity . . . it is a rare work that does not contain a variation of this motif".[49] It is in the complex dialogic interrelationship between chronotopes that the depth of plot and counter-plot emerge.

One of the problems I have with utilizing the chronotope too slavishly is that it leads to an intrinsically generic approach to fantasy which, as I have already argued, is a restrictive, even reductive, reading of the fantastic. As Bakhtin acknowledges, "The chronotope in literature has an intrinsic *generic* significance. It can even be said it is precisely the chronotope that defines genre."[50] My usage of the chronotope, then, takes no account of it as a classificatory system for texts, but looks at its relevance to what is surely the polychronotopic structure of the grotesque utopia as explored within contemporary women's fiction. This brings us on to Lynne Pearce's primary project in *Reading Dialogics*, in which Pearce selects *Sexing the Cherry* as one of the novels upon which to focus her challenge to what she perceives to be Bakhtin's own gender-blindness in his reading of the term.

In her analysis of Winterson's novel Pearce isolates a series of key chronotopes, which she itemizes in the following manner: "two 'historical presents', 1630–66 and 1990; the 'enchanted cities' inhabited by Fortunata and her sisters and 'visited' by Jordan; and the sea voyages undertaken by Jordan and Nicholas Jordan". At the same time, she observes, these discrete units are further complicated by all of the characters, across chronotopes, simultaneously co-existing in the chronotope of "romantic love". Pearce's overall task at this stage of her argument is to demonstrate, as she succeeds in doing, that individual chronotopes in a text such as *Sexing the Cherry*, cannot be parcelled up in any neat manner. Instead, she continues:-

> Since Jordan's sea journeys are the means by which he arrives at his "enchanted cities", should they not be regarded as part of the same continuum rather than a discrete chronotope? Alternatively, perhaps they should be classified as simply part of the time-space belonging to the historical present of seventeenth-century England.[51]

Thus far Pearce's reading of the polychronotopic novel is in perfect synchrony with my own. Where we start to come adrift from each other is in our respective readings of the role played by the fantastic in Winterson's novel. Pearce, rather like Bakhtin himself, is noticeably suspicious of anti-realist modes of writing. For Bakhtin, the one exception to this reservation is that of the folktale, which he applauds for maintaining its mimetic relationship with the spatio-temporality of the everyday: "[T]he fantastic in folklore is a *realistic* fantastic . . . it does not stitch together rents in that world with anything that is idealistic or other-worldly . . . ". Pearce's own ideological mistrust of the fantastic is manifest from her uncertainty about what she sees as the "utopian" stance on dialogics taken by Robert Stam and Barry Rutland for reading polyphony in an intrinsically democratic manner (many voices contributing to the ensuring of multiple viewpoints), through to the detail of her reading of the role played by the fantastic in *Sexing the Cherry*.[52]

Pearce's stance on the work of Jeanette Winterson is, by her own admission, that of the disappointed zealot. An early advocate of Winterson's writing in the case of her first novel, *Oranges Are Not the Only Fruit* (1985), Pearce has become increasingly disappointed with what she believes to be, in Winterson's later novels, a determination to explore the universality of the chronotope of romantic love at the expense of what she would prefer to see: greater attention paid to the material realities and difficulties of living out lesbian desire within a largely hostile and heterosexist patriarchy. In fact, on occasions Pearce cites the fantastic as the root-cause of what she reads as dubious ideology in *Sexing the Cherry*: "It could be argued that it is by removing her characters to the realms of fantasy . . . that Winterson has left behind the question of what it is to be a woman and/or a lesbian in any more material sense." In contrast to her disappointment with *Sexing the Cherry* is the enthusiasm with which Pearce embraces Toni Morrison's *Beloved* (1987), a novel which we will look at in more detail in Chapters 3 and 4. For the time being it is sufficient to note that, for Pearce, *Beloved* is everything *Sexing the Cherry* is not, right down to its oppositional ideological stance: "where [Morrison] rewrites nineteenth-century American history from the perspective of the slave, Winterson writes seventeenth-century British history from the perspective of the colonizer". In fact Pearce goes further, charging Winterson's novel with being ideologically duplicitous on the very issues Morrison chooses to foreground: "Although [*Sexing the Cherry*] designates its male characters 'explorers' whose sole quest is the discovery of exotic fruits, we know that the most rapidly expanding trade at that time was not in pineapples or bananas but in slavery". Though this is a succinct summary of contrasting ideologies in the two novels, it does not do full justice either to Winterson's overall narrative concerns or to what I have already argued to be its profound political significance in feminist terms, not least because Pearce criticises its inspirational qualities for *being* inspirational. When, instead, she praises Morrison's novel on the grounds that "most of the characters are even more wary of the future than they are of the past, and would never trust that a leap into the unknown would bring them happiness", she seems to be suggesting that any novel that deliberately sets out to look positively towards future possibilities should be brought back down to earth for being "unrealistic".[53]

Pearce's argument regarding *Beloved* is convincing and informative and of course it is fitting that a novel about the brutal horrors of slavery should prioritize "grim materiality" over flights of fancy. But that is a very different issue from condemning another novel for taking a utopian (even a grotesque utopian) stance. Further developing this discussion of the ideological basis of the chronotope, its very definition ("the representation of time/space in the literary text") and, in Bakhtin's own words, their "intrinsic connectedness"[54] surely implies, in itself, that those works of fantasy and the fantastic in which time and /or space-travel play a central role must have an important contribution to make in the utilization of the chronotope for specifically feminist ideological purposes. In Chapter 2 I set out to demonstrate the significance such fantastic texts have upon the material reality of women, continuing my discussion of Russ's *The Female Man* in conjunction with Octavia Butler's *Kindred* (1979), Fay Weldon's *The Cloning of Joanna May* (1989) and Marge Piercy's *Body of Glass* (1991).

# 2
# Chronotopes and Cyborgs: Octavia Butler, Joanna Russ, Fay Weldon and Marge Piercy

> The very notion of compression refers to diminished distance among parts . . . Such mechanisms are related to technological speed-up and . . . the rate of transport of people, sound, pictures and any other forms of information . . . [1]

## The Polychronotopic Text: *Kindred* (1979)

Octavia Butler's *Kindred* and Joanna Russ's *The Female Man* (1975) are obvious examples of what Pearce terms the "polychronotopic" text. Picking up on what she reads as one of Bakhtin's most suggestible phrases, "Time, as it were, thickens, takes on flesh, becomes artistically visible",[2] its application to Butler's novel adds a further dimension to its gendering. Dana, the central protagonist of *Kindred*, is a Black woman writer who, on her twenty-sixth birthday, the day after she moves house with her white husband Kevin, is suddenly projected back in time into a nineteenth-century slave America. There she comes face to face with two of her distant ancestors: Rufus, the white son of a plantation owner and Alice, the Black "free-" woman who will be bought back into slavery by him for choosing the "wrong" man and, later, bear Rufus's children. In the process Dana comes face to face with a mirror image of her own relationship with Kevin, projected backwards into a new chronotope that has a significant material effect upon both her own subjectivity and personal relationship.

Dana, too, is born "free", but works for a temping agency colloquially known as the "slave market" and has been "bought" by Kevin on the marriage market, a contract some feminists have equated with slavery and which Angela Carter has referred to as "fuck[ing] by contract".[3] While K.K. Ruthven sounds the cautionary warning that, while "feminists might find it helpful to think of marriage as slavery for women, no abolitionist would think of slavery as rather like marriage", the irony is not lost on either Dana or Kevin when Rufus asks him, "Does Dana belong to you now?" and he replies, "In a way ... She's my wife".[4] Dana's relationship to temporal subjectivity undergoes a number of shifts during the course of the narrative journey, including the optimistic midway belief that "Some part of me had apparently given up on time-distorted reality and smoothed things out" [*K*, 127]. Nevertheless, their shared confrontation with a world, at the end of the text, which in itself embodies the harsh chronotopic juxtapositions symptomatic of postmodern urban life, reminds us that such chronotopic shifts *can* take on "material reality":

> We flew to Maryland as soon as my arm was well enough. There, we rented a car ... and wandered around Baltimore and over to Easton. There was a bridge now, not the steamship Rufus had used. And at last I got a good look at the town I had lived so near and seen so little of. We found the courthouse and an old church, a few other buildings time had not worn away. And we found Burger King and Holiday Inn and Texaco and schools with black kids and white kids together and older people who looked at Kevin and me, then looked again. [*K*, 262]

This passage is a detailed fragment of a travelogue, part of that crucial "road" motif Bakhtin finds all-pervasive. One of the reasons for that all-pervasiveness is the fact that travel directly impinges upon the coherence (actual or perceived) of subjectivity. In the opinion of Bakhtin, " ... both the hero and the miraculous world in which he acts are of a piece, there is no separation between the two".[5] This returns me to Pearce's point that space and time are intrinsically gendered and that our journeys through them impose those gendered-orientations upon us. I have already countered that opinion by claiming that it is our subjectivities that are gendered, not our travel through space and time, and hence it is the act of moving through space and time that causes the latter, on occasions, to *appear* gendered. The major difference between these two stances is the amount of agency attributed to the traveller (including the reader who voyages through the text) in each case. Dana's experiences in the nineteenth century demonstrate that the chronotope of the road is certainly defined in racial terms. Whites can travel freely, while Blacks must have written papers to allow them to travel at all. Nevertheless, the novel is full of Blacks travelling, runaways, chained coffles, and the seemingly accepting elderly Black man driving a wagon, "humming tunelessly, apparently fearing neither patrollers nor any other dangers of the night" [*K*, 172]. Admittedly the road motif appears silent on the theme of white women travelling alone, but then the gendering of the road chronotope is far less clearly defined in this novel, despite the fact that, overall, *Kindred* is as deeply involved with interrogating issues of gender as it is of race.

How might that compare with Dana's own relationship to terrestrial travel in the twentieth century? Once again, her relationship to the chronotope of the road is based upon her role as voyager across time, not as a woman. As soon as Dana comprehends the reason for her journey she realises that she will be called between chronotopes repeatedly and, importantly, against her own will. Her immediate response hinges directly upon this issue of to what extent we carry baggage with us through time and to what extent the baggage of time is imprinted upon us as we travel through it:

> I decided not to go to the library with Kevin to look for forgeable free papers. I was worried about what might happen if Rufus called me from the car while it was moving. Would I arrive in his time still moving, but without the car to protect me? Or would I arrive safe and still, but have trouble when I returned home – because this time the home I returned to might be the middle of a busy street? [*K*, 58]

While Dana's anxieties here are proven to be misplaced (gradually we learn that she always leaves from and returns to her own home), it substantiates my point. We have more agency about what we take through time and space than we may realise. At the same time, we have seen that Pearce's key reservation about Winterson's novel revolves around its usage of the polychronotopic in a manner that suggests that we can free ourselves from our material circumstances and float through time and space at will. As she puts it: "What some readers, myself included, may find problematic about this reincarnating time travel is that it is conceived as a wholly positive, 'painless' experience".[6] This qualm certainly cannot be levelled at *Kindred*, for Dana's shifts between chronotopes are always stimulated by violence and ultimately result in actual and irreversible bodily mutilation: "I lost an arm on my last trip home. My left arm. And I lost about a year of my life and much of the comfort and security I had not valued until it was gone." [*K*, 9] In fact, one might even argue that far from moving between chronotopes, Dana ends up caught fast between their shifting plates:

Something harder and stronger than Rufus's hand clamped down on
my arm, squeezing it, stiffening it, pressing into it...melting into
it, meshing with it...Something cold and nonliving.
Something...paint, plaster, wood – a wall...I was back at home – in my
own house, in my own time. But I was still caught somehow...I looked
at the spot where flesh joined plaster, stared at it uncomprehendingly.
It was the exact spot Rufus's fingers had grasped. I pulled my arm
toward me, pulled hard.
And suddenly, there was an avalanche of pain, red impossible agony!
And I screamed and screamed. [*K*, 260–1]

Where both novels upon which Pearce bases her discussion, *Beloved*
and *Sexing the Cherry*, are complex examples of the literary fantastic,
*Kindred* is far more straightforward in structural terms, being genre fantasy. As such one might expect it to be found wanting in the manner in
which Pearce finds the fairy tale wanting: "One could argue, of course,
that...realist 'causality' is not the responsibility of the fantasy text". At
the same time it is also far more disruptive in a chronotopic sense than
*Beloved*, which Pearce praises for the restrictions it places upon spatio-
temporal shiftings: "we rarely see characters exploring a time-space outside their own...Their travel across time is nearly always a rememorying
of a chronotope they once occupied."[7] Yet despite the greater degree of
disruption in *Kindred* "realist causality" remains at its core, amalgamating what might otherwise seem to be a form of textual irresponsibility
with the type of "grim necessity" Pearce applauds in *Beloved*. It also
reclaims a problem Pearce has with the mannner in which travel
between chronotopes is effected in Winterson's text. Where, in *Sexing
the Cherry*, Pearce claims the sole purpose of "slipping through the 'black
hole' (p.137) of time" is "to (re)discover our 'missing part' (heart)",[8] in
*Kindred*, despite the central motif of Dana's romantic relationship with
Kevin, Dana's "missing part" is her own genealogical complexity, first
encountered face to face as Rufus nearly drowns by falling into a hole
in the river-bed, a moment he describes in the following words: "and
then I couldn't find the bottom any more. I saw you inside a room. I
could see part of the room, and there were books all around – more
than in Daddy's library." [*K*, 22] This *Alice in Wonderland*-style fall
into the "rabbit-hole" of the text initiates most fully the traditional
fantasy devices at play here. But far from eluding or evading any
larger ideological issues, Rufus is also forced into a series of violent
encounters which, by taking the shape of Dana, also embody the
flesh-and-blood substance of "the bloody spectre of our ancestors'

oppression",[9] but here displaced through a topsy-turvy temporal and racial alter ego.

Mary O'Connor focuses upon the domestic arena as the presiding means through which the chronotope becomes gendered in contemporary women's fiction, a chronotope which, Pearce observes, depends upon "presentness" for effect.[10] In *Beloved* one might argue that 124 is the space within which Beloved attains, if not presentness, then at least "presence" and, in part, it is Sethe's positively creative relationship to the house that fosters such manifestations. In contrast, for Dana domesticity is never "home" in the way in which it functions for the majority of female protagonists in contemporary fiction. Neither shelter nor enclosure, Dana's "home" is simply a location, a base-point "touched" between chronotopic zones. As she and Kevin find themselves firstly transported together and then separately across time(s), the house becomes less and less *home* in any connotative sense: "For one thing, Kevin and I had lived here together for only two days. The time, the year, was right, but the house just wasn't familiar enough." [*K*, 191] That, too, carries ideological assumptions regarding their respective positions in the nineteenth-century culture, where the house, if not the home, connotes far more positively:

> I could recall walking along the narrow dirt road that ran past the Weylin house, shadowy in twilight, boxy and familiar, yellow light showing from some of the windows . . . I could recall feeling relief at seeing the house, feeling that I had come home. And having to stop and correct myself . . . [*K*, 190]

## Splitting the Subject across Space and Time

In a more obviously technological science fiction novel such as Marge Piercy's *Body of Glass* (1991), houses are run by a computerized unit which co-ordinates security, the type of encyclopedic function one would expect from a library, and communication facilities (internal and external). But, we note, "Most houses had female voices" and, although entirely automotive, the humanoid attributes that the house has leads Piercy's central protagonist Shira to acknowledge that she had always perceived the house (particularly as a child) as a surrogate mother figure "perhaps ten years younger than [her grandmother] Malkah".[11] Even as an adult she repeatedly finds herself attributing a personality to this machine, much as she early on finds herself confused by her dealings with the cyborg Yod. In fact the house gradually forms a rivalrous relationship with Yod, which Shira interprets historically as the "pique" of "a servant [who] would have expressed disgust and dismay at another servant who had become involved with the mistress of the house, leaving behind his own class" [*BG*, 251]. It is intriguing that, in this technologically oriented novel the house (especially the house of the good mother Malkah) is, unlike that in *Kindred*, the founding principle of the text, source of nurture and warmth. It also becomes a metaphor (and metaphorical substitute at times) for the absence of the maternal. So, for example, Shira's young son Ari learns early on that, when Shira is plugged into the Net, the house functions as a palatable companion [*BG*, 506], a point worth comparing with her own problematic feelings following on from what she believes to be her mother Riva's death: " ... she longed to crawl away and collapse around a missing that felt larger than her body, as if the depression *surrounded* her rather than *inhabited* her" [*BG*, 343 – my emphasis]. Here it is almost as if Shira has become a house-like empty shell, missing an owner/occupier. This is highly resonant of Malkah's final reference to herself as "an old house about to be remodelled" [*BG*, 565]. In other words the house is, as with so many motifs of this text, intrinsically connected firstly with the woman's body and secondly with the melancholic. Perhaps this also explains Piercy's rather hard-line attitude towards the former occupation of housewife as a means of "wasting" women. For in this novel we still find small girls (the text is gender-specific in this case) playing house long after such obsolescence [*BG*, 323] and it is interesting that only in the male scientist Avram's private dwelling does play find a space (which is clearly, here, a site of loss):

> The house was strange, a sort of museum of antique toys ... Machines ate obsolete coins ... in hand-held games, tiny silver balls floated over holes on cartoon faces and scenes ... It was as if Sara's death had freed Avram for a second sedate childhood of games. [*BG*, 70]

Despite their differing perspectives on domesticity, *Body of Glass* is similar to *Kindred* in its treatment of multiple chronotopes, shifts between them being relatively stable and clearly traced. The same cannot, however, be said for Joanna Russ's *The Female Man* (1975), which not only deals in time- and space-travel but also, like *Sexing the Cherry*, the possibility of the simultaneity of alternate universes:

> Sometimes you bend down to tie your shoe, and then you either tie your shoe or you don't ... Every choice begets at least two worlds of possibility ... or very likely many more, one in which you do quickly, one in which you do slowly, [etc.] ... To carry this line of argument

further, there must be an infinite number of possible universes . . . Every displacement of every molecule, every change in orbit of every electron, every question of light that strikes here and not there . . . [12]

What is most interesting about Russ's perspective on the chronotope is that she seems to follow Bakhtin quite closely in her equally clear prioritization of time over space in such spatio-temporal shiftings:

> . . . the paradox of time travel ceases to exist, for the Past one visits is never one's own Past . . . or rather, one's visit to the Past instantly creates another Present . . . and what you visit is the Past belonging to that Present – an entirely different matter from your own Past. And with each decision you make (back there in the Past) that new probable universe itself branches, *creating simultaneously a new Past and a new Present, or to put it plainly, a new universe.* [*FM*, 7; my emphasis]

In other words, while we tend, in common parlance, to make sense of this and other universes in terms of space (usually Outer space), here Russ implicitly defines the universe in temporal terms. Moreover she equates it with a type of inner temporality which we, as subjects, carry along with us. It is perhaps in the context of shifting subjectivity, as well as shifting spatio-temporal planes, that Whileaway, the major alternate society/universe/utopia Russ sets up in her text, is to be understood. It is, we read, "the Earth ten centuries from now, but not *our* Earth . . . [I]n the future. But not *our* future." [*FM*, 7] In that context it may take on a more material definition in terms of a space, time and topography of its own, or may be understood as landscaped by our own ideologies.

To a large extent the role played by the romance chronotope in *The Female Man* is identical to its application to Winterson's character Jordan and his own searches, being described by Russ as "the fourth-dimensional curve that takes you out into the other who is the whole world, which is really a twist back into yourself, only a different self" [*FM*, 70]. The chronotope of romance is, in this novel, associated with Jeannine, a character from Earth in the late 1960s. The choice between worlds is offered here as a straight choice between partners and, as in Pearce's opening in *Reading Dialogics*, finds its central focus in the telephone. For Pearce, the telephone is both the perfect embodiment of Bakhtin's "dialogic contract" and the mainstay of romance; from her own epigram to her text, "To 76305 and all the other lines I've hung on", through to the cited instance of telephone betrayal taken from an article in *The Guardian*: "I remember exactly where I was when I found out about my husband's adultery – I was sitting in the loo on the first floor landing..."[13] In *The Female Man* this dialogic function is maintained, but here it shores up Pearce's later development of the dialogic to include the dialogic interrelationship between the chronotopes in a text, the chronotope of the "receiver" and the chronotope of the recipient being further distanced than normal by an implied chronotope known first as "telephone never-never-land" [*FM*, 128] and secondly as "Telephoneland" [*FM*, 130].

Like Winterson, Russ assigns different characters to different chronotopes, but she does so in a manner that is far more fixed and definite than in *Sexing the Cherry*. Janet, for example, the first character to whom we are introduced, is from the future or, more precisely, from Whileaway. Jeannine is from the here and now of the recent past or, more precisely, the United States of 1969. Many critics jump to the conclusion, through their shared first name, that Joanna is the stand-in for the author in this text. On the contrary, it seems to me that she is the implied author's desired mirror-image: the ideal *reader* and, in that guise, like Manastabal for the character Wittig in *Across the Acheron*, functions as our guide and primary identification-point throughout the text. She is also, therefore, a representative not just of the present, but of *our* present, what we will come on to see as Donna J. Haraway's version of the Modest Witness in that she reflects upon others (primarily Jeannine and Janet) rather than having an opacity of her own. She is also, as we have seen in Chapter 1, the "female man" of the title and, in that respect, exists as the paradoxical embodiment of that chronotope which defines the text in which she is situated. Jael, the last of the four Js, is the futurist, cybernetically enhanced creature of the future who exists at the meeting-point of all other chronotopes. If anybody it is Jael who is the author's stand-in, embodying desire in its most abstract sense – not sexual desire, but the same desire that fuels Jordan: the quest or compulsion to move between chronotopes to look for one's own other self in fantastic others (the characters in novels). Far more similar to *Sexing the Cherry* than to *Kindred*, transportation between chronotopes in *The Female Man* seems relatively painless:

> [Janet] had us stand close together, all within one square of the sidewalk...It would have been better to leave from some less public spot, but [the Whileawayans] don't seem to care what they do; Janet waved engagingly at passersby and I became aware that I remembered becoming aware of the curved wall eighteen inches

from my nose. The edge of the sidewalk, where the traffic. Had been. [*FM*, 88]

One is reminded here of Pearce's own observation regarding terrestrial travel in Winterson's text:

Most of us would expect to experience some stress, anxiety and discomfort on a journey from London to Paris, together with a period of cultural readjustment when we arrive at our destination and when we return. How, then, can [these characters] cross oceans and centuries so effortlessly?[14]

The answer to Pearce's question is different in each case. Though Russ's *characters* are as easily uprooted as Winterson's, Russ's reader is far less so. Certainly Winterson's novel requires an active, fully-engaged reader to follow the various narrative shifts and competing polyphonies, but *The Female Man* takes this difficulty into a further dimension. In fact, having read Russ's novel many times over the years, it still remains a struggle for at least this reader to work out not only which chronotope we are "in" at any one time but who is speaking, to whom and, perhaps above all, how that particular chronotope relates to all the others in the text. In other words, and in this respect unlike any of the other novels discussed in this chapter, it is not simply characters and the reader who shift between chronotopes: in *The Female Man* chronotopes themselves seem to be continually on the move.

Most unstable of all is the one chronotope in Russ's novel upon which, in mimesis, we commonly believe we can rely: namely that of the "I" itself, which shifts in status continually between the subject of enunciation and the subject of the enunciating. Lacan's famous claim is that the subject who enunciates the "I" is not identical with the "I" which is enunciated, because we project our own self continually onto a perceived other/self called "I" (the linguistic equivalent of our own mirrored image). The signifier "I" is, in that context, one of mediation as much as one of connection.[15] Russ delights in playing havoc with this post-structuralist metaphor, the subject who is enunciating frequently being disguised behind a cloak of anonymity, but one that shifts continually between fictive selves, "As I have said before, I (not the one above, please) ... " [*FM*, 19]. This takes us right back to Virginia Woolf's treatise on the gendered implications of the narrator's use of the first person pronoun, discussed in detail in the Introduction. But rather than Woolf's "I, I, I," which resonates through its text under the name of

Mr A,[16] here we have the phallus "queered" (a term we will find central to Haraway's own work on fantastic subjectivity) to provide a more inquisitive "J". In the context of the speaking subject of the novel, unless given reason to believe otherwise, the reader tends to assume the speaking subject to be Joanna, the reader's pseudo-omniscient representative. At the same time we are equally aware that Janet addresses us in the first person as, later on, will Jael, so our presumption always carries with it an air of provisionality. In addition to all three, a fictionalized version of the author introjects directly at times, also using the "I" persona, in order to address us from behind a veil. Towards the end of the narrative this instability of the "I" comes most evidently to the fore: "I said goodbye and went off with Laur, I, Janet; I also watched them go, I, Joanna; moreover I went off to show Jael the city, I Jeannine, I Jael, I myself" [FM, 212]. What this endlessly unstable chronotope sets up, then, is the afore-mentioned issue concerning whether chronotopes are explicitly gendered. Ironically, although the "I" in isolation may be taken to be non-gendered, in *The Female Man* it is an alternative generic – a generic that is always and can only be female.

It is in this context that the apparent ease via which characters shift between chronotopes comes under further scrutiny for, as we journey towards the end of the novel we find that characters here do not move at will. Instead they have been drawn together by Jael, the apparently unifying entity of the text, who demonstrates the lack of ease via which such shiftings occur:

> It came to me several months ago that I might find my other selves out there in the great, gray might-have-been...It was very hard work...You, Janet, were almost impossible to find. The universe in which your Earth exists does not even register on our instruments ...I had located Jeannine and not Joanna; you very obligingly stepped out of place and became as visible as a sore thumb; I've had a fix on you ever since... [FM, 160–1]

Again, this proves vital to the larger ideological issues of the novel. If each character represents a different reality for women, then the difficulties involved in tracking each of those possibilities relates directly to our ability to envisage as possible alternatives those societies to which our own present materiality blinds us as better options. These difficulties are also represented by the inability of any one "I" to unify this novel, despite at least three individual attempts to do so. I have already identified Jael as a possible unificatory figure in the text. Certainly she pulls together all three central female protagonists and draws them, like a magnet, into her own chronotope. But she is careful to differentiate between them, showing that Joanna, Janet and Jeannine are not and never can be one "whole" self:

> We are less alike than identical twins ... but much more alike than strangers ... we are the same racial type, even the same physical type ... We ought to be equally long-lived but we won't be ... We ought to think alike and feel alike and act alike, but of course we don't ... even I can hardly believe that I am looking at three other myselves. [*FM*, 161–2]

In part this is a discussion regarding the interface between biology and cultural determinism in the shaping of the self, but it is also an argument that points to the need for diversity among women: we are not one whole, unified, "I", but different within our samenesses. Precisely the same concerns are central to Fay Weldon's more recent novel *The Cloning of Joanna May* (1989).

## OncoMouse™ and Other Monsters: *The Cloning of Joanna May* (1989)

As the title of Weldon's novel makes clear, this is a novel about doubling (indeed quadrupling) and, inevitably, in the context of cross-generational cloning, raises issues relating to genetic experimentation and in vitro-fertilization. Carl May punishes his wife, Joanna, for what he sees as her secret desire to have a child against his will (manifest in what proved to be a phantom pregnancy). Despite learning from a friend in the medical profession that Joanna's pregnancy is fake – information withheld from her – he insists on putting her through the ordeal of a staged termination. Once under anaesthetic he arranges for one of her ova to be removed and artificially inseminated. It is then split and sub-divided in order to produce four clones. Reimplanted in the wombs of four other women, these monstrous offspring of a monstrous creator finally produce Joanna Mays in quadruplicate – but younger, hence endlessly desirable, alternatives with whom Carl plans to taunt Joanna in later life. This is, once again, a novel of multiple chronotopes. Each of the four clones of Joanna May carries her own chronotopic world with her, allowing it to gradually become intercepted by those of the others. Jane Jarvis is an independently minded career woman who reads drama scripts for a living and [knows] herself to be free"; Julie

Rainer is the disenchanted wife of an infertile husband, who displaces her desire to have children onto looking after animals; Gina Herriot is a mother of three children, with a violently abusive husband whom she does not leave because "where can she go, she hasn't got the courage" and Alice Morthampton, a fashion-model, is "in love with herself... would do anything for herself".[17]

Additional chronotopes can be seen to be identified with levels of fantasy and speculation: genetic research, Eyptology and astrology, culture as simulacrum. Most disturbing of all these fantasy chronotopes is the "otherspace" to which Carl banishes his murder victims. Fantasizing about the nature of his young lover Bethany's punishment, should she ever prove unfaithful, he muses "She would not die, or only so far as friends and relatives were concerned, *and up to a point herself*... No, she would merely be put off to some other time, as Joanna's [lover] had been" [*CJM*, 238 – my emphasis]. A third series of chronotopes emerges in relation to tense-usage. We begin with a retrospective narrative voice which moves back into the recent past in order to gradually access the present. Events are recounted out of order, or more than once. Most discordant of all is the realization, voiced collectively by the four clones towards the end of the narrative, that Joanna has been "born at the right time. They were a generation out." [*CJM*, 251] Like Jael in *The Female Man*, here Joanna is the harness for all these various competing chronotopes: "I wake... to face a day now peopled with the ghosts of the past: they throng around me, reminding me, instructing me" [*CJM*, 198].

One could be forgiven for thinking that Weldon's novel is a revisioning of Russ's own, set in a different set of chronotopes. This narrative similarity to (one might even say cloning of) *The Female Man* is even evident down to the naming of individual characters. Once again the "I" of the text is central, apparently harnessed/unified but actually deconstructed by coming into conflict with a presiding set of Js. Again it is the name Joanna which is selected as the hub of the character connection, but rather than this hub of a wheel being surrounded by Russ's Janet, Jeannine and Jael, in Weldon's novel it is Julie, Jane and G[J]ina. Only once we encounter Alice does the break in the mirror effect cut in – at least until we recall that even Russ's character Jael's full name is actually Alice-Jael. The major difference between the formatting of these two texts lies in their respective ideologies. Whereas the various "Is" and "Js" of Russ's novel stamp or brand themselves upon every page of the text, in Weldon's novel the superficially assertive phrase "I, Joanna May", which also recurs frequently, does so in the face of perpetual effacement from the husband who gives her the ironic name "May" in the first place. In the guise of handing out permission in fact he takes away any agency she may have. In that sense she can be compared with one of Haraway's notoriously fantastic creatures, OncoMouse™.

OncoMouse™, central protagonist of Haraway's book, *Modest_Witness @Second_Millennium* is, Haraway informs us, "my sibling, and more properly, male or female . . . my sister". A "real-life" transgenetic hybrid of woman and mouse, this is a breasted creature/monster injected with an "oncogene" programmed to stimulate the development of breast cancer. As scientific apparatus, however, OncoMouse™ is a child with an impressive family tree: "Beginning with the rats who stowed away on the master ships of Europe's age of exploration, rodents have gone first into the unexplored regions in the great travel narratives of Western technoscience."[18] At face value, the existence of OncoMouse™ in chronotopic terms may therefore appear to defy Pearce's gendering of the chronotope of the sea-voyage as inescapably masculine, for surely Onco-Mouse™ is defined by the specifically female grotesque: "Her essence is to be a mammal, a bearer by definition of mammary glands". And yet a closer look reveals that OncoMouse™ is not descended from these seafaring rodents at all. As her trademark makes clear she is the child of capitalism, and as Haraway demonstrates in detail, this is a capitalism that places women's breasts firmly in the "safe-hands" of patriarchy:

> Inventions do not have property in the self; alive and self-moving or not, they cannot be legal persons, as corporations are. On April 12 1988, the U.S. Patent and Trademark Office issued a patent to two genetic researchers, Philip Leder of Harvard Medical School and Timothy Stewart of San Francisco, who assigned it to the president and trustees of Harvard College . . . Harvard [then] licensed the patent for commercial development to E. I. du Pont de Nemours & Co . . . Du Pont then made arrangements with Charles River Laboratories in Wilmington, Massachusetts, to market OncoMouse™.[19]

*This* is the genealogy of OncoMouse™, a genealogy that, though aping the type of Biblical begetting we find in the Book of Genesis and manifesting itself in a "passion" akin to that of the Messiah ("S/he is our scapegoat; s/he bars our suffering; s/he signifies and enacts our mortality in a powerful, historically specific way that promises a culturally privileged kind of salvation"),[20] is one of pure pedigree: "value-added" at every stage. This is also the genealogy of Weldon's Joanna May.

Joanna, we are told, allowed Carl to banish her own mother as too much of a rival for her attention. Then denying Joanna her own chance to be a mother, he cuts her adrift from what we find to be a crucial marker (good and bad) of women's identity in relation to other women throughout this book. Once he has severed her from that two-way female genealogy he believes it his right to take full possession:

> How desperately I, Joanna May, tried to be myself, not Carl May's wife. Even in exile, even divorced, I was married to him, linked to him... Even in Isaac King's arms, I was Carl May's wife, his employer's wife... Therein lay the excitement... [*CJM*, 246]

This is a truer statement than even Joanna herself recognizes for, like OncoMouse™, Carl has *bought* her, not just metaphorically through marriage, but as his own patented property and, in the process, reduced her to her essence, an "instrument of reproduction, a walking womb; the pulsing, gurgling, bloody redness inside the whole point of her being" [*CJM*, 200]. In the name of the same kind of pseudo-religious trickery, Dr Holly plays Lucifer to Carl May's God (although, of course, to the alert reader there is some perverse satisfaction taken from their feminization through their own "brand names", May and Holly). Neither any of the characters nor the reader is taken in by Holly's disclaimer: "We are not in the business... of creating monstrosities, but of removing disease" [*CJM*, 195]; he is less ruthless than Carl simply because he is less successful ("He wished [the clones] out of existence, but they failed to dematerialize" [*CJM*, 233]).

In these terms Joanna, Carl May's own OncoMouse™, has an even more uneasy relationship to subjectivity than do most women. Whereas Russ tries to enlist Woolf's phallic assertiveness for her own ends, Joanna's pseudo-Lacanian initial observation on identity constrains her within the role of eternal child, one who bears Daddy's name like a badge:

> Small children (so I'm told) start out by confusing "me" with "you" ... But is the "me", the "I", really the same as that initial "you" with which we all begin...? [*CJM*, 6]

In Weldon's novel the recurrent usage of both first and surnames in relation to both Carl May and Joanna May resonates irritatingly throughout the novel. But this is in keeping with Carl's own role within the cloning game and, like the artificial irritant by which May and Holly fertilize Joanna's eggs, so "May" also resonates differently in different contexts. To Carl, the great "I am", May combines with "I" to produce "I May", a homonym for Carl's belief in his right to have his own way about all things at all times. Joanna, on the other hand, wears the name like an identity bracelet, "I [branded] May", chaining her to Carl as firmly, we are told, as he was chained to his kennel as a child by his own abusive mother. Only by the end of the book does she finally sever the bonds: "I, Joanna May. Or perhaps now, just Joanna" [*CJM*, 248].

Both narratives deal, head-on, with the grotesque effects of a patriarchy which reads all women as monstrous. Nevertheless, despite Haraway's observation that *The Female Man*'s original date of publication was "a couple of years after the first gene-splicing successes inaugurated the practice of deliberate genetic engineering",[21] in fact it is Weldon's novel which is the more literal in its exploration of science *as* fiction. Ultimately, *The Female Man* evades the nitty-gritty of embryonic splitting by supplanting it, as we have seen, with a series of chronotopic superimpositions. This is true even if it does emphatically assert an assumption implicit throughout *The Cloning of Joanna May*, namely that research into genetic engineering and primatology is the sole preserve of men: "the chimpanzees with their hierarchy (male) written about by professors (male) with *their* hierarchy, who accept (male) the (male) view of (female) (male)" [*FM*, 135].

Certainly one can empathize with the anger expressed in *The Female Man*, particularly in relation to the manner in which patriarchy pulls women into internal conflict between their variously imposed cultural roles. But Joanna's conclusion that, under patriarchy, "You can't unite woman and human any more than you can unite matter and anti-matter" [*FM*, 151], is less than uplifting. It is also a claim Haraway struggles hard to disprove. As we have seen in the previous chapter Russ's notion of the "female man" is extremely problematic in feminist terms, not least because in its apparently androgynous (if not oxymoronic) naming, for all its grotesquely utopian possibilities it is the word "man" that is the defining term, "female" simply functioning as a qualifier. More positively, nevertheless, Russ's position does call the bluff of a patriarchy that claims that the generic term "man" applies as much to women as it does to men.

Haraway recognizes some of the drawbacks of Russ's image, but welcomes her(?), nevertheless, as a prototype for what she sees as a technologically-inspired heroine of deconstructed gender relations. Offering a radical rereading of Russ's eponymous hero/ine, she redefines him/her as part of a multi-national corporate identity, the FemaleMan©, "Elder Sibling [to all ] other sociotechnically-genetically/historically-manipulated creatures... ". Haraway's version is, like Russ's, a concept that inter-rogates the relationship between men and women, while resituating women at the centre of those narratives where men are always pre-sumed to be active. As Haraway implies, it is not by latching onto pat-riarchy *per se* that women will challenge their own position, but by considering closely what woman's agency *as actants* within patriarchy involves: "doppelganger to the coherent, bright son called man"[22]. Along-side the FemaleMan© comes the concept of the brand name. Again taken from Russ's novel, Haraway uses as her inspiration for this coinage the activating character Jael, whom Haraway describes as a "techno-enhanced warrior woman".[23] At the beginning of Parts II and VIII Jael asks "Who am I? I know who I am but what's my brand name?" [*FM*, 19 and 157]. At once she highlights the political implications of how women are "branded", "named", "appropriated", bought and sold. While one might like to claim that ravelled up in the term "brand name" is an apparent promise of the "brand new", as polychronotopic novels super-impose slices of history one upon another, they show there is absolutely nothing new under *the Son*.

In their differing ways *The Cloning of Joanna May*, *Body of Glass* and Haraway's *Modest Witness* are all retellings and rereadings of Mary Shel-ley's novel *Frankenstein* (1818). Like Victor, Carl May usurps scientific experimentation for his own aggrandizement, but unlike Shelley's prot-agonist, lacks any ameliorating positive aims. Once again mirroring the debate between the monster and his creator, he asserts "if you'd loved me properly... I would [have] create[d] a sinless race... [But] woman makes man bad... if I'm the devil it's your fault" [*CJM*, 111]. In Weld-on's text Carl May is rightly depicted as the monster of the text in moral terms but, again as with Frankenstein, it is what comes into con-tact with him that takes on the stigma of the grotesque/monstrous:

> ...if he had Bethany cloned, he could perhaps undo the effects of her upbringing. If he... had the egg implanted in a womb as stable as that of Joanna's mother... [Or] If he reimplanted the egg in Beth-any herself – but no, that would be hopeless; she was spoiled, sullied, somehow she would reinfect herself. [*CJM*, 78]

Though far from monstrous as individuals, monstrosity is imposed upon the four clones once they collectively come together to embody the female grotesque, in the process forming a double-visioned replica of one of Mary Russo's fascinatingly freakish politicized forms: "As a model of sociality, the configuration of the Siamese twin suggests to me the possibility of an odd sisterhood worth considering in place of the failed, unitary model of female solidarity which spent so much time defending its normalcy."[24] This new-found assertiveness is never clearer than when the four clones collectively confront Dr Holly for an explanation: "'we're waiting,' or rather 'w-we-we'r-we're wait, waiti, waitin, waiting.' Odd that; the ripple effect...Did it follow the same sequence as the initial cell division?" [*CJM*, 233]. Though Holly's thought-sequence demonstrates patriarchy's reluctance to endow these women with fully-developed human status, going beyond infantalization to "embryonize" them, reducing the clones to plasma on a laboratory slide; nevertheless he is overtly threatened by their presence.

Despite the importance Haraway places upon Russ's figure of the Female Man, it is with *Body of Glass* that she opens *Modest_Witness @Second_Millennium*. *Body of Glass* is, like *Kindred* and *The Female Man*, polychronotopic and, in its usage of superimposed time scales, differs from those chosen by Winterson in *Sexing the Cherry* only insofar as where Winterson juxtaposes seventeenth-century England with late twentieth-century Britain, Piercy juxtaposes seventeeth-century Jewish Prague with twenty-first century Jewish North America. According to Haraway, "Cyborgs are not about the Machine and the Human, as if such Things and Subjects universally existed. Instead, cyborgs are about specific historical machines and people in interaction...." As if to prove it she even gives cyborgs their own ancestry, parented by two scientists whose own "brand names" sound as connotative of cloning as either of the two sets of four Js:

> The term cyborg was coined by Manfred Clynes and Nathan Kline (1960) to refer to the enhanced man who could survive in extraterrestrial environments. They imagined the cyborgian man-machine hybrid would be needed in the next great technohumanist challenge – space flight...[25]

In the process she answers the rhetorical question asked, by Yod the cyborg, of Malkah and Shira: "You are embedded in history...What leads to me? Legends, theories, comic books. All my destroyed brother machines." [*BG*, 365] In fact, through the polychronotopic shifting of the text Yod is given a highly-developed, historical genealogy shared by OncoMouse™, namely that of the archetypal scapegoat – in his case within Jewish history. In the seventeenth-century chronotope Malkah tells Yod the story of Judah who, encountering the angel of death in a dream, finds him writing down on parchment a list of people due to die during the next twelve months [*BG*, 534]. Snatching the list from the angel's hand, he leaves behind the final stub on which only his own name is written. The angel gives him the choice of exchanging his own life for the deaths of all the others, or saving the others at the expense of his own death. Judah chooses the latter, heroic option, injesting the rest of the parchment which "was bitter in his mouth and burned" [*BG*, 534], as if to secure his own state of abjection. The fate of not just Yod but also OncoMouse™ is inherent within such litanies, its own suffering being the price paid for "our" salvation. And yet, in the context of ethnic difference, *can* we all huddle under the protection of this word "our"? Haraway suggests otherwise:

> For whom does OncoMouse™ live and die...when, between 1980 and 1991, death rates in the United States for African American women from breast cancer increased 21 percent, while death rates for white women remained the same...Who fits the standard that OncoMouse™ and her successors embody?[26]

As the Maharal also observes, in the context of Jewish scapegoating, "This is how the friendly rulers usually act when faced with a threat to the Jews. They regret, they temporize, they mitigate, and then they stand aside" [*BG*, 423–4].

Like *Frankenstein*, Haraway's project in *Modest Witness* is both an ethical rereading of science through gender and a rereading of gender through the ethics of science. Her originary historical epoch is, again, the seventeenth century, her key focus being the scientist Robert Boyle and, in particular, his experiments surrounding the invention of the air-pump. It is the figurative aspects of Boyle's invention that enable her to adopt it as the primary trope for rereading subjectivity through accountability. In essence, Boyle's public demonstrations of the workings of the air-pump simultaneously aped and yet evaded accountability. Hence:

> ... [at] a demonstration attended by high-born women...small birds were suffocated by the evacuation [of air from] the chamber in which the animals were held. The ladies interrupted the experiments by demanding that air be let in to rescue a struggling bird. Boyle reports that to avoid such difficulties, the men later assembled at night to conduct the procedure and attest to the results.[27]

The issues at stake here are nicely replicated by this image of not one but two bodies of glass, a connection with Piercy's novel that Haraway misses simply because she reads the differently titled American edition, *He, She and It*. The first echo relates, metonymically, to the transparency of the glass shell of the air chamber. The second inference is metaphorical and relates to the lack of "transparency" in the tactics adopted by the men involved. In their duplicitous guise of "modest men", these are scientists whose "self-invisibility" ensures that "their reports could not be polluted by the body" (read culpability). In fact, Haraway argues:

> Much more than the existence or nonexistence of a vacuum was at stake ... The experimental philosopher could say, "It is not I ... it is the machine" ... The world of subjects and objects was in place, and scientists were on the side of the objects ... As men whose only visible trait was their limpid modesty, they inhabited the culture of no culture.[28]

At first glance, what makes this perspective so interesting in gender terms is that it appears to reverse what we by now take as the normal identification under patriarchy between masculinity and the (active) subject and femininity and the (passive) object. Here, and throughout Haraway's book, it is Boyle and his followers (representing "Science" as patriarchal metanarrative) who stand as bodies of glass at the heart of the text. But of course, what these scientists claim for themselves is not the status of object, but the mantle of object*ivity* and, along with it, truth, knowledge and power (in the most unaccountable guise of no power at all). And yet as we have seen, this particular vacuum is quickly filled by gendered intervention and not just on the basis of animal liberation. These birds are inhabiting the type of glass coffins we will come to see women, from Snow White onwards, inhabiting so frequently in literary texts. They too are spectacles to be watched, suffocated, controlled by a patriarchy that simultaneously, and paradoxically, wants to show them off as monsters.

Perhaps the closest equivalent this demonstration/experiment has in *Body of Glass* is the intriguing use of boundary demarcations employed to control the seventeenth-century golem Joseph by the Maharal. As well as framing the terms of Joseph's construction and deactivation, these invisible limits exist as urban boundaries with as direct an anatomical consequence as Boyle's suffocation of the birds:

> As soon as [Joseph] passes out of the gates ... a sudden uneasiness comes over him ... He feels weak ... By the time he has reached the midpoint of the bridge ... he can barely push through the thick spongy

air ... When he has passed through the gates of the ghetto, he is once again strong, vigorous. Joseph does not understand what has happened to him ... [*BG*, 540]

Such bodies of glass are alluded to through inference on many occasions, not least perhaps when, at the end of the text, Ari witnesses the corpse of a bird whose neck has been broken by a window-pane, finding in it an epitome of the death of Yod. From the same historical chronotope as Boyle, Joseph's own "birthing" via alchemical metamorphoses evokes a similar metaphor: "He has become transparent with power that is power through him. His flesh is blackened like glass that has stood in a fire ... " [*BG*, 88]. Importantly, the "him" of this passage is not Joseph, but his creator the Maharal. Just like Boyle, this body of glass is a figure in a state of transmutation, but not from the inhuman to the subhuman (as are Joseph, Yod and Frankenstein's monster), so much as from the human to the supernatural/divine/magical. The Maharal is also a reincarnation of Frankenstein, although projected backwards through chronotopic trickery as a historical ancestor. Irrespective of the chronotopic complexities, the dilemmas remain clear-cut:

> The Maharal is speared through by what he has conceived, a task he can neither persuade himself to proceed with nor allow himself to abandon ... Is he afraid to risk himself in that ultimate attempt to harness the power of the word in creation? [*BG*, 79]

## The Post-Nuclear Family: *Body of Glass* (1991)

At first glance the American title of Piercy's novel, *He, She and It*, seems to relate to what is, early on in the text, a primary triadic rivalry between Gadi (He), Shira (She) and Yod (It). As Hannah succinctly observes to Shira, "I've had the impression ... that you and *he or it or whatever* had a relationship" [*BG*, 549 – my emphasis]. Alternatively, however, "He" could be Avram himself, in which case the "She" would be Malkah and "It" their child, Yod, for this is a novel of interconnecting three-way rivalries. So Gadi, the despised son of the overreaching Avram (who creates Yod to fill the disappointing absence his own son has left), sets up a rivalrous same-sex triadic dynamic between himself, Yod and Avram, referring firstly to himself as "Son of Frankenstein" and, on being questioned by Yod, "Who is Frankenstein?" replying "He built a monster ... Like my father has" [*BG*, 199–200]. Despite Shira's rapid defensive intervention here, an intervention that demonstrates her own assumptions that Gadi is calling Yod the monster in question, Gadi himself is not quite so sure. As self-proclaimed "Son" of Frankenstein he is also identified as monster. Certainly he is equally cybernetic, his array of artificial implants and chosen methods of self-adornment enabling his own body to take on almost the sheen of Yod's: "Hot and cool, curly and sleek, firm and silky, wiry, metallic" [*BG*, 60] while, at a festival attended by all the main characters, Gadi's costume and presence are almost literally magnetic: "The entire party was a fantasy garment swirling around him as the centrepiece. His metallic eyelids caught the flashing lights. His eyes were gleaming mercury." [*BG*, 335]

This image evokes the second "body of glass", which is Yod's own physiognomy, a series of flawless surfaces which function as the reflection of Shira's feminine desires: "Everything [about Yod] was smoother, more regular, more nearly perfect. The skin was not like the skin of other men she had been with, for always there were abrasions, pimples, scars, irregularities. His skin was sleek as a woman's." [*BG*, 227] Note the feminization this brings with it and the resulting impact on Shira's own desires. Here, as in certain lesbian novels, this smooth reflection is a reflection of sameness within difference. Malkah's sensuality (particularly in the context of Yod) lies in his feminine side. She programmes him to fulfil desire in a manner entirely evading Freud's belief in woman's sexuality being driven by the castration complex. Here, Yod satisfies the woman by giving her a reflection of herself, but couched in an outwardly masculine physique. This is a realization that is worth comparing with one of Shira's rare moments of insight (again cast in the guise of a glance into the glass surface of a mirror):

> So often she found that with Yod, when she moved into her usual behaviour with men, she was playing by herself. Whole sets of male-female behaviour simply did not apply . . . Small pleasures, small anxieties, sources of friction and seduction, all were equally stripped out of the picture. [*BG*, 331]

This returns us to Malkah, the third body of glass. Unlike Avram and his forerunner the Maharal, Malkah learns to become "queered" in the manner affirmed by Haraway, refusing to uphold "clear distinctions between subject and object . . . living and dead, machine and organisms, human and nonhuman, self and other as well as of the distinction between feminist and mainstream, progressive and oppressive, local and global."[29] In conclusion, a variety of conflicting fragments: fragility, beauty, ease of destruction, and the potential to be a weapon itself, are embodied in the phrase "Body of Glass". How significant, then, that all Shira has left of that body by the end of the novel are a handful of crystals – the essence of flesh prohibited from being made manifest through "the word".

*Body of Glass* also mimics *Frankenstein* in its usage of narrative embedding. One of the most positive depictions of archetypal femininity derives, in Piercy's text, from the role of woman as storyteller. Malkah and Shira alternate narrative points of view at an average ratio of two chapters by Malkah for every one by Shira, narrative embedding thus being controlled from within an entirely female domain, the duality sharing the "Double Midwiving" explored in a different context in the seventeenth-century chronotope in chapter 13. In Devon Hodges's terms this multiply layered feminine embedding would set *Body of Glass* apart from *Frankenstein*, in which "[Shelley] adopts a [series of] male voice[s] while assigning her self-effacing female characters ... to a marginal position".[30] Hence, while at the centre of Shelley's text one finds a storytelling monster who, though feminized in the manner discussed in the Introduction is still anatomically male, at the centre of Piercy's novel one finds another who is a double-headed woman, the epitome of both the split subject and the female grotesque. Yod's origins and *raison d'être* are, therefore, intrinsically textual: existing on one level simply as a character constructed by Malkah, it is fitting that he dies once Malkah's story is complete.

In *Modest Witness*, Haraway identifies herself with Piercy's character Malkah, whom Haraway describes as a "writer of stories and software, spend[ing] her days making monsters and fiction".[31] Although we find other characters fleetingly telling stories among themselves in Piercy's novel – Yod to Ari, Nili to Malkah, Riva to Malkah – just as we do in Shelley's original, Malkah is clearly the main storyteller: "A mother and a grandmother, I have been telling stories for fifty years. As the children grow, so do the tales ... " [*BG*, 23]. The juxtaposition, in the context of Malkah, between what is an archetypal (grand)motherly task: the telling of stories and the mothering of children, and what so clearly is not: the writing of computer programmes, is what makes her so suggestible to Haraway. But as Haraway consistently observes, science *is* storytelling: "We exist in a sea of powerful stories ... There is no way out of the stories ... [although] there are many possible structures, not to mention contents, of narration".[32] Mary Shelley's *Frankenstein* is, in these terms, Malkah to contemporary feminist SF. On the one hand a novel about mothering and foremothering, it is also a novel about the cybernetic effects of genetic technology filtered through a specifically gendered set of voices.

The vast majority of critical scholarship that has accrued around Mary Shelley's novel has tended, in recent years, to focus on the mother/child bond, amalgamating biographical readings of Shelley's fears and desires relating to her own children, the wording of her 1831 Preface to the novel, and the depiction of the relationship between Victor and the monster within the text. Midwiving is thus a powerful subtext handed down to *Body of Glass* via *Frankenstein*, Shelley "bid[ding her] hideous progeny [to] go forth and prosper",[33] while Piercy's Chava "thrusts her hands and face right into the screaming and the bleeding, the hot smelly brew of birthing, our brute entrance into the violence of being alive" [*BG*, 500]. As we have seen this is an image that pulls together the potency of narrative and/as technological reproduction. In her earlier science fiction novel, *Woman on the Edge of Time* (1976), Piercy divorces biology from reproduction, giving us instead the "Brooders", aquarium-like buildings in which, "joggling slowly, upside down, each in a sac of its own inside a larger fluid receptacle... babies bobbed. Mother the machine."[34] In *Body of Glass* she returns to anatomical reproduction, at least in part, all teenage girls in Tikva being given an implant at puberty to prevent pregnancy, although in the context of the society of the cybernetically enhanced Nili, as in the Mattapoisett of *Woman on the Edge of Time*, "The little ones are raised by several mothers" [*BG*, 489]. In essence, therefore, Piercy remains seemingly committed to an idea radically different from Shelley's own, namely that female creativity in a larger sense must be divorced from biological childbirth, even if they remain figuratively bonded.[35]

Sex and mating are as crucial in *Body of Glass* as in Shelley's original, and far more positively depicted than in any of the other novels discussed in this chapter. But Piercy reverses Frankenstein's monster's preferred option for a mate "of the same species and [with] the same defects".[36] Instead of desiring to pair off with Nili (the closest this text comes to a female cybernetic equivalent for Yod), he asserts his desire for an ongoing master/slave dialectic in the form of transgenetic identification: "I doubt attraction between cyborgs could occur, we would both yearn towards the type of being who made us" [*BG*, 441]. In that sense similarities are set up with Franco Moretti's analysis of the monster as an example of industrial labour relations (methods of production rather than reproduction). Moretti reminds us that, "Like the proletariat, the monster... belongs wholly to his creator (just as one can speak of a 'Ford' worker)... He is not found in nature, but built."[37] In his relationship with Shira, therefore, Yod's threat to the establishment is less reproductive (the threat posed by Frankenstein's monster) than aimed at the validity of master/slave relations, in that Yod refuses to remain dehumanised. At a meeting of the Town Council to decide Yod's future, the discrepancies between these two ideologies is endemic: "'This cyborg is the property of the town?' Avram wavered. Finally he simply nodded. 'He is not the property of anyone,' Malkah insisted. 'But he's a citizen of the town'" [*BG*, 531]. As far as Malkah and Shira are concerned, however, this is an ontological debate once again based on that universalizing chronotope of romance, a chronotope which, even here, takes an age-old poetic form:

> Yod extended a hand gingerly. It took hold of one rose and deftly plucked it, bringing it towards its face. "It has colour, fragrance and form, just as my memory instructed me. But it also has a curiously pleasant tactile quality. I think you might describe it as . . . like velvet, perhaps? Am I using a simile correctly?"
> "Excellent, Yod." [*BG*, 123]

Increasingly Yod, like Winterson's Jordan, falls under the sway of his own femininity, identifying with Malkah and Shira as much as we have seen them identify with him. Though always overturned by his innate masculine programming to kill as required, this cybernetic femininity is the real threat to the status quo and, as ever, must be made abject. Compare this with Gadi who, though often associated with the parodies of camp, threatens Shira with a form of contamination that approximates to technological reproductive intervention: "Why was she suddenly afraid, as if someone had jammed a needle into her spine and were injecting a cold dangerous liquid?" [*BG*, 339]

Haraway reads "reproductive technology" in its widest sense, to include not only "artificial milk . . . the human body itself . . . sonograph machines, caesarian surgical operations" and, of course, "*in vitro* fertilization techniques", but also "agribusiness seed technologies . . . [and] marketing systems for national and international customers". Nevertheless, as a biologist by training, mothering is never far from the surface. What she refuses to do is set up so-called "natural" mothering as a superior option. Reminding us of the artifice of such nature/culture binary polarities, she observes, "Breast milk is not nature to the culture of Nestlé's formula. Both fluids are natural-technical objects, embedded in matrices of practical culture and cultural practice".[38] It is the primary point-of-view character Shira who exists as the main point of maternal identification in the text and interestingly she is a poor substitute for her more interesting, anti-conventional grandmother. For Shira biological birthing is the starting-point in the determination of the distinction between human and cyborg forms within the specific context of the feminine. She perceives Nili, for example, to be "real . . . all the way through" because she witnesses her to be more than "a mother . . . in name only" [*BG*, 506]. In contrast to this is the suspicion, rivalry and resentment she holds towards her own biological mother, Riva, and her determination to assert "I am Malkah's daughter, not yours" [*BG*, 270]. Nor has Shira, for all the reproductive enhancements on offer, evaded the tyranny of the biological clock. Although technology has replaced the type of biologically essentialist obsessions with fertility that we will find structuring a novel such as Margaret Atwood's *The Handmaid's Tale* (1985), in *Body of Glass* we see, from the start, that time and the body, far from being separate from each other, are actually conjoined in the form of an "internal clock . . . [located] in the corner of her cornea" [*BG*, 1]. In fact it is this cybernetic conjunction that first identifies Shira in maternal terms and, ultimately, as a figure of melancholia. Hence, confronting the difficulty of adequate mourning for Riva's death, Shira "felt as if she had taken a spiny ball into her body which remained in her tissues, giving an occasional sharp twinge" [*BG*, 407].

As so many critics have by now observed, one of the most controversial aspects of Piercy's earlier, so-called utopian state of Mattapoisett in *Woman on the Edge of Time* was the treatment given to reproductive technology as a liberating force for women, one obvious drawback being inherent in Piercy's character Luciente's words:

> It was part of women's long revolution. When we were breaking all the old hierarchies. Finally there was that one thing we had to give up too, the only power we ever had, in return for no more power for anyone.[39]

A similar problem is raised by all of these novels and succinctly summarised, in addition, by one of Haraway's rhetorical questions: "Is the computer womb now female, or is gender one of the many things at stake?".[40] Despite Haraway's hopes for the cyborg as a fantastic way forward for women, few obviously clear-cut advantages spring from the "hope" of this chapter. Where women such as Nili are cybernetically enhanced, the effect is to render them masculinized: "She had a way of smiling . . . with a little twist of power that reminded Shira of a few men she had met. Dangerous men" [*BG*, 255–6]. At the same time Shira's comparatively natural biological state makes her feel " . . . as natural as seaweed and mud . . . ashamed, as if her unaltered, unenhanced body were something gross" [*BG*, 168–9]. Ultimately, in fact, it is difficult to avoid the inference that what we read as cybernetic perfection is, in actuality, *masculine* perfection writ large. Hence Avram, on being quizzed by Shira about the relevance of giving Yod a male member, retorts: "I could see no reason to create him ... mutilated" [*BG*, 96], and the Maharal, giving his Golem a cloak with which to conceal his nakedness, recognises that "the three of them had formed him as a *man* ... without thinking about it or discussing it ... he did not think he could improve on the design" [*BG*, 110 – my emphasis]. Not surprisingly, therefore, Haraway has as many feminist critics as she has feminist followers, Nicole Ward Jouve, among others, expressing a problem with which I have some sympathy:

> There is – as has always been recognized in the plural mode of "the women's movement" ... a crucial "hiatus between Woman and women" ... From Monique Wittig, who wants to substitute lesbian thinking for the "straight mind" ... to Donna Haraway who hails the cyborg as half technological, half human ... to Teresa de Lauretis who substitutes the term "feminist" for the worn and discredited term woman – a formidable array of theorists' aims to subvert and even dispose of, the very ... reality? ... which makes me want to call myself a feminist ... Linda Alcoff asks very pertinently, it seems to me, "What can we demand in the name of women if 'women' do not exist ... "[41]

Haraway flirts with and delights in her cast of fantastic creatures and endows them with a clear ideological trajectory: "Getting out of the Second Millennium to another email address is very much what I want for all mutated modest witnesses". But she resists the temptation to settle for easy answers, choosing instead some very tricky questions:

> Who are my kin in this odd world of promising monsters, vampires, surrogates, living tools, and aliens? How are natural kinds identified in the realms of late-twentieth-century technoscience? What kinds of crosses and offspring count as legitimate and illegitimate, to whom and at what cost? Who are my familiars, my siblings, and what kind of livable world are we trying to build?[42]

*Body of Glass* and *The Cloning of Joanna May* are both novels which intermesh discourses which might at one stage have been thought of as necessarily discrete: techno-science on the one hand and supernaturalism and the gothic on the other. Only, perhaps, in the twentieth century have we felt the need to segregate futurist techno-fiction off from the possibilities allowed by the supernatural. This is something Haraway works hard at reintegrating, identifying herself with creatures such as the vampire who, along with siblings such as the illegitimate spawns of the (post-) nuclear scientific family, those "(onco)mice of all species and (female)men of all genders", will "force a revaluation of what may count as nature and [as] artifact, of what histories are to be inhabited, by whom, and for whom".[43] In the following chapter we look at the application of this concept to the work of Margaret Atwood, Toni Morrison and Bessie Head.

# 3
# Vampires and the Unconscious: Marge Piercy, Margaret Atwood, Toni Morrison and Bessie Head

> We pursue objects which sustain our fantasies, but the origins of FANTASY...are unknown and can only ever be encountered as a boundary beyond which nothing can be said.[1]

The vampire can, it seems, be put to any (perhaps every) use. James B. Twitchell cautions us to "Witness poor Dracula: in our century he has been sent from Transylvania into outer space, into corporate finance, into the antebellum South, into California encounter groups...".[2] As part of what we have seen to be Donna J. Haraway's playful use of fantastic tropes in her work on the ethics of science and technology, in *Modest Witness* the vampire takes over from the cyborg as a player who flirts with boundary-negotiations such as "category-crossing" and "the pollution of natural kinds". But the vampire is also intrinsically related to OncoMouse™, both existing as "an invention who/which remains a living animal...subsisting in the realms of the undead". This preoccupation, in itself, suggests that the fantastic carries along with it an intrinsically ideological aspect which can accommodate speculations beyond the realm of mimesis for, as Ken Gelder claims, "The vampire is not an arbitrarily conceived invention; rather, it is a way of imaging what in a sense has already been vampirized by prevailing ideologies".[3] As all these readings assert, despite the vampire's impressive historical lineage, Dracula is a figure before his time whose "home" is the twentieth century in which he is "reproduced, fetishized, besequeled, and obsessed over" and hence "less a specter of an undead past than a harbinger of a world to come...".[4] Thus as much a time-traveller as many of the characters we encountered in Chapter 2, the vampire's ongoing relevance to the contemporary is sealed in its importance to recent women's fantastic fiction.

Auerbach, retrospectively analysing her own adolescent attraction to vampire culture, insists that while "Vampires were supposed to menace women ... to me at least, they promised protection against a destiny of girdles, spike heels, and approval".[5] In other words in twentieth-century terms they have become part of a larger sub-culture that incorporates punk and goth fashions as masquerades involved in defying dominant role-playing for women, as opposed to its earlier, late-nineteenth-century misogynist manifestation in the cultural superstition that "woman's blood lust came from her need to replace lost menstrual blood".[6] As the title of Auerbach's book, *Our Vampires, Ourselves* implies, though projected outwards onto an eternal stranger (paradoxically, Gelder claims "it is by being so 'at home' with other languages that Dracula remains always a 'stranger'...signify[ing] nothing less than his irreducible Otherness"),[7] the vampire's inherently problematic relationship to abjection, with his/her fluid excesses leading to the difficulty of distinguishing between the I and the not-I, always tells us more about our own bodies, identities, state of belonging than it does the monstrosity of the demon.[8] So the vampires of the early nineteenth century were, she argues, "indeterminate creatures who flourished, not in their difference from their human prey, but through their intimate intercourse with mortals, to whom they were dangerously close".[9]

In addition to what Kristeva reads as women's innate connection with the process of abjection, further ideological paranoia surrounds cultural readings of their mouths, lips and teeth. From the *vagina dentata* through to Irigaray's labial metaphors and Patricia Parker's work on literary fat ladies, both discussed in Chapter 1, patriarchal culture is obsessed with the dangers which lie in women's orality. According to Klaus Theweleit, engulfment by the woman's body is a fear right at the root of the destructive fantasies and actions of the *Freikorps* and one which targets the mouth as the pivotal focus of the woman's body as wounded space:

> 'Mouth' : a woman is punched in the mouth; she is clubbed in the teeth with a rifle butt; a slot is fired into her open mouth. The mouth appears as a source of nauseating evil. It is 'that venomous hole' that spouts out a 'rain of spittle'... [So m]ouths can symbolically represent the vagina, and the spittle pouring out of them, its secretions.[10]

Intriguingly, it seems such fears are so entrenched, even in the late twentieth-century, that the fear of the mouth proves more powerful than its "real" potential:

> ... theorists of the AIDS years tend to excise "the bloodsucking part", turning instead to a slithery, polymorphous creature ... a Dracula

potent in his *non*-traditional eros... [which, l]ike Lewis Carroll's Cheshire Cat, expresses his dynamic contradictions in a mouth so significant it scarcely bothers to bite: it simply *is*.[11]

Because of these possible psychoanalytic readings the vampire, like other horror monsters, can actually take on a cautionary function within a narrative, particularly in cinematic narratives, warning adolescents (male and female) of the possibly damaging consequences of destructive sexual encounters, a finger-wagging notion with added currency in the current climate of HIV and AIDS. It has also led to a variety of racist and homophobic reactions which have fastened on to fears of impure transactions involving border-zones. One of the most pervasive and culturally disturbing readings of vampire imagery in fiction and film derives from the precise geography of Dracula's "homeland" of Transylvania. Multilingual, wealthy and potentially corrupting, the vampire finds its apotheosis in racist readings of the Eastern European Jew.

## The Vampire, the Jew and the One-Sex Body

Returning in this context to Marge Piercy's *Body of Glass*, for Sherry Lee Linkon, one of the most important aspects of the novel is its foregrounding of Piercy's own Jewish ethnicity in a manner which is often less evident or even erased in her earlier novels. Here, she claims, Piercy directly addresses a key problem faced by Jewish Americans, namely "a sense of being different from their white, Christian (whether religious or not) neighbours and... a sense of uncertainty about what being Jewish might mean. They are different but not always sure exactly how."[12] The geography of the futurist chronotope of Piercy's novel largely shifts between North America and Western Europe, with occasional references to what Shira refers to as the Black Zone, namely Israel and the Middle East (homeland to Shira's estranged husband Josh). But the historical chronotope is set in Central Europe and the city of Prague, until recently the extreme edge of Eastern bloc territory. According to Gelder, Dracula's fascination with acquiring multiple languages can be interpreted as an attempt to confuse or erase his own origins, a characteristic the critic associates with Armenius Vambery, a Hungarian traveller and scholar of the period, whom he reads, following Friedrich Kittler, as the original inspiration for Stoker's protagonist. Though born a Jew, Gelder claims that Vambrey was keen to dissociate himself from that ethnicity:

He enrol[led] in a Protestant school; later he gains a Catholic education ... still later he converts to Islam. He learns German, Hungarian,

Slavic, Hebrew, French and Latin; moving to Budapest, he learns Turkish, Danish, Swedish, Spanish, Russian and Arabic. His Jewish identity becomes, now, thoroughly dispersed. A 'polyphonic' figure, he no longer has an essence . . .[13]

Jewishness is central to *Body of Glass*, but for Linkon this does not prevent Shira, Piercy's main protagonist, from experiencing her own Jewishness as simultaneous "belonging" and "difference". In both the historical and futurist chronotopes of the text Jewish culture represents home, friends, neighbours and thus belonging. But this cannot be divorced from the negative associations with the ghetto, which offers only a facade of security surrounded by hostile forces. In the chronotope of the future the world beyond Judaism also becomes a world of "corporations rather than nations",[14] requiring a series of complex boundary negotiations, a system of negotiation quite familiar to Jews of both the past and the present day, with their endlessly problematic placement regarding nation state.

For Linkon, Yod the cyborg functions as the major interrogative factor in forcing Shira to confront her own sense of Jewishness as difference. An obvious embodiment of boundary negotiations in his own anatomy, Yod is identified as "Jewish" in certain conventional ways. Firstly he is "born" to Jewish parents, Avram and (more importantly for the purposes of the matrilineality of Jewish descent) Malkah. Secondly, in terms of his "alternate" origins in history and myth, he has another ancestor in the form of the seventeenth-century Golem, "born" out of Kabbalah, Jewish mysticism. As Linkon observes, citing a review by Arthur Waskow, "'Yod' is linguistically close to the word yid, the Yiddish 'generic word for Jew' . . . [and] one of several derogatory terms used by non-Jews to refer to Jews".[15] This raises a new issue relating back to our discussions in the previous chapter, regarding Yod's masculinity and Avram's assumption that perfection equates with *masculine* perfection.

For Cyndy Hendershot, the replicant, icon of postmodernism and that favourite gothic monster, the vampire, share what she reads as a lineage based upon the "One-Sex Body". Deriving the foundations of her argument from Thomas Laqueur's *Making Sex*, Hendershot elaborates: "from the time of the ancient Greeks to the eighteenth century, European society viewed anatomy as a one-sex model".[16] In other words, man's body is held up as a model of both perfection and perfectedness, in relation to which woman's anatomy failed to signify at all, except as a lesser, provisional form. Even following the supersession of this model with a two-sex version in the later eighteenth century, the one-sex model continues to haunt us, raising its ugly head in response to two specific moments of cultural crisis centered upon shifts in gender relations. For Hendershot two fictional texts function as foci for such fears, Bram Stoker's *Dracula* (1897) in *fin-de-siècle* Britain and Jack Finney's *The Body Snatchers* (1955) in post-World War II United States of America. In the first case fears surround the emergence of the New Woman and in the second a nascent American female workforce. In "unhing[ing] gender from biological sex",[17] both moments encapsulate what Mary Russo would read as grotesque female activism propelling patriarchy back into precisely the type of atavistic terror that fuels horror narratives.

In Hendershot's terms the replicant, though a different order of creature, signifies primarily as a surrogate vampire in that its hollow shell of humanity becomes "Possessed by another life form" and, in the process, rendered "but a parody of itself".[18] To read Yod as a surrogate vampire is in some ways bizarre. After all, as we will come on to see, vampires are intrinsically predatory and, despite their currency among writers of popular lesbian novels, still maintain their standing in stereotypical terms as a predominantly paternal predator, a connoisseur of women's blood. In that sense the vampire is perhaps the patriarch *par excellence*, virile masculinity writ large. With Yod, on the other hand, "Whole sets of male-female behaviour simply [do] not apply", because he is a creature of mutuality who takes upon himself the Jew's famed ongoing mobility where boundaries are concerned, negotiating between masculine and feminine perceptions of gender despite being sexualised as consistently male. And yet, in conjunction with the work of Sander Gilman and Cyndy Hendershot we see a manner in which Yod does share this presumed "One-Sex" model of "human" perfectedness and, in the process, the same dilemma that faces the vampire seducer, namely how to relate fully to the desired other when "the troubling one-sex body prevents 'normal' heterosexuality from occurring".[19]

This image of difference within sameness is never clearer than in Shira and Yod's genital encounters, for although Shira is reassured, having "feared a giant penis... [and being] relieved Avram had not been carried away" [*BG*, 229], difference nevertheless remains firmly in place:

> Going down on him, she discovered he did not taste like a human male. There was no tang of urine or animal scent to him. She missed the biological, but certainly he was clean, the pubic hair softer than a man's. Perhaps Avram had been thinking of female pubic hair. [*BG*, 247]

Compare this passage with Hendershot's observation that "Although vampires are, socially, both men and women, they all, as it were, possess the same body...Possessing only one sex organ – the mouth – the vampire introduces a one-sex body into a two-sex world."[20] We notice here that it is Shira who seems in possession of what Hendershot sees as the single sex organ of the mouth, a possession which helps project Yod into a feminized and (hence?) dehumanized status. Returning to the scene in which Shira questions Avram's decision to endow Yod with a phallus and his retort that without one he would be mutilated, a further irony enters into the equation. Despite the addition of the male genitalia, Avram is determined to maintain Yod's ontological status as that of the non-human, hence the final act of "voluntary" self-destruction. But Linkon reads Avram's determination as one in which he does not maintain Yod's status as non-human, but as "non-Jew". In this manner Piercy both confronts and complicates her earlier affirmed belief that "A Jew may be anyone the society defines as a Jew and anyone who defines herself as a Jew". Instead she adopts a less definitive stance, refining her earlier position to the more interrogative recognition that there is an inherent complexity involved in "negotiating between external and internal definitions of Jewishness, especially when Jews argue with each other about what it means to be Jewish".[21]

Such an argument raises itself immediately in the interface between Piercy's stance and that of Gilman, for in his terms to be Jewish one has to be male:

> The gender designation of the term 'Jew' as used in [this book] is masculine. While some women (and images of women) are present in the various investigations, the central figure throughout is that of the male Jew, the body with the circumcised penis...it is *this* representation which I believe lies at the very heart of Western Jew-hatred.[22]

In one fell swoop, then, we are back to Hendershot's "One-Sex" model. Or are we? If Yod's existence as human depends upon his possession of the phallus the key question must revolve around that of circumcision, the very issue which, for Gilman, complicates the model: "The Jew is the hysteric; the Jew is the feminized Other...the altered form of his circumcised genitalia reflecting the form analogous to that of the woman".[23] What most critics agree upon, despite the many and varied available interpretations of vampire culture, is that during the nineteenth century a social downgrading of the vampire took place in which what was once the representative of a leisured aristocracy feeding off not just the blood, but also the sweat and toil of the ordinary people, became a representative of a new, capitalist bourgeoisie for whom "blood" meant less than circulating currency. It is this particular class dynamic that fed, in its turn, the consulting rooms of *fin-de-siècle* psychoanalytic practitioners. According to Elaine Showalter, the patients themselves became vampiric, "the hysteric, the feminist intellectual whose sicknesses drain her family's energies".[24] One important question to consider is whether analysts like Freud were the source or the cure of the "contamination". For Gilman, Sigmund Freud and Joseph Breuer's case-histories of female hysterics offer intriguing revelations about the status of Jewishness in their work; for us they will prove symptomatic of vampiric reading strategies. Freud's case-history of Dora is, Gilman claims, "the classic example of the transmutation of images of gender and race (masculinity and 'Jewishness') into the deracinated image of the feminine". In fact, as Gilman goes on to explain, what reveals itself behind Dora's facade is Freud's fascination with the diseased Jew:

> There is a detailed medical literature which links the very act of circumcision with the transmission of syphilis . . . to newly circumcised infants through the ritual of *metsitsah*, the sucking on the penis by the *mohel*, the ritual circumciser, in order to staunch the bleeding . . . For Freud the act of fellatio would . . . be a sign which incorporated his own relationship between his racial identity, with his co-religionists, and indeed, with other male authority figures.[25]

The sucking, bleeding and contagion in this passage already alerts us to vampiric stereotypes, but a similar intervention into one of Freud's famous cases, that of Emma Eckstein, infers this might not be an isolated instance of comparison.

William Fliess, the interventionist in question, was preoccupied with nasal disorders, a part of the body obviously connected with Jewish ethnicity. For him it was a crucial source of hysterical symptoms, particularly when related to sexual disorders, basically because he believed "The nose was the developmental analogy to the genitalia".[26] That this is an analogy that can only apply to the *male* genitalia may appear too obvious to be worth mentioning here, but it does seem to have been lost on some very eminent thinkers. Though Gilman is not among them, the inference he draws from Fliess's repeated acts of nasal disfigurement is not without its own ideological problems. In words that strikingly echo those in which Hendershot delineates her reading of the

"One-Sex" model, Gilman reaffirms his belief that to be Jewish is to be male and therefore to have one's Jewishness threatened is to be emasculated: "While [Fliess's] theoretical material covered both males and females, his clinical material . . . focused on the female's nasal cavities as the clinical substitute for the Jew's nose".[27] Certainly, as several cultural critics affirm, when Jewish figures turn away from their Jewish origins it is not unknown for them to turn to anti-Semitism as a means of underlining that split. Karl Marx and Armenius Vambrey were both guilty of this type of oppressive self-loathing as, according to Gilman, was Freud. For our purposes, however, irrespective of the motivation behind Freud's demonization of his female patients, demonize them he did, and in a manner that appears explicitly vampiric, not least in the counter-transferences which one might read as hysterical contagion: "the carrier of disease can only be eliminated by one who is equally corrupt and diseased".[28]

Collaborating with Freud in the diagnosis of Emma Eckstein, Fliess performed surgery on her nasal passages, purportedly as a means of curing her "hysteria". Far from improving, however, the patient found herself in "severe pain", developed a "'purulent secretion' coming from her nose, had a dreadful, sickeningly foetid smell coming from the wound, and had haemorrhaged badly". Freud, accompanying another physician from whom he sought a second opinion, peers into the bloody chamber:

> There was moderate bleeding from the nose and mouth; the foetid odour was very bad. R . . . cleaned the area surrounding the opening, removed some blood clots . . . and suddenly pulled at something like a thread. He kept right on pulling, and before either of us had time to think, at least half a metre of gauze had been removed from the cavity. The next moment came a flood of blood . . . [29]

Between the two of them, Freud and Fliess transform this woman into a gothic fantasy. Though Freud initially accepts that Fliess is at fault, he quickly reverts to type: "you were right [Fliess]; her haemorrhages were hysterical, brought on by 'longing' probably at the 'sexual period'".[30] It is not just the blood and the infection that are significant here, but also the implications that wound has for the fetishized orifice of the mouth and the immediate connection Freud draws with the vagina from which her menstrual haemorrhages flow. Famously, for Freud the vagina dentata is the taboo behind cultural readings of the Medusa's head, an association deriving from what Freud sees as the young boy's vision of the mother's genitalia, "surrounded by hair" at the original site/sight from which the castration complex derives. Once we attribute this laughing Medusa with teeth we find the belief of the gynecologist William J. Robinson, that "just as the vampire sucks the blood of its victims in their sleep, so does the woman vampire suck the life and exhaust the vitality of her male partner".[31] The dynamic of two-way vampiric transactions between clinician and patient is therefore in place: but in the context of contemporary women's fiction, the equation becomes reconfigured in certain important ways, as we will now come on to see.

## Covering the Traces: *The Robber Bride* (1993)

Margaret Atwood's eighth novel, *The Robber Bride*, gives us an archetypal late-twentieth-century reading of the vampire in the role of the literally "undead" Zenia, the vamp *par excellence*. Like Vambrey, Zenia has plenty of circulation but few traceable national origins, overlaid as they are with multiple and multi-lingual possibilities:

> ...*Xenia*, a Russian word for hospitable, a Greek one pertaining to the action of a foreign pollen upon a fruit; *Zenaida*, meaning daughter of Zeus, and the name of two early Christian martyrs; *Zillah*, Hebrew, a shadow; *Zenobia*, the third-century warrior queen of Palmyra in Syria, defeated by the Emporer Aurelian; *Xeno*, Greek, a stranger, as in *Xenophobic*; *Zenana*, Hindu, the women's quarters or harem; *Zen*, a Japanese meditational religion; *Zendic*, an Eastern practitioner of heretical magic – these are the closest she has come.[32]

The dynamic in this text is not, as it might appear, between a predatory man-eater and three naive, desiring males (the partners whom Zenia "steals" from Tony, Charis and Roz), but between a vampire and these three female "other selves", all of whom, in age-old tradition, invite Zenia over the threshold only to find her here to stay. A clear sense of mutual responsibility is felt by all three women for Zenia, initially in relation to their decision to take her under their wing and later in feeling partly responsible for the continuing influence she holds over them. As Tony, the academic historian, acknowledges: "The dead return in other forms...because we will them to" [*RB*, 468]. With her cosmetically enhanced body and sensuous form, once Zenia "returns", she is "hungry for blood" [*RB*, 191]. It is in Tony's eyes that Zenia takes on, in glimpses, the most stereotypically vampiric form, "with her bared incisors and outstretched talons and banshee hair" [*RB*, 193]. This point is never made more clearly than when Tony concludes, towards the end of the novel, that Zenia's story is "a rumour only, *drifting from mouth to mouth* ... She did it with mirrors ... but there was nothing behind the two-dimensional image but a thin layer of mercury" [*RB*, 462 – my emphasis]. Notice that the contagion of the "mouth to mouth" dynamic here is simultaneously that of the vampire's mode of contagion and the resuscitation that endlessly brings beings back from the dead. But the mirror iconography is also conventional vampire mythology and feeds into the fact that Zenia is, for each of the protagonists, a monster in the shape of their own reflected anxieties, while failing to cast a firm shadow of her own. Hence, though Zenia's physique is ubiquitously present throughout the text, it is repeatedly reconfigured in a manner that continually evades definition. Roz, for example, self-conscious about her own obesity, focuses upon Zenia's artificial nips and tucks, while the diminutive, child-like Tony sees only Zenia's extreme voluptuousness.

However, while Zenia is certainly the *central* vampire of this text, she is neither the only nor the most powerful one. Rivalling and ultimately surpassing her in this role is Karen, Charis's childhood self and the *doppelganger* who most clearly embodies, in her parasitic duality with Charis, the type of all-female vampiric dynamic Auerbach names in her own title. Charis splits from Karen as a defence mechanism after being repeatedly sexually abused by her Uncle Vern as a child. In the process she packages all the self-hatred she feels into this lost jettisoned self. Even prior to this point in the narrative, however, Karen is seen to have inherited a form of witchcraft from her maternal grandmother. In a reverse vampire dynamic, Karen's grandmother has the supernatural ability to staunch the flow of blood from severed limbs, an ability which leads the child Karen to muse "She would like to touch blood too" [*RB*, 250]. Her uncle's fear of blood is manifested in him leaving her alone after the onset of menstruation. Recognizing the nature of this fear, Karen exacts a specifically vampiric style of vengeance:

> it's as if she's reaching in through his ribs and squeezing his heart so it almost stops. He says he has a heart condition, he takes pills for it, but they both know it's a thing she's doing to him ... [*RB*, 264]

However, keeping Karen at bay from Charis takes all the strength Charis has, a burden that turns Karen into a form of succubus and leaves Charis easily the weakest and most ineffectual of the three main protagonists. It also makes her the most fearful of Zenia, because unlike Tony and Roz, Charis genuinely believes in the vampire's supernaturally invasive powers. Not only does she fear for herself [*RB*, 50], she fears that her daughter, Augusta, might become similarly contaminated: "'Hey that was different,' Billy says ... (That was the night her daughter was conceived ... She has always known who the father was ... But the mother? Was it herself and Karen, sharing their body? Or was it Zenia, too?)" [*RB*, 266].

In the context of Karen's abuse at the hands of Uncle Vern, Zenia's own shape-shifting ability to move between genders should be observed. Though it is Roz who dreams of Zenia in male guise, Charis's belief that Zenia's return constitutes her having "taken a chunk of Charis's own body and sucked it into herself" [*RB*, 68] horribly reconstitutes that childhood violation. Hence while Charis is part of a nurturing adult triumvirate of three friends, she is simultaneously assaulted by one comprising three fiends: Uncle Vern, Karen and Zenia. Her response is a determination to do her own possessing, suffocating Augusta and Billy, her childish lover.

Where Charis's psychological damage is understandable, it does not alter the disturbance one feels about her determination to metonymically elide the excised/exorcised Karen with dirt, poison and the "goose turds" she believes Uncle Vern's semen has implanted within her. Nor does it prevent the horror of her past sticking to her skin like glue. As Tony, describing her initial impressions of Charis at university, recalls, she "was slippery and translucent and potentially clinging, like soap film or gelatin or the prehensile tentacles of sea anemones. If you touched her, some of her might come off on you. She was contagious and better left alone" [*RB*, 119]. Charis's own status as primary deject may offer one explanation for her particular attraction for Zenia who, like all vampires, is the very definition of abjection. But it is less feasible as an explanation for her relationships with Roz or Tony. Instead, several important features are *shared* by all three women. The first is what we have already seen to be the vampire's evasive relationship with his/her own originary mythology, for all four women are the product of uncertain origins and difficult or damaged parental relationships. The second, related to this, is that all three change their names to signal a severence from that past. So Antonia becomes Tony, shelving the prefix she shares with her mother Anthea; Karen becomes Charis for the reasons given, and passes a similar determination for change onto her own daughter August, who "normalizes" it to Augusta. Rosalind Greenwood is a Western Caucasian version of the originary Jewish self, Roz Grunwald.

What these name-changes also indicate are the strategies these women have adapted to survive, for despite Charis's apparent feebleness at times, all four *are* survivors of genuine atrocities. Zenia tells Tony that her mother was a White Russian and that she escaped with her to Poland as a refugee. As an addendum she informs her that she was prostituted out by her mother from the age of five or six and that her mother, living in poverty, eventually died of tuberculosis. The appeal of this fabrication for Tony lies in the fact that Tony really has survived a past characterized by maternal distance and eventual neglect and, in Zenia, Tony hopes to reconnect herself with her lost twin who died in the womb. The nature of Charis's survival has already been given, and in this case Zenia matches it with the claim that she is suffering from cancer, having been in remission once and the growth having returned. Adding that she had to have a hysterectomy in order to remove the tumour on the first occasion, Zenia simultaneously manages to focus upon the type of bodily contamination Charis feels within herself, while ensuring that her own claimed inability to have children appeals to Charis's own insufferable desire to (s)mother. But it is in relation to Roz that Zenia plays dirtiest. Encountering Zenia working as a waitress in a restaurant and remembering her from university, Roz asks her what she is doing there. Claiming to be a freelance journalist working under-cover on cases of sexual harassment, Zenia begins to lure Roz into her confidence:

> Zenia must be different ... if she's writing about that stuff. She even looks different. She can't place it at first, and then she sees. It's the tits. And the nose too. The former have swelled, the latter has shrunk. Zenia's nose used to be more like Roz's. [*RB*, 315]

It is, of course, the final sentence of this quotation that is the key reference and one that Zenia knows how to exploit. Roz, Jewish by birth, disguised as a Catholic with her convent education, finds herself face to face with the same erasure of difference imposed upon herself as a child and that Gelder links up with the vampire. But there remains one crucial imbalance. Whereas Roz comes to accept that "Zenia doesn't have a jugular. Or if she does Roz has never been able to figure out where it is, or how to get at it" [*RB*, 103–4], Zenia wastes no time in going in for "the kill":

> "You know, Roz ... [Your father] saved my life ... During the war" ... Roz hesitates ... this is what she's longed for always – an eyewitness,

someone involved but impartial, who could assure her that her father really was ... a hero ... "It's a long story", says Zenia, "I'd love to tell you about it ... If you want to hear it, that is." She smiles ... and walks away ... as if she knows she's just made the one offer that Roz can't possibly refuse. [*RB*, 316–7]

The cumulative effect of these multiple mythologies is that, like the three main protagonists, the reader concludes the text knowing as little about Zenia as we did at the beginning:

> [Zenia] doesn't seem to have been born, at least not under that name; but how can anyone say, since so much of Berlin went up in smoke? Inquiries in Waterloo produce nothing. She didn't go to school there, or not under her present name. Is she even Jewish? It's anybody's guess ... [*RB*, 372]

But perhaps it is not what we learn of Zenia that counts but what Zenia shows us about Tony, Roz and Charis. What gradually becomes clear is that it is not Zenia who searches out these three women but, like the purportedly hysterical patients of Freud, they who seek out her. And it is a psychoanalytic role that Zenia takes on, forcing all three to face up to their unconscious repressions. In the process Charis comes face to face with the ferocious Medusa that is her other self and who, in the apparent guise of Zenia, has hair which "twists like flames ... [and] crackles with static electricity; blue sparks play[ing] from the tips ... " [*RB*, 398]. For Tony, Zenia is the vampiric mother, simultaneous source of adoration and neglect and whose womb becomes a coffin for Tony's other self. Most powerfully of all, for Roz Zenia is the manifestation of a transgenerational haunting which recurs in literal fragments, sometimes in dreams, and patently relates to the horror of the Holocaust:

> Roz is walking through the forest ... There's a track ahead of her ... Many people have been that way; they've dropped the things they were carrying, a lamp, a book, a watch, a suitcase fallen open, a leg with a shoe, a shoe with a diamond buckle ... there's something in there, something frightening she doesn't want to see. [*RB*, 399]

As a child at Jewish Summer Camp, Roz remembers the number tattooed on the arm of the pastry cook and the silence surrounding that bodily articulation. A similar silent message is sent out by the behaviour of Roz's mother who, eventually uprooted from her social origins by her husband's suddenly acquired and seemingly dubious wealth, turns into one of Freud's stereotypically domesticated hysterics, thrust back into an endless mobility which acts out what Gilman reads as the Jews' problematic relationship to belonging: "She wandered around in her housecoat and slippers, from room to room, as if she was looking for something" [*RB*, 343]. Determined to use Zenia to beat back this past, Roz uses her position of executive power to impress her own "brand" upon the horrors of history, and does so in a manner that takes Zenia as its inspiration. Considering, "Maybe I'm getting hooked on blood... Blood and violence and rage" [*RB*, 73], Roz harnesses the oral fascinations that characterize her desires for food in the novel and combines them with capital and, in the range of lipsticks she devises, blood-like oral traces:

> *Rubicon*, a bright holly-berry. *Jordan*, a rich grape-tinged red. *Delaware*, a cerise with a hint of blue ... *Saint Lawrence* – a fire-and-ice hot pink – no, no, out of the question, saints won't do. *Ganges*, a blazing orange. *Zambezi*, a succulent maroon. *Volga*, that eerie purple ... And there's one final shade needed ... a sultry brown, with a smouldering, roiling undernote. What's the right river for that? *Styx*. It couldn't be anything else. [*RB*, 101]

Zenia lacks origins, appears invulnerable, does not reproduce except in and of herself, and resists intervention within the patriarchal master–slave sexual dynamic. Failing to trace Zenia on ethnic terms, Roz settles for her mythology as *femme fatale*. One thing Roz has learnt from her own Jewish experiences is that it is in Zenia's body that the traces of her covered tracks will be found:

> When you alter yourself, the alterations become the truth ... Zenia is no longer the original, she's the end result. Still, Roz can picture the stitch marks, the needle tracks, where the Frankenstein doctors have been at work. She knows the fault lines where Zenia might crack open ... a magic word – *Shazam!* ... [might] cause time to run backwards, make the caps on Zenia's teeth pop off ... melt her ceramic glaze, whiten her hair, shrivel her amino-acid-fed estrogen-replacement skin, pop her breasts open like grapes so that their silicone bulges would whiz across the room and splat against the wall. What would Zenia be then? Human, like everyone else. [*RB*, 102]

Roz's phrase "everyone else" here strikes the reader as being noticeably ambiguous. On the one hand, if it is to be taken to include Roz as an amorphous "all of us", it becomes a gesture of self-acceptance as much as an acceptance of Zenia being "just like us". But somehow everyone *else* seems more likely to mean "everyone other than me", a more common identification in Roz's case which always returns to Roz's sense of her own cultural difference. If Zenia's purported Jewish identity is shown to be as much a fiction as her breast implants, only Roz is left in the liminal position as being somehow less than human. For, as Gilman has claimed, anti-semitism takes various parts of the Jew's body in isolation and fetishizes them as connotative of difference – hence not fully "human".

This issue of the problematic interface between humanity and inhumanity in racial terms is never clearer, however, than in discourses of slavery. Again, Gilman tells us, the Jews share with Black races their African originary status and thus, he claims, "The Jews are black, according to nineteenth-century racial science".[33] These same "scientific" findings are, of course, those to which Morrison's character Sethe falls foul in *Beloved* as the White character Schoolteacher documents on paper, written in ink mixed by Sethe, what he sees as the bestiality of all Black slaves. Sethe tells her daughter Denver, "It was a book about us but we didn't know that right away. We just thought it was his manner to ask us questions . . . I still think it was them questions that tore Sixo up".[34] What we find, however, is that the Jew and the Black slave have more than their African roots in common and the resultant dehumanization inflicted upon them by Caucasians. Like contemporary readings of vampirism, contemporary readings of slavery depend upon their nineteenth-century lineage for authenticity. In *Beloved* we find the slave and the vampire brought into similar contact as the European Jew and the vampire in *Body of Glass* and *The Robber Bride*.

## The Succubus: *Beloved* (1987)

Of all the novels discussed in this book, *Beloved* is the one I approach with the greatest trepidation, being a novel by which I always feel kept at a distance, and not just because I am a white, late-twentieth-century reader reading about nineteenth-century Black slavery told by a Black writer for, as we saw in Chapter 2, identical mechanisms are at work in Butler's *Kindred*, where the same effect is not produced. Equally significant and augmenting this always/already state of cultural and historical difference is *Beloved*'s disruptive relationship with the fantastic. *Kindred* is, we have seen, genre fantasy. This enables us to enter, with Dana, a very separate world of nineteenth-century slavery and, like her, leave it behind at the end of the text. We do not return unscathed by what we have read and nor does she, as the amputation of her arm makes quite clear. Her future remains a scarred one, scarred by a past that is both hers and not hers, written onto her body, but lived fully by others. Nevertheless, in *Beloved*, slavery is never left behind, albeit that the characters we meet are, at the time at which we encounter them, technically "free". Instead we are thrust into slavery's midst, no frame-text being there to contain it and, in the flashbacks and chronotopic disruptions of the text, it therefore continues to surround us on all sides. Horror film and fiction, it has long been claimed, works via a paradox whereby viewers and readers are rendered psychologically "safe" by the violent and tyrannizing material being safely contained by the screen or book-cover.[35] By removing the parameters of genre fiction, Morrison renders the violence of *Beloved* out of control, its polyphonic structure left clamouring in our ears. Structurally, the treatment of narrative subjectivity is not unlike that found in Russ's *The Female Man* as discussed in Chapter 2. But here the result is even more violent in structural terms, as the reader is left struggling to make sense of what does not and cannot make "sense": the horror of slavery.

This distancing technique is particularly painful, perhaps even hurtful, because it excludes us from that aspect of the text by which we hope to be consoled and comforted: Sethe's reunion with the daughter she murdered to save her from future brutality from white men. This mother/daughter bond is therefore defined by a blood-bond that simultaneously divides and defines mother and child, Sethe slitting Beloved's throat in terrorized panic. Their coming together again, as Beloved reappears as an avenging demon, the ghost of that child transformed into a fully-grown woman, is one bonded equally viciously in blood. According to Meredith Skura, this is a common foundational premise for all adolescent relations with the mother, reacting against an infantile state of bliss which, though desiring complete union with the mother, "threatens to become a hellish suffocation if the mother is too possessive and prevents the child's development as a separate being".[36] As we have seen, Sethe is not too possessive; on the contrary, she lets her child go. But she does so in a manner that inevitably prevents "the child's development as a separate being", figuratively separating/splitting her head from her body. It is part of Beloved's revenge that, in answer to that early brutality inflicted in the name of escaping brutality, she is the one who will do the possessing, aiming her point of focus at that very part of the body upon which the original severance took place. As Pamela Barnett observes:

> When Beloved kisses Sethe's neck in the clearing, Sethe is transfixed but suddenly becomes aware that the act is inappropriate. Perhaps she also senses the danger of a kiss on the neck as a prefiguration of a vampiric attack. This haunting is marked by an infantile sexual desire for the mother, as Sethe's reprimand suggests: "You too old for that" ... [37]

In avenging her mother by feeding off her body, Beloved re-enacts Sethe's abuse by two white boys, in which they forcibly suck the milk from her breasts, holding her down while the whole event is documented by the white school-teacher. The cross-racial connection with Beloved is of course part of the disturbance, but this is just one of the many ways in which the ambivalence of this violent mother/daughter dynamic is explored.

Denver, Beloved's sister, is equally implicated by this ambivalence. Present as a babe-in-arms when Sethe murders Beloved, Denver instinctively keeps on sucking, apparently oblivious, "swallow[ing] her blood right along with my mother's milk" [*B*, 205]. But this surface oblivion masks a fierce repressive drive, one which is accounted for by Franco Moretti's reading of the vampire. Like Skura, Moretti takes the origins of the vampire back to the mother/infant bond, but adds an element of infantile aggression that Skura postpones until adolescence: "We know that babes which, while toothless, are content to suck the breast, no sooner cut their first teeth than they use them to bite the same breast".[38] Fearing later retribution for this early, instinctual, moment of aggression, the blood on the breast injested by Denver is somehow confused and written over as the blood *of* the breast, where Moretti reads the vampire as a conscious, safely-controlled manifestation of this maternal vengeance, masking our unconscious terrors of that being who is, to the infant, almost infinite in size and strength. Denver's own childhood fears again reflect the lack of safety-mechanisms here:

> I love my mother but I know she killed one of her own daughters, and tender as she is with me, I'm scared of her because of it ... All the time, I'm afraid the thing that happened that made it all right for my mother to kill my sister could happen again ... I need to know what that thing might be, but I don't want to. [*B*, 205]

Not just Beloved, then, but also Denver, is vampiric in this text, a dynamic that throws responsibility for all three women's roles uncomfortably back on themselves, even as they are projected outwards onto the horrors of slavery. Nina Auerbach's observation that "psychic vampires in the late twentieth century can shrink to a whisper or expand to fill ... history"[39] is never truer than in the context of *Beloved*, in which we find a late-twentieth-century vampire who comes to embody the full horror of nineteenth-century slavery, yet is simultaneously as tiny and intimate as a whisper in her guise as mother's child.

So Beloved is not just as figure of vengeance she is also a figure of extreme sensuality. In this manner, too, she fulfils her vampiric script, for, according to Moretti, "Dracula ... liberates and exalts sexual desire. And this desire attracts but – at the same time – frightens".[40] Compare Moretti's reading and Denver's afore-mentioned suckling of blood at the breast, with James B. Twitchell's reference to a scene in the late 1960s Hammer Horror film *Dracula, Prince of Darkness*, in which he perceives the breast to stand in as substitute for the phallus:

> ... Christopher Lee first slowly draws his razor-sharp finger talon across his breast, leaving a foot-long serration, and [then] grabs his victim by the hair, forcing her to his chest in an unsubtle-enough way to titillate the audience and also get past the censor.[41]

One of the most important areas of Pamela Barnett's reading of Morrison's novel concentrates on what she calls the "breakfast" scene in which Black male slaves are forced to perform fellatio upon White male guards, which Barnett reads as a literalization of the requirement slavery inflicts upon these men to "go down" or debase themselves in social terms:

> After the prisoners line up, they must kneel and wait "for the whim of a guard, or two, or three" ... "Breakfast? Want some breakfast, nigger?" ... [so] deflect[ing] the guards' appetite onto the prisoners and forc[ing] the prisoners to name it as their own ... [42]

Once we compare Skura's description of the infant's unconsciously repressed rage at being "tied down, moved, filled, and emptied by someone too strong to resist – an invasion of the body which has its logical culmination in cannibalism and vampirism"[43] we recognise the immediate similarity with the way in which the slaves are habitually chained ("tied down"), made to walk miles in gangs ("moved"), forced into fellatio ("filled"), starved ("emptied"), all to ensure that the white guards remain "too strong to resist". Here, then, we find neither an infantile nor an adolescent fantasy of vengeance embodied by the iconic phantasy representative of the vampire, but an adult realization of those violent desires, one in which Black men are projected into what the White men see as the necessarily debased place of the mother.

I have said that the character Beloved embodies a sensual presence; Barnett defines her more precisely as the embodiment of the succubus, a specifically Afro-American blood-relation to the vampire, "a female demon and nightmare figure that sexually assaults male sleepers and drains them of semen". As in the case of the white guards, Paul D is the victim of Beloved's attentions in this context, a parallel that enables her not only to seduce Paul D, but also feed off "her victims' horrible memories of and recurring nightmares about sexual violations that occurred in their enslaved past". Barnett's reading, though persuasive, is extremely problematic in terms of the degree of complicity manifested in her reading of Beloved's role *vis-à-vis* Black oppression. Ultimately, for Barnett, Beloved remains a dangerous scapegoat, explaining the necessity for her final exorcism: "Beloved's child would represent for the community of women something they wish to exorcize, something they will not tolerate in the future – the memory of children forced on their bodies in the past."[44]

## The Viennese Witch Doctor: *A Question of Power* (1974)

Like *Beloved*, Bessie Head's novel *A Question of Power* examines the torture of the woman's psyche and body under a hostile ideology. As a mixed race South African in exile in Botswana, Head was writing through an awareness of similar horrors to those which haunt Sethe and, through her writing, Morrison. As a child Elizabeth, Head's central protagonist, is told that her own mother, a white woman, was stigmatized for allowing herself to become impregnated by a black stable-boy. Though distinct from Morrison's Sethe in these terms she shares their alienation from the mother/daughter bond and its political implications. Elizabeth is told, "Your mother was insane. If you're not careful you'll get insane just like your mother...."[45] So Elizabeth comes to perceive herself as the inheritor of a wound which, though focused on the head, inflicts itself in phantasy upon the vagina.

It is perfectly possible to read Head's novel purely as an exploration of madness, under the terms of which Elizabeth is a schizophrenia sufferer. Certainly, as Jacqueline Rose observes, the narrative itself is powerfully affective in psychological terms: "I am not sure that it is possible to read this book without feeling oneself go a little bit mad. It is, I think, part of the wager... "[46]. As a novel of/about madness, the reader is called upon to directly experience the central protagonist Elizabeth's breakdown, a mechanism effected by the narrative being glued to the central protagonist's narrative point of view as she is affected by recurrent nightmare hallucinations. Emerging at the end of the text whole, healed, ready to tell her story (the narrative is retrospective, told by the "cured" protagonist) some degree of resolution is offered. But to read the text only in this way shelves off one of its most powerful aspects, which is its simultaneous relationship with the horror genre and the powerful supernaturalism of traditional African witchcraft. In the terms of this reading Elizabeth is "possessed" by two hostile masculine predators.

In fact *A Question of Power* operates as a very good illustration of the workings of what Tzvetan Todorov defines as the essence of the fantastic, namely that:

> In a world which is indeed our world... a world without devils, sylphides, or vampires, there occurs an event which cannot be explained by the laws of this same familiar world. The person who experiences the event must opt for one of two possible solutions... Either the devil [or vampire] is an illusion, an imaginary being; or else [s/]he really exists... The fantastic occupies the duration of this uncertainty.[47]

As Rose indicates, Head's own perspective on conventional African occultism is at best sceptical, a stance that is understandable in the face of White Western readings of the Black woman as the "'dark continent' (Africa): the figure/witch of mystery".[48] This scepticism appears to be reflected in the novel when Elizabeth refers to local neighbours' grievances against each other as an "adult game that should really have been relegated to children: 'I'll betwitch you and you'll bewitch me'" [*QP*, 21]. In this context political realism wins out over superstition as Elizabeth continues, "...people seemed to survive [this game]...but not malnutrition and other ailments. As soon as these struck, they remembered the witchery" [*QP*, 21]. Nevertheless, cultural difference also plays a significant role in the decision to privilege a reading of mental illness over one of horror. A White Western reader who pays no heed to the occult possibilities raised by the text may also miss out on an important aspect of its politics. As Head discovered when researching for a subsequent book:

> ...there are two kinds of witches in the society...The day witches are people in the society who are evil and can be identified. The

night witches are hidden. They are the baloi. They enter the body of
a sleeping victim and from then on the victim feels a pain ... The hideous and the obscene is the great joy of the night witch/wizard. The
other great joy of the wizard is to open the mouth of a sleeping
person and poke his finger in it.[49]

Two aspects of this quotation are particularly noteworthy. The first is
that Head acknowledges this information came to her after writing
*A Question of Power*, but in doing so highlights a point that is clear at least
to this reader: there is a tangible unconscious (in fact uncanny) trace of
the supernatural here underlying what we might otherwise read as pure
psychoanalytic preoccupations. The second, not unrelated observation
raised by Head's research, is the similarity between Head's description
of the "night witch" here and Barnett's succubus or vampire already
encountered in relation to *Beloved*. Rose's observation that Elizabeth's
narrative is a form of "talking cure" feeds perfectly into the centrality
psychoanalysis holds to this text, but I disagree with her observation
that the one "crucial difference" in Head's novel is "that there is no
analyst present".[50] On the contrary, once we compare the dynamics of
Freud's case-study of Dora with Elizabeth's narrative it becomes clear
that Freud ("the Viennese witch doctor"[51]) and his ilk *are fully* present
in what we have come to see as their familiar role as vampire/succubus/
night witch of the text.

In his "Fragment of an Analysis of a Case of Hysteria ('Dora')", itself
a retrospective narrative distanced by time if not by a "cure", Freud is
quick to recognise the degree of sexual intimacy which the analytic
situation sets up: "I will simply claim for myself the rights of the gynae-
cologist – or rather, much more modest ones ... ".[52] The caesura, followed by the qualifier "or, rather ... " after the strikingly assertive "I
will simply ... " says it all. This woman has, in contrast to Freud's
"rights", no rights at all. She must lay all bare for his inquiring gaze,
while he may penetrate ("claim for myself") her depths with impunity.
The context for Freud's original disclaimer was the criticism he had
already received from colleagues, who deemed this level of vocal sexual
"intimacy" with young, inexperienced women to be professionally uneth-
ical. But what also emerges from Freud's desire to slip between vagina,
mouth (the source of the voice) and psyche is the vampiric dynamic
involved. The focus of Dora's encounter is, to Freud, a kiss on the lips
by a lakeside, a gesture in itself which Freud invests with a great deal of
sexual innuendo; but then so does vampire mythology: "Dracula's own
language conflates erotic desire and feeding; the mouth both kisses and

consumes, the same organ gratifying two distinct hungers".[53] Freud, having been invited over the threshold once, will seduce Dora into returning again and again, offering up her mouth/voice to his penetrating analysis. In the process her "complicity", like that of the male slaves in *Beloved*, is made to "own" an appetite that is all Freud's.

The notorious misreadings attributed to Freud in the Dora case usually cohere in flagrant examples of counter-transference, a factor usually directly or indirectly involved in switches of "complicity". Jacques Lacan reveals a crucial example of such "switching" when he points out that Freud reverses the accepted terminology when he refers to oral sex between Frau K. and Dora's impotent father as fellatio rather than cunnilingus and, in the process, reverses the dynamics of "blame". For Rose, *A Question of Power* is a novel in which "It is not [always] clear whether we are dealing with an outside-in or inside-out situation – the writing does not let you decide".[54] Nor, quite honestly, does Freud in his Case-Studies. All one can say is that in the following claim Freud's projection outwards seems more revealing of his own self-delusions:

> Neurotics are dominated by the opposition between reality and phantasy. If what they long for the most intensely in their phantasies is presented them in reality, they none the less flee from it; and they abandon themselves to their phantasies the most readily where they need no longer fear to see them realized.[55]

The demonic female is one of the prevailing topics of horror narratives, a point of little surprise once one considers that one of the key roles played by horror fiction derives from its ability to effect the cathartic expression of repressed socio-cultural fears and taboos. Freud's fascination with the image of Medusa, already encountered in connection with the castration/decapitation dyad, manifests itself centrally in *A Question of Power*. Patriarchal fears aside, Elizabeth undoubtedly *is* in need of healing, for when she skids on the slime of female mutilation herself (*QP*, 116), we remember that her relationship with the fantastic is not only defined by a tormented obscenity that all too frequently takes on a damaged and damaging female form, but that it equally frequently manifests itself as negatively overt female arousal intent upon the reduction of women themselves:

> ... [Medusa] sprawled her legs in the air, and the most exquisite sensation travelled out of her towards Elizabeth. It enveloped Elizabeth from head to toe like a slow, deep, sensuous bomb. It was like falling

into deep, warm waters... 'You haven't got anything *near* that, have you?' (*QP*,44)

This destructive and dark force is similar in form to the maliciously destructive force employed by Dan against Miss Pelican-Beak and the mannequin version of Elizabeth and hence, though manifesting itself in the form of a perverse distortion of active female sexuality, is really a patriarchal force. Like the black slime that Dan forces from Miss Pelican-Beak's breasts, Medusa's thunderbolts "...seemed to ooze out of her hands" (*QP*, 92) and, like her orgasm, threaten to explode in Elizabeth's face. On one level Head's depiction of Medusa is a different version of what operates, in *Beloved*, as the figure of the succubus and, like Morrison's eponymous character, feeds off female as much as male flesh. But Sello as incubus also plays a role here, emerging as a monster out of Elizabeth's own flesh:

> A filament-like umbilical cord appeared. Attached to its other end was Sello. The filament glowed with an incandescent light. As she looked at it, it parted in the middle, shrivelled and died. The huge satanic image of Sello opened its swollen, depraved mouth in one long scream. (*QP*,140)

This horrifying image, through its parodying of female biological creativity, also feeds into the type of misogynist horror we have seen revealed in Theweleit's study, in which women are repeatedly transformed into "castration wound[s]".[56] In Head's narrative this is given explicit treatment through the nightmare manifestations of masculine fears of failing to "stand up" to the superior sexual prowess of the *fantastic* woman:

> As she closed her eyes all these Coloured men lay down on their backs, their penes in the air, and began to die slowly. Some of them who could not endure these slow deaths simply toppled over into rivers and drowned, Medusa's mocking smile towering over them all. (*QP*,45)

Multiple references to heads being cut open or smashed to pieces often directly link in with horrifying vaginal images of the type Theweleit mentions: "She found herself faced with a deep cesspit. It was filled almost to the brim...It was so high, so powerful, that her neck nearly snapped off her head at the encounter" (*QP*, 53). In her Foreword to Theweleit's analysis, Barbara Ehrenreich refers to male perceptions of women's bodies as "holes, swamps, pits of muck that can engulf"[57]. In *A Question of Power*, by means of a horrific metonymy mirrored by Theweleit's own study, characters such as Madame Squelch Squelch and Miss Body Beautiful (whose orgasm is like "a small child wetting her pants" over Elizabeth (*QP*, 164)) demonstrate how masculinist fantasies of sexually active women are equally permeated by swamps of slime and filth which transform the secretions of the vagina, through nightmare, into frighteningly contagious festering tissue: "The flesh of [Miss Body Beautiful's] private parts had a raw, red look as though the surface skin had been rubbed off by many hands" (*QP*, 164). This returns us to Freud's case-studies on hysteria, its perceived connection with syphilis and, by extension, vampirism.

The relationship between purity and contagion in Head's text follows a similar trajectory not just to Freud's phantasies, but also Gilman's analysis of the relationship between Victorian pimping and prostitution:

> The seducer [of prostitutes] is parallel to the image of Bram Stoker's *Dracula* (1897). For in the act of seduction he transforms the innocence of the female into a copy of himself, just as Dracula's victims become vampires. She becomes the prostitute as seductress, infecting other males ... [58]

In essence Gilman offers a corrective to James B. Twitchell's affirmation that "Horror monsters exist without explanation. Jack the Ripper, The Boston Strangler, and Charles Manson just are; likewise, the vampire, the Frankenstein monster, the werewolf, the zombie".[59] On the contrary, Gilman insists, there are cultural explanations for everything, including the anti-Semitic nineteenth-century belief that the East End location for the murders was sufficient to cause widespread public speculation that "Jack" was a "*shochet*" a Jewish ritual butcher.[60] In *A Question of Power*, the brutal and ritualized woman-hating we witness is epitomized by Dan and Sello who, in equating their variously fetishized images of women with filth and degradation, simultaneously taunt Elizabeth with her prudery and castigate her for being like them:

> ...he had a masterpiece of his own to produce...she could see him wiping up the legs a bit because they were too dirty. Then supposedly, since he was God, he breathed into it the breath of life. The model stood up and turned to face Elizabeth. They were identical replicas except that what stood before Elizabeth was a demon of sensuousness...Her legs were so weak she could hardly stand on them. (*QP*, 192–3)

One of the many astonishing claims Freud makes in his case-study of Dora is that her choice to resist Herr K.'s advances is sufficient, in itself, to effect a diagnosis: "I should without question consider a person hysterical in whom an occasion for sexual excitment elicited feelings that were preponderantly or exclusively unpleasurable".[61] Like Dora, Anna O., Frau Emmy von N., Miss Lucy R., Head's Elizabeth is repeatedly confronted by a variety of soiled and contaminated phantasy forms in an attempt to force her to "shape up" once and for all:

> Pelican-Beak was too pushy . . . He broke her legs, he broke her jutting spindly elbows . . . Out of her breasts which were small, round and hard, he forced a black slime . . . Then he decided that [she] was too dangerous; she'd better quiet down totally. He'd redesign her pelvis area along the lines of Elizabeth's, which was extraordinarily passive . . . There, sure enough, at Elizabeth's side appeared a feminine pelvis with passive legs, nearly a replica of Elizabeth's. Poor Pelican-Beak had her own slashed off and was fitted out with a new pelvis. (*QP*, 167–8)

Significantly, three areas of the woman's body form the foci for this destructive act: the breasts, the pelvis and (it is implied) the mouth/vagina. In dismembering her breasts and pelvis Dan effects a Jack-the-Ripper style assault which aims itself explicitly at woman's ability to reproduce. In attempting to render her passive (mute) Dan indirectly aims a blow at her mouth. As Rosalind Coward observes:

> . . . the mouth seems to be woman's . . . most intimate orifice . . . Source of gratifications, illicit and delicious intimacies, the organ of confession, the mouth is strangely crossed by the structures of eroticism and prohibition which touch on women . . . Is it that . . . lipstick has condensed the eroticisms and the prohibitions around the mouth? For blood on a woman's orifice reminds me of another orifice which bleeds.[62]

The silencing of one orifice here undoubtedly functions as an implied (and far more ferocious) attempt to render another impotent, for it is the vagina which is the real source of threat, a space too horrifying to confront. Hence although Angela Carter claims that woman's "symbolic value is primarily that of . . . a dumb mouth from which the teeth have been pulled",[63] we know it is not an engulfing by the mouth which Dan fears, teeth or no teeth, but that orifice which gives her definition: "her passageway, which was long and tough like the bird's beak" (*QP*, 167).

One important additional connection between vampiric penetration and Freudian psychoanalysis resides within the role of the needle in this novel. Like the teeth of the vampire, this pointed incisor perforates the skin in order to inject an alien contamination. Like the vision we have been constructing of the psychoanalyst, the needle is a simultaneous source of healing and contagion. Though in its hypodermic, soothing quality it lulls Elizabeth back into a calming sedation, beneath the surface of both the narrative and the skin it becomes, like the penis of Dora's father, a "dirty squirter" which has ruptured and is destroying her mind:[64] "It had taken such a drastic clamour to silence the hissing record in her head, but it had left a terrible wound. She could feel it bleeding and bleeding, quietly. Her so-called *analytical* mind was being shattered to pieces." (*QP*, 52–3 – my emphasis) It is through a combination of the intervention of Miss Sewing-Machine and the phallic needle which "rattles up and down" all night long, that the threads of Elizabeth's nightmare world bind together and tighten around her like a noose. The ultimate horror of Elizabeth's nightmare world, however, is that unlike Theweleit's analysis hers is a projection of a female mind turned destructively inward upon itself. A similar problem is at work in Atwood's *Alias Grace* (1996).

## Freud, Dora, and *Alias Grace* (1996)

*Alias Grace* is a novel about the ideological power of storytelling, a point that is made clear from the first 20 pages of the text, which juxtapose extracts from Susanna Moodie's *Life in the Clearings* (1853), which is a piece of social history surrounding the case of the real Grace Marks, the protagonist of Atwood's novel, alongside newspaper articles of the period, poetry written about the "real" events and the first chapter of the text. The treatment of history *as* fiction is a point Atwood is careful to justify in her "Author's Afterword":

> I have of course fictionalized historical events (as did many commentators on this case who claimed to be writing history). I have not changed any known facts, although the written accounts are so contradictory that few facts emerge as unequivocally 'known' ... Where mere hints and gaps exist in the records, I have felt free to invent.[65]

Where we have seen Winterson unapologetically "fictionalize" history to suit her own purposes in *Sexing the Cherry*, Atwood feels a greater need to spell out and hence justify her own stance regarding the boundaries between the real and the unreal in *Alias Grace*. As part of the blurring of fact and fiction the work of Mrs Moodie is referred to inside the text, by Dr Samuel Bannerling, a medical consultant, as "the concoction of convenient fairy tales" and "the 'eye-witness reports' of a goose" [*AG*, 435]. Atwood is also sceptical of Moodie's study and its findings outside the text, but perceives her book to be important in terms of asserting the presence of female influence upon social concerns and reforms of the day. Like Grace, she is another female writer written over by Atwood. *Alias Grace* is an explicitly intertextual novel, not just in its rethinking of pre-existing source material but in the reading of stories within stories which takes place within it. Nancy's reading to Mr Kinnear of Sir Walter Scott's *The Lady of the Lake* is one example of this, as is Mr MacKenzie's comparison between Grace and the Scheherazade of *The Thousand and One Nights*. As in *Beloved*, although we are reading a late-twentieth-century novel, the reader must resituate herself in nineteenth-century terms (at least partially). Also like *Beloved*, *Alias Grace* is composed of a combination of linear and anti-linear modes. The effect of this is, at times, unsettling, not least for the reason that we are left to juggle between science, religion, superstition and psychology – all of which our own culture tends to read (and treat) quite distinctly, in order to experience history's own complexities at first hand. But although we, as readers, need to partially situate ourselves within a nineteenth-century framework in order to follow the text, it is not a nineteenth-century novel we are reading. We are now so well versed in twentieth-century psychoanalysis that the work of Dr Jordan and the other clinicians in this text seems retrospectively prototypical of the findings and trickery of twentieth-century psychoanalysis and must, to some extent, be read in this regard. Grace could be articulating the words of Head's Elizabeth when she observes:

> When you are in the middle of a story it isn't a story at all, but only a confusion; a dark roaring, a blindness, a wreckage of shattered glass and splintered wood . . . [*AG*, 298]

The same oscillations between the supernatural and the psychological are central to this text as were central to *A Question of Power*. Grace, it turns out, is possessed by the phantom of Mary Whitney, a friend who dies from a botched abortion and whose soul parasitically attaches itself to Grace's body and speaks through her mouth like a ventriloquist. Under the influence of Mary's demonic drive she murders Nancy Montgomery, the housekeeper and lover of her employer Mr Kinnear. Failing to recall anything about the murder, the text joins Grace as she is incarcerated under a life sentence, the death sentence having been revoked on the basis that Grace was suffering from delusions and thus not in full control of her faculties at the time of the murder. Dr Simon Jordan, interested in her case, uses her as an experiment for testing his own reformation theories about how to treat and understand the insane. He believes that, through delving into the depths of her psyche, Grace will ultimately recall and narrate to him the precise events surrounding Nancy's death. Only at the end of the novel, Grace having been put into a mesmeric trance by the charlatan "quack" Dr DuPont, does Mary reveal her presence and, along with it, Grace's innocence. In that regard *Alias Grace* is simultaneously a novel of the occult and a narrative centrally involved in the workings of nineteenth-century psychiatric practice. Grace is not *just* possessed, she is also a speaking subject with a psyche, whose dreams and patterns of free association are Dr Jordan's fascination:

> Every day he has set some small object in front of her, and has asked her to tell him what it causes her to imagine. This week he's attempted various root vegetables, hoping for a connection that will lead downwards: Beet – Root Cellar – Corpses, for instance; or even Turnip – Underground – Grave. [*AG*, 90]

So Atwood draws attention to the ways in which the discourses of mesmerism, medicine and spiritualism, otherwise so keen to disassociate themselves from each other, come together at the one meeting point of their speculations upon women. At the final *dénouement* scene, a perfect illustration of such a meeting point, despite the presence of both women and men, the dynamics are identical to those not only of conventional psychoanalytic practice but also of Boyle's experiments with the air chamber discussed in Chapter 2. Only the men are directly addressed, the women being either the passive object of speculation or mere onlookers.

Storytelling and its complexities, then, interpreted by the type of struggling reader we are conceptualising in this chapter, follows a sort of distorted psychoanalytic dynamic. Freud is notoriously circumlocutory in his telling of his own tales, but in a manner that seems destined to put the needs of a "good story" before genuine findings:

> I cannot help wondering how it is that the authorities can produce such smooth and precise histories in cases of hysteria. As a matter of

fact the patients are incapable of giving such reports about themselves. They can, indeed, give the physician plenty of coherent information about this or that period of their lives; but it is sure to be followed by another period as to which their communications run dry, leaving gaps unfilled, and riddles unanswered... The connections ... are for the most part incoherent... [66]

In essence, Freud's tracing of his methodology is one which sets himself up as the embodiment of order there to dispel chaos. But where he hopes, as primary narrator, to disappear largely from view and allow his story to tell itself, he disconceals his own trickery, revealing himself as the central figure early on in his text: "Even during the course of their story patients will repeatedly correct a particular or a date, and then perhaps, after wavering for some time, return to their first version". This, it turns out, is exactly what he does; as Angela Richards observes,

It is curious that in his later writings Freud more than once assigns his treatment of "Dora" to the wrong year – to 1899 instead of 1900. The mistake is also repeated twice in the footnote which he added to the case history in 1923... There can be no question that the autumn of 1900 was the correct date... [67]

This meta-textual preoccupation reveals itself in *Alias Grace* in Mr MacKenzie, Grace's lawyer's determination to turn Grace's story into his own:

He wanted me to tell my story in what he called a coherent way, but would often accuse me of wandering... and at last he said that the right thing was, not to tell the story as I truly remembered it... but to tell a story that would hang together. [*AG*, 357]

Perhaps MacKenzie's most Freudian moment, however, one which even shocks the narcissistic Dr Jordan, is when he tells Jordan that Grace's inability to resolve her analysis is due to her romantic fascination with him:

The poor creature has fallen in love with you... You are doubtless the object of her waking daydreams... I had the experience myself, or the twin of it; for I had to pass many hours with her, in her jail in Toronto, while she spun out her yarn for me to as great a length as it would go. She was besotted with me, and didn't wish to let me out of her sight. [*AG*, 377]

In this context of self-delusion it is worth pausing to consider the real status of the word "Alias" in Atwood's title. On one level it refers, of course, not to the central protagonist but to Mary, who hides behind Grace (and her name) in committing "her" crime, hence operating under the alias, Grace. But there is another sense in which the term does relate directly to Grace herself. Following Grace's ultimate reprieve and attempt to begin a new life, she considers "to those who do not know my story I will not be anybody in particular" [*AG*, 443]. Taking on a new identity, like Freud's famous case histories, the alias becomes more literalized, purportedly designed to protect the "real" identity of the subject, but in the process helping to effect the disappearance of the "real women" behind the names and hence render Dora and the others the total property of the text, author/ized by a patriarch named Freud or Simon Jordan. The story of "Dora", as seems to be clear to most critics, is really the story of Freud, hence his lack of scruples about obtaining her permission prior to publication.[68] These convolutions and power relations implicate the reader, for whereas, in *A Question of Power*, our point of identification lies with Elizabeth throughout, here narrative point shifts between analyst and analysand. So, while Grace is the character with whom we sympathize, our point of readerly identification lies with Dr Jordan who, like us, treats Grace's case as a complex puzzle to be unravelled/made sense of.

The vampire dynamic is again the major pattern, implicit in *Alias Grace* via the clinician/patient dyad and explicit in Mary Whitney's possession of her body. At times there are difficulties in deciding where Dr Jordan's predilections end and Mary's parasitism begins: "*Murderess, murderess*, he whispers to himself. It has an allure . . . He imagines himself . . . draw[ing] Grace towards him, pressing his mouth against her. *Murderess*. He applies it to her throat like a brand" [*AG*, 389]. We have seen that, for Freud, it is the kiss on the mouth which functions as the crucial metonymy in Dora's story, operating to signify both the stimulation of sexual secretions through masturbation or fellatio and oral repulsion signalled by vomiting. But here Simon does not fantasize about their lips meeting. Instead his simply imprint themselves upon Grace like a tattoo. He has as much autonomy over her body in this scene as he has over her story throughout the text and just as he draws the threads of her story together like the cord on a drawstring bag, here he sucks her story out from under her skin. Earlier on her lips are the focus of his eyes, not his mouth:

> [Grace] was threading the needle now; she wet the end of the thread in her mouth, to make it easier, and this gesture seemed to him all at

once both completely natural and unbearably intimate. He felt as if he was watching her undress, through a chink in the wall, as if she was washing herself with her tongue, like a cat. [*AG*, 91]

The sexual dynamics of this scene are abundant and Grace is cast in a partially complicit light. But she will not accept, as Freud affirms, that "there is no such thing at all as an unconscious 'No'".[69] Instead she is quite clear where to draw the line, refusing to comply with Dr Jordan's suggestions at those moments when she perceives him to have taken advantage of her in some way: "I should not speak to him so freely, and decide I will not, if that is the tone he is going to take" [*AG*, 161].

But Grace is not the only victim of Dr Jordan's perverse desires. Lacking Grace's (or is it Mary's?) deep sense of self-protection, it is through Rachel, his landlady cum mistress, that Dr Jordan's own Jekyll and Hyde duality comes to light:

During the day, Rachel is a burden, an encumbrance, and he wishes to be rid of her; but at night she's an altogether different person, and so is he. He too says no when he means yes. He means more, he means further, he means deeper. He would like to make an incision in her – just a small one – so he can taste her blood ... [*AG*, 365–6]

Jordan's desires for incisions here mirror the stabbing of Nancy, the sheets upon which they writhe reminding us of those upon which his daylight self writes up stories of Grace, his night-time self feeding off Rachel's self-loathing.

Another way in which day- and night-time selves come together here is, in purely narrative terms, via the *mise-en-scène* of the analytic situation, which might be said to follow what Twitchell defines as the formula of early gothic narratives:

The sexual assault usually takes place in a confined setting ... [and] tells the story of a single and specific family romance run amok; "father" has become monstrous to "daughter". It seems to make little difference if the father role is shunted to uncle, priest, duke, landlord, devil [or analyst?], as long as his relationship with the young female is one of paternal dominance.[70]

Grace we find situated in a variety of "confined settings": a prison, servitude in other people's households, the consulting room, the asylum. In all of them she is assessed and analysed by a variety of older, supposedly authoritative, masculine figures. The same can be said for Rachel, who ultimately becomes a prisoner in her own gothic household as the maid (ironically also named Dora) delights in broadcasting:

> What [Dora] had to tell, you would scarcely credit . . . screams and groans and horrifying goings-on at night, as bad as a haunted house . . . I must say she made a good story out of it. But I thought myself she got carried away. [*AG*, 427]

Here, Grace plays the role of the doubting Freud, but in another reversal the "family romance" aspect of Twitchell's observation seems to apply more to Jordan's own situation, for while we read about Grace's own difficult, poverty-stricken upbringing it is Jordan's that appears to attempt further concealment.

On the surface Simon Jordan is afflicted with an overly possessive mother who is determined to see him marry the "right" kind of woman and banish all unsuitable rivals at any cost. Rachel, a mature woman, simultaneously threatens the mother with the determined predatory ways that appear to match her own and offers Dr Jordan a form of effigy upon which he acts out the horrifyingly violent fantasies that imply his own deep-seated hatred for such women. His father being dead, this might appear to be the central "family romance" and one which largely follows Freud's purportedly Oedipal structures. But in fact, as a chance aside seems to reveal, it is actually his father who may hold the key to his use and abuse of younger, more vulnerable, possibly socially "inferior" women. This revelation is cast within the parameters of a dream deriving from another potentially gothic scenario:

> Simon is dreaming of a corridor. It's the attic passageway of his old house, the house of his childhood; the big house they had before his father's failure and death. The maids slept up here. It was a secret world, one as a boy he wasn't supposed to explore, but did . . . When he was feeling very brave he would venture into their rooms, knowing they were downstairs . . . he'd examine their things . . . In his dream the passageway is the same, only bigger . . . But the doors are closed, and also locked . . . There are people in there though . . . Women, the maids . . . their lips parted . . . waiting for him. The door at the end opens. Inside it is the sea. Before he can stop himself, down he goes, the water closing over his head . . . Past him, just out of reach, various objects are floating . . . Things that were his father's once, but sold after his death . . . He watches in horror, because now they're gathering,

twining together, re-forming. Tentacles are growing. A dead hand. His father, in the sinuous process of coming back to life. He has an over-whelming sense of having transgressed.

He wakes, his heart is pounding... After he's lain quietly for a time, reflecting, he thinks he understands the train of association that must have led to such a dream. It was Grace's story, with its Atlantic crossing, its burial at sea... and the overbearing father, of course. One father leads to another. [*AG*, 139–40]

Despite his haste to parcel up this lengthy testimonial as Grace's story, the outline of a cryptonomy appears to emerge. The narrative turns, like Roz's dream about the Holocaust and its detritus in *The Robber Bride*, into an example of transgenerational haunting involving his own dead father and, presumably, surreptitious meetings with the maids. That Jordan is in "over his head", suggested by the drowning imagery, infers a piece of voyeuristic repression at the centre of his unconscious among what he refers to elsewhere as "the forest of amnesia, where things have lost their names" [*AG*, 291]. The originary phant-asy at the source of the repression might well revolve around a primal scene involving the lost/fallen father and these maids, while the "one father" who "leads to another" discloses his acknowledgement of his own likely future as a predator upon fallen women (akin to the situ-ation involving the Victorian pimp and prostitute noted earlier in this chapter). Naturally it also recalls Dora and her sense of betrayal at her father's defence of Herr K.

The longing for clean sheets that perturbs Jordan at times in the text is only partly explicable in terms of a guilty conscience. In the context of sheets of paper it is also an awareness that he sullies Grace with his written inscriptions as much as he does Rachel with his/her bloody trails. Sheets are everywhere in this novel, from shrouds to the multiple references to hanging out laundry (equated in general with the "wash-ing of Grace's dirty linen in public"). Just like the winding sheet in which Grace's mother's corpse is buried at sea, as we delve down through the layers of both characters' unconscious and Grace's story gradually unravels, what one expects to see revealed gradually comes to resemble another form. "[As] the sheet began to come undone at the top... her hair floated out... [But] the hair was over her face so I could not see it, and it was darker than my mother's hair had been ...." [*AG*, 167] Dr Jordan, like the later Freud, in perceiving no irregularity in read-ing anatomical symptoms as apparently "hysterical" data, acts out the reversal of the head and body imagery so frequently inflicted upon women under patriarchy. But in a similar reversal he also comes to learn the manner in which his own professional status becomes sexualized for women. So, though claiming to be "unprepared" for the attraction his status holds for women [*AG*, 81], he obviously relishes the ease with which this gives him access to their bodies and the power it affords him to judge and to classify. Nor is he slow to endow his intimate knowledge of Grace's psychology with the type of fantasy fleshly significance we find Freud attributing to his female analysands:

> He has been where they could never go, seen what they could never see; he has opened up women's bodies, and peered inside. In his hand, which has just raised their own hands towards his lips, he may once have held a beating female heart. [*AG*, 81–2]

In this narcissistic response, coupled with the kiss to the proffered hand, we hear further echoes of Dora's case-history. Freud, analysing her awareness of the pressure of the man's embrace "upon the upper part of her body", determines to reread this symptom in the manner most flattering to his own theory:

> *I have formed in my own mind* ... [the belief] that during the man's passionate embrace she felt not merely his kiss upon her lips but also the pressure of his erect member against her body. This perception was revolting to her; it was dismissed from her memory, repressed, and replaced by the innocent sensation of pressure upon her thorax, which in turn derived an excessive intensity from its repressed source.[71]

It is via this focus upon "pressure upon [the] thorax" that Freud accounts for what he sees as Dora's chief hysterical symptom, "a complete loss of voice", coupled with "a cough and ... hoarseness".[72] Like Dr Jordan's recurrent fascination with the "whisper" which seems to him to hold the key to the secrets of Grace's alleged crime, the voice is both sexualized and later demonized in its connection with the opening from which it emanates. Just like Dora's own choked orifice, so for Grace this emanation is choked/stopped/blocked by Dr Jordan's intervention, among others. Irony surrounds the role of Mary's voice in this context. When Grace continues with the words: "*I* was shut up inside that doll of myself, and *my* true voice could not get out" [*AG*, 295 – my emphasis] we cannot be sure if the first person pronoun here relates to Grace speaking as herself or to Mary speaking through Grace's narrative psyche. Certainly Grace is the doll/dummy to Mary's ventriloquism, passively parroting Mary's own insights throughout.

We have seen that one of the many acts of doubling which take place in *Alias Grace* involves Jordan's desires to conjoin Grace and Rachel into the archetypal virgin/whore duality so popular in nineteenth-century fiction. Ironically, not until the final revelation scene does he learn that an identical and equally sexualized double has been facing him, day after day, within Grace's own form. Mary's ultimate choice to reveal her true identity through the words and music of the hymn "Rock of Ages, Cleft for Me" underlines her occult status simply by rendering a Christian hymn profane in the name of "grace"; but the specific choice of hymn is also significant. The words do not just draw attention to the means of possession ("Let me hide myself, in thee") but also the "cleft" which indicates the centrality of vulvic imagery. Grace, feeling early on in the text that Dr Jordan's interventions into her case involve a sense that she is being " ... torn open; not like a body of flesh ... but like a peach; and not even torn open, but too ripe and splitting open of its own accord" [*AG*, 69], reminds us that the perceived presence of this vampiric, sensualized other who knows Simon's desires better than even Rachel does would be, in conjunction with the idealized Grace, Jordan's epitome of the phallocentric masturbatory fantasy of possessing two women simultaneously. Day-dreaming of keeping Grace as a secret mistress closeted away for his private use, he considers, "But why only mistress? It comes to him that Grace Marks is the only woman he's ever met that he would wish to marry." [*AG*, 388]

What seems a respectful desire here drags at its heels a reminder of another Grace, Grace Poole, and her own charge, Bertha Mason, likewise "closeted away" for Rochester's personal convenience in Charlotte Brontë's *Jane Eyre* (1847). But Grace is no accepting Jane Eyre and, confronting the horror of this duality head on it is actually Simon who responds in the type of hysterical fashion Brontë attributes to Bertha: "his brain [felt] like a roasting chestnut, or an animal on fire. Silent howls resound inside him; there's a dashing and frenzied motion, a scrambling, a dashing to and fro ... " [*AG*, 407]. According to Haraway, for many in the first decades of the twentieth century, race mixing was a venereal disease of the social body, producing doomed progeny whose reproductive issue was as tainted as that of lesbians, sodomites, Jews, overeducated women, prostitutes, criminals, masturbators, or alcoholics.[73] Firstly we notice how similar so many of these categories are to the women branded (or "brand named" in Haraway's terminology) by Freud as hysteric. Secondly we see in that inheritance the nineteenth-century fascination with vampires. So many fantastic forms that we tend, in contemporary terms, to think of as recognizably different and stable in their various identities prove to derive from interchangeable terms. Phantoms, fairies and vampires all, for example, derive from their usage as synonyms for "the dead". In the ensuing chapter we consider the role played by the phantom (beginning with its proximity to the vampire for certain critics) with particular reference to psychoanalytic readings, not of Oedipal relations, but with regard to relationships between women, revisiting *Beloved* and *The Robber Bride* alongside Jeanette Winterson's *Written on the Body*.

# 4

# Ghosts and (Narrative) Ghosting: Margaret Atwood, Jeanette Winterson and Toni Morrison

It was not I that answered, I was not there at all. I was following a phantom in my mind, whose shadowy form had taken shape at last. Her features were blurred, her colouring indistinct, the setting of her eyes and the texture of her hair was still uncertain, still to be revealed.[1]

A great deal of work has, by now, been published on the gothic (including the female gothic), but until recently relatively little of that has focused upon the role played by the contemporary ghost story as a way of exploring female subjectivity. From the start this task may appear an atavistic one. In one of his characteristically sweeping statements, Freud confidently asserted in 1919, "All supposedly educated people have ceased to believe officially that the dead can become visible as spirits", but this is not to say that he advocates their redundancy as objects of phantasy. On the contrary, he acknowledges:

... the primitive fear of the dead is still so strong within us and always ready to come to the surface on any provocation ... Considering our unchanged attitude towards death, we might rather inquire what has become of the repression, which is the necessary condition of a primitive feeling recurring in the shape of something uncanny.[2]

As is well known, what Freud goes on to argue in his essay is that the mother's body is the ultimate taboo which deflects us away from a recurrent confrontation with the dead, the mother's genitals forming the all-pervasive embodiment of the uncanny: "what was once *heimisch*, familiar; the prefix 'un' ['un-'] is the token of repression". Though the origins of life, for Freud the castration complex reconfigures the mother's body as the space of death to the phallus and hence death in general.[3] Freud's analysand/protagonist in this essay is presumed to be male. What happens in the context of fiction when both protagonists (the alive and the dead) are female?

Within a more specifically gendered context, Jenni Dyman's work on the ghost stories of Edith Wharton asserts that so called "popular" women's writing always engages with a double-voiced discourse that inevitably functions as narrative "ghosting" (as in the double-image of a television screen). This, she argues, produces "a dual text, a text in the dominant language observing traditional forms, and a subtext which, breaking the bonds of the dominant language through a sub-language, conveys [the woman writer's] perspective".[4] This observation sites the point of subversion at a level underlying a surface (and superficially conformist) popular narrative form, emerging from between the lines and articulating itself only to the ear that can hear it. In a more contemporary context, what interests me about Dyman's position is that it seems to be focusing upon a fleeting space and moment of contiguity. Her interest actually lies in the point at which both layers *speak together* to give voice to the "real" ghost of the text,which might be read as a form of *écriture féminine*/writing the body which, in this case, also functions as a body of articulation – the underlying, occluded voice speaking through a surface level of conformity.

## *Rebecca*: The Ghost(ed) Text

First published in 1938, Daphne du Maurier's novel *Rebecca* can neither, in all conscience, be claimed to be contemporary nor obviously feminist. Nevertheless it acts as a form of close ancestor to all the contemporary novels discussed in this chapter not least because, underlying the apparently conformist nature of its heterosexual romantic plot is precisely the type of latently subversive – even feminist – ghosting strategy outlined by Dyman. In the same way that Mary Shelley's *Frankenstein* operates as the originary source text for so many of the issues raised by Haraway, Piercy, Russ and Weldon in Chapter 2, so in this chapter we will find *Rebecca* carving out space for a far more explicitly political version of the contemporary feminist ghost story, a form of narrative in which, among the many doublings that take place within such works, the ghost both is and is not a literal spectre.

In the previous chapter we examined the extent to which Freud's relationship with his own monster, the female hysterical subject, can be seen to operate as a type of vampire dynamic. In their own reading of du Maurier's novel, Avril Horner and Sue Zlosnik analyse the role played by the eponymous heroine as that of a contemporary vampire figure. Beginning with a reassessment of Alison Light's own reading of Rebecca as vamp or femme fatale, Horner and Zlosnik continue by claiming that these two terms are not as interchangeable as they at first appear: "'vamp' is defined by the Oxford English Dictionary as a Jezebel figure who is deliberately destructive, whereas the femme fatale is often perceived as having 'power *despite herself*'". Noting the direct etymological derivation of vamp from "vampire", they continue, "Rebecca is also associated throughout the novel with several characteristics which ... traditionally denote the vampiric body: facial pallor, plentiful hair and voracious sexual appetite ... And, like the vampire, she has to be 'killed' more than once: the plot's excessive, triple killing of Rebecca (she was shot; she had cancer; she drowned) echoes the folk belief that vampires must be 'killed' three times".[5]

My own reading of *Rebecca* takes a different line to Horner and Zlosnik's, but to some extent can be seen to be playing around with similar tropes. In particular, what both share is their recognition that the crucial relationship in the novel is not, as might appear, that between the unnamed second wife and Maxim de Winter, but that between two women joined by their negation in patriarchal terms: the woman with no name and the woman who has nothing and is nothing *but* her name, Rebecca. Luce Irigaray's influential if controversial essay "This Sex Which Is Not One" is, of course, a direct answer to Freudian readings of female sexuality and, in those terms alone, is a useful rejoinder to what has gone before.[6] Picking up on Freud's negation of female sexuality through his theory of penis envy, Irigaray recasts woman as an autoerotic being whose dual set of labia, always in contact with each other, are ruptured by the intervention of the phallus in a manner that severs woman into two parts that are unnaturally severed, one from another. The well-known paradox of Irigaray's essay is that woman is neither one nor two. Her two sets of lips prevent her ever from being "singular" in her eroticism, but their contiguous relationship, one with another, means that they continually push towards a unity of the self. The importance of her argument on a cultural level, of course, is that it operates as a dynamic explaining the difficulties of female-female bonding under a heterosexist patriarchy that is insistent upon reading the man as the target of all female desire. Woman will turn away from herself, turn her back upon her sister self, in order to compete for the man whose attentions will, we are told, make us (w)hole.

On the surface *Rebecca* is an archetypal patriarchal text. Effaced by the more wealthy, more beautiful, more accomplished first wife, the name-less heroine, whose very lack of identification makes her everywoman in her perceived inability to compete with the idealized other at a stage of removal, encourages the reader to identify and join with her in her successful attempt to banish the dead rival, firstly by discrediting her and secondly through Maxim's affirmation that he loves the ordinary woman, not the impossibly beautiful one. But this superficial conform-ity does not account for the all-pervasive fascination this novel holds for so many women readers. One of the central themes of *Rebecca* lies with the pleasures of storytelling itself. The opening:

> Last night I dreamt I went to Manderley again. It seemed to me I stood by the iron gate leading to the drive, and for a while I could not enter, for the way was barred to me ... Then, like all dreamers, I was possessed of a sudden with supernatural powers and passed like a spirit through the barrier before me [*R*, 5]

is that of the typical traveller's mystery and, in its status as best-seller, the book appeals to many women as the possible adventure story of themselves. But that opening also infers a delving back into repressed material, a point made particularly clearly by the opening of Alfred Hitchcock's cinematic version (1940), in which the disembodied voice of the nameless protagonist speaks over a moonlit entrance to Mander-ley, where these famous words are accompanied by the image of an apparently impenetrable wrought-iron gateway which, as we (through the eyes of the camera lens) push against its outer limits becomes trans-formed into a veil-like curtain, immediately swaying aside and beckon-ing us within. Manderley thus exists as the site of unconscious desires *couched* in the guise of unconscious fears, at the centre of which stands that inviting woman Rebecca.

In order to understand the full dynamics of the rivalrous relationship between the first and second Mrs de Winter, we need to recognize that the second wife is not simply *jealous* of Rebecca, she wants to *bond inseparably* with her. In reading this book about an absent eponymous heroine, it is all too easy to follow the narrative dynamic set up, again, by nineteenth-century novels like Charlotte Brontë's *Jane Eyre* and unthinkingly elide the unnamed character with the name of Rebecca. Like the point of contiguity that Irigaray identifies between the two sets of lips, this name brings the two women to the closest point of proxim-ity, while at the same time indicating their point of absolute severance.

In other words Rebecca is, to the nameless protagonist, both the "other woman" and the desired "other self", as the following looking-glass moment implies:

> In a minute Rebecca herself would come back into the room, sit down before the looking-glass ... I should see her reflection in the glass *and she would see me too* ... I went on standing there waiting for something to happen. [*R*, 173 – my emphasis]

In drawing attention to this moment of reciprocity involving the looking-glass, here we notice that the viewer who stares into it and the face one sees in it are, in essence, both "I" and "not I", inescapably conjoined by that glass surface. This is, of course, the metaphor of much lesbian fiction, in which the desired other is a vision of one who is simultaneously self and other, embracing sameness and difference at the same time. Later on in the text, the desire to reflect the other within the self takes on a form of fleshly materiality as the unnamed protagonist is granted her wish. But here she gazes on as if returning the initially returned gaze:

> I did not recognize the face that stared at me in the glass. The eyes were larger surely, the mouth narrower, the skin white and clear? The curls stood away from the head in a little cloud. *I watched this self that was not me at all* and then smiled; a new, slow smile. [*R*, 221 – my emphasis]

In *The Apparitional Lesbian*, Terry Castle documents the image of the apparition as a key *leitmotif* for closet lesbianism in literary history, a study that begins with a statement highly evocative of both passages from *Rebecca*: "When it comes to lesbians ... many people have trouble seeing what's in front of them."[7] For Castle the apparition or spectre is at the centre of cultural explorations of lesbian desire, simply because the historical determination, most notorious during the Victorian era, to render lesbianism "disappeared" in cultural terms, does not succeed in killing it off. On the contrary, she claims, lesbianism haunts patriarchal culture more than any other form of difference, simply because it renders its basic tenets (that women are the focus for exchanges between men) totally redundant. The fantastic element evoked by the spectre is also crucial to Castle's concerns, for the anti-mimetic identity of the ghost reminds us that only by moving beyond the ideologically-constrained realms of patriarchal reality are new and renewing avenues opened up. The main focus for Castle's study lies in what she deems the central paradox of this (and all) spectral images, namely that what is ghosted in order to be exorcised can, under the right stimulus, manifest itself out of thin air: "Strictly for repressive purposes, one could hardly think of a *worse* metaphor [than the phantom] ... To become an apparition was also to become endlessly capable of 'appearing'".[8]

Once Rebecca is dead, Mrs Danvers the housekeeper keeps her desires alive. Implied to be lesbian in orientation and thus another (perhaps successful) rival for Rebecca's affections, on one of the rare occasions where Mrs Danvers allows the mask of servile duty to slip from her face, she coerces the second wife, not just into dressing-up as Rebecca at the fancy-dress ball, but, on a separate and more fleeting occasion, to step into her shoes: "Sometimes, when Mr de Winter is away, and you feel lonely, you might like to come up to these rooms and sit here. You only have to tell me" [*R*, 180]. The second wife's demurral, like the presence of the looking-glass itself, reminds us that though providing the intimacy of mirroring, the glass surface remains like a membrane separating the two women in their difference just as they are conjoined.

Paradoxically, contiguity *requires* such a severance in order to bring about the site of alignment, presence partly depending upon absence for its effect. In all ghost stories it stands to reason that this "space of severance" is the determining factor. And this explains the mystery behind the second wife's determination to refer, repeatedly, to Rebecca as if her name is "no one" (arguably a mirror image of her own naming). So, she tells us, "No one" lived at Rebecca's beach-house [*R*, 119] and, calling a second time, "No one" answers [*R*, 161], despite the presence she feels in the room. On asserting that "No one" calls her husband Max [*R*, 167], despite having already told us that this is Rebecca's name for him, her double-voiced discourse is finally understood. To her, of course, Rebecca is indeed "no(t) one" – she is two, but not divisible into one(s). On the surface the second wife obeys every word Maxim utters. But underneath we find her own occluded text: for it is the nameless protagonist's *own* spell(ing)s that write Rebecca across every page and surely this is the fascination this novel holds for its women readers. In her ghostliness Rebecca is the rebellious, anti-patriarchal def(v)iant self we most wish to be.

## Apparitional Geometries: *The Robber Bride* (1993)

Many of these dynamics apply also to Margaret Atwood's *The Robber Bride*. As in *Rebecca*, a seemingly heterosexual narrative rivalry based around two or more women competing for the same man actually transforms itself into an ongoing fascination between two or more women, for which men prove to be a mere catalyst.

Atwood is to some extent controversial in feminist terms for her refusal to idealize the nature of the relationships between women. But although these relationships are not idealized, their importance is absolute in her works. It is the precise and powerful nature of female-to-female bonding and its obstructions, within or beyond rivalries, that is always Atwood's major theme. In *The Robber Bride* the male characters are strikingly inconsequential. Either phantom-like in their own insubstantiality or just plain unappealing, Mitch, West and Billy lie at the periphery of a narrative that follows a very similar geometrical patterning to that set out in *The Apparitional Lesbian*. In her book Castle takes issue with Eve Sedgewick who perceives the structures of desire within heterosexual narratives to actually function between men, women simply functioning as their go-betweens.[9] Castle's concern with this approach is that it succeeds, yet again, in leaving the lesbian in the position of the "disappeared" or spectre of culture. Rethinking this dynamic within "women only" terms leads to the following modifications in the model:

> ... the male-female-male erotic triangle remains stable only as long as its single female term is unrelated to any other female term. Once two female terms are conjoined in space ... an alternative structure comes into being ... In the most radical transformation of female bonding ... the two female terms indeed merge and the male term drops out. At this point ... not only is male bonding suppressed, it has become impossible – there being no male terms left to bond.[10]

Like *Rebecca*, *The Robber Bride* is not, of course, an overtly lesbian novel. In fact its explicitly sexual parameters are heterosexual. But covertly it is definitely a homo-erotic novel, in that all Tony, Charis and Roz can think of is Zenia's erotic form and the profound and dangerous fascination she holds for them. As in *The Apparitional Lesbian*, then, Zenia is the fantasy spectre hovering compulsively between Tony, Charis and Roz. The question Atwood's novel raises is just how different women's rivalrous fantasies of women are from the sexual fantasies (so often based on similarly competitive tenets) men project onto women?

Of the three central female protagonists Roz is the one who represents most obviously the power of the marketplace. A senior business executive, Roz has money and (corporate) power in abundance. Ironically, however, it is the negation of these assets that makes her relationship with Tony and Charis so positive for her. Placing herself at the apex of an isosceles triangle with Tony and Charis as the two additional co-ordinates, Roz delights in the *lack* of power these women grant her over them. Apparently similarly positioned in marketing terms, Charis is far more sterotypically disabled by the patriarchal libidinal economy. Though working within a shop called "Radiance", which sells crystals, essential oils, and other "alternative" products, her job continually teeters on the brink of redundancy and, often choosing to take home products in lieu of her wages, Charis is far more happy with her role as currency in the game. This resistant placing in marketing terms also impacts upon the geometric nature of her relationship with the apparitional Zenia:

> [Their] history . . . began on a Wednesday in the first week of November in the first year of the seventies. *Seventy* . . . A zero always means the beginning of something and the end as well, because it is omega: a circular self-contained O . . . And seven is a prime number, composed of a four and a three – or two threes and a one, which Charis prefers because threes are graceful pyramids as well as Goddess numbers, and fours are merely box-like squares.[11]

While Charis begins with a numerological reading of the patterns of her relationship with Zenia, once she comes on to geometry, with the "graceful pyramids" winning out over the "box-like squares", Zenia has been squeezed out of the equation, which is completed by a return to the isosceles imagery. Momentarily, towards the end of the text, the isosceles triangle reconfigures itself as equilateral, facilitated by the literal expulsion of Zenia as all three women are rendered equal by the shared ritual: "[Charis] takes the hands held out to her, one on either side, and grips them tightly . . . Three dark-coated middle-aged women; women in mourning . . . " [*RB*, 469]. But at the very end the isosceles structure reasserts itself, this time with Tony: "From the kitchen [Tony] hears laughter . . . and goes in to *join* the others" [*RB*, 470 – my emphasis]. Narrative point of view lies always with the apex, which is perhaps why Zenia is never one of the co-ordinates – she is always the object, never the subject of the narrative. Only via a type of hexagonal structure with Zenia at the hub can Zenia join in the dance, Charis, Tony and Roz circling around her as the various subdivisions into sections pair up alternately one with another within the frame, but never enclosing Zenia within them.

The crux of du Maurier's *Rebecca* resides in the interface between female silence and female articulation, an articulation understood in specifically graphological terms. Rebecca is, on the surface, silenced through death and replaced by the poor substitute through whom Maxim has "blotted out" the past [*R*, 43]. This is, then, a novel about rewriting, retracing and the erasure of the signature, for Maxim appears to have simultaneously "rubbed out" and "written off" Rebecca. Most defiant of all, then, is the signature that refuses to be erased, for its curves and flourishes are signed across every page. This returns us to Maxim's motivations for the murder. Overtly, Maxim claims that he was driven to killing Rebecca by her vampishly promiscuous infidelity and the shame this brought upon his family's name. As Irigaray's work illustrates, the concept of inheritance etc. allows for man to pass his power on to another man. Women function simply as mediators, vessels and commodities which enable this transaction to take place:

> It is out of the question for them to go to "market" on their own ... speak to each other, desire each other, free from the control of seller-buyer-consumer subjects. And the interests of businessmen require that commodities relate to each other as rivals.[12]

Thus, the father who "gives away" his daughter to another man, does so only as part of a bargain that will enable him to gain a son and, hopefully, a grandson upon whom inheritance will fall. In du Maurier's novel, Maxim is duped into believing that Rebecca is carrying another man's child, a strategy she adopts to goad him into murdering her, to save her from her own fears of dying slowly and painfully from cancer. Illegitimacy is, of course, the greatest sin against the Law of the Father, robbing him of his status by robbing him of his right to appropriate the other as self. This brings us back to the notion of masculine intervention as a severance that alienates woman from her (sister) "self". Rebecca sells Maxim a fiction, but it might as easily be the case that Maxim sells a similarly fictive account to her replacement. Beneath this superficially credible story lies a more "undercover" motivation for the murder. Rebecca's phantom is a simple metonymy for what she was when alive: a woman of letters. Hence her real failing in Maxim's eyes is not her sexuality *per se*, but their respectively unequal relationships with language.

As the second Mrs de Winter has no name, it stands to reason that, in an eponymous novel, her role will remain that of a ghost-writer. And yet, the eponymous tradition that encloses her ensures that the voice of the point of view protagonist and the present/absent other are truly inseparable. Not only are they part of the same text, but neither can exist without the other. Rebecca needs her nameless other in order for her story to finally come to light. In that sense both women truly are part and parcel of the same body/text and, in the process, fulfil Irigaray's claims that woman "within herself...is already two – but not divisible into one(s) – that caress each other".[13] It is in this context that a further significant act of spectrality comes to light in Atwood's character Tony's own relationship with ghost-writing. Early on in the text, this takes its most literal form in Tony's naive desire to become "Zenia's right hand, because Zenia is certainly Tony's left one" [*RB*, 169], a desire that leads Tony to agree to "ghost-write" an essay for Zenia and, in one fell-swoop, lay herself open to the blackmail that most threatens her own sense of self. Tony's perceived inferiority is as tangible in Atwood's text as is the unnamed protagonist's in *Rebecca*. In du Maurier's text, in contrast to "the tall and sloping R dwarfing the other letters" [*R*, 37] Rebecca's desirous carbon-copy notes, "how cramped and unformed was my own hand-writing..." [*R*, 93]. In Atwood's novel, in contrast, Tony's written skills are a compensation for her general sense of inferiority in comparison with the other women in McClung Hall of Residence:

> ...they would get her to write their names for them, backwards and forwards at the same time, one name with each hand; they would crowd around, marvelling at what she herself felt to be self-evident, a minor and spurious magic. [*RB*, 116]

Perhaps the most interesting aspect of Tony's bizarre talent, however, is noted as an aside towards the beginning of the novel: "Her two halves are superimposed: there's only a slight *penumbra*, a slight degree of slippage" [*RB*, 8 – my emphasis]. Here, rather like Irigaray's notion of contiguity as the defining point of femininity, in appearing to stress superimposition, the introduction of the penumbra, the meeting-point of light and shadow, "resulting from the partial obstruction of light by an opaque object",[14] clearly signals the point of fissure into which Zenia inserts herself as disruptive other within the self. Zenia is not Tony's missing twin in that sense, she is the shape that fills the space of fantasy left by Tony's sense of self-loss:

> What had beckoned to Zenia, shown her an opening in Tony's beetle-like little armoured carapace? Which was the magic word, *raw* or *war*? Probably it was the two of them together; the doubleness. That would have high appeal, for Zenia. [*RB*, 130]

As with the eponymous Rebecca, the very name "Zenia" is part of her fascination and includes, as we have seen in the previous chapter, its etymological significance. But the most clear parallel with *Rebecca* is Tony's discovery of the signature, like a ghost of the past, scrawled across West's jotter pad:

> On a hunch, she gets up and tiptoes over to West's desk...on the back of a discarded sheet of musical notations she finds what she's afraid of. Z. – A. Hotel. Ext. 1409. The Z floats on the page as if scrawled on a wall, as if scratched on a window, as if carved in an arm. Z for Zorro, the masked avenger. Z for Zero Hour. Z for Zap. [*RB*, 39]

The A in question here is the initial letter of the hotel at which Zenia is staying. But as it is set out on the page, "Z. – A.", we see the real significance of Zenia. She is Alpha to Omega and back again, to these women whose own origins are so clearly lacking in definition. For Charis, too, it is in the pages of a notebook that Zenia manifests herself:

> The notebook is for [Charis] to write her thoughts in, but so far she hasn't written any. She hates to spoil the beauty of the blank pages ...But now she uncaps her pearl grey pen, and prints: *Zenia must go back*. She once took a course in italic handwriting, so the message looks elegant, almost like a rune. [*RB*, 69]

For Roz, the manifestation of the signature is rather more prosaic. Returning to her Mercedes Benz after the fateful lunch in the Toxique at which the revenant Zenia manifests herself for the first time following her "death", she finds "a little message scratched in her paint, on the driver's door. *Rich Bitch*" [*RB*, 104]. The reader feels the act to be one written with Zenia's flourish, her presence being the main focus of Roz's mindset as she returns to the car. And perhaps this is underlined by the fact that Roz, despite being a down-to-earth, no-nonsense woman, keeps a secret "Z file" on Zenia which takes on, in part through the etymological riddles of Zenia/Xenia's own name, a striking resemblance to the X files. Hiring a private detective, Roz is determined to prove "the truth is out there".

In many ways this book anticipates the concerns of ghosting and doubling explored in a more strictly historical context in the later *Alias Grace* (1996). The most obvious connection between the two novels is their shared preoccupation with after-death doubling in the form of the ghosting of one woman upon another. As is the case with Mary Whitney in *Alias Grace*, so Charis in *The Robber Bride* knows, through her own psychic fascination, that Zenia is still present, even after her (first) funeral. But it is not just the Zenia/Mary doubling that connects the two texts. There is also a double ghosting, this time between Charis and (Alias) Grace herself. When Charis muses, "Zenia was not in that canister [sic] ... Zenia was loose, loose in the air but tethered to the world of appearances ... it's Charis who won't cut her free" [*RB*, 50], she mimics Grace's nineteenth-century concerns that omitting to open the window on Mary's death results in her soul becoming trapped like a fire-fly in a glass jar.

Not surprisingly, amid these doubling dynamics, mirrors feature as significantly in *The Robber Bride* as they do in *Rebecca* and again imply the binding of and tension between the various characters in the text. Karen, for example, prior to splitting off from Charis, utilizes "a space ... a presence, transparent but thicker than air" [*RB*, 264] to protect herself from Uncle Vern's advances once puberty is reached. This may explain why the adult Charis deems mirrors in general to have specially "deflective" properties for warding off negative or disturbing presences. But Zenia gives the lie to this belief right from the start, first manifesting herself to Tony as a reflected image in the women's toilet of the Toxique bar, suggesting that she does have the archetypal spectral ability to cross over from "the other side". Perhaps this also reflects Tony's own position as one half of a mirror image, the other half her own dead twin, her own death-defying potential involving transcending her original status as the Snow White-like prisoner: "a premature baby ... kept in a glass box" [*RB*, 135].

Only for Roz do mirrors have a more mimetic function. The least open to fantasy of all four protagonists, it stands to reason that, for Roz, the mirror maintains its mimetic properties, failing to function, as it does for the other key protagonists, as a space within which fantastic power struggles take place. How significant, then, that as a woman who has successfully broken through the "glass ceiling" holding so many careerist women back from the most senior of management positions, the mirror continues to trap Roz in other ways, not least in the context of her aforementioned Jewish ethnicity: "There was something about her that set her apart, an invisible barrier ... like the surface of water, but strong nevertheless ... " [*RB*, 325]. Ultimately, in the hands of the oppressors, she may even be transformed into a "body of glass":

> Little Rozzie-lind ... If they got their hands on you ... they'd make
> you into a lampshade ... She has a picture of her entire body ... with

a lightbulb inside it and the light beaming out from her eyes and nostrils and ears and mouth. [*RB*, 334–5]

Throughout *The Robber Bride*, then, occultism is simultaneously evoked and rejected. In a bizarre reversal of even gothic norms, Zenia begins the novel as a fake phantom who has feigned her own death and burial and ends the text a corpse lying face-down in an ornamental fountain. In that sense the supernatural aspects of this novel (unlike those of *Alias Grace*) appear to be a hoax. And yet Zenia *is* a true phantom in that she proves to be as insubstantial, ultimately, as any wraith-like ghost: "The Zenia's of this world ... are fantasies for other women, just as they are for men. But fantasies of a different kind" [*RB*, 392]. As all three women acknowledge, Zenia is the cement that binds them together, in the guise of splitting them from their male "other half". It is perhaps this dynamic that explains what is otherwise an anomaly in the text. The loss of Zenia is a source of obvious melancholy to these women, not a source of retribution or long-lasting triumph. She is necessary quite simply because, without her, there can be no Tony, Roz and Charis – the three sides of the triangle would simply come apart from each other. This is the realization with which the novel concludes: "Somewhere ... Zenia continues to exist" [*RB*, 464].

In that sense Zenia is a form of mother figure, idealized when absent, problematic when in competition with her three other selves. Note that Tony's relationship with West is haunted by two hovering ghosts: Zenia in the form of one who "hovers ... like the blue haze of cigarette smoke" [*RB*, 181] between them and her mother Anthea, who "hovered just out of reach, a tantalizing wraith, an *almost*..." [*RB*, 154]. As a student Zenia takes on the image of Tony's dead mother (at least in Tony's eyes) as the latter wakes from sleep to find Zenia standing in her college bedroom:

> ... it's her mother ... Tony goes cold all over. *Where are my clothes?* Anthea is about to say, out of the middle of her faceless face. She means her body, the one that's been burned up ... [*RB*, 171]

In an important dream sequence, Zenia undergoes an obvious anatomical metamorphosis in the process, yet remains recognizably Zenia:

> Tony is playing the piano but no music comes out ... [Her mother's] leather hand, cool as mist, brushes Tony's face ... A tall man is standing in the corner. It's West ... There's a suitcase beside him ...

*Reverof*, he says sadly ... Zenia is at the door ... In her neck there's a pinkish grey gash, as if her throat's been cut; but as Tony watches, it opens, then closes moistly, and she can see that Zenia has gills. [*RB*, 397]

Here, not only are Zenia and Anthea conflated as haunting women who leave Tony in a presiding state of loss, Tony also regresses into an infantile state in two ways. Firstly, in playing the piano but no sound emerging, Tony acts out the wailing of the incubated infant whose mouth opens and closes endlessly but whose crying cannot be heard. Secondly, at the end of the passage, Tony's nickname "Guppy" is doubled in the gills with which Zenia is attributed. In the process Zenia doubles the doubling of mother and child, the parasite of the parasitic. Again, this is similar to *Alias Grace*, in which Mary Whitney is actually the second of two ghostly doubles, the first of which (often confused in Grace's mind with Mary Whitney) is Grace's mother who dies onboard ship. It is this fascination with a competing other who both is and is not the self, lost through death, that takes us on to Jeanette Winterson's *Written on the Body*.

## A Ghostly Romance: *Written on the Body* (1992)

Exploring the text as a site of articulation in which language remains inseparable from the contours of the flesh, the effect of Winterson's narrative is to give a full fictive voice to a newly-born woman who exists throughout, paradoxically, as the writer written: "Articulacy of fingers, the language of the deaf and dumb, signing on the body body longing ... You have scored your name into my shoulders, referenced me with your mark ... Your morse code interferes with my heart beat".[15] Returning to Castle's reading of the "Apparitional Lesbian", we notice several points of particular relevance to *Written on the Body*. To some extent Winterson's work floats as the primary spectre at the edge of Castle's book. Repeatedly cited, but only in passing, Castle's specialism in the eighteenth century seems to dissuade her from taking on Winterson in detail, but what is interesting, particularly in the context of *Written on the Body*, are a number of points she makes that dove-tail (though not always seamlessly) with my own. *Written on the Body* is, to some extent, a less overtly fantastic text than *Sexing the Cherry*. But Castle is right:

Precisely because it is motivated by a yearning for that which is, in a cultural sense, implausible – the subversion of male homosocial desire – lesbian fiction characteristically exhibits, even as it masquerades as "realistic" in surface detail, a strongly fantastical, allegorical, or utopian tendency.[16]

The manner in which this masquerade primarily manifests itself in Winterson's text is through gothic intertextuality with novels like *Rebecca*. For some critics *Written on the Body* is a narrative told by a "genderless" narrator who prevents the old binary polarities (subject/object, passive/active) from reproducing the inequalities of the lover/beloved pairing. For others, myself included, this claim for genderlessness fails to ring true. According to Castle, *Written on the Body* is a novel in which lesbian desire is cloaked in the role-play of surrogate "male rakery", as "the main character ... though apparently a woman, is named Lothario". Lynne Pearce goes further, claiming that the narrator is not just masculinized but seemingly male: "Lothario isn't a very convincing woman to me: his/her role in the heterosexual economy of marriage/adultery is too prototypically masculine ... ". But Nicole Ward Jouve takes the opposing view:

> ... it is interesting that [the novel] is called "written" on the body rather than "writing" on the body ... that title in itself makes the narrator, the lover, very much a she for me, because I don't think a man writing about love would be writing about "written" on the body. I don't think he would be trying to find the traces in his body of the loving.[17]

Like Ward Jouve, I find it impossible to read *Written on the Body* through the voice of either a masculinized or a genderless narrator. Less a distinction between "writing" or "written" *on*, for me it is simply the presence of "writing the body" (*écriture féminine*) that circumscribes this text within all-female terms, male characters such as Elgin functioning as the archetypal phallic threat that severs woman from her sister-self: "'The facts Elgin. The facts.' 'Leukaemia ... ' 'Will she die?' 'That depends.' 'On what?' 'On you.' 'You mean I can look after her?' 'I mean I can.'" [*WB*, 101–2] Winterson's narrator's voice, though certainly belonging to the "sex that is not one", never could belong to one who has no sex (or gender). Instead, these two women, simultaneously lover and beloved in the one skin, truly fulfil Irigaray's claims that woman "within herself ... is already two – but not divisible into one(s) – that caress each other",[18] and articulate a story in which lips "speak together": "The lining of your mouth I know ... The glossy smoothness of the inside of your upper lip is interrupted by a rough swirl . . . There's a story trapped inside your mouth . . . where the skin still shows the stitches" [*WB*, 117–8]. Only with the rupturing of this "self-caressing" by "a violent break-in" does the seam between the stitches start to split apart, and certainly this novel is not without its rivals and banishments. Structured entirely in terms of adulterous liaisons, not only is the beloved Louise married, the narrator has also chosen to abandon her own lover Jacqueline for Louise. Just as the murderous phantom is elsewhere identified with an articulating female presence determined to write herself back into the script, *Written on the Body* reproduces this "literary" role:

> The bathroom looked like it had been the target of a depraved and sadistic plumber . . . The walls were covered in heavy felt-tip pen. It was Jacqueline's handwriting . . . Pasted like an acid-house frieze around the ceiling was Jacqueline's name over and over again. Jacqueline colliding with Jacqueline. An endless cloning of Jacquelines in black ink. [*WB*, 70]

Only when the mirror is once again shattered as Jacqueline threatens to inscribe her name in glass upon Louise's face, is the former's signature fully and finally erased from the text [*WB*, 86]. Almost immediately there *is* no name but Louise:

> I was sitting in the library writing this to Louise, looking at a facsimile of an illuminated manuscript, the first letter a huge L. The L woven into shapes of birds and angels that slid between the pen lines. The letter was a maze. On the outside, at the top of the L, stood a pilgrim in hat and habit . . . How would the pilgrim try through the maze . . . ? I tried to fathom the path for a long time but I was caught at dead ends by beaming serpents. I gave up and shut the book, forgetting that the first word had been love. [*WB*, 88]

In du Maurier's novel the revelation of the cancer in the heroine's body is the only point at which her signature is temporarily erased. Concealing her identity under the pseudonym Danvers, Rebecca almost succeeds in covering her traces, disappearing as successfully as the word "cancer" itself, for only the disreputable Favell is "indiscreet" enough to give voice to what he calls "This cancer business" [*R*, 385]. In *Written on the Body*, the narrator's determination to go to the other extreme and speak of Louise through writing her cancer ironically results in an identical erasure. Replacing her are a series of narrative (cross-) sections which slice-up the text into bodies of knowledge: "The Cells, Tissues, Systems and Cavities of the Body", "The Skin", "The Skeleton" and "The Special Senses". Only by the final sub-section, centred on vision, do the scales fall from the narrator's own eyes and, finally refusing to play along with Elgin, she re-inscribes her resurrection across the pages of the text, breathing life back into Louise through the power of the writer/written: "Green-eyed girl . . . come in tongues of flame and restore my sight" [*WB*, 139]. As Castle observes:

> . . . within the very image of negativity lies the possibility of recovery – a way of conjuring up, of bringing back to view, that which has been denied. Take the metaphor far enough, and the invisible will rematerialize; the spirit will become flesh.[19]

But does this revelation truly take place in *Written on the Body*? Pearce takes issue with what she perceives to be a universalizing phenomenon in Winterson's fiction in general which, she claims, evokes lesbianism as an ideology only to allow it to disappear in a universalizing cloud of romantic love. Surely Castle's own theory is not dissimilar: "Once the lesbian has been defined as ghostly . . . she can then be exorcized".[20] Pearce's *Feminism and the Politics of Reading* (or rather its organizational framework) is, as noted in my Introduction, especially productive in relation to my reading of *Written on the Body* because of her conceptualizing of her own reading process in spectral terms. Pearce begins from a position of the ghosted and ghostly self: ghosted because she begins with a duality articulating the contradictions felt between the professional, academically-oriented reader and the "gullible wanderings of our off-duty selves"; ghostly because, in her own words, "the most suggestive and enduring characterization of the reader that has formed in the course of this book is . . . her ghostly *insubstantiality* . . . how she is logistically situated in relation to her textual other(s)".[21] The overall project in which Pearce engages is a revisiting (one might say a haunting) of previous reading positions adopted at various stages of her own career and a rethinking of them in a manner that involves a dialogic engagement with herself as simultaneously self and other. As if to formalize this division of the subject, she interweaves in her text passages of reading in *sans serif* which the reader encounters as the voice of *an-other* in the guise of the same. Throughout, Pearce turns her textual encounters back and forward onto a reflection upon the self. Articulating her textual desires and disappointments, she observes that her relationship with the texts she addresses amounts to a "ghostly romance".

For Pearce, unlike Castle, the fantastic (as opposed to Pearce's notion of the process of the "reading fantasy") manifests itself solely as rhetorical strategy. This explains why, turning to the reader's desirous relationship with her text(s), Pearce utilizes "enchantment" simply in the sense of seduction, and the transgressive potential inherent in the spectre as a figurative device:

> The ghost-metaphor...is a successful trope for enabling readers to "explain" their ability to enter texts from which they are notionally excluded. My ghost...relishes her ability to wander amidst the scene of her past *ravissement*, while all the while feeling the discomfort and excitement of the trespasser...[22]

Nevertheless, in connection with my reading of *Written on the Body* as reworking of *Rebecca* Pearce's reading becomes particularly persuasive as a strategy opening out onto the fantastic. As I have argued in Chapter 1, many critics read Winterson on politics and sexuality rather than on the fantastic and Pearce is no exception to this. But in Pearce's case the spectral metaphors she sets up operate as an important midway stage. Introjecting her own ghostly reading self, Pearce cites a former reading positon held regarding Jane Campion's film text *The Piano* (1993). In it she articulates her own position regarding reader pleasure through identification with the text's own speaking subject as simultaneously self and other:

> ...I quickly discovered a means by which I could relate to [the protagonist's] story without either fully occupying her subject position or fully displacing it with my own. The solution...[was] to align myself with the..."voice-over": the ghostly persona who narrates not what happens to her, but how she remembers it from a point of view that is both "above" and (in temporal terms) "beyond".[23]

As I read through this passage it is not *The Piano* that comes into my mind, but the faceless, retrospective and introspective narrator who provides the viewer with the afore-mentioned "voice-over" at the start of Hitchcock's *Rebecca* and beckons the ghostly visitor (who is both the viewer and the faceless narrator) into the dream-text/text of the unconscious. This makes my own intertextual connections between *Rebecca* and *Written on the Body* particularly uncanny in the context of Pearce's reading, for *Written on the Body* is the novel that haunts Pearce's book the most obsessively. Unable to leave it behind, like a revenant of the melancholic Winterson's novel recurs like the return of the repressed – as Pearce herself readily admits, "In some respects my reader-experience of Winterson's *Written on the Body* could be said to be wholly consumed by the anxiety of waiting for the missing (textual) other of my memory/ expectations to (re) appear."[24] In her rereadings of this novel Pearce self-consciously articulates her sustained compression of the narrative itself with its own implied author. Her romance with Winterson's work was, she asserts, in part a romance with the idealized image of Jeanette Winterson herself. In this book of readings, the author as much as the text is "read":

> Unable, it seems, to articulate my own loss (of "Winterson"), I let the text do it for me. In the same way that Lothario waits for Louise, so do I wait for "Winterson". Both of us have kept up the search long after we know it to be "hopeless", and both of us share the mourner's inability to accept that "it" (this life, this romance) is finally over.[25]

Just like the ghostly (because faceless) reading/writing protagonist in *Rebecca*, Pearce looks to exorcize her demon ("Winterson") by cloaking herself in the disguise of the apparently hating but actually desiring other. Certainly, Pearce as reader articulates her own sense of lack of empowerment in ways that evoke that faceless narrator/reader/writer of du Maurier's text: "My frustrations . . . are well illustrated by the meta-phor of the ghost who can never make her presence felt". Her stance on the text even mirrors that of Hitchcock's cinematic version when she identifies her reading position as "both *inside* and *outside* the textual action . . . *I can see but not be seen*". Finally, in Pearce's fascinating con-cept of "reader jealousy", we hear echoes of du Maurier's narrator's response to Rebecca's own lettering: "How alive . . . how full of force" [*R*, 62]:

> . . . I was, at different times, both jealous of the author, "Winterson" [Rebecca?], for having written . . . [what/how] I would have like to have written, and of other members of the feminist writing com-munity [Maxim, Mrs Danvers] who also claimed a special relation-ship with her . . .[26]

Pearce concludes, "I both wish[ed] to be the exclusive interlocutor of [her] texts . . . and to be (to displace) 'Winterson' [Rebecca?] herself".[27] *Rebecca* leaves us with Manderley ablaze, lighting up the sky, telling its own version of the writer/written: "The sky above our heads was inky black. But the sky on the horizon ... was shot with crimson, like a splash of blood. And the ashes [of Rebecca?] blew towards us with the salt wind from the sea" [*R*, 397]. Though outwardly conformist, du Maurier's nameless protagonist is as hell-bent on resurrecting the story of this woman as is Winterson's nameless lover/beloved. In neither novel can the one woman exist without the story of the other. After all, although I have so far talked of Louise, the beloved, in apparitional terms, it is the narrator of whom we might say, "she epitomizes 'not-thereness': now you see her, but mostly you don't".[28]

## Writing Black in White Ink: *Beloved* (1987)

Where one feels relatively little compunction about playing fast and loose with a text such as du Maurier's *Rebecca*, one treads far more warily in the context of a novel documenting nineteenth-century slavery from a late-twentieth-century (even postmodern) perspective. In fact the minute one uses a term such as postmodernism in the context of a novel like *Beloved* one feels potential hackles rising. Paul Gilroy's is presumably among them: "Morrison savours the irony that black writers are descending deeper into historical concerns at the same time that the white literati are abolishing [them] in the name of something they call 'postmodernism'."[29] Certainly the politics of the postmodern can be notoriously irresponsible, throwing the cards of history up to the ceiling and allowing them to cascade into intriguing mosaics on the floor. But postmodernism need not be innately depoliticized, as a novel like *Beloved* so clearly shows; for like it or not, its narrative structure does follow a postmodern "mosaic" style. Linda Hutcheon rightly cautions us not to overreact:

> To say the past is only *known* to us through textual traces is not ... the same as saying that the past is only textual ... This ontological reduction is not the point of postmodernism: past events existed empirically, but ... we can only know them today through texts.[30]

In fact it is through challenging postmodern texts like *Beloved*, which reread the nineteenth century through a late-twentieth-century narrative filter, hence giving it simultaneously the authenticity and authority of the past and the immediacy of "presentness", that we are forced to look slavery right in the eye. But if the charge of postmodernism is sufficient to create ideological disturbance among critics of *Beloved*, its connection with the fantastic seems to have caused even greater mistrust.

Repeatedly, critics go to great lengths either to explain away, render metaphorical, or blindly ignore the powerfully fantastic elements of *Beloved*. Plasa's editorial summary of Shlomith Rimmon-Kenan's reading of *Beloved* traces what is at best an ambivalent perspective when he notes that "what is 'supernatural' from one perspective can equally be seen as 'natural' from another: what might 'be called superstition and magic' in the West is for Morrison and the Afro-American tradition ... just 'another way of knowing things'".[31] As Barnett's essay, discussed in the previous chapter, illustrates, taking account of Afro-American "way[s] of knowing things" does not necessarily conspire against those ways being read in supernatural or fantastic terms. On the contrary, it is the very centrality of fantastic narrative strategies that makes *Beloved* the powerful text it is.

In the middle of section II of *Beloved*, the logical, linear structure of the style and syntax starts to fracture. This process begins by juxtaposing three interrelated passages. All told in different voices, the first begins "Beloved, she my daughter. She mine." The second opens "Beloved is my sister. I swallowed her blood right along with my mother's milk". The third begins "I am Beloved and she is mine" and the fourth, "I am Beloved and she is mine".[32] The first is obviously Sethe's voice, the second Denver's, and the third and fourth Beloved's voice. Beloved is doubled/ghosted in herself here because she is not just the ghost of one child, but also the ghost of slavery, which haunts these supposedly free black characters who, in the major historical chronotope of the text (1873–4), have imprinted on their bodies the literal and figurative scars of a past which continues to name both them and their children. As Sethe's own mother, Baby Suggs, recognizes: "Not a house in the country ain't packed to its rafters with some dead Negro's grief. We lucky this ghost is a baby" [*B*, 5]. Elizabeth B. House uses these passages for rather different purposes, however, namely to try and convince us that readers who want to find any type of ghost in this text are suffering either from delusional naivety or, at the very least, mistaken identity. There is no ghost in this text, she claims, and Beloved "has no blood relation to the family she enters and comes to control". Instead she is just an orphan looking for anybody who will take her in: "Beloved is haunted by the loss of her African parents and thus comes to believe that Sethe is her mother. Sethe longs for the dead daughter and is rather easily convinced that Beloved is the child she has lost."[33] This reading angers me in its almost wilfully reductive determination to transform this powerful novel into pure social mimesis. In novels like this one the supernatural carries the socio-historical along with it: "If *Beloved* is a story about a ghost, it is also a story which itself has a ghostly status or existence, haunting, as it does, the gaps and silences of the tradition on which it draws, seeking release".[34]

That *Beloved* is a ghost-story should be self-evident to even the most recalcitrant reader. The text opens: "124 was spiteful. Full of a baby's venom. The women in the house knew it and so did the children" [*B*, 3]. Even the house-number is based upon the mathematical principle of doubling/ghosting (1(+1=)2(+2=)4). Immediately, then, ghosting is situated in familial terms, more specifically following a female genealogy which is innately linked with oral (popular) storytelling approaches. As Linden Peach observes, along with the other symbolic patterns of the text, the "novel itself is [structured] like a quilt and it is important to remember that the quilt, a feminine art form, was used to map the ancestry of a family as each successive generation added to it".[35] In this relationship to narrative fabrication *Beloved* is a novel of enchantment in the dual sense of seduction and spells. However we must differentiate between the status of the supernatural in a novel such as Butler's *Kindred* (1979) and the status it holds in *Beloved*.

*Kindred* is fantasy in its most generically absolute sense. Dana moves from the twentieth-century realm of mimesis into a nineteenth-century chronotope which, in its self-containment, forms the space of nightmare. The supernatural exists in this novel only as an anachronism, so that whereas for Dana and Kevin their uncertainties over their experiences can only be one of two choices, time-travel or insanity, for Rufus they exist either as ghosts or as demons rendering himself possessed: "'Oh no!' he said softly. He stared at me the way he had when he had thought I might be a ghost...'I heard a voice, a man...And someone else – you – whispered...'" [*K*, 30–1]. As even Tom Weylin tells Dana at one stage, "You're something different. I don't know what – witch, devil, I don't care...You come out of nowhere and go back into nowhere...You're not natural!" [*K*, 206].

*Beloved* is not fantasy in this neatly "finished off" manner. Instead it is a form of magic realism which, as we will see in more detail in Chapter 6, is a mode of writing which disrupts the commonly held ideological and material assumptions about "the real" by subverting its codes from within. *Beloved*'s status as magic realism is what allows the fantastic to be so inseparably woven through with substantial political significance, including colonial and postcolonial discourses. In essence, as Barbara Hill Rigney succinctly observes, "Morrison's historic world is so unnatural, so horrific and brutal, that the only 'natural' element is the supernatural".[36]

Clearly, like so many magic realist texts, *Beloved*'s treatment of the domestic interior places it in a directly contiguous relationship with the gothic. In an early review of the novel A.S. Byatt makes an astute observation:

> ...in a curious way [*Beloved*] reassesses all the major novels of the time in which it is set. Melville, Hawthorne, Poe wrote riddling allegories about the nature of evil, the haunting of the unappeased spirits, the inverted opposition of blackness and whiteness. Toni Morrison has...showed us the world which haunted theirs.[37]

This is an important and interesting piece of contextualization. But critics have been extremely cagey about connecting *Beloved* with anything other than Black literary traditions, concerned that in some way differential contextualizations detract from its testimony to its own racial ancestry. Surely the very fact that the panorama of *Beloved* lies in its polychronotopic immensity means that it is capable of coming to life in a variety of ways depending on different contextualizations and Morrison has ensured that none of these can ever lose sight of the powerful Afro-American identity which gives *Beloved* both its direction and, in the most basic sense of the term, its "meaning". Reading Morrison's novel alongside other contemporary women's ghost-narratives with which it shares significant tropes and concerns does not render the blackness of *Beloved* invisible. On the contrary it helps to render transparent some of the ideological assumptions inherent in Eurocentric feminist thinking as well as demonstrating the points of contiguity Morrison's novel shares with those by other contemporary women writers of the fantastic. With this in mind I want to consider how the contemporary fascination with the spectre as a form of female-female bonding takes us to Hélène Cixous's figure of the "Newly Born Woman", whose own paradoxical title already carries resonances of the character Beloved.

Though formerly thought of as dead, Morrison's spectral protagonist Beloved is "newly born" through Sethe's experience of the breaking of her waters, and she is certainly a "woman" rather than a child, as her seduction of Paul D testifies. Cixous's exhortation to all women to "write her self...[by] return[ing] to the body which has been more than confiscated from her"[38] appears to have been realized in Sethe and Beloved's reunion, for *Beloved* is a novel centring upon maternal melancholia. But just as there are dangers in over-idealizing this mother/ child dyad (as seen in the discussion of its vampiric dynamic in the previous chapter), so we also have to avoid falsely idealizing the relationship between Sethe and Paul D. Pamela Barnett's otherwise excellent essay on the use of the succubus in Morrison's text is, as we have seen in the previous chapter, very disturbing in the conclusions it draws about gender politics, conclusions that focus upon Paul D's image. For Barnett, rape is the central motif of *Beloved* but it is a rape that is identified on racial rather than sexual grounds. Of course Barnett is right to focus on Paul D's sexual abuse by the white guards in the prison camp and to remind us, as Morrison does, that black men suffered sexual abuse and humiliation too. One might go further and observe that the songs sung by the chain-gang are not dissimilar to the cryptic elements of Dyman's ghostly femininity: "They sang it out and beat it up, garbling the words so they could not be understood; tricking the words so their syllables yielded up other meanings" [*B*, 108]. In this sense the abuses of slavery certainly "feminize" the black men in this text, but Barnett does not rest with defending their position. Through her reading of the character Beloved as succubus she starts to tilt the scales of blame towards Beloved as the abuser. Concentrating upon the passage in which Beloved seduces Paul D in the cold house, Barnett claims Paul D is raped by this woman who, though "a black perpetrator... *embodies* memories of whites' assaults on blacks". In other words, though Black on the outside, Beloved has become a white rapist on the inside through her own metonymic contamination as an infant. In the most extraordinary of ways this victim of all victims is being read as a rapist:

> He tries to resist... and he is frightened when she lifts her skirts... He imagines telling Sethe, "it ain't a weakness, the kind of weakness I can fight 'cause 'cause something is happening to me, that girl is doing it... she is doing it to me. Fixing me. Sethe, she's fixed me and I can't break it".[39]

One wonders how many women like Sethe have heard such excuses before and how many women like Beloved have been similarly blamed. It does not seem to occur to Barnett that Paul D's disclaimers may be testimony to his sexual guilt rather than his sexual innocence.

More convincing is Pearce for whom, despite the relatively positive way in which the black men are portrayed in this novel, they remain outsiders to the presiding female chronotope which is 124 itself. This is even (perhaps especially) true of Paul D:

> The various thresholds, then, that Paul D must pass through before he arrives at the chronotopic core of 124 may be seen to represent the cultural and linguistic barriers separating women from men in the historical period covered by the novel. Men and women, in this nineteenth-century slave community, cannot easily pass into one another's worlds... [40]

Hence, for all the similarly palimpsestic nature of the male slaves' subversive vocabulary, "Mixed in with the voices surrounding the house, recognizable but undecipherable to Stamp Paid, were the thoughts of the women of 124, unspeakable thoughts, unspoken" [*B*, 199]. He is, as Irigaray would say, listening with the wrong ear: "And there you have it, Gentlemen, that is why your daughters are dumb".[41] According to both Cixous and Irigaray, woman's relationship with her own sexuality directly impinges upon definition through the voice. Drawing a direct connection between promiscuity and verbosity, Irigaray utilizes the metaphor of vaginal and oral lips to clarify this connection. Beloved's voice is, in itself, an *unheimlich* presence in the novel, but it is not the only mother-daughter bond which shares this quality. In Denver's case contiguity expresses itself most forcibly in the contact of chalk upon slate:

> For a nickel a month, Lady Jones did what white people thought unnecessary if not illegal: crowded her little parlor with the colored children who had time for and interest in book learning. The nickel, tied to a handkerchief knot...thrilled [Denver]. The effort to handle chalk expertly and avoid the scream it would make; the capital *w*, the little *i*, the beauty of the letters in her name...Denver practiced every morning; starred every afternoon. [*B*, 102]

Nevertheless, in a reversal of the "norm" regarding a mother's eager anticipation to share in the successes of her daughter's schooling, or hear her young child's first words, after the arrival of Beloved in the house "Denver notice how greedy [Beloved] was to hear Sethe talk" [*B*, 63]. And, as Deborah Horovitz argues, "Although Sethe has forgotten the words of her mother's language, they continue to exist inside her as feelings and images that repeatedly emerge as a code that she relies on without realizing it".[42]

Secrets and the secrets of history are keystones of Morrison's narrative, but here this follows a dynamic whereby the (black) oral tradition is shown to be directly in tension with the (white) written text. Sethe tells us that she mixes the ink in which Schoolteacher inscribes his false testimonial upon paper. In a specifically gendered moment she notes that the ink is mixed from a recipe developed in the kitchen. This ink, then, originates in that space that Sethe is shown to love so much and with which she is so consistently associated in a positive, creative, archetypally motherly way:

> Quickly, lightly she touched the stove. Then she trailed her fingers through the flour, parting, separating small hills and ridges of it, looking for mites. Finding none, she poured soda and salt into the crease of her folded hand and tossed both into the flour. Then she reached into a can and scooped half a handful of lard. Deftly she squeezed the flour through it, then with her left hand sprinkling water, she formed the dough. [*B*, 16]

It is, to all intents and purposes, Sethe's ink, "Black" ink and woman's work. And yet, in white hands, it becomes none of these things. According to Linden Peach, "The backbone of [*Beloved*] is an occluded text buried within the surface narrative which the reader has to recover in order to make sense of the whole ... ".[43] This strategy, strikingly similar to that Dyman witnesses in Wharton's texts, includes a type of friction dynamic between so-called authoritarian and non-authoritarian discourses. Those authoritarian discourses are not dissimilar to those found in *Alias Grace*, but also include a form of white "anthropology" of the nineteenth century and fundamentalist readings of the Bible, both used to shore up racial inequalities. In tension with this lie the invisible because oral traditions of nineteenth-century Black culture, manifest in *Beloved* through the metaphors of quilting, the presence of songs and syntactic dislocations of standard English. Sethe is to some extent as victimized by the latter as she is by the former as conflicting oral tales – hearsay and gossip – revolve around this loss of the "good mother". But the worst instances of so-called "black" ink inscribing a white story across Sethe's skin is the schoolteacher's aforementioned orchestration and documentation of Sethe's rape. It is in this trope of black being superimposed upon white that another metonymy of the racial dynamic of the novel emerges.

Returning to the scene of Sethe's violation we recall that the main focus for horror is upon the theft of her breast milk, that fluid by which

Cixous claims the woman writes her own self. With horrible irony Cixous positively renames this milk "white ink", conceptualizing it figuratively as the secreted presence of an invisible trace element, inscribing the otherwise silenced presence of the feminine from within the lines of the printed page. As post-colonial critics have warned us, "whiteness ... has been associated historically with a certain invisibility, regarded simply ... as a 'normative state of existence: the (white) point in space from which we tend to identify difference'".[44] These words ring particularly true in the case of *Beloved*, in which the "invisibility" of the whiteness of the ink derives less from the secret inscription of a ghostly femininity and more as the type of inscription the chiseller's phallus traces across her own body as she uses herself as currency to pay for the carving of the word "Beloved" across her daughter's headstone.

According to Cixous and Clément, it is only in "writing, from woman and toward woman ... that woman will affirm woman somewhere other than in silence ... ".[45] In producing a series of double-voiced interactions the phantom in these texts joins hands with the newly-born woman to produce a playful site of contiguity and severance all in one. This is not dissimilar to the closing dynamic of *Beloved* in the frequently cited "pass on" section. The paradox of the phrase is that, as far as contagion or gossip is concerned, one must come together with another in order to transitively "pass on" something. In its intransitive sense, however, one passes on only through the final severance of death. A third connotation stands at the edges of the term, in that "this is not a story to *pass* on" (have no opinion about). Overall, what is true of the dynamic of female-female contiguity in *Beloved* is that it is, itself, "passed on" by means which are sometimes oral and sometimes "stitched together". Hence Sethe talks of obliging her own mother's wishes "with anything from fabric to her own tongue" [B, 4] and, in the process, reminds us that storytelling is another way of spinning yarns. Denver, seeing Sethe with the sleeve of a white dress wrapped around her, uses this as a means of "Easily ... stepp[ing] into the told story" [B, 29] of her mother's past, as if it were she around whom the fabric was wrapped. Repeatedly, from Amy's search for Carmine velvet (which results in this white woman becoming midwife for Denver's birth) to Sethe's stealing of scraps of fabric to make a bedding dress, fabrication intertwines the lives of women into the same space, from across generations and between Black and White [B, 59].

In conclusion, where du Maurier's superimposition of black on white resides entirely within the dead woman's signature, "A little blob of ink marr[ing] the white page opposite" [R, 37], for Sethe the scarred and scarring injustice of white inscriptions upon black skin shouts out loud, despite the final exorcism, continuing to leave the last word of the novel with/as "Beloved" [*B*, 275]. Both *Beloved* and *Rebecca* are eponymous narratives defined by a violent spillage of women's blood, effected at the hands of those who escape justice through their supposedly superior (whiter than white) social standing. Sethe, like the second Mrs de Winter, operates less as the transgressor and more as the silenced witness who, in the guise of telling her own story, is named by the presence of a "significant other" whose death is insufficient to silence her. In their shared relationship to the gothic, all of the novels discussed in this chapter situate a specifically female bonding at the centre of a house that refuses, despite itself, to be mere hearth and home. In Chapter 5 we remain with this intimidating arena and its relationship with "alternative knowledge" and women's bodies, but here we examine it in the context of ancient folklore and superstition.

# 5
# Fairies and Feminism: Alice Thomas Ellis, Fay Weldon and Elizabeth Baines

> As a matter of every-day practice we cannot ... go back to that infant-
> ine state of mind which regards ... all objects animate and inanimate
> around us, as instinct with a consciousness, a personality akin to our
> own.[1]

A great deal of research has been undertaken into the conventional
fairy-tale (or, as Edwin Sidney Hartland calls it, the nursery-tale) and its
relationship to women, feminism and gender. But in doing so this
research tends to look at only half of the fairy tradition as it impacts
upon even contemporary literary texts, and in doing so overlooks that
type of writing which deals with ancient fairy folklore or mythology in
favour of those tales in which genuine fairies rarely, if ever, feature.
Although "faery", as defined by Lewis Spence, has long been with
us, one possible derivation coming from medieval Latin "*fatare*, 'to
enchant' ... [and its] past-participle *fáe*, which resolved itself into *fée*
... form[ing] a derivative noun *fäerie*, or *fëerie*, meaning 'enchantment'",[2]
Maureen Duffy is at pains to point out that the current usage of the
term "fairy" "didn't come into general use until the thirteenth century
... through Norman French possibly because of a verbal association with
'ferly' which ... came to mean 'a marvel'". The only direct legacy of fairy
mythology in the fantasy genre we know as the "fairy"-tale, is that
nineteenth-century eroticized "good fairy" who remains transmuted as
a fairy godmother.[3]

For Hartland, the key issue with fairy-lore and its narratives derives
from its powerful storytelling qualities, a feature shared by the nursery-
tale. But he starts to tread on very dangerous ground when he associates
nursery-tales with being better told by women (because of their association with the nursery), implying that "genuine" fairy tales are better

told by (male) travellers who have witnessed enough of the world to have such tales to tell.[4] The novelists in this chapter breach this divide by demonstrating what happens when the conventional nursery-tale becomes reconnected with its genuine mythological and occult roots, revealing the "powers of horror" underlying both seemingly innocuous forms.

There is a tendency to believe, in the late twentieth century, that fairies were washed up in the Victorian period as part of the larger cultural ethos of the child and remain stranded there as part of the sentimental detritus we, often wrongly, associate with children's literature. Few of us still believe in their relevance in cultural terms, and yet there has been a minor renaissance of interest in fairy mythology, particularly as it impacts upon contemporary and historical readings of gender. Nicola Bown, for example, situates representations of fairies as a key early-twentieth-century signifier of the way in which pre-pubescent and adolescent femininity is positioned and positions itself in regard to the adult world, while Maureen Duffy's still excellent 1972 study, *The Erotic World of Faery*, goes a long way to explaining why fairies may appear obsolete to adults, but in fact have merely been superseded by other fantasy modes, such as science fiction, which basically fulfil the same cultural needs.[5]

One of the key commonalities of all fairy mythologies is that by which human adults or children encounter fairies, only to be lured into another world which works to an entirely different time-dimension. Having been seduced by this contact with fairydom, the human in question is, if adult, allowed to join in the "games" of that world until, what may seem hours or days later, s/he decides to return to her/his family. Two possible scenarios then occur. The first is that they are not allowed back at all, a belief which permitted the development of a new consolatory mythology surrounding women who died in childbirth, namely that they "were not dead but taken to suckle fairy children: a thought as comforting as that they were in heaven but with the added advantage that they might return".[6] The second involves returning to their former dwelling-place and/or family and finding it/them immeasurably changed, or even dead. What seemed a few hours or days to the enchanted party has been years, decades or generations to those whom they left behind, the parallel with the current mythological trend for stories of alien abductions being clear.

To emphasize the pertinence of such legacies to contemporary modes of fantastic fiction, fairy mythology is even incorporated into Joanna Russ's *The Female Man* and Jane Palmer's *The Watcher*. In Russ's novel her character Jael relates an extended scene in which she tells us that one of her time-travelling metamorphoses involved taking on the persona of a "Prince of Faery" (Lancelot?) to a King who, with his "festive Kingly board", sounds very much like Arthur. As Jael informs her sceptical audience, teleportation is no different to many fairy ceremonies, in which incomers are often spirited away never to return [*FM*, 188–91]. In Palmer's narrative the opposite occurs, Alfred Tobias Wendle being left stranded in a state of protracted immortality, waiting for the death that is denied him through an encounter with a science fiction being called the Kybion who wears "a long shroud, like monk's habit, the material of which they noticed was instantly dry as soon as air touched it" [*TW*, 18]. As Wendle waits he acts out precisely the same type of fairy ceremony that typically splits characters across chronotopes in fairy lore, leaving at least one stranded beyond their own time, while the same instantaneous dryness of the fabric worn by the Kybion will be found characteristic of encounters with the "fair-folk" in Alice Thomas Ellis's *Fairy Tale* (1996).

For children, Duffy claims, fairies offer promises of larger than life experience transcending the child/adult hierarchy of power, such as the ability to "cross seas, fly, invisibly observe, assume different shapes, juggle time as we wish". Paradoxically, of course, this might be the very explanation behind their loss of appeal for adult readers, for now, with mass access to transglobal travel most of us, finances permitting, can choose to "cross seas" and "fly", "invisibly observe" through television and even, most recently, "assume different shapes" thanks to cybernetics and virtual reality. Indeed virtual reality in the shape of computer games has also perhaps contributed to children's own lack of interest in fairydom, now that the screen enables their full immersion into an Other World out of which they can emerge far later than we may have wished to believe possible. Previous warnings surrounding fairyland are still with us in this context: "The censor warns that [fairydom] is unreal and that those who spend too much time there, that is in fantasy, will be unable to return successfully to the real world".[7]

The association with winged flight, so important to the discussion of the grotesque utopia in Chapter 1, is interestingly "inauthentic" in the context of the historical development of the fairy, demonstrating the power of representation over traditional mythology. Duffy attributes the first winged fairies to Inigo Jones, the Renaissance stage-setter, who brought from Italy the expertise to produce theatrical costumes incorporating, among other things, "elaborate stage machinery".[8] Gradually wings became a primary cultural signifier separating fairies (since the Victorian period fictively feminine) from pixies, elves and brownies (fictively masculine). Immediately we witness the same sexual/anatomical inference we found in the context of the grotesque utopia, namely the analogy between the labia and the "diaphanous folds" of fairies' wings. Where sexuality (particularly female sexuality) is feared, fantasy creatures either become sexless (as in angels who are conventionally androgynous) or, more complicatedly in the case of nineteenth-century flower fairies, both sexed and unsexed simultaneously. So their poses and posies situate them as children, but in the process they leave the disturbing possibility remaining that they fuelled what Duffy refers to as "the Victorian leaning towards suppressed paederosity".[9]

Flying in the face of this presiding cultural scepticism, the novels discussed in this chapter take on fairy mythology in entirely contemporary and adult concerns. Ellis sees fairy mythology as an influential part of the perceived "otherness" of Celtic cultures in Britain. An Anglo-Welsh writer herself, her reading of the Welsh Tylwyth Teg (fair folk) in *Fairy Tale* is an important metaphor for larger discussions of cultural marginalization and border territory. In Fay Weldon's *The Cloning of Joanna May* (1989) and Elizabeth Baines's *The Birth Machine* (1983) such mythology works differently as "alternative" women's knowledge set up in contradistinction to the interventionist reproductive technology inflicted upon the central protagonists by patriarchy in each case. All three collude in a feminist critique of phallocentric appropriation of the birthing process, using fairies and related occult forms to do so.

Children and their relationship to their parents and, in particular their mothers, is the key concern of this chapter, one that will also lead us to an analysis of the connections between traditional fairy lore and more recent readings of the insider/outsider debate as analysed by Julia Kristeva. One point that might be lost on those of us used to reading fairies as little more than kitsch calendar decor, is that, as far as traditional belief is concerned, little distinction is drawn between fairies, ghosts or other spirits of the dead. Hence, Duffy claims, the underground barrows or mounds traditionally believed to be fairy dwelling-places point to the melancholia which is the flip-side of fairy-lore: "The underground siting recalls not only Hades but the simple fact that the dead are in the ground". Although Duffy also offers other, more optimistic, alternatives relating to death and barrow imagery, life and death remain hand in glove as she claims "The corpse in the barrow [to be] an emblem of the child in the swollen belly". Finally, she notes, "Ghosts...are themselves ancestors, therefore parents, come back to warn and accuse...".[10] Hence there is a long-established mythology surrounding the relationship between fairy-folk and human birth and motherhood.

## Border-Crossings: *Fairy Tale* (1996)

*Fairy Tale* is a novel dealing with a young couple, Eloise and Simon, who move from the city to take up "the good life" in rural Wales. Ellis's use of the chronotope functions well in this text, facilitated by the split between country and city, England and Wales. Rural Wales is set up as the space of dream, legend and the supernatural here, while London is the world of so-called common-sense and the technologized present. Wales is also, in this context, in ongoing contact with the "space" of the past, an issue linking space and time in a chronotopic entity. More controversial, perhaps, is the related issue of the status of Celtic mythology in this text, which provides a fantastic extension of the incomer debate that is as alive in Wales today as it has always been. At one point, the four men who accost the central protagonist Eloise are believed, by her partner, to be Welsh Nationalists and Eloise reveals her own stance on national identity and border-territory when, on their first departure, "she could hardly remember their words – as though they had spoken in a half-known language".[11]

Three separate factions interconnect in this text, at least two of whom might well perceive themselves to be rivals for "originary" status. One is the local, native Welsh community, the second are the Tylwyth Teg themselves, whose presence is always perceived in terms of malignant foreignness,[12] and the third are the English incomers, represented by Eloise, Simon, Clare and Miriam. Ellis continually stresses the halting (almost artificial) accent in which communications across these divides take place, as well as the reluctance to breach those divides shared by all parties. So Miriam, first crossing the threshold of Eloise and Simon's house, wonders "what others said when they arrived . . . Italians, Zulus, Serbs, Welshmen" [*FT*, 60]. Later, having become immersed more fully into the fantasy scene of the text, she dreams of the Kings on the heights, and observes: "She understood not a word they said but she knew they meant no comfort to humankind" [*FT*, 90]. The Kings in question are "the watchers" of this text, ancient pseudo-deities whom the Tylwyth Teg serve. Despite her sense of linguistic difference it is Miriam, and only Miriam, who knows and uses the correct term, "Tylwyth Teg"; Eloise is oblivious, being an archetypal outsider, musing that she moved here to escape people in general, irrespective of their social or ethnic characteristics. It is this last point, however, that also makes her so useful to the Tylwyth Teg who, though named as Welsh, set themselves up as being as distinct from native-born Welsh humans as from any other kind of being. Only once she is in face-to-face contact with them does Eloise have a rare moment of insight, perceiving "a painful sense of the inadequacy of [*any*] human language" [*FT*, 47] in her communications with them.

On the first page of the novel Eloise articulates her desire for a child as she sits at her needlework in the sunshine of her cottage garden. The opening is conventional nursery-tale, a combination of Briar Rose and Snow White, which begins with the mother sitting spinning, blood falling from her finger to spoil her dress, just as it does for Eloise. But though Eloise is "away with the fairies" and as irritatingly passive in a romantic context as any Snow White, she is less passive in the context of both the traditional world of fairy lore and what Mary Daly sees as a renewed image of the spinster "participat[ing] in the whirling movement of creation . . . spinning in a new time/space".[13] Though no radical feminist, Eloise does utilize traditional female crafts as a means of forging an identity deliberately distinct from that of her own mother, and her handiwork, much admired by the Tylwyth Teg, is one of the major motivations behind them choosing her to give birth to "their" child. This is the manner in which the "new time/space" is set up. Described as "sew[ing] in fantasy with each stitch, for she was, in her way, an artist" [*FT*, 6], several intertextual connections are established between Eloise and Tennyson's poetic figure of the Lady of Shalott (1831–2). Like her, Eloise dreams of a passing man who will gaze upon and admire both her beauty and her artistry, turning her into a living work of art.

The very first words of the novel do not attribute narrative point of view to Eloise, however. Instead it opens with "the watchers" and their supernatural gazing powers, their eyes being described as "cold and flat and incurious", while:

> Whenever they moved – be it ever so slightly – there was a brief darkness, a shadow behind the leaves, a hint of something that humanity might call loss . . . [*FT*, 3]

The relationship between fairies and sight is conventionally loaded with supernatural powers. Fairies have *second* sight, a power that can also be invested in humans if they rub their own eyes with a fairy balm usually applied by human mothers to the infants of fairies. In fairy-lore, as in Ellis's novel however, trouble always ensues when humans usurp these fairy-gifts for their own purposes, fairies conventionally punishing such intervention with the blinding of the affected eye (and sometimes both). Though Eloise does not literally lose her sight, she is figuratively blinded by a combination of her own egotism and the fairies' superior insight.

Discussing, with Simon, the possibility that the group that accosted her might have been Jehovah's Witnesses, the irony of a publication named *The Watchtower* becomes apparent. In fact Eloise *is* being watched from on high, and by several different observers: the Watchers themselves; a variety of spies in disguise as shepherds and gamekeepers; the reader; and, at least possibly, a category A sex offender who is on the prowl in the area, creeping across each faction's territory while remaining apart from all of them.

As Nicole Ward Jouve observes, for women the fear of such predators is often expressed in terms of the relationship between the seen and the unseen, a fear she experienced at first hand, living in Yorkshire during the Ripper years:

> ... my particular fear focused on having to get coal from the shed after sundown ... as I bent to shovel coke into the scuttle my back and neck bristled. Black on black mound, coal in the dark, the most unseeable thing there is. Taking a torch didn't help: it simply made me more visible.[14]

Fairy lore proves Ward Jouve wrong in painting "black on black mound" as "the most unseeable thing there is", for as various personal testimonies reported to W.Y. Evans Wentz at the beginning of this century affirm, the Tylwyth Teg are renowned for their full or partial invisibility.[15] Here this characteristic manifests itself in their presence, though visible to Eloise, being somehow inexplicable by the ordinary laws of physics, casting no shadow and emanating first from a voice rather than from a body, Eloise only "seeing" them as the first of their group articulates them into visibility. Staring from her bedroom window during the night, Eloise perceives, as if by second sight, the presence of another world, one in which her own fantasy of motherhood will be realized:

> There was no one to be seen in the moonlight and nothing moved, yet Eloise knew that somewhere in the far shadow something was crying for [her]. [*FT*, 11]

According to Duffy, "Rejection of modern society becomes a metaphor for the rejection of father; return to a primitive naturalism a desire to return to the exclusiveness of the natural mother and baby situation".[16] Certainly there is an element of this pattern throughout *Fairy Tale*. Simon, a woodworker, leaves the house every morning for work and, in the process, the house closes off from him, as illustrated when, by the end of the novel, he has to struggle to reach the house and fight his way through the hedgerow that has almost closed the road, recalling the prince's fight to reach sleeping beauty in the castle, "protected from intrusion by an equally magic growth of brambles and thorns".[17] The house itself, Ty Coch, is symbolically and mythologically significant too, being a strange amalgam, in narrative terms, of the enchanted castle under siege and the house of the witch in the story of "Hansel and Gretel": "a fairy-tale house sprung up by chance in a strange landscape" [*FT*, 60]. But it is also a maternal space, hence one to which Simon seems to have only peripheral access. One of the first things we learn about Simon is that he calls "I'm home" on drawing "*near* the door" [*FT*, 9 – my emphasis], almost as a warning that he is approaching, or as permission to enter, rather than as a simple greeting to his wife.

That the house is part of a larger connection with matrilineal inheritance is affirmed on a prosaic level once Eloise's mother Clare and her friend Miriam come to stay. But the issue is far more deep-rooted than this arrival, although they are undoubtedly drawn there to bring it to a head. "Ty Coch" translates into English as "The Red House" and hence, on one level, picks up on the traditional association between the Tylwyth Teg and "redness", this being the colour traditionally adopted for their clothing when emerging for their nocturnal dancing rituals.[18] But although this is the literal translation of the name, it is not the one used either by the locals or the text. Instead it is named "The Queen's House" and described by one local as "a house of women ... A house of blood" [*FT*, 89–90], a point that seems to point positively towards the female reproductive cycle and reveals, through the work of Kristeva, precisely what the Tylwyth Teg have to fear:

> Fear of the archaic mother turns out to be essentially fear of her generative power. It is this power, a dreaded one, that patrilineal filiation has the burden of subduing. It is thus not surprising to see pollution rituals proliferating in societies where patrilineal power is poorly secured, as if the latter sought, by means of purification, a support against excessive matrilineality.[19]

Where, to the original inhabitants, its most uncanny aspect is its connection with "the Red people", to the Tylwyth Teg the fear comes from its association with women.

The legend surrounding the house offers a further explanation for this fear and is proffered towards the end of the text by the gamekeeper, himself a member of the Tylwyth Teg in disguise. The manner in which he tells us the tale gives it an additionally intriguing dimension: "[T]he men of the Tylwyth Teg had been out hunting and a peripatetic holy man had come across the Queens dancing with *their* women and banished them, exorcized them with one stroke" [*FT*, 198 – my emphasis]. What is interesting here is the lack of specificity attributed to the gendering of the term "their" and the nature of the so-called "dancing" involved. Fairy dances are one of the most common of all traditional fairy activities and their profane affiliations are sufficient to merit the exorcism from an unsuspecting, witch-hunting missionary-man. But we must not overlook that this is an all-female gathering and that he draws a distinction between the Queens and the Tylwyth Teg: the former, though related to the latter mythologically, seem somehow distinct here. To precisely *whose* women is he therefore referring? Does he mean the women who "belong" (in his terms) to the male members of the Tylwyth Teg, away hunting at the time, or the Queens' own women, members of the Tylwyth Teg whom the Queens seduce once their male members are out of sight? In essence this is just as much a tale (and a novel) about so-called sexual deviancy and the potency of assertive feminine sexuality as it is one about the perceived evils of fairy folk. That ever since, the Tylwyth Teg have chosen to mate with human women to perpetuate their own lineage does not, therefore, just make a statement about the absence of "their women", it also implies that the Tylwyth Teg have ensured that no more women are born to them (otherwise the continuing need for human involvement would be removed). To the Tylwyth Teg, *all* women are trouble, including those humans who subsequently inhabit Ty Coch/the Queen's House, a point reinforced by Evans Wentz's citation of the real-life testimony of "a Welshman ninety-four years old", who affirms that though abductions by the Tylwyth Teg were common, "They took only boys, never girls".[20]

## Spinsters and Stepmothers

Eloise's desire to join such a matriarchal genealogy is introduced into the text shortly following her articulated desire for a Lancelot-style passer-by. Revising the original wish, having become disturbed by the cat's apparent fear of an unspecified presence, Eloise considers a seemingly safer option:

> A woman should walk past. A wise woman who would praise her sewing and tell her that in all her life she had never eaten pastry . . .

as light and delicious . . . A woman who would say, "But of course you must have a baby" . . . . [*FT*, 5]

Three figures unsuccessfully vie for this role: Clare who, far from praising her sewing, complains endlessly about Eloise's "shapeless frocks" [*FT*, 137], Miriam, who has more insight into the supernatural events surrounding the house but is clearly not the fairy godmother in question, and the mysterious Moonbird, whose name again evokes the type of gynocentric modes of alternative knowledge Daly propounds in her text, but whom we never encounter face to face, despite the obvious hold she has over Eloise. It is telling that, for Simon, Eloise's desire for a baby immediately translates into a desire to see her biological mother, because in reality this connection is one of two-way disappointment. Eloise and Clare inhabit very different chronotopes, as is made abundantly clear throughout and emblematized by Eloise retreating into a fairy ring so that she is not in the house to greet Clare and Miriam on their arrival. Later, it is suggested, it is her retreat into this space that causes the conception of her child, not the scene earlier on in the novel, in which we witness her fruitless searching under gooseberry bushes. Eloise's own matrilinearity resides, in its most meaningful sense, with the Queens and witches that are her forebears among the Tylwyth Teg. Towards the end of the novel a further twist emerges, as Clare demands to know from the fairy gamekeeper the whereabouts of her daughter, Ellis observing that she has "remained in the sort of Greenwich Mean Time she was familiar with" [*FT*, 199]. In using the phrase "my daughter" rather than "Eloise" the narrative suggests that Eloise, too, might be a fairy changeling, perhaps not the "real" daughter of Clare at all. This is a point raising obvious questions about Clare herself and her own relationship to the Tylwyth Teg.

Both older women are more interesting than they at first appear to be and are certainly a great deal less one-dimensional than their role in a conventional nursery tale would permit them to be. Though an inhabitant of London, Clare never quite fits in there, as is evidenced by her superstitious attitudes towards machinery such as the telephone, which takes on a kind of toad-like structure as it "crouche[s] on its desk, triumphantly, wickedly silent" [*FT*, 39–40] earlier having "mocked her" by twice "ringing urgently and then speaking with voices in which she had no interest" [*FT*, 33]. Importantly, according to Jacqueline Schectman the toad is not the mother's but the *step*-mother's symbol, with her "croaking voice . . . heard in the castle grounds", an early clue we are invited to pick up on and consider, regarding the legitimacy of Eloise being Clare's "natural" child. According to Maria Tatar, the Grimm brothers swopped the word "Mother" for "Stepmother" to "preserve the image of Good Motherhood", a point Schectman reads slightly differently, perceiving the two images to be one and the same character: "The difficulty comes with the reality of birth . . . When the longed-for baby cries all night . . . the Good Mother may indeed die, to be replaced by an impatient, angry, exhausted Stepmother".[21] In the context of *Fairy Tale*, what this paradigm reveals is that Clare's maternal function is secondary to the difficult identification she feels *with* Eloise, which is consistently shown to be simultaneously too stifling and yet never close enough. It is Gilbert and Gubar's famous reading of "Snow White" that is of relevance here, they also reading the dyadic connection between the child and the wicked stepmother as a struggle to divorce the self from the *other* who is the self:

> . . . Snow White is not only a child but . . . the heroine of a life that *has no story*. But the [stepmother], adult and demonic, plainly wants a life of 'significant action' . . . And therefore, to the extent that Snow White, as her daughter, is part of herself, she wants to kill the Snow White *in herself* . . . [22]

In Ellis's text, however, this dynamic is reversed. It is not Clare who wishes to separate off from Eloise, but Eloise who wishes to become the "plotter . . . plot-maker . . . schemer . . . witch . . . artist . . . woman of almost infinite creative energy", the role which Gilbert and Gubar read as belonging only to the stepmother.[23] In that sense Clare articulates what proves to be the fears of *Eloise's* other self, locked into the reductive, nursery-tale version of the fairy-text in believing herself to be "incomplete without a man" [*FT*, 101]. In the process, the *unheimlich* encounter Eloise grasps with both hands frees her from the inferior *heimlich* one Clare chooses to have, one in which she passively waits for a handsome prince complete with white charger. Except (as she herself unwittingly learns when she becomes a character in her own daughter's story) in this text horses are not something to play around with.

The long-held association between the Tylwyth Teg and horses is well rehearsed in all the anthropological surveys of fairy-lore, which sees them as avid hunters on horseback eager for the chase. In *Fairy Tale* Ellis adds to this feature the *ceffyl dŵr* (a mythological water-horse), hence connecting up with another commonly held belief that the Tylwyth Teg are water-dwellers who live in an enchanted/invisible island in the middle of a lake. Though, in this novel, we never see any of the Tylwyth

Teg mounted, the infant changeling, at the sound of the hooves, "rose to its feet, swaying as the cradle rocked...want[ing] to go into the night and leap on the neck of the *ceffyl dŵr...*" [*FT*, 180]. Clare herself also spots a *ceffyl dŵr* on two separate occasions, once from the top of the waterfall, and secondly when, finding her daughter in the woods chewing on a human knuckle-bone, Clare's gaze is prevented from fixing on this evidence of her daughter's cannibalism by a vision of the supernatural in the form of "a brief glimpse of a white horse which instantly transmuted itself into the fallen, whitened branch of a rowan" [*FT*, 200]. Though Eloise may well have "something of the Tylwyth Teg in her – more than [the fairy gamekeeper] had suspected was possible in a so-called human" [*FT*, 201], Clare's own position in this regard is far from innocuous. After all, it is she whom the gamekeeper feels the need to stun with fairy dust; Eloise is rather more prosaically "clouted... behind the ear with a nice round stone" [*FT*, 201].

Gradually we start to become suspicious about Clare's supposed innocence of fairy lore, not least in her confrontation with the gamekeeper towards the end of the novel, a scene very much in keeping with traditional reports of the searches of bereaved mothers looking for their kidnapped children. Having encountered him, Clare only *appears* not to realize the significance of her own words:

> Clare was the taller and as terrible as any mother seeking her child. The wind died down for a moment and he said he knew nothing of daughters. Clare stepped even closer so that for a moment they shared a breath. She said in a voice that neither the wind nor the water could overcome that... wild horses would not get her off this mountainside without her daughter.
> The gamekeeper seemed inordinately affected by the mention of wild horses: he looked inquiringly into Clare's eyes as though wondering how much she knew... [*FT*, 197–8]

For Miriam, too, the relationship with fantasy is more developed than we first believe, although our initial introduction to her does suggest that this might well prove the case. Referred to as Clare's "oldest friend and familiar with Eloise's oddities" [*FT*, 11], the reader's eyes tend to pause after the phrase "friend and familiar" (a witch's side-kick), before moving on to reread "familiar" as an adjective not a noun. Though we correct ourselves, the connection has been made, and it is one that proves salient to Miriam's later development, when she gradually discovers that she too has more knowledge of Welsh mythology than she consciously realizes:

"It's a very old landscape" ... That outcrop of rock down there is far
older than any to be found over the border, and that long narrow
stretch where the grass is greener is where they dragged a dragon
from the mountain top, where the Kings had killed him, to the lake
at the bottom of the valley ... The dragon transmuted into a *ceffyl
dŵr* ... and it terrorized the local inhabitants ... so they emptied the
lake and he sank into the mud. That darker bit down there where the
reeds grow, that's where he lies." ... she was not really sure where
she had heard this improbable tale nor why she knew it so well. [*FT*,
125–6]

Notice how we move in this passage from a register of tourist-guide
style explication to one of self-interrogation, but one which emphasizes
rather than undermines the consistently authoritative tone which
Miriam adopts. At first we can consign the legendary aspects of the tale
to the realms of the "marvellous" (closed fantasy). Even the shepherd,
who appears at one stage in the guise of the Grim Reaper, holding "a
knife with a long, curved blade that gleamed with the sheen of water"
[*FT*, 174], can be explained away as a farm labourer intercepted as he is
about to engage with his everyday duties. But, like the fantasy registers
overall in the text, such safe readings gradually have to take on a more
dynamic, fantastic status: "The lane became a torrent ... Once, over the
drumming of the rain, [Miriam] thought she heard a great splashing as
though some swift beast were passing by" [*FT*, 167].

The mythic elements that fuel the fantastic here also relate to phantasy
in its psychoanalytic sense and do so primarily through Oedipal relations. Where these first intersect with the world of the fantastic is in the
Kings' decision to instantly assassinate the sex offender as he crawls
through the bushes towards the unknowing Clare. This is not, it is made
clear, out of a desire to protect Clare; it is simply that the Kings refuse to
have their authority usurped by another male. This dynamic returns us
to Simon, of course. Their attempts are wasted. On each occasion the
antagonists are deemed to be male (no female police officers are men-
tioned in the text), thus fuelling the Kings' ongoing Oedipal struggle for
dominance with other (albeit less powerful) contenders.

Already under threat from the matriarchal inheritances of the cottage,
the apparently unseeing Simon knows more than he lets on. His fears
are far more readily aroused than Eloise's at the start of the text, as is
shown in his response to her story of four strangers. Later we witness
his greater insight into the significance of fairy gifts. Early on, the Tylwyth Teg leave Eloise a basket of herbs and mushrooms and some leaf-

lets informing her of "the riches, the undreamt of riches burgeoning unknown in your fields and hedges" [*FT*, 47]. Traditionally, fairy gifts are both a blessing and a curse. When the help of the fairies is spurned (as it is when Miriam insists on Eloise throwing the mushrooms away), trouble will always ensue. The leaflets relating to "riches" are a clear reminder of the mythology surrounding fairy gold which, Hartland tells us, when paid to humans by fairies will be later "changed", transformed into "withered leaves of oak", left behind in a drawer.[24]

Although no money changes hands in this novel, Eloise's response to the gifts is non-quizzical: "Gifts, she had always assumed, were due to her" [*FT*, 47] and, in this case, she is right; they are the payment she receives for doing the fairies a service. Hartland's reports of withering transformations are realized in what happens to the leaflets Eloise stores away in the kitchen drawer and the prescription issued to Eloise by the two supposed social workers that later visit her. Simon, taking the prescription to the chemist feels in his pocket "nothing there but his pen and a dry, faded leaf... *that was when the sadness had seized him...*" [*FT*, 150 – my emphasis]. As the italicized phrase reveals, Simon is fully cognisant of the fairy lore in which Eloise has become embroiled and knows that only tragedy can come of it. He also knows that "There are eyes everywhere" [*FT*, 138], a phrase reiterated later as a recognition of a returned gaze by the watchers themselves. Unwilling to leave Eloise to die in the woods because they too feel "There were eyes everywhere" (this time human ones) [*FT*, 202], Hartland is shown to be correct in his assertion that "supernatural personages... dislike not merely being recognized and addressed, but even being seen, or at all events being watched".[25]

So we find that the supernatural, in this novel as in most others of its type, functions as a kind of veiled omnipresence which, in keeping with the sewing imagery that runs throughout the text, often coheres in scenes relating to gauze and other filmy substances. To offer a parodic example, great mirth is expressed by the Tylwyth Teg when former New Age inhabitants of Ty Coch "contriv[ed] to extrude, from parts of their persons, lengths of muslin which they called ectoplasm" [*FT*, 204], but elsewhere it is far less easily dismissed. So Eloise, stepping outside her door, is immediately "wrapped in mist... it felt as clinging and clammy as wet butter-muslin" [*FT*, 57], and later, falling asleep in her recurrent role of Briar Rose, she almost becomes a mummified corpse as a similar substance coheres around her face:

> Something like a fine, broken veil lay across her eyes, barely perceptible except where the lamplight glinted on its strands... [*FT*, 142]

This connection between death and (after-)life, wet and dry fabric is also frequently the marking point signalling a movement between real and fantastic worlds. As Eloise returns inside from a deluge of rain on the day Miriam and Clare arrive at Ty Coch, Miriam wonders at Clare's apparent failure to see "what she herself had noticed first – that Eloise, her face and her hair and her long dress . . . were completely, and terrifyingly, bone dry" [FT, 79]. Nor is this the only point at which Miriam witnesses cloth as uncanny. Entering the parlour she sees, on a chair:

> A newly made nightdress . . . [which] looked, she thought, as though it might get up and walk . . . [She] threw it down untidily so that it seemed only like a crumpled piece of cloth . . . The room smelled faintly of that old scent; a scent that, once familiar, might remind a child all through life of its mother's touch . . . [FT, 126–7]

Clothing is a key trope of traditional fairy lore, repeatedly used as a decoy to keep fairy kidnappers away from human infants. In this context Eloise's refusal to give up her child to the Tylwyth Teg, hence breaking her part of the bargain, results in them trying to take the child by force. Here the nightdress is left to confuse the fairies and leave them to believe that this is the child they are looking for. The effect is identical in a scene which appears ridiculous until its mythological origin is explained. Simon, disturbed in sleep by the sounds of intrusion downstairs, an intrusion motivated by violent desires for his death, puts on the nearest piece of clothing to hand, which turns out to be Eloise's nightgown. As he confronts the Tylwyth Teg cross-dressed in this manner, far from attacking him they run away in fear. Without recourse to traditional folk mythology their response seems unlikely. But it is Hartland's observations about the gullibility of fairy folk that give much-needed credibility to this otherwise inexplicable scene. Arguing that fairy folk are "easily tricked", Hartland explains that "It appears to be enough to lay over the infant, or on the bed beside the mother, a portion of the father's clothes . . . [to convince the fairies] that he himself is present watching over his offspring".[26] Here the father appears in the mother's clothes and, in an ironic reversal of gender norms, implies that she is simultaneously capable of looking over/after him while also being elsewhere. The obvious implication takes us back to the supernatural powers and influence of the Queens, setting up maternal transgression as the most terrifying (and hence empowered) of all.

Eloise's unworthiness for this role means that she, unlike Simon, though eventually banished from her fantasized Eden, never really connects sufficiently with the Tylwyth Teg to confront them. Instead, such encounters are left to all three peripheral characters. So, in an incident that happens concurrently with Simon's gowned encounter with his assailants, Miriam takes it upon herself to negotiate a strategy for their collective retreat, complying with the Tylwyth Teg's insistence that the baby be returned to them on their terms. This is done, again, in keeping with traditional mythology which, Evans Wentz affirms, "As a rule, [requires] treating the fairy babe roughly and then throwing it into a river...", the result of which should be the "restor[ation of] the real child in return for the changeling".[27]

Miriam lures Clare and then Eloise and her child on a picnic, taking them to the head of the waterfall (waterfalls being another common location for fairy activity) where all three imbibe a form of charmed vodka which, as is known only to Miriam, has been supplied for the purpose by the Tylwyth Teg. As the resulting trance starts to affect all three, Eloise feels the child kicking and struggling in her arms and finally realizes its lack of affinity with her before allowing it to hurl itself over the edge and into the water. Conscious once more, all Eloise sees is what she believes to be a lamb caught in some rushes, although she is left with a persistent, unconscious sense of loss: "'We've forgotten something,' she said", as they drive away [*FT*, 193]. What they have forgotten, of course, is the "real" child Eloise should gain in return, the loss of which is what prompted the liaison in the first place. According to Schectman, "The Step- in Stepmother derives from the Middle English *steif*, meaning bereaved... A Stepmother, then, is the mother of a bereaved child".[28] As gradually becomes clear the "child" in this case is not the baby but Eloise herself who, as we have seen, desires a child only to fill the loss left by her own mother. Simon was right all along: it *is* a mother Eloise desires, but a mother whom Clare can never be. Instead of the obligatory happy-ever-after ending of the nursery tale, then, fairy mythology enables Ellis to explore the mother/child bond in a manner that reveals an ongoing melancholy desire.

Thus Eloise's "trip" to fairyland is a search for the unattainable, the good mother who can only exist as "a dream of infant limbs and downy heads, of milk and honey" [*FT*, 42–3]. The difficulty set up in this text is that Eloise's withdrawal from society ends up following the old trap of feminine wish-fulfilment conspiring against engagement with the nitty-gritty world of the real, despite the fact that she takes the adventurous route in the process. Ultimately, Eloise and Simon have to return to the late twentieth century, not knowing whether that modern world will have moved on, in typical fairy tradition, at odds with the timescale they have witnessed in fairyland. Duffy's reading of the negative aspect of fairy lore reflects heavily on this novel:

> [The] fear reflects the guilt of fantasising. We shouldn't want to get away and if we do we may be punished by never being able to get back ... [parents] may be dead or gone away. Who doesn't remember this fear, half-guilty wish, when returning from a long day's playing out, forgetful of times and meals ... Timewarp can let us play out for hours and still be home in time for tea.[29]

## Tennyson and the Tarot: *The Cloning of Joanna May* (1989)

In Chapter 2 we looked at *The Cloning of Joanna May* as an exploration of cybernetic reproduction. But, as noted above, in women's writing what one might assume to be oppositional discourses (cybernetics pointing towards the future and women's traditional knowledge the past) are often brought into an interrogative relationship with one another, deconstructing the binary divides upon which such oppositions are based. In Weldon's text one might separate out the cybernetic and the supernatural as separate chronotopes identified with Carl May and Isaac King, Joanna's husband and lover respectively, but Joanna continually oscillates between the two. The novel opens, "This has been a year of strange events", a point followed by an encounter with a magic mirror that projects Joanna immediately into the role of the wicked stepmother: "[T]hat evening when preparing for bed I looked into my mirror and saw the face of an old woman looking back at me, and that was very strange and terrible".[30] Such ambivalent disturbance is perpetuated when events are broadened out to include the reactions of the four clones to these same events. The night is stormy, a typical setting for the uncanny, and Jane Jarvis knows this only too well: "[She] thought the wind was alive: that it was some kind of vengeful spirit: that it whined and whinnied like the ghost of her aborted baby, long ago" [*CJM*, 7]. At this reference to the termination the reader feels a stab of poignancy, wondering how this ghost will develop through the text, but little is made of this memory elsewhere, except as a means of perpetuating the ongoing but inconclusive discourses about presence and absence related to the mother/child dyad. Jane is born out of Joanna's purportedly phantom pregnancy as well as being mother to a ghostly child. Ben, Gina's young son, fears "bangs, crashes and screams in the night" [*CJM*, 173], but is actually shown to be immune to ghosts; his fears relate to his father's violent abuse of his mother. Nevertheless, looking at Julie, the double of his mother [*CJM*, 170], the *unheimlich* strikes Ben as powerfully as it directs both Gina and Julie who, for separate and unknown reasons, find themselves turning away from home (the *heim*), a piece of disorientation that directs their joint (if unlikely) encounter in a branch of McDonald's. Of course Gina and Julie and, later, Jane and Alice, on staring into each other's face as if looking into a mirror, experience that absent glassy pane as the entry-point into the worlds of Joanna. It is at this point that the initial mirror scene involving Joanna becomes clear: she is the witch who conjures up her own selves, just as if she had been staring into a crystal ball.

Astrology is given credence right from the start by the omniscient narrative voice of the text. Introducing the four clones in turn, this voice suggests that fate has as much of a hand as culture upon our shaping and, indeed, even influences biology: "As for Alice Morthampton. . . in the womb a week longer than . . . expected, the great wind bypassed her: of course it did. Alice was smiled upon by different stars" [*CJM*, 19]. Does this explain the different phonemes of her naming? Her surname, we are told, means literally "house of death" [*CJM*, 177], a naming that adds weight to the battles over domestic territory by the Kings and Queens in *Fairy Tale*. Even to Carl the supernatural is a force to be reckoned with. To him, living a life of eternal presentness, history itself is uncanny, associated purely with the dead and turning an art gallery into a graveyard. In continuing to play out games of vengeance with the Tarot pack, mocking its signifying potential by reading the cards purely as parodic representations, he inevitably invokes *their* revenge upon himself. First he becomes a "dead white face on [a] TV screen" [*CJM*, 247] and then his lover Bethany, playing with the realm of the spectral in the medium of virtual reality, foreshadows her own survival, but only at the expense of his death: "'I have the highest score ever,' she said. 'There's this little figure you have to guide through rooms full of demons and ghosts. I'm really good at it'" [*CJM*, 256]. Proving herself far more accomplished at playing games than Carl, their joint dousing in the cooling pool of Carl's reactor plant kills him while leaving her fantastically unscathed.

The Lady of Shalott connection, so important to Ellis's novel, is also present in *The Cloning of Joanna May*, and links Weldon's eponymous character with Ellis's Eloise. Carl, picking up on the powerfully incantatory qualities of Tennyson's poem, recites:

> On either side the river lie . . .
> Long fields of clover and of rye –

"Barley," said Bethany, and Carl May chose to ignore her. Once.

> ... And through the fields
> The road runs by
> To many-towered Camelot.

"That's where my ex-wife lives," said Carl May, "in Camelot."
"I thought she lived at the King's House, Maidenhead," said
Bethany ... He ignored her. Twice.

> ... Gazing where the lilies blow
> Round an island there below
> The island of Shalott –

"Shallots, onions," said Bethany.
Thrice.

> ... And the silent isle embowers
> The Lady of Shalott.

"Yes, I know," said Bethany, "'She left the web, she left the loom, she
made three paces through the room' – we did it for diction – 'the
mirror cracked from side to side, the curse is come upon me, cried
the Lady of Shalott'... Which reminds me that the curse has not
come upon me. What are we to do, Carl?"
Carl was silent. [*CJM*, 148–9]

This passage is intriguing for what it implies about the magical arts and
the two characters' relationships with them. Bethany is here set up as
the uncultured "bimbo", a social inferior to Carl but, towards the end
of the passage, she reveals that she does know the poem, she is just
not prepared to play games by his rules, only her own. Interspersed
within the lines of the poem is Weldon's description of Bethany's growing *ennui* with Carl. He has served his purpose, and this is literally
the beginning of the end for him. The three occasions on which he
ignores her in the passage are also important in this regard, because the
"Once ... Twice ... Thrice" is as much a reference to the magic number
of witchcraft as it is the incantatory quality of the lines *Bethany*, not
Carl, recites. On one level the three points at which Carl ignores her
could imply that his own patience is running out, particularly once she
informs him that "the curse" has not come upon her. As his past attitude
towards Joanna has already amply demonstrated, even the threat of
pregnancy is sufficient to secure "redundancy" on this count. But, if we
look closely, here we find the trick behind this version of Tennyson's

text. If the curse has not come upon Bethany, it must have come upon Carl, and Bethany is sick of being ignored:

> ...the auspices for the day of the projected PR event in Wales were bad indeed. The common pack had produced the Ace of Spades 40 per cent above probability: the Tarot pack the Tower 90 per cent likewise; the *I Ching*...No. 23 (Splitting Apart) four times running with mention of Tears of Blood...and the teacups came up repeatedly with coffins on the rim. Carl May laughed aloud. "Gobbledygook," he said..."If you have foretold anything it is the death of your own department: the end of your payslips..." [*CJM*, 254]

The card motif is also an important, yet understated one in *Fairy Tale*. In a reworking of a common fairy motif, Eloise's dabbling with fairies catches her out as Simon returns home before he is expected, his and her own chronotopes having come adrift from each other:

> she felt as a card-player who had let his attention wander might feel: cheated yet uncertain as to precisely who had broken the rules... [*FT*, 48]

The main significance of this card motif to the novel as a whole, however, derives from its main instigators being kings and queens and the fact that Eloise is visited, not by her desired suitor Lancelot, but by "four suits" in the form of the Tylwyth Teg. Later, reinforcing this connection, Miriam refers to her own plans (couched in conjunction with the Tylwyth Teg) as "a carelessly dropped deck of cards" [*FT*, 190]. In Weldon's hand this analogy is far more explicit and, as we have seen, actively deals with the Tarot pack, where the common pack is that employed by Ellis's work. In the Tarot pack the four suits are Swords, Wands, Pentacles and Cups. Later in the text these various suits are linked in with each of the clones: Jane is Queen of Wands ("power of the intellect"), Julie is Queen of Pentacles ("the strength of the material world"), Gina is Queen of Swords ("the capacity for endurance"), and Alice is Queen of Cups ("aesthetic and sensual perception") [*CJM*, 102 and 161–2]. Again, as in Ellis's novel, both Kings and Queens are in play, the King in question being Isaac King, while Joanna is the "Ice Queen" [*CJM*, 69] and again the combination spells out death and intimidation. As Isaac deals the cards for Joanna, they are seen to comprise "the four Queens" accompanied by "the Hierophant" and "Death". The next time we see these, they spell out a literally deadly combination, as

Joanna's neighbour Trevor finds Oliver, the gardener with whom Joanna is having an affair, strung up by his feet in the garage:

> On the floor, beneath the hanging body . . . lay a single card . . . The Hanged Man . . . And above, below, and to the left and right of the signifier, the Hanged Man in person, were the four Queens. Oh kinky, thought Trevor: what is going on? [*CJM*, 146]

As far as Carl is concerned, the supernatural is only there to be dispelled, hence his literalization of Joanna's tarot reading here and his development of a Department of Divination in his corporation, setting it up only in an attempt to have it discredited. But the fact of the matter is, as in Ellis's novel, the supernatural is far from discredited. Instead it parallels scientific findings, setting up an alternative but credible body of knowledge. The details of Oliver's death are highly realist, Carl, motivated by jealousy, having paid five contract killers to dispatch him. But like Ellis's Tylwyth Teg, their visitation as a force from an "otherworldly" elsewhere later manifests itself in genuinely supernatural terms:

> The car that followed [Julie and Gina] was white, all white . . . a vehicle fit for angels from some phantasmogorical heaven and on the front seats, grey-suited, prosperous and clean, two young men who might have been God's accountants. [*CJM*, 174]

As I have already suggested in Chapter 2, critics disagree about the extent to which Weldon can be genuinely considered a feminist writer. But for Elaine Tuttle Hansen *The Cloning of Joanna May* is a positively assertive women's text that helps to move feminist readings of the mother/daughter bond on beyond what might be read as its three major historical phases: "harsh repudiation; sentimental recuperation; and confusion, conflict, and a silencing sense of impasse". Instead, she claims, Weldon offers us "The vision of a frankly better but not fully utopian future for female identity and motherhood".[31] I would like to add to this that the cloning aspect of the text permits a reversal of what, in Ellis's text, is the oppositional tug of war between Clare and Eloise. Here, rather than fighting to divorce the other from its malignant presence within the self, Joanna finds that the female principle is always stronger when women are collectively bound:

> When I acknowledged my sisters, my twins, my clones, my children . . . I found myself: pop! I was out. He thought he would diminish

me: he couldn't ... for all of a sudden there was more of me left ...
Joanna May was now Alice, Julie, Gina, Jane as well. [*CJM*, 246–7]

It is this utopian realization that makes Joanna's last-minute capitula-
tion (so similar to Eloise's) such a profound disappointment, considering that the patriarch and his interventions have been so absolutely
defeated. Agreeing with Carl's dying request that he be cloned and thus
live on beyond the boundaries of his own death Alice, formerly the
house of death, suddenly agrees to become a source of new life, be
impregnated, and give birth to Little Carl. The name is again significant. Allowing the "little man" (the phallus) renewed life at the end of
the text conspires against what is otherwise a victory of the womb over
the tomb. Instead, just as Eloise leaves the cottage with the feeling that
something important is calling to her from just out of reach, so an earlier passage of Weldon's novel is left ringing in my ears:

> ... if the four Queens of the Tarot pack ... are seen together they
> denote nothing worse than arguments ... [But i]n conjunction with
> the Hanged Man ... things don't look good ... [*CJM*, 152]

## Briar Rose/Dead Dolls: *The Birth Machine* (1983)

We have seen, in the case of both novels already discussed, direct intertextual connections with Tennyson's "The Lady of Shalott", a poem
which begins as a fascinatingly fractured interrogation of the gaze, not
least in the apparent gender reversals it contains. By the end of the
poem this complexity is submerged as the Lady falls foul of a watery
death, a cliché reminding us that fluidity is essentially linked with cultural representations of women throughout history:

> A river without end ... flows through the world's literature ... the
> women-in-the-water; woman as water, as a stormy, cavorting, cooling
> ocean, a raging stream, a waterfall; as a limitless body of water ...
> woman as the enticing (or perilous) deep, as a cup of bubbling body
> fluids; the vagina ... as a dark place ringed with Pacific ridges; love as
> the foam from the collision of two waves ...[32]

This inherent link between fluidity and fear is taken a stage further in
Baines's *The Birth Machine*. Zelda, the main protagonist, is pregnant and
married to a medical consultant, Roland. The narrative tracks her progress, from early pregnancy to birth, a birth in which she is set up as a

model for interventionist experiment. As in *The Cloning of Joanna May*, technology goes hand in hand with superstition, here in the form of the "Briar Rose" fairy-tale. The version of the tale employed by Baines is that referred to, in the epigram, as "the classic English version", in which "one day as the queen was walking by the side of the river, a little fish lifted its head out of the water, and said, 'Your wish shall be fulfilled, and you shall soon have a daughter'".[33] In this context the fish in question operates as a metamorphic version of the thirteenth fairy at the christening of the child in the traditional tale, for as well as pro-claiming happiness, in Baines's novel it emerges out of the depths to pronounce judgement, doom and foreboding. In the process the water is transformed into an "unreal" and threatening world of its own, not dissimilar to the waterfall imagery of *Fairy Tale*. So Zelda becomes Theweleit's "woman-in-the-water" and what begins as a wish-fulfilment fantasy of being able to enter her own womb and caress her child, both of them bathing in the amniotic fluid together, is transformed, rather like Carl and Bethany's swim in the reactor plant, into a nightmare confrontation with the monster within:

> The water steeps, meets above her ... warm sphere, two eyes, nestled to her rib-cage ... Something knocks them in the darkness ... What is that nudging? ... Something bird-like, a reptile. An underwater liz-ard. The face opens and grins. Not that. She thrashes up, up and out ... [*BM*, 97]

Throughout this text Zelda is submerged by fluids imposed upon her by patriarchal representatives, connected up to more and more drips and catheters. In contrast there is a clear resistance, on the doctors' part, to sanction any role for the woman's body as a flooding rather than a drowning entity. Zelda, projecting through fantasy a vision of herself upon the operating table, considers "There must be blood. But [she] can't see, over the mound ... " [*BM*, 76]. As Chris Turner and Erica Carter acknowledge, it is "The 'concrete' (and not merely 'fantasized') bodily flows ... [that] are the source of antagonistic currents of pleasure and unpleasure" in the patriarchal body of society.[34] In this respect Zelda's own body operates as a censoring mechanism through fantasy here, preventing the display of the unclean fluid, forced into a state of complicity by means of anaesthesia.

Initially Zelda's perceptions of her own creativity are positively defined through references to her "round, fruity belly". But as the con-nection between food, cookery and gestation is further developed,

Zelda's nightmare surrounds her recognition that her culinary creativity is flawed and hence so might be her reproductive creativity:

> She picked up a swede, icy-cold, buried all winter and yanked that morning from the hardened soil. She began to peel it. Her knife stuck on a knot, a place where the tense yellow flesh had gone woody... She was suddenly terribly, desperately afraid... [*BM*, 44]

Zelda's father, passing a large joint of meat on the kitchen dresser, pinches and admires it in a manner that suggests his wife's fecund form is interchangeable with that of the food she prepares. More reductively still the medical consultants treat Zelda *herself* as a plate of meat and her hapless husband Roland, taking Zelda out to a restaurant, fails to realize that what he is encouraging her to digest is an image of the "smothered hump" of her own body, which she fears is also "rotten", "sour and musty" even if, like the pheasant on the plate, it is camouflaged as creative and succulently fruitful [*BM*, 89–90]. This is a fear which cannot be concealed by the end product of her cooking or, she fears, the resulting child: "A piece of undercooked carrot caught in her throat... she thought most likely she'd been wrong with her timing – also, there was something lacking in the swede... They scraped their plates in silence. She felt deflated, not relieved" [*BM*, 52–3]. In a novel where roundness and swelling is perceived so positively, Zelda's state of deflation here is highly significant, as is the introduction of the subject of timing, which has implications for the progress of the developing foetus and arouses suspicions in Zelda's mind that her body may be inadequate as a time-piece.

In both psychoanalytic and mythological terms, food is a sacred or totemic force. Kristeva places strong emphasis upon tribal rituals surrounding raw and cooked food indicating, aptly enough, that "In contrast to a ripe fruit that may be eaten without danger, food that is treated with fire is polluting and must be surrounded with a series of taboos". The really crucial point, however, is her observation that "Food becomes abject only if it is a border between two distinct entities or territories",[35] for this is also true of traditional fairy offerings. In particular Hartland emphasizes that the consumption of fairy-food is to be avoided because it effects a metamorphosis from within the self (hence forcing one to involuntarily cross limits one would otherwise not cross) which is almost always harmful and threatens to efface the self when confronted by the other within the self.

Ellis uses this strategy directly in *Fairy Tale* where Eloise, a vegetarian for much of the book, is transformed into a voracious carnivore by her encounter with the Tylwyth Teg, desperate for "meat, red and sanguine, iron-rich liver and protein-laden steaks" [*FT*, 172]. Later, demonstrating how, once one limit is crossed the next crossing is simply a matter of time, she becomes a cannibal who gorges herself on the human flesh of the category "A" sex offender in a bizarrely unintentional revenge attack. In *The Birth Machine*, therefore, Zelda's food-related fears are not only related to the metaphorical connection between two traditionally feminine forms of creativity, but also to the belief that they prevent her from having a satisfactory food sacrifice to leave as an offering for the thirteenth fairy. As Spence cautions, "Offerings or oblations to fairies are, of course, on a similar basis as offerings to the dead, and intended to avert their vengeance".[36] Bearing in mind that all fairies are reputed to have a particularly voracious appetite for milk, Zelda fears the direct consequences of this lack as one which might starve or provoke the repugnance of her child:

> Food loathing is perhaps the most elementary and most archaic form of abjection. When the eyes see or the lips touch that skin on the surface of milk ... I experience a gagging sensation and, still farther down, spasms in the stomach, the belly ... [37]

Zelda's fears and perceived inadequacies are repeatedly set up in contradistinction to the talents of her own mother. It is significant that, remembering climbing into bed beside her mother as a child, Zelda's perceptions of the latter's body which "stirred closely, giving off a faint odour like ripe fruit" [*BM*, 17] are notably similar to those of her own pregnant self in adulthood. But as we repeatedly find in this study of the fantastic, such mother/daughter inheritances are frequently ambivalent. Like the "witch" from whom the children shy away in the woods, and Zelda's childhood friend Annie with whom she plays with dolls in the den, Zelda's mother is an ambivalent figure who gathers and mixes together a variety of natural ingredients in a manner that is as suggestive of the cooking up of harmful potions as it is delicious meals. In particular, the growing and gathering of herbs forms the focus for this, a focus which reminds us, again, that herbs might heal but they can also often poison. Cooking up a dish of faggots, the disturbing similarities with the witch's spell or the ritual slaughter are very clear in Zelda's mind:

> ... Zelda passed the bundle [of sage], furry as an animal, and Mother brought the knife down. The leaves bounced, she trapped them,

dragging them back again . . . No mercy. Now the liver: the dark mass shivered as she scooped it, little tongues of it licked her wrist. She pushed it into the mincer . . . and slapped back the little arms that flailed . . . The air was filled with the high metallic stink of blood. [*BM*, 17]

Eating is inseparable from violent death here. Although the sage is vegetable tissue, the imagery of the passage compares it to a slaughtered animal and though the meat is already dead, Baines's comparison of it with references to various body-parts and the ability to lick and flail combine with the vital evocations of the word "live-r" to add to the murderous connotations. Referring to the Stepmother's demands for the huntsman to bring Snow White's liver, Schectman observes:

> The Queen is not content to merely kill the beautiful usurper; she wants to ingest her strength and vitality . . . The lungs and liver, stewed in salt, are to be a massive dose of Vitamn E, a preserved and preserving elixir of youth. For the Queen, this cannibalism is, in a sense, a religious act: to partake of Snow White is to be in communion with the Divine Child . . . [38]

As the final sentence of this quotation illustrates, one of the drawbacks with Schectman's approach is that her fixation upon the therapeutic at all costs means that she oftens forces readings of even cruelty towards children to take on synthetically sickly-sweet proportions. Her reading of "Hansel and Gretel" is typical in this regard:

> When we can move past our fear of being eaten up alive, we may well find treasure in the Witch's house . . . If, in returning to the sweet and bitter prisons of our childhood, we look carefully enough, we may find unexpected riches where there once seemed only traps and cages . . . [39]

Consuming the child is far from consoling in *The Birth Machine*. On the contrary, as we journey through the text the fears of infant deformity that tyrannize the pregnant Zelda gradually reveal themselves, through a series of flashbacks, to be a conscious manifestation of a buried horror, long repressed, effected upon another child by cruel means. Again, as in Ellis's novel, it involves the presence of a monstrous criminal who presides alongside the presence of other, seemingly sanctioned tyrannies. But whereas, in *Fairy Tale*, the sex offender is shown to be a poor substitute for the threat posed by the Tylwyth Teg, in *The Birth Machine* this horror seems impossible to exorcize.

The scene in question concerns a flashback in which the childhood Zelda and her friend Hilary discover the skull of a dead boy in their den, refusing to articulate any knowledge of the incident to any of the authorities, becoming mute in the face of the horror they have seen. That both girls believe this terror to have a supernatural rather than a criminal source is made clear by the role played by bird imagery in the text. Prior to the death of the boy the children find a desecrated bird's body in the den, a vision which, in their childhood naivety, they perceive as evidence of the presence of a witch who has left the bird's corpse as a warning. Refusing to abide by the laws of the totem, the boy disturbs the bird's body, immediate retribution seeming to emanate from its form as "angry life welled up out of its feathers: green and blue flies welling up and shooting off at tangents into the air" [*BM*, 58]. Returning home to take refuge, Zelda is further horrified to find what she believes to be *the* bird alive again and perched on her roof, eyeing her threateningly. At this point the uncanny elements of the bird's apparent ability to return to life and its traditional role of witch's familiar ("A black shape was poised on the roof" [*BM*, 59]) suggests that it is the witch itself in alternative guise as it/she flies off "with a cackle" as Zelda's mother appears on the doorstep.

Irrespective of this apparent surveillance by a magic bird where, in *Fairy Tale*, Eloise is bombarded by "watchers", in Baines's novel, by and large, the treatment of eye imagery takes on a haunting sense of blindness associated with guilt and mutilation. This explains Zelda's adult fear of bringing forth a child whose "mouthless face cannot cry" [*BM*, 92] and who "Had only one eye. No nose. Its eye folded inwards to the centre, and the single eye looking out, like the eye of a bean." [*BM*, 83] And yet, for all this turning of blind eyes, the feelings of guilt which the child Zelda suppresses through a prohibitive silence do ultimately find expression through visual form. In an attempt at displacement, she immerses herself into creating a detailed drawing of a village, packing the page with shopkeepers and merchandise. As she does so the "Two dots, a dash, a half-circle like a moon" [*BM*, 93] which represents the butcher's face seem more than a little reminiscent of the defamiliarized reference to the living boy's "face split open, a straight gap between the freckles" [*BM*, 99].

In terms of fairy mythology this returns us to the theme of the changeling, here projected onto a sleeping-beauty-style doll, which increasingly comes to stand in as a mediating image between the dead boy and Zelda's baby:

Absently, [Hilary] stroked the doll's head...curling the wisps that had escaped from the plaits. Annie suddenly shrieked. "Look what you've *done!*" Hilary looked down. The doll's hair had come loose. It flapped, above the forehead. She peeled it back...The doll's bald head glimmered. It was pitted all over with rows of holes...Furiously Annie grabbed the doll back...her eyes gleaming wickedly...She slopped her hankie in the saucepan and dabbed the doll's head... The green-brown liquid dribbled through the holes in the skewered head. [*BM*, 37]

This incident, which begins by taking the conventional creative lines attributed to children's play, is very quickly transformed into a destructive act as, once again, the ritual forms of cookery and healing are transformed, in their turn, into a ritual death. The green-brown "stew" which doubles here as a fantasy embrocation to heal the doll's head will, in reality, bring about the destruction of the doll and transform it into a horrifying effigy of the dead boy's body. Thus, long before the latter is discovered, the smell of the rotting doll's head acts as a very clear portent of the nightmare vision that is to come:

Something stank in the den...The smell was in the pram. They lifted the doll and brown liquid dripped from the joint in her neck. Her body came upright and a pivot in her head moved her eyes open. Annie jabbed them shut with two fingers. This wasn't the moment for her to waken. The spell had gone wrong...[*BM*, 50]

Most interesting of all, however, is Zelda's cryptic response, only really explicable in terms of the tradition of fairy changelings: "...who'd have guessed the inversion? Who'd have guessed it would be the boy who died?" [*BM*, 82]. In adulthood she finds this dynamic repeated as she offers herself up as a sacrifice, or wax effigy, hoping to buy her child's health in return: "A human shape embossed. A torso and legs...Zelda's arm is outstretched, her hand still pinned" [*BM*, 99].

That Zelda perceives herself to be "pinned" down here recalls the significance of needles to the nursery tale. Mimetically, Zelda's nightmare world is often set in motion by the plunging of the hypodermic needle into her veins, the drugs sending her as effectively into a confrontation with fantasy as if she, too, had drunk fairy vodka. These needles are part of the gender struggle of the text, on the one hand the property and trademark of the representatives of patriarchal intervention as Zelda is *stitched up* by the consultant and made "Good as new" with "magic stitches that disappear all by themselves in a week. Invisible mending" [*BM*, 79]. But on the other they return us to our nursery tale opening to this chapter because, of course, needles remain a staple of fairy tales, and the incantations of alternative knowledge continue to echo through her mind: "You can't bury the bird ... you can't bury all the spindles, there'll still be one hidden, closest to home, obsolete, forgotten ... all that will be needed is one little prick...." [*BM*, 72]. Amusingly, Zelda's trauma does indeed begin with the "one little prick" closest to home – Roland, but he is as easily dispensed with as the doctors. More serious are Zelda's fantastic fears, which remain deep-rooted in her body, the same preoccupation with spinning and weaving imagery encountered in Ellis's novel erupting here as the crying of new-born babies becomes "an elongated thread of sound that picks up another and draws it behind it; more threads spinning under them, then the whole together, a tangle of sound" [*BM*, 86].

But this is where the vicious circle starts to break down, for where Eloise and Joanna finally capitulate or retreat from taking a stand, Zelda determines to take control of her own future and, it is inferred, along with it her past. Ironically, this involves a final recognition that she is, in the most positive sense possible, an "unnatural" mother. Roland Barthes's claim that "The writer is someone who plays with *his* mother's body" suggests both, as Suleiman claims, that "Mothers don't write, they are written" and, moreover, that writers are implied to be male.[40] But at the end of *The Birth Machine* Zelda recognizes that her only means of purging herself of her nightmare world is by forging her own reality through becoming "her own author"(ity) [*BM*, 119]. As an interim stage she must break out of the taboo of silence which has locked her into Snow White's glass coffin and, in addition, "suffer no guilt. It was that, after all, that was the power of the witch ... the upper floor drops away and back, a receding space-ship ... And then outside" [*BM*, 118–20]. We have seen that Schectman utilizes the characters and tropes of fairy-tale forms primarily to offer an allegorical reading of behaviour patterns within the family unit. Zelda determines to break free from those patterns, but also knows that such rebellion is never an easy choice. As Jennifer Waelti-Walters has observed:

> Any woman, then, who speaks out, who thus has control over her own situation and over her children's lives, who makes choices, and carries them out with authority, who recognises and fulfils her own desires ... runs a great risk of being labelled ... mad by [the men

around her] as they attempt to ... prevent her speech from being heard. Return to the fairy-tale: do not believe the witch, she will tell you lies or cast a spell on you. Her language is taboo.[41]

Where Hartland encourages women to tell stories of consolation to their children, all mothers who warn their children not to "tell fairy stories" recognize that, in their conventional, nursery-tale form, these tales and their emphasis upon the imprisonment of women or their silence render the woman a mute and muted object. Throughout *The Birth Machine*, many of the manifestations of Zelda's nightmare existence typify the dilemmas of the truly creative woman: "Guilt, desperation, splitting of the self ... these are some of the realities ... that writing mothers live with".[42] At the end, however, Zelda's determination to be her own author demonstrates the empowerment that can be attained when our creativity is allowed to forge our own fantasies, including those of "alternative knowledge" through mythology, legends or the occult, rather than taking on board those we are encouraged to assimilate.

# 6

# Magic Realism Meets the Contemporary Gothic: Isabel Allende and Angela Carter

> ...the marvelous begins to be unmistakably marvelous when it arises from an unexpected alteration of reality...from a privileged revelation of reality...or an amplification of the scale and categories of reality...[1]

In comparison with ancient folklore, magic realism is a more recent form of fantastic fiction still relatively unfamiliar to many contemporary readers in Britain and Europe. Its very name associates the term with oxymoron (how can something simultaneously be "real" and "magical" at the end of the twentieth century?) and, in that regard, provides a perfect framework for many of the concerns of postmodern writers of the fantastic, while also being integrally concerned with the impact of post-colonialism upon narrative theory. The etymology of the term is repeatedly emphasized by all critics of the field. To reiterate this in brief, its origins lie in art history, first being coined in 1925 by Franz Roh, actually as a counter-response to what Roh saw as the "exaggerated preference for fantastic, extraterrestrial, remote objects" typical of the Expressionist movement.[2] In literature it can be seen to take the opposite trajectory, rooting itself in the real, but allying magical realism with the extraordinary *within* the real, evoking a type of double-edged *frisson* not dissimilar to the concerns of the post-colonial, in that both actively resist turning what one might define as "the Other" (the fantastic/foreign/native) into "the Same" (realism/empiricism/empire).[3]

Intriguingly, once the magic realism of Latin America is situated alongside its Anglo-American siblings, what evolves is a dynamic which, in recognizing the Otherness of the Same, reveals a nascent gothicism in both traditions, yet one that rethinks some conventional gothic tropes in a new, more collectivized, ideological manner. Pearce's comments about the ending of *Beloved*, a novel I signalled up as magic realism in Chapter 4, reflect this interface:

> In the years which follow, in which it is disputed whether there really was a ghost at 124, it is significant that ... only the women of the town ... claim to have seen 'it' (p.265). And this is clearly because 'Beloved' came from a time/space that, deep in their 'unspoken' hearts (p.199), all slave mothers have visited.[4]

Pearce, we have seen, is unconvinced of the suitability of fantastic tropes as capable signifiers for material politics, but magic realism takes this interface for granted and I think it is this, rather than a differing treatment of time-travel or polychronotopic structure in general, that leads Pearce to feel more at ease with *Beloved* than *Sexing the Cherry*.

For critics such as William Rowe and Vivian Schelling, women's role in the history of the magical real in a *South* American context is crucial, not least because the "magic" in question has always been understood as an alternative mode of knowledge not dissimilar to the form it took in the previous chapter, one particularly sustained in the cultural role played by indigenous women. This social phenomenon directly impacts upon a collective consciousness and, being "a syncretism of native Indian, African and popular European belief",[5] also impinges directly on an understanding of the post-colonial as a mode of thought directly engaged with the "project of dismantling the Centre/Margin binarism of imperial discourse".[6] In its originary usage as "women's work" or "alternative knowledge" it is not, perhaps, intentionally part of such a project, simply continuing to exist as a discredited form of superstition at odds with Imperialist doctrines of "Enlightenment". This is part of the significance of magical realism in a fictional context, because it gives a centrality back to those modes of thought, while remaining "ex" of centre itself. Typical of this dynamic is the central figurehead of Scheherazade, the storyteller from *The Thousand and One Nights* who, though ex-centric to the power base (the Sultan himself), simultaneously uses and usurps that power base for her own purposes. As the eponymous character of Allende's *Eva Luna* (1988) informs one such representative of the establishment, General Tolomeo Rodríguez:

> Reality is a jumble we can't always measure or decipher, because everything is happening at the same time ... behind your back Christopher Columbus is inventing America, and the same Indians that

welcome him in th[at] stained-glass window are still naked in a jungle a few hours from this office . . .[7]

Simon Sleman relates the narrative foregrounding of "gaps, absences, and silences" so common to magic realist texts to those "produced by the colonial encounter . . . display[ing] a preoccupation with images of both borders and centers . . . [and] destabilizing their fixity".[8] Such gaps can be understood in different terms. One possible interpretation derives from the formal lacunae in Beloved's own testimony in part two of Morrison's novel, a formal technique that mirrors the gaps of knowledge that open up at the point at which Sethe's memories of her dead baby connect with the young woman who returns as the embodiment of that infant. But they are also disruptive spaces which open up from within the formally seamless, smooth surface of social realism and thus illustrate the manner in which, as Wendy B. Faris claims, "The mysterious character of Beloved . . . slithers provokingly [and provocatively?] between . . . two options, playing with our rationalist tendencies to recuperate, to co-opt the marvelous . . .[9] Another interpretation centres on the importance Rowe and Schelling place upon the role of technology as a signifier of cultural disruption, as epitomized by the mediations written into its very terminology.

One of these moments of confrontation can be seen to take place in Allende's *The House of the Spirits* (1985) as Esteban Trueba, trying to build up the mining community of Tres Marías, orders "a short-wave radio with two enormous batteries" as a means of maintaining contact with so-called civilization. Instead of civilization, however, he finds his own remote location invaded by news of international warfare. What is particularly salient to Sleman's point about cultural "gaps" is the manner in which Trueba silently allows the news to *media*te his own response to it:

[He] was able to follow the advances of the troops on a map he hung on the school blackboard, which he marked with pins. The tenants watched him in amazement, without the foggiest idea of why anyone would stick a pin in the color blue one day and move it to the color green the next. They could not imagine the world as the size of a piece of paper . . .[10]

The map is the ultimate signifier, always at a stage of removal from its signified, simultaneously able and unable to capture the entirety to which it relates. In an ironic reversal of colonialist "norms", the peasants' reaction recognizes the space between the signifer and the signified without being equipped to fill in the space. The map, commonly read as a marker of mimetic representation, becomes instead a piece of fantastic mysticism, "alternative knowledge"and even the uncanny.

A second instance, taken from Allende's *Eva Luna*, revolves around the *telenovela*, a form of serialized drama which Eva writes, adding a further layer of storytelling to the narrative she recounts to us. For Rowe and Schelling the *telenovela* is a crucial mediating space in cultural terms which, for all its disparagement at the hands of the mainstream, fulfils an important function in interrogating the political through the popular. Firstly it directly draws upon the collective historical consciousness of ordinary Latin American people and weaves that shared knowledge and storytelling structure into its own form. Secondly it encourages a form of active participation which literally causes the characters to become projected into people's everyday lives in a manner endowing them with extra-textual status. The result is politicized through the filter of the problems of the viewing audience, projected onto the scenario witnessed.[11] Eva's own *telenovela* functions in precisely these terms, but added to them is an explicit framing of magic realism which opens up spaces within the mimetic for explicit ideological critique. Having subverted the system through Mimí, a transsexual, having seduced the Director of National Television, hence enabling ideologically subversive material to be shielded under the protection of the State Authorities, Eva writes a politically-loaded script, gripping her audience through a complex blend of enchantment and political revelation, simply by telling her own story (the one we have already read) in visual mode:

> I doubt that anyone understood [it, but] ... they went off to bed every night with their heads spinning from clashes of snakebitten Indians, embalmers in wheelchairs, teachers hanged by their students, Ministers of State defecating in bishop's plush chairs ... The government warned *señor* Aravena ... [and] I had to omit several of La Señora's bawdy activities, and to muddy the Revolt of the Whores, but everything else survived nearly intact. [*EL*, 263]

Even her own house is directly affected by the screening of the drama, Eva herself claiming that the characters start to invade it, a claim we read metaphorically as Eva's own compulsion with her writing, until we read of the effect they have on a third party:

> [They] upset Elvira's routine; she spent much of her time arguing with them and cleaning up the chaos of hurricane they left in

passing...but when she saw them at night, fulfiling their roles on the television screen, she would sigh in pride. In the end, she considered them all members of her family. [*EL*, 264]

For Rawdon Wilson, space is attributed with a similarly materialist essence in the context of magic realism. Storytelling takes up not just conceptual but literal space in which the tale mediates between an addressor and an addressee. Hence, in *The House of the Spirits*, Blanca does not just help her childhood sweetheart Pedro Tercero García with his reading, she enables him to join her in another world, one populated by "gnomes, fairies, men stranded on islands who eat their comrades after casting their fate at dice...Oriental countries with genies in bottles, dragons in caves, and princesses held prisoner in towers" [*HS*, 165].

What sets magic realism apart from other fantastic forms, however, is that the precise nature of its polychronotopic structure results in "two distinct geometries...inscribed onto the same space", much like the effect produced when Angela Carter's Dr Hoffman inscribes his own cartography of the unconscious across a pre-existing cityscape:

Cloud palaces erected themselves then silently toppled to reveal for a moment the familiar warehouse beneath them...A group of chanting pillars exploded in the middle of a mantra and lo! they were once again street lamps until, with night, they changed to silent flowers. Giant heads in the helmets of conquistadors sailed up like sad, painted kites over the giggling chimney pots...[The city] had become the arbitrary realm of dream.[12]

In post-colonial terms, the ideological dimension of the magical real derives from the fact that "plural worlds...approach each other but do not merge". This has implications, also, for time. According to Carpentier, "buildings and spaces also speak to us of a past forever suspended".[13] Fewer more salient examples of this exist than Carter's depiction of Big Ben in *Nights at the Circus* (1984), a monumental time-marker which seems, in this novel, to operate as a synecdoche for London.

Returning to the discussion of the media as a force capable of reassessing global paradigms, the superimposition of Big Ben upon the ITN news broadcasts in Britain succeeds in communicating it as an icon representing both the new and the eternal. Something will never change, it implies, and London remains at the centre of global communication, just as the world is changing around it – hence making news. Literally attached to the seat of government, it is easy to effect a slippage in this text that superimposes Big Ben upon the Greenwich meridian, implying that the whole world takes its time and meaning from this magnetic point of the Northern hemisphere. But Carter's character Lizzie gives the lie to this truth at the same time as she parodically reinforces its emphasis. As we move towards the cusp of a new century in the novel, all is about to change, but Lizzie forces millennial time to stand still. As if to reinforce a moment of stasis prior to the headlong hurtling over the precipice of the new world, Walser listens, expecting Big Ben to strike one in the morning:

> Big Ben concluded the run-up, struck – and went on striking... Lizzie, chattering with rage, snatched the papers from him and stuffed them away in the corner cupboard. Odd, that – that she did not want him to examine her old newspaper.
> But, odder still – Big Ben had once again struck midnight. The time outside still corresponded to that registered by the stopped gilt clock, inside. Inside and outside matched exactly, but both were badly wrong.
> H'm.[14]

For A.A. Mendilow, a critic whose perspective on fantasy and the fantastic is less than enthusiastic, there are only four different categories of fiction, each with their own relationship to time:

> ... the impossible, the improbable, the possible, and the probable, the novel proper claim[ing] from the beginning to have eliminated from its field the first two, and so to have clearly marked itself off from the romance. The third was at first held by many to be legitimate, but the greater novelists maintained that they were writing within the limits only of the fourth.[15]

As with all of the texts discussed in this chapter, at face value we might think *Nights at the Circus* capable of scraping into at least the "third" category of the "possible". After all, it begins with a realist setting, an interview between a journalist and a circus perfomer in her dressing-room and the larger time-frame of the text, with tremendous historical specificity, locates itself in the year 1899, as "the world tilt[s] away from the sun towards night, winter and the new century" [*NC*, 200]. In this sentence lies the hinge upon which the ideology of this novel pivots. On the one hand associated with night (darkness, unease and the unknown) and winter (coldness, bleakness and depression), this new century, as the terrorist encountered in Siberia affirms, also stands for a new start, or at least renewed hope. Yet despite the fact that the novels discussed in this chapter cumulatively seem to prove Mendilow's point that "In a sense our age has seen the conquest of space by time[, t]he four quarters of the world have drawn together, and to reach them has become not merely quicker and easier but more common",[16] in fact both Allende's and Carter's use of the bizarre, the "unnatural" and the fantastic puts both writers well beyond Mendilow's ideal frame of reference, choosing to revel in the improbable, while flirting with impossibility.[17]

Using the fantastic, Carter plays with the idea of time as a manipulable concept. Lizzie, a specialist in "household magic", returns us (albeit within a Western European tradition) to that issue of women and alternative knowledge already addressed in the context of Latin America. Her own hybrid nationality as London-born Italian facilitates this ability for, within the terms of conventional British xenophobia, this will always emphasize the kind of marginal status associated with "alternative knowledge". Hence her description as "a tiny, wizened, gnome-like apparition" [*NC*, 13] who, in "crackl[ing] quietly with her own static ..." [*NC*, 28] evokes echoes of the word "cackles" and hence witches' laughter. Almost by default, Lizzie becomes a mother substitute to Fevvers, just as, in Allende's work, the mother is always the source of fabulous tales and other household tricks:

> ... able to camouflage herself against the furniture or to disappear in the design of a rug ... [But when] she talked about the past, or told her stories, the room filled with light; the walls dissolved to reveal incredible landscapes, palaces crowded with unimaginable objects, faraway countries ... She placed at my feet the treasures of the Orient, the moon, and beyond. She reduced me to the size of an ant so I could experience the universe from that smallness; she gave me wings to see it from the heavens; she gave me the tail of a fish so I would know the depths of the sea. [*EL*, 21]

## Evoking The Strange(r): *The House of the Spirits* (1985)

What we find in magic realism (particularly at the dark end of its spectrum where it meets the gothic), is a double-edged *frisson* which oscillates around the disturbing aspects of the everyday. As an illustration of this interface between the ordinary and the extraordinary and the interrelationship between visual and literary representation, one could find fewer more salient examples than the portrait of the central female protagonist, Clara, in *The House of the Spirits*:

> The canvas shows a middle-aged woman dressed in white, with silvery hair and the sweet gaze of a trapeze artist, resting in a rocking chair that hangs suspended just above the floor, floating amidst flowered curtains, a vase flying upside down, and a fat black cat that observes the scene like an important gentleman. Influence of Chagall, according to the catalogue, but that is not true. The picture captures precisely the reality the painter witnessed in Clara's house. [*HS*, 306]

*The House of the Spirits* is a deeply political novel dealing with concepts of nationalism, inter-class warfare and the undermining of democracy by a totalitarian regime. But it is also and equally a novel about the supernatural, this dialectical combination of the numinous and global politics being a feature common to magic realism.

Despite the disparities in the origins of the two modes, magic realism's amalgamation with the gothic brings to light a surprising narrative similarity. We might anticipate Alejo Carpentier's belief that the traveller is the reader's representative in works of the magical real, epitomizing our sense of wonder as we turn page after page. Speaking of a visit to China, he considers:

> ... in spite of having spent hours ... at the fish counters watching the fish whose colors blur in the enveloping motion of their lightly fanning fins ... I return to the West feeling somewhat melancholy ... I am not sure that I have understood ... [18]

What we may well have missed, in a different context, is that this same stance of wonder is at the root of the reading process in Freud's essay, "The 'Uncanny'", preoccupied as it also is with the discourse of foreign travel and the mystification deriving from seemingly mundane, everyday details. Hence we find passengers who find their cabin door, railway compartment and hotel room marked with the same number; walkers who find themselves embarking upon various "voyages of discovery" which always end up back on the same spot; or recipients of letters from two different countries, both signed by a name about which one has been reading. In both contexts, then, travel is a metaphorical phenomenon which shares an addiction for journeys into the unknown. Hence Carpentier's similarly *unheimlich* perspective on "home" (Latin America): "Here the strange is commonplace, and always was commonplace."[19]

*The House of the Spirits* is certainly a novel about travelling, from Uncle Marcos and his fantastic voyages in the first chapter, through to Jaime and Alba's expedition into the mountains to hide Esteban Trueba's stash of armaments in chapter 12, and Blanca and Pedro Tercero García's removal to Canada at the end of the text. But as well as literal travel within and beyond geographical boundaries, magic realism fuels fabulous stories from across the world, such as those Clara tells of "[Tibetan] lamas who take salt tea with yak lard ... the opulent women of Tahiti, the rice field of China, or the white prairies of the North, where the eternal ice kills animals and men who lose their way ... " [*HS*, 29]. In effect, in magic realism narrative itself is a fabulous panorama, whereas in the gothic landscape is inevitably claustrophobic. Part of the clashing world-views in *The House of the Spirits* revolves around the tension between the allure of the agoraphobic, manifest in the many adventures into new territory, and a type of gothic magnetism which continually drags characters back to a nodal grouping of oppressive houses.

The first of these is the derelict mansion at Tres Marías, Esteban Trueba's mining and agricultural site, with its "broken shutters ... and spider-webs ... carpeted with a layer of grass, dust, and dried-out leaves" [*HS*, 66]. The second is the mansion Trueba buys for Jean de Satigny as a dowry for marrying his estranged daughter Blanca, which de Satigny transforms into a Bluebeard's Castle, and from which Blanca ultimately flees in terror. The third, and most significant, is the "big house on the corner", built by Esteban Trueba on his marriage to Clara and subsequent home to several generations of the family. Haunted by the spirits of the living and the dead alike, in the most traditional of gothic fashions this third house is an architectural manifestation of the eccentricities and fallibilities of its generations of inhabitants. This is largely due to Clara, who has numerous annexes built on to house the various incompatible groupings who take up residence within its walls:

> The house filled with political propaganda and with the members of [Esteban's] party, who practically took it by storm, blending in with the hallway ghosts, the Rosicrucians, and the three [spiritualist] Mora sisters. Clara's retinue was gradually pushed into the back rooms of the house, and an invisible border arose ... the noble, seigneurial architecture began sprouting all sorts of extra little rooms, staircases, turrets, and terraces. Each time a new guest arrived, the bricklayers

would arrive and build another addition to the house. The big house
on the corner soon came to resemble a labyrinth. [*HS*, 259]

Allende's comparison of the house with a labyrinth here recalls Fred
Botting's discussion of such images in the context of the eighteenth-
century gothic and its role as conveyor of dark political intrigue. Such
tropes, seen as particularly suspicious in the hands of the female novelists of the time, whose dabbling in politics was, to their contemporaries,
an "unsexing" practice, set up ironic historical resonances between past
and present. According to Botting, labyrinths are "places of radical
politics and confusion ... [l]inked to novels that raise the spectre of
democracy ... [and blur] proper national and sexual identifications".[20]
These points, originally set against the backdrop of the French Revolution and British fears for its contagion, are shown to have lost none of
their resonance for a writer such as Allende, who employs identical
tropes two centuries on, for identically pro-democratic reasons. Within
this house are two apparently separate worlds, the world of politics and
the world of the supernatural. But as we have seen, in Latin American
magic realism the one directly impinges upon the other. Elsewhere I have
defined the gothic in terms that emphasize such a conflict between
worlds, the world inside the gothic mansion being "an interior dream-
(or rather nightmare-) space" and that beyond its walls forming "the
outer world of daylight order". Once this dichotomy is in place, "a
Gothic text *becomes* a Gothic text only when such fixed demarcations
are called into question by the presence of an interloper who interrog-
ates their existence".[21] The magical realist basis of *The House of the Spirits*
gives this interrogation a particularly acute political edge. Hence, as
Clara's son Nicholás enters the world inhabited by his working-class
lover Amanda, he does so on one level as the unsuspecting interloper of
a gothic interior, but on another in the manner of a privileged man
repulsed by the masses:

Poverty to him was an abstract, distant concept ... he had never had
any direct contact with it himself. Amanda, his Amanda so close and
so well known, suddenly became a stranger ... It was another world.
A world whose existence he had not even suspected. [*HS*, 270]

As part of the larger political dimension of Allende's work, the numinous is less possession than *re*possession. Speaking, herself, from a position allied with relative marginality in cultural terms, in Allende's hands
history becomes fable and the phantom the presence of the formerly

silenced whose pasts, in P. Gabrielle Foreman's words, have been "too often trivialized, built over or erased". Lois Parkinson Zamora elucidates further on the nature of ghosts: "They are always double (here and now) and often duplicitous (where?)".[22] The apparition in *The House of the Spirits* of Férula, Esteban's sister, is crucial in this context because, paradoxically, the whole family experiences her manifestation as if she is a living visitor, some characters greeting her with words, one even rising to acknowledge her entrance. But in fact her appearance paradoxically signals her disappearance, for it is the first manifestation of the knowledge of her death, as Clara immediately recognizes.

A similar moment occurs towards the end of the novel as Esteban Trueba, desiring to understand if and how his son Jaime has died in the political coup that tries to depose him, finally evokes his spirit as confirmation of the news. In the first of the two scenes Férula's apparition is a family rebuke. Jealous of Férula's closeness to his wife, Esteban gradually starts to believe that "she was stealing forbidden kisses that properly belonged to him" [*HS*, 155], hence once more returning to the labyrinthine structure of the house as, in Botting's terms, not just likely to stand in for the transgression of political, but also sexual boundaries. Finding Férula in Clara's bed, having taken refuge there from her fear of the earthquake which starts to rumble around them, Esteban reacts like a betrayed lover, throwing her out of the house and threatening her with a death that is realized as he faces her apparition. In the second scene, the presence of the phantom gives visual manifestation to the fact that Jaime dies a horrible and prolonged death at the hands of torturers. Just as Esteban is shown to be too preoccupied with his own concerns to heed the physical suffering of his dying mother, with her "two bruised, elephantine [legs] . . . rotting alive" [*HS*, 107], so here he is immune to the suffering of his dying son, "open[ing] a bottle of French champagne to celebrate the overthrow of the regime . . . never suspecting that at that very moment his son Jaime's testicles were being burned with an imported cigarette" [*HS*, 423]. This second scene is both a personal and a political rebuke, the ultimate reminder that Esteban has sacrificed his whole family for his own political aggrandisement. Finally, as Allende spells out, "History itself is a ghost to be confronted, exorcized, used, overcome".[23]

## Originary Tales: *Eva Luna* (1988)

As its title suggests, *Eva Luna* is, in many ways, a novel about origins and their relationship with narrative in a variety of forms. Eva's mother tells her that her first name means "life", the name Luna relating to her unknown father's origins, he belonging to a tribe known as the Children of the Moon. In that sense Eva brings together two originary mythologies, the Genesis story of Adam and Eve, and one marking her own relationship to native Indian ancestry. In the process she straddles the post-colonial divide, reminding us that origins are not simply familial in this novel, though family is again a powerful influence upon characters and their personal and political destinies. Also originary are the mythologies out of which Eva tries to rewrite the histories of the oppressed, here in the form of her lover Rolf:

> ...she had to invent it all – from his birth to the present day, his dreams, his desires, his secrets, the lives of his parents and his brothers and sisters, even the geography and history of his homeland ...when she felt her spirit as empty as that of a newborn child, she understood that in her desire to please him she had given him her own memory... [EL, 249]

In the early chapters of *Eva Luna*, a new chronotope is set up with every chapter and with it, a different set of fabulous tales. Chapter 1 introduces Eva and her mother and concerns itself with her origins and her childhood destiny. Chapter 2 opens on the other side of the world, in Austria, and concerns itself with Rolf Carlé's childhood, particularly in relationship to trauma at home and the wider political climate. When Rolf travels to Latin America following the death of his tyrannical father in chapter 4, he finds a simulacrum of Austria overlying that of Latin America in the form of the Alpine colony geared towards Latin American tourists. Chronotopes exist within chronotopes in this novel in a way that mystifies national and geographical boundaries. So simulated snow is superimposed upon tropical heat; Kamal the Turk travels to that part of Palestine inhabited by North Americans and finds there "gringas ... washing their cars ... dressed only in shorts and scoop-neck T-shirts", bemused by the so-called "optical illusion" of "men swathed in tunics, with dark skin and beards of Prophets" watching them [EL, 143]. Still wider disjunctions occur, such as when Rolf starts work with Aravena "the same month the Russians launched a space capsule containing a dog" [EL, 153], and yet, in his own land, "In many places people did not learn of the overthrow of the dictatorship because, among other things, they had not known that the General was in power all those years" [EL, 158].

The alternation between these chronotopes reinforces the cultural superimpositions taking place within the main romance plot of the text, so that for the reader it is as if Eva and Rolf already belong to the same story even before they meet in chapter 10, a perspective shared by Eva herself, who looks into her past, but is "sure I had not known him" [*EL*, 228]. In fact we discover, as already implied, that Rolf is the product of her own projections. Hence, in chapter 3, long before she meets Rolf and hears his childhood stories, Eva tells Huberto Naranjo a story about a bandit which pulls together chronotopes which will later, unbeknown to her, become connected in the novel. In part this bandit is a version of the outlaw that Huberto will later become, but far more present in her tale is the ghost of Rolf's father, Lukas Carlé, whom the reader has already encountered by this point, but whom Eva certainly has not:

> [He was] a real jackal who resolved even minor disagreements with bullets, strewing the landscape with widows and orphans ... When he showed up at the house it was like a gale from hell ... [and] terrified youngsters ran to hide in the wardrobe ... [*EL*, 59]

The paradox of this novel, later made evident in the writing of the *telenovela*, is that the characters are simultaneously products of this text by Allende and products of one of her own products, Eva, who writes them into her own text as well as telling her own story to us. Eva is therefore simultaneously within and beyond the narrative frame. It is an intriguing analogy for magic realism itself, in that she is both born out of and transcends/explodes the boundaries of the text, just as magic realism is born out of and transcends/explodes the boundaries of the real. One disturbing and haunting illustration of this process involves Eva's witnessing of her employer's wife Zulema and his brother Kamal, making love right in front of her, believing their lack of concern over her presence to be evidence of her own invisibility: "Only a few steps from me ... his masculinity pointed directly at me ... for a second our eyes met, but his passed on unseeing" [*EL*, 147]. Only in a magic realist text could the reader pause to consider the possibility of the *literal* truth of this statement. Eva's invisibility here is a figurative manifestation of her storytelling role and our readerly involvement in the novel for, like us, she is unseen, watching the couple within the covers, while we are unseen watching from beyond the covers. Unlike us, though, Eva feels implicated by her proximity in a manner that leads to a fetishistic haunting: "A huge nose pointing at me, unseeing ... poking into her, not me, no, only her ... " [*EL*, 176].

Frequently, and characteristically for magic realism, there is an explicit political motive for the haunting of characters. Following his father's murder, Rolf Carlé is haunted by guilt, despite not being one of the perpetrators, because he sees in that act the manifestation of his own desires. But this haunting is also related to a larger atrocity witnessed just prior to his father's return from the war when, as a child, he and the other available villagers are forced to bury dead bodies at the nearby prison camp, an incident "they would try to forget, to tear . . . from their souls, resolved never to speak of it, with the hope that time would erase it" [*EL*, 32]. Where *The House of the Spirits* takes its central protagonists from the aristocrat classes, in *Eva Luna* it is the ordinary people. One of the more mystifying instances of the manifestation of the ordinary people is in their representation by significant buildings, one of which is the mirage-like presence of the Palace of the Poor, manifesting itself to Eva on two occasions in the text. Originally the home of the dictator, on his death "indigents began to take it over, timidly at first, and then in droves . . . they invaded bathrooms of onyx, jade and malachite; and finally settle in with children, grandparents, goods and chattels and livestock" [*EL*, 122–3]. What is typically magic realist about this is the manner in which political activism quickly shifts over into the realms of the fabulous while never undermining its ideological import: "Invisible lines divided the commodious rooms, and each family staked out its place . . . They could not evict the occupants because the palace and everything inside it had become invisible to the human eye; it had entered another dimension . . . " [*EL*, 123]. In this context the subsequent manifestations of the Palace to passers-by along the road reminds them of the ongoing need to keep exorcizing this particular demon if they are to be freed from extreme poverty.

It is partly in this context of exorcism that abjection, a recurrent theme in the text, takes on its political dimensions. Central to debates about the "I" and the "Not-I" its relevance to post-colonial and other political encounters becomes clear, from the "statue of [Columbus,] the Father of the Nation . . . humiliated by the irreverence of pigeon shit" [*EL*, 56], to the vengeful peasants who, following the death of a poor child by a wealthy landowner, cram his house so full of mangoes that "the juicy fruit burst open, soaking the walls and running across the floor like sweet blood" [*EL*, 129]. It also functions to symbolize Huberto Naranjo's metamorphosis into Commandante Rogelio, while simultaneously legitimating his belonging to the surrounding environment, as we gain a vision of him "becoming one more animal in the jungle, nothing but instinct, reflex, impulse, nerves, bones, muscles, skin, frown, clenched

jaw, tight belly. The machete and rifle... natural extensions of his arms."
[*EL*, 163] It is against this background that other transformations (personal and political) are set and it is perhaps pertinent that it is the transsexual Mimí, him/herself a fantasy creation, who treats Commandante Rogelio's revolutionary plans as if they belong in the realm of the hyperreal:

> ...she forgot they were trying to free prisoners and thought of it as a kind of parlour game. Fascinated, she drew maps, made lists, imagined strategies...when Comandante Rogelio set Tuesday of the following week as the latest possible date for the attempt, Mimí... realiz[ed] for the first time that he was truly serious... [*EL*, 241]

For Jan Nederveen Pieterse, who focuses upon the role of urbanization in Latin America, the city there often exists as a site or space in which "the fusion of pre-capitalist and capitalist modes of production ...may give rise to 'cities of peasants'" and what he refers to as "*mixed times (tiempos mixtos)*", which he defines as "the coexistence and interspersion of premodernity, modernity and postmodernity".[24] La Colonia negates this evolutionary model being, like the Disney World of the United States, a deliberately constructed society, based on static and uniform principles. Founded in the nineteenth century, Allende's fictive site is built by 80 immigrant families from Austria, "selected on the basis of merit and good intentions", who travel to this magical landscape to begin a new life in a "promised paradise" set in the cooler, hill country, creating in microcosm "a replica of the villages of their homeland: wooden-trimmed houses, Gothic-lettered signs, window boxes filled with flowers, and a small church where they hung the bronze bell they had carried with them on the ship" [*EL*,79–80]. Compare this with Walt Disney's original vision for the Orlando Disney World development:

> It will be a planned, controlled community, a showcase for American industry and research, schools, cultural and educational opportunities ...there will be no landowners...No slum areas...People will rent houses...at modest rentals. There will be no retirees. Everyone must be employed.[25]

Both communities, then, strive to homogenize development and lifestyle within the parameters of these closed "utopian" spaces. The original vision of La Colonia is that of a closed community that will allow for neither emi- nor immigration. Soon forced to open its borders by the national government, resistant to the existence of an autonomous community within national boundaries, however, La Colonia becomes a simulated site of tourist pilgrimage. Similarly, Sharon Zukin informs us, Disney World "was not built exactly to Disney's original specifications" and becomes, instead, "a temporary haven ... a resort colony". With sweeping confidence, Zukin continues, "Frederic Jameson is wrong about the postmodern landscape of visual consumption. Disney World suggests that architecture is important, not because it is a symbol of capitalism, but because it is the capital of symbolism".[26] The same might be said of La Colonia.

A type of Baudrillardian reading of culture as simulacrum runs throughout this text, but always as a commentary either on the post-colonial or magic realist readings of otherness in general. Take, for example, the activities of the sinister embalmer, Professor Jones. Though alone in his refusal to believe in the spirit world that surrounds him, his fascination lies with mummifying corpses. In a bizarre reworking of originary mythology, towards the start of the text Eva's mother reports that the gardener has been bitten by a serpent. Rather than trying to save the man, Professor Jones announces he will await his death, delightedly anticipating turning him into "an indigenous mummy posed as if pruning the Malabar plums" [*EL*, 17]. In all of these contexts, there are a multiplicity of ways and means whereby magic realism can render the real bizarre. This is just one of the ways in which *Eva Luna* can be compared with Angela Carter's *The Infernal Desire Machines of Dr Hoffman*.

## Magically Gothic: *The Infernal Desire Machines of Dr Hoffman* (1972)

Elsewhere I have discussed the interface between Carter's depiction of images of desire and the simulated "skin" of celluloid in *The Passion of New Eve* as one of many illustrations of Baudrillard's claims that America has "*one single passion only: the passion for images*".[27] In *Dr Hoffman* this fascination functions slightly differently, although the same preoccupation with spectrality is central. Though Dr Hoffman's creations appear to have material existence, and are certainly experienced by the population as verifiable (hence the panic caused when he transforms the entire Opera House audience into a collective gathering of peacocks in chapter 1 [*DH*, 16–17]), in fact he is effecting projections, not just in a cinematic or spectral sense, but also in a psychoanalytic one. This is not the realm of simulation we find in Allende's La Colonia, it is a realm in which fears and desires are *magically* realised. This is the problem the Minister of Determination, representative of the rational, fails to accept and thus fails to counter:

> The Minister spent night after night among his computers ... But it seemed to me that he sought to cast the arbitrarily fine mesh of his predetermined net over nothing but a sea of mirages for he refused to acknowledge how palpable the phantoms were ... [*DH*, 24–5]

The fact that magic realism is never a mode of the fantastic that sits easily on British territory may explain, in part, why *The Infernal Desire Machines of Dr Hoffman* is among the most critically neglected of what is becoming, almost notoriously, "the Carter industry". This is to some extent Carter's most "foreign" novel, not because of its cultural location, but because of the precise nature of its relationship to the fantastic.

While it is commonly accepted by critics of the text that *Dr Hoffman* is set in an unspecified region of South America, I would argue that Carter refuses us even this much precise orientation. The same "America" is at work in this text as is at work in *The Passion of New Eve*, namely, not that/those tied to grid references composed of longitude and latitude, but the one to which she refers in her epigram to that novel: "In the beginning the *whole world* was America", no differentiation even being made between North and South continents.[28] It is this simultaneous allusion to South America and its magic realist traditions and the type of Baudrillardian simulacra typical of the "northern continent" that makes Carter's topography so ripe for flights of fear as well as those of fancy. Just as Allende's writing typically evokes a sense of "nation" while often refusing to name it as her own country Chile, so the central paradox of *Dr Hoffman* is that Desiderio's territory is simultaneously evocative of two continents while only ever being one unnamed country. The effect in both cases is the successful retention of the tangibility of actual topography while maintaining the mystification of fantastic tropes. The reader remains dissatisfied with this stance, continually engaging in our own quest for topographical and cultural clues, but all our resolution dissolves, precisely at the point that it seems to come most closely into view:

> The Portuguese did us the honour of discovering us towards the middle of the sixteenth century but they had left it a little late in the

day, for they were already past their imperialist prime and so our nation began as an afterthought, or a footnote to other, more magnificent conquests ... [T]hey left it to the industrious Dutch a century later to drain the marshes and set up that intricate system of canals, later completed and extended during a brief visit by the British, to which the country was to owe so much of its later wealth.

... it was principally the Ukranians and the Scots-Irish who turned the newly fertile land into market gardens while a labour force of slaves, remittance men and convicts opened up the interior ...

During the next two hundred years, a mixed breed of Middle Europeans, Germans and Scandinavians poured in to farm the plains and ... enough black slaves ran away from the plantations of the northern continent to provide cheap labour in the factories, shipyards and open-cast mines which brought the country prosperously enough into the twentieth century. [*DH*, 67]

This presiding sense of Otherness, so important to the "foreignness" of the magical real, also defines Desiderio, the central protagonist of the text. His mother is of "middle-European immigrant stock", a prostitute "of the least exalted type". His father, though personally unknown, shares the same native Indian ethnic background with Eva Luna's father, going by "his genetic imprint on my face" [*DH*, 16]. In that respect Desiderio simultaneously represents the centre and the margin, being ethnically "ex" of centre, but employed by the establishment in the form of the Board of Trade. All the characters he encounters on his quest turn out to be outsiders like (and yet importantly unlike) himself. Even to the River People, who share his Amerindian descent, he is an outsider to be duped, killed and eaten, thus quelling his sentimental affirmation that he "felt the strongest sense of home-coming" [*DH*, 76] in entering their community. But it is the circus people whom he encounters in chapter 4 of the novel that personify most clearly the interrelationship between the magical real and the perpetually "foreign" for, though cosmopolitan in origins, they rise above issues of national boundary in the process of going about their business of transcending the laws of gravity, "for everywhere we halted was exactly the same as where we had stopped last, once we had put up our booths and sideshows" [*DH*, 98].

Desiderio himself travels great distances and by multiple modes, "through space and time, up a river, across a mountain, over the sea, through a forest" [*DH*, 13] but, for all the talk of nation, culture, society and belonging, it is the realm of a specifically Freudian unconscious that lies at the centre of this text and it is this that ultimately separates the gothic (intrinsically psychoanalytic) off from magic realism (fantastic in a truly Todorovian, "hesitant" sense). As in Allende's work, *Dr Hoffman* is a novel in which we oscillate, sometimes dizzyingly, between the vast panoramas of geography (topographical and psychological) and suffocating claustrophobia, the most extreme example of which is perhaps the immense chimney via which Desiderio plans his escape from imprisonment within the Town Hall in chapter 2:

> The sweep had used a child to clamber up and down the chimney for him with the brushes but I was a grown man and it was a chamber of unease to me...my overwrought senses soon convinced me the passage was steadily growing narrower and the walls were shrinking to crush me. [*DH*, 64]

It is these claustrophobic spaces, sites of unconscious repression as much as physical oppression, to which we always return and the archetypal Gothic icon of Dr Hoffman's Castle to which Desiderio is ultimately drawn. In the Introduction, Desiderio informs us that he and the Minister of Determination "did our best to keep what was outside, out, and what was inside, in" [*DH*, 12], but as we have seen, this dichotomy and the apparently futile attempt to maintain it is at the basis of all gothic texts.

It is impossible to read the title of Carter's novel without thinking of E.T.A. Hoffmann's own gothic stories and, bearing in mind the explicitly Freudian anchor point for desire in this novel, most obviously Hoffmann's "The Sandman" (1816), which stands so centrally within "The 'Uncanny'". In Hoffmann's story we find Nathaniel, a character who is "dreamy", "fantastical" and perhaps (although not necessarily) "crazy" and who is haunted by a variety of infernal desires of his own, including the hallucinated loss of his beloved Clara's eyes, as they are dashed from her head "like blood-red sparks, singeing and burning on to Nathaniel's breast", before he is himself thrown into "a flaming circle of fire" by the evil Coppelius, a figure that haunts his childhood and adult world. In contrast to Nathaniel, Clara, as her name suggests, is a clear-thinking, rational woman whose love he ultimately betrays. That this Clara shares her name with Allende's own protagonist is worth observing, simply because what is shown to be a recognition of clear-sighted clairvoyant powers in *The House of the Spirits*, in Hoffmann's nineteenth-century text turns into a form of intuition closely related, in later decades, to an analysis of the unconscious:

Perhaps there does exist a dark power which fastens on to us and leads us off along a dangerous and ruinous path which we would otherwise not have trodden; but if so, this power must have assumed within us the form of ourself, indeed have become ourself, for otherwise we would not listen to it, otherwise there would be no space within us in which it could perform its secret work. But if we possess a firm mind ... then that uncanny power must surely go under in the struggle ... [29]

The specifically Freudian stance of *Dr Hoffman* could be seen to offer a new, analytical role for Scheherazade for, as Beate Neumeier claims, "Whereas earlier Gothic/fantastic texts had to be interpreted in psychoanalytic terms by readers and critics, [*Dr Hoffman*] provides its own reading".[30] So Desiderio tells his own story as a means of delaying his own death, simultaneously analysing the relationship between the pleasure principle and the death drive as he goes. Though Desiderio's relationship with his own text is identical to Allende's Eva's, it being a story in which he is both a character within the text and the teller of it beyond its covers, the effect of this reading is different in each case. While we never lose faith in Eva as a reliable character within her own tale, Desiderio is far more slippery, as his own name suggests (and we have repeatedly seen the effect naming has upon understanding of character in this type of text). Hence, for David Punter, Desiderio's narrative role in the novel renders him "an allegorical figure for the object of desire", but this purported role of objectivity (itself, of course, ironically undercut by the subjective nature of the visions revealed) is, he claims, complicated by the etymology of Desiderio's own naming: "'Desiderio,' the desired *one*, is also anagrammatically ambivalent: the name contains the 'desired I,' but also the 'desired O'".[31]

In purely psychoanalytic terms, Desiderio's subjectivity as "I" persona shifts and fades as the counter-transference between "self as self" and "self as other" kicks in. This returns us to "The Sandman" and Coppola's initial invitation to buy: "lov-ely *occe*, lov-ely *occe!*". Bringing from his coat-pockets multiple pairs of spectacles, the narrator informs us that:

... the whole table began to sparkle and glitter in an uncanny fashion. A thousand eyes gazed and blinked and stared up at Nathaniel, but he could not look away from the table, and Coppola laid more and more pairs of spectacles on to it, and flaming glances leaped more and more wildly together and directed their blood-red beams into Nathaniel's breast. Unmanned by an ungovernable terror, he cried: "Stop! stop! dreadful man!"[32]

What Hoffmann gives us here is a scene in which Nathaniel is penetrated repeatedly by the infernal desires ("flaming glances") of a myriad "eyes" which are simultaneously, in the blood-like spatterings upon his chest, splintered fragments of glass(es). "Unmanned" by the action, Nathaniel experiences the event as a figurative sexual violation. Compare the following rape scene in Carter's novel, in which Desiderio is attacked by the acrobats of desire:

> The mirrors reflected not only sections of the Arabs; they reflected those reflections, too, so the men were infinitely repeated everywhere I looked and now eighteen and sometimes twenty-seven and, at one time, thirty-six brilliant eyes were fixed on me...I was surrounded by eyes. I was Saint Sebastian stuck through with the visible barbed beams from brown, translucent eyes...I was filled with impotent rage as the wave of eyes broke over me.
> The pain was terrible...I ceased to count my penetrations but I think each one buggered me at least twice. [*DH*, 117]

Although Desiderio experiences the same gaze that he inflicts upon the peep-show exhibits as a direct and violently penetrating social weapon, he is repeatedly informed by others that his experiences are nothing but the products of his own imagination (ironically mirroring the manner in which Freud inflicts "hysterical" motivations upon very real suffering among his female patients). But despite its clearly Freudian basis and the similarities between Desiderio and Hoffmann's Nathaniel, Carter also has a new narrative motivation for the comparison, taking the tropes of Freud's texts and stringing them together into a novel of the magical real, not just conveying a cartography of the unconscious but also the topography of the fantastic. This is a landscape and combination she develops more fully in her later and most accomplished novel, *Nights at the Circus*.

## Agoraphobic Reflections: *Nights at the Circus* (1984)

Where *Dr Hoffman* mystifies imaginary locations, *Nights at the Circus* could not make their geographical placement or their relationship to Imperialism clearer. Fevvers may break free on numerous occasions, but she always does so in relation to particular places and times, and, in that regard, the methodological encounter personified by Fevvers as representative of an oral tradition and Walser as one of a written tradition, parallels Rowe and Schelling's understanding of the relationship between landscape and the magical real:

> ...the oral universe as a historical continuity [is] 'written' on the land, [while] that of writing, whose meaning can break free from a particular place and time, creat[es] its own space rather than needing the land to be inscribed on...[33]

Moving from London to Imperialist Russia, and then on to the *tabula rasa* of Siberia, Carter directly uses landscape as a commentary on Empire and its limitations. A novel in which travel is its *raison d'être*, the centrality of the circus (the world in microcosm) is its centre point and the *fin-de-siècle* (reread as fin-du-globe by some[34]) its temporality.

As Sarah Gamble observes, *Nights at the Circus* is an "expansive" novel, a quality she perceives to derive less from its actual word length and more from its use of space, "for the narrative itself mimics Fevvers's leisurely pace through the air, 'potter[ing] along the invisible gangway between her trapezes'".[35] This reading backs up the novel's status as magic realism, but ducks the role played within it by the gothic. Where, for Gamble, *Nights at the Circus* bids farewell to "the lurking sense of claustrophobia" commonly identified with Carter's earlier fiction, for me, it remains as what we have seen to be the dark or under-side of the magical real. In these terms Ma Nelson's whorehouse, Madam Schrek's museum of woman monsters, Mr Rosencreutz's gothic mansion all cohere as the points of stasis Fevvers only *apparently* leaves behind in running away with the circus to St Petersburg. Furthermore, once there, others are "lurking". In St Petersburg these are clown alley (in many ways the most powerful chronotope of the text) and the Grand Duke's Palace. In Siberia, the most agoraphobic landscape of all, they constitute Walser's burial alive in the wreckage of the train, the sub-plot surrounding the revolt at the female penitentiary, and finally the place selected for the eventual reunion of Fevvers and Walser: the "most official-looking building" in the Siberian village, which Fevvers and Lizzie enter via a "creaking door", only to find inside, "No sign of life...traces of blood, of fur and of feathers...[and] a *nightmarish sense of claustrophobia about the place*" [*NC*, 286–7 – my emphasis].

It is this role played by the journey as a commentary on the fantastic that leads me to prevaricate over Magali Cornier Michael's claim that, in the text overall, "The movement toward increasingly foreign and remote places parallels a movement away from any stable grounds of reality and toward the ever more fantastic".[36] On the contrary, as I hinted at in Chapter 1, the magic realist status of *Nights at the Circus* demonstrates quite clearly that it is in the realm of the everyday and the close at home that the "ever more fantastic" can be found and, for both the reader and Walser, we are never more disorientated by the apparent lack of "stable ground" than when Lizzie plays the afore-mentioned tricks on both Big Ben and Father Time, as if to realize the storyteller's magical ability to enable us to move outside time and space by means of her magic words. But of course I am not suggesting that the agoraphobic does not have a magic of its own, and here it is one with the greatest resonance. Stranded in Siberia by the train-crash, Fevvers's well-established flirtation with a variety of mirrors meets its zenith:

> ... amongst the ruins of the 'wagon salon', I beheld a great wonder. For the tigers were all gone into mirrors ... of those lovely creatures, not a trace of blood or sinew, nothing. Only pile upon pile of broken shards ... as if Nature disapproved of them for their unnatural dancing ... As if that burning energy you glimpsed between the bars of their pelts had convulsed in a great response to the energy released in fire around us ... On one broken fragment of mirror, a paw with the claws out; on another, a snarl. When I picked up a section of flank, the glass burned my fingers and I dropped it. [*NC*, 205–6]

The tigers are a bizarre and complex element in this novel. Earlier on in the text, Walser gazes into Fevvers's eyes and finds himself hopelessly disorientated, a scene with its own mirror image when he is later forced to plumb the depths of the tigress's eyes, finding reflected back at him, not his own image, but "the entire alien essence of a world of fur, sinew and grace in which he was the clumsy interloper" [*NC*, 164]. Echoes of Susanne Kappeler's work resonate through this passage, implying that the woman and tiger are interchangeable to Walser: "Woman, in the history of culture, has occupied a place on a par with animals. She has been recognized as similar but different: in her look man recognizes himself. In her look, however, he experiences fear and ignorance ... ".[37] But in the context of this novel's treatment of the fantastic we should also bear in mind that the scene is perfectly analogous with Jon Thiem's reading of the mirror as a primary metaphor of the magical real. In his terms the particular realm of impossibility associated with magic realism is comparable with

... entering into the world *inside* a mirror or a painting. At best you might break the mirror or poke a hole through the canvas with your finger, but with a text the very means of literal entry seems especially elusive. How *do* you get in?[38]

Is it enough, in this context, to say that the type of otherness that features in circus reflects the bizarre distortions of the everyday that characterizes the magical real? For similar trickery is inflicted on the clowns, who are also under threat of being consumed by their reflected circus personae, as the grotesque spectacle of Buffo's madness reveals. These mirrors literalize the dark side of circus, which traps its performers in a freakish status, the bars of the tigers' cage grotesquely mirroring the "bars of their pelts" rendering their natural power unnatural.

In general terms, the significance of the symbol of the mirror to the relationship between fantasy and reality is that the mirror less reflects reality than forges an image which resembles our interpretation of reality (and is often amended and distorted by how we wish this to look). In generic fantasies such as *Alice Through the Looking-glass* (1871), the world of the mirror is the world of fantasy into which we are immersed and then resurface, as if through water. In the terms of magic realism the boundary between the two is one of more ongoing fluidity, as Wendy B. Faris illustrates in her reading of magic realist depictions of death:

> Fluid boundaries between the worlds of the living and the dead are traced only to be crossed ... If fiction is exhausted in this world, then perhaps these texts create another contiguous one into which it spills over, so that it continues life beyond the grave, so to speak.[39]

In *Nights at the Circus* it is the smouldering shattered remains of the tigers, or the clowns' diabolical obsessions, which come closest to symbolizing this transcendence between worlds and their ongoing flirtation with death. For Buffo and the tigers the dangers win out, but women, for once, seem to gain the upper hand.

Fevvers is not, as we have seen, entirely unscathed by the hostile reflections of the mirror, but on occasions she proves herself wise to these dangerous flirtations. Early on it seems her greatest ally, preventing her from being consumed in the manner of Freud's Dora or Atwood's Grace Marks: "As Walser scribbled away, Fevvers squinted at his notebook in the mirror, as if attempting to interpret his shorthand by some magic means ... 'Come on, sir, now, will they let you print that in your newspapers?'" [*NC*, 21]. We have seen that *Nights at the Circus* can be read, in the repeated set of encounters between Fevvers and Walser, as an anthropomorphic exploration of the meeting point of oral history and written culture. As Fevvers shrieks, guffaws, bawls and belches her way through her own oral history Walser dutifully scribbles notes on white paper, trying but failing to capture the "essence of Fevvers" as tangibly as he sniffs it in the rank atmosphere of her dressing-room. In that sense Carter effects a trick in her own text, Walser's ability as hack journalist being outsmarted by Fevvers's own ability to transcend the power of any written word. It is this element of their relationshp that makes it difficult for me to fully accept Linda Ruth Williams's reading of Fevvers as a Dora figure, although it is certainly the case that early descriptions of Walser are not unlike the mystery persona Freud likes to construct for himself within such case histories:

> ...there remained something a little unfinished about him...There were scarcely any of those little, what you might call *personal* touches to his own being...he had a propensity for 'finding himself in the right place at the right time'; yet it was almost as if he himself were an *objet trouvé*, for, subjectively, *himself* he never found, since it was not his self which he sought. [*NC*, 10]

The source of my resistance to finding Freud's character Dora within Fevvers derives, not from a false idealization, but from the manner in which magic realism and the gothic interact in this novel. As I argued in Chapter 3, Freud's sinister reading of female hysteria is always pure gothic, while here Carter captures the gothic at precisely the moment it lets fly from the page, allowing Fevvers to pursue that paradigm of empowered subjectivity that Williams herself associates with everybody's desires: "We narrate ourselves into existence as subjects, and continue explaining and rewriting that existence through fantasy scenarios which can be conscious, unconscious, or somewhere in between".[40] Fevvers, refusing to be "put down on paper", leaves Walser floundering like "a kitten tangling up in a ball of wool it had never intended to unravel in the first place" [*NC*, 40]. In *Wise Children* another Dora has much the same effect upon us.

## Dancing with Death: *Wise Children* (1991)

In contrast to the exotic locales with which *Nights at the Circus* leaves us, *Wise Children* opens with a description of London of all-too-mimetic proportions: "wind-swept bus-stops ... marital violence, breaking glass and drunken song" and yet out of even this prosaic setting develops a recurrent blurring of the real and the unreal as this Dora warns us from the start, "you can't trust things to stay the same", and lures us in with clairvoyant possibilities: "Sometimes I think, if I look hard enough, I can see back into the past."[41] Born, we hear, "Out of a bottle, like a bloody genie" [*WC*, 223], *Wise Children* self-consciously situates itself within magic realist terms and delights in the magic and trickery of the storytelling voice. As their various sexual exploits imply, Dora and Nora know that one form of enchantment frequently leads to another – seducing us into the terms of their tale so we no more see the join between the realms of mimesis and the magical real than we do the line where pan-stick joins flesh.

For Gerardine Meaney, the presiding theme of Carter's work is always "unrepresentability", a facet she reads as Carter's means of resisting stereotypical or homogenizing readings of femininity.[42] Certainly, in Nora and Dora, we find perfect examples of Meaney's "(un)like subjects", twins who, Dora assures us, are "Identical, well and good; Siamese, no" [*WC*, 2]. But there is more to it than this; the whole novel deals in the paradox of representing the unrepresentable, and it uses a variety of magical representations in order to do so. Like Desiderio, Dora treats us to a "Retrospective", but unlike with Desiderio her "I" does not dominate. Instead she puts on a show, giving us within that singular voice, a mutiple cast of *dramatis personae*. As we return to London, having journeyed to Hollywood, and Perry having returned from the dead as well as South America (where else?), we resurface, finally understanding that what we have come face to face with is not, as Clare Hanson would have it, "a pub bore",[43] but a genuine latter-day Scheherazade, even more fitted for the role than Fevvers, for Dora, like Desiderio, is literally effecting one more stay of execution, dressing up in the seemingly immortal guise of "Dora Chance in her tatty old fur and poster paint, her orange (Persian Melon) toenails sticking out of her snake-skin peep-toes, reeking of liquor ... " [*WC*, 227]. For Kate Webb she is also another incarnation of the Freudian namesake, but in this case one who "suffers very little psychic damage from lusting after her father ... or a string of father substitutes ... with whom she has affairs". In addition, where we have seen Freud drag from "his" Dora's own narrative a variety of salacious details that seem as much of his own making as hers, Webb observes of Carter's protagonist's tale that it is "a spilling of all the family secrets, bringing the skeletons out of the closet and exposing them to bright lights. This is a comment in itself: no more family secrets, no more lies, no more illegitimacies."[44] Most of all, of course, it means no more Freuds – or even Jack Walsers.

Though this is a loud, brassy novel with fun at its core, its central theme is truly gothic, namely death itself. The Chance sisters live in a house which, like the archetypal gothic mansion, is "nothing but spare rooms" [*WC*, 36], largely inhabited by phantoms of the past. Be they "skeletons [in] the closet" [*WC*, 5] or "batty old tarts with their eyes glued on their own ghosts" [*WC*, 125], Nora and Dora themselves are always at least partially undead. Their mother is nothing but a "ghost without a face" [*WC*, 164] and, in the process, ghoulishly mirrors the de-faced corpse, wrongly believed to be their niece Tiffany, fished from the river towards the start of the novel. Even the class structures are ripe for gothic tropes, the age-old aristocrat "Wheelchair" (Lady Atalanta Hazard) living in their basement like a subterranean reincarnation of Bertha Mason or, as Dora comically observes, "not so much Miss Haversham, more the ghost of Christmas past" [*WC*, 192]. There are a number of *unheimlich* connections and resurrections in this text, including Perry's description of himself and the twins as "Birnan wood . . . just now creeping up on Dunsinane" as they approach Melchior for the first time in his dressing-room on Brighton pier [*WC*, 69]; and the "phantom caller" in Hollywood, whose "unseen eyes" Dora feels upon her and who turns out to be the Brooklyn wife of the film director Genghis Khan, transforming herself into "A hand-made, custom-built replica [of Dora], a wonder of the plastic surgeon's art" [*WC*, 155] in order to trick her own husband into taking her back.

Ultimately *Wise Children* gives us a carnivalized camping-up of the type of family apparition scenes we encountered more darkly in *The House of the Spirits*. Central to these is Nora and Dora's encounter with the ghost of Grandma Chance:

> Something leapt off the shelf . . . No, not leapt; "propelled itself", is better because it came whizzing out like a flying saucer . . . It was her hat . . . And as we nervously inspected it, there came an avalanche of gloves – all her gloves, all slithery leather thumbs and fingers, whirling around as if inhabited by hands, pelting us, assaulting us, smacking our faces . . .
> "Grandma's trying to tell us something," said Nora in an awed voice. [*WC*, 189–90]

As resistant to linearity as Dora's tale ("they float free in time, not just here and now but then and there, eternal and everywhere"),[45] the ghosts of magic realism help to bring traditional and anti-traditional readings of subjectivity into confrontation with each other and, in this case, prefigure a revelation that will take place in the final chapter. The catalyst to Grandma's manifestation here is Nora's own sadness about having no child to love and no mother to love her. But Perry, having come back from the dead himself and gleefully burst, not out of a birthday cake, but out of a tempest that blows up as the cake is to be cut, reminds Dora that visibility is not only proof of life, it can also function as the only proof of death: "has it ever occurred to you that your mother might not be your mother? . . . Did you ever see your mother's grave?" [*WC*, 222–3]. Grandma, it turns out, was their mother all along.

But if gothicism has the edge over magic in *Dr Hoffman*, in *Wise Children* the scales always tip in the other direction. Irish may portray a less than flattering pen-portrait of Dora as "the treacherous, lecherous chorus girl with her bright red lipstick that bleeds over everything, and her bright red fingernails and her scarlet heart" [*WC*, 119], but Dora is no vampire, even if she does carry a box of earth to Hollywood, "like Dracula!" [*WC*, 113]. Nor is the role of gothic aristocrat one Melchior ever quite gets right, for all his efforts to the contrary:

> He wanted a house that looked as if each leather armchair in the library had been there at least half a century . . . but the Mayfair peeress he'd got in to do [the interior] . . . incorporated just that little bit [too much] . . . So the aged leather was cracked and fissured a little bit more than was absolutely necessary; the mirrors were distressed so much as to look quite marbled; and the walls turned out the colours of very rare roast beef and gravy . . . [*WC*, 95–6]

Above all it is Uncle Perry, with his tablecloth tricks in which, at one tug, everything ("the fine china, the knives and forks . . . the bones, the crusts, the empties") disappears [*WC*, 62] and who desperately tries to fill the space of loss felt by two children at being spurned by their errant father, who takes the credit for celebration at any price:

> I have a memory, although I know it cannot be a true one, that Peregrine swept us up into his arms . . . spread his arms as wide as wings . . . Or perhaps he slipped us one in each pocket . . . And then, hup! he did a back-flip out of the window with us, saving us. But I know I am imagining the back-flip and the flight. [*WC*, 72]

As Paul Magrs rightly observes: "Perry may come back from the dead repeatedly, never age, grow to the size of a house and excrete tropical butterflies, but we never stop believing in him"[46] because for Nora and Dora he is that idealized father of fantasy they never had. In addition, if the ghost in magic realism is conventionally there to give voice to those whom society has silenced or rendered "disappeared", then Uncle Perry is *it*, not just in his protection of the illegitimate Nora and Dora, but in spilling the beans about Grandma Chance.

For those critics who believe the post-colonial to be an essential ingredient of magic realism *Wise Children* will never easily fall into the category. After all, Hollywood lies right at the core of that branch of privileged Western capitalism which is the one remaining legacy of White Western colonialism and also sits right at the core of this text. But *Wise Children* camps up Empire as unmercifully as any Carry-On film, cocking a snook at nationalistic fervour while simultaneously (and this is the complication) seeming genuinely to regret its loss as just one more aspect of childhood nostalgia. It is this aspect of the text that is accommodated by Melchior, the serious Shakespearean actor, left clinging to a childhood momento of his father, the pasteboard crown he wore in the title role of *King Lear*, that "key play for the late 20th century".[47]

But Melchior also answers the call for post-colonial intervention. For Homi K. Bhabha, the Sacred text and its introduction to indigenous cultures is a crucial signifier of the colonial encounter, symptomatic of power in its most "transparent" of guises, and yet carrying along with it a recognition of its own diffident relationship with authority in this foreign context: "for it is in between the edict of Englishness and the assault of the dark unruly spaces of the earth . . . that the colonial text emerges uncertainly". Rowe and Schelling develop this point further in a specifically Latin American context, adding the weight of a more localized secular authority to that of the universally divine. In their terms this particular combination derives from:

> . . . the *requerimiento* (requirement), a written document explaining the history of the world from Adam, justifying the authority of the Pope and the Catholic monarchs, and requiring the Indian populations to submit and be converted. The *requerimiento* was designed to be read out by the Conquistadors before making just war on the Indians, who were unlikely, of course, to have understood a single word of it.[48]

This is a scene well worth comparing with Carter's humorous treatment of a very similar moment, endowed simultaneously with sacred and secular authority, as Melchior consecrates the kitsch set of *A Midsummer Night's Dream* in Hollywood:

> I bear here, in this quaintly shaped casket . . . only a little bit of earth. Nothing more. Earth. And yet it is especially precious to me because it is English earth, perhaps some of the most English earth of all, precious above rubies . . . For it is earth from William Shakespeare's own home town, far away, yes! Sleepy old Stratford-upon-Avon . . . Welcome to our great enterprise . . . to all of you come together here . . . to ransack all the treasuries of this great industry of yours to create a glorious, an everlasting monument to the genius of that poet whose name will be reverenced as long as English is spoken . . . who left the English language just a little bit more glorious than he found it, and let some of that glory rub off on us old Englishmen too, as they set sail around the globe, bearing with them on that mission the tongue that Shakespeare spoke! [*WC*, 134–5]

We have seen that, for some critics, the post-colonial elements of magic realism are inseparable from its deconstruction of the binary oppositions between high and low culture. Paradoxically it is through the great iconic symbol of Shakespeare that Carter pulls all three things together, using her particular brand of reverential mischief:

> . . . the Forest of Arden was a lovely, flimsy, fantastic place, where you could live in grand, two-dimensional style among the hissing lawns – those incessant sprinklers! – and there was a pool, shaped like an acorn leaf, of bright turquoise, planted with shocking pink flamingos, everso As You Like It . . . [*WC*, 121]

Thanks to Jon Thiem, such parodic aspects of the postmodern can be fed directly into our reading of ghosts:

> Often, the postmodern writer is haunted by the feeling that if something has not already been written, then it is probably not worth writing. Many of the characteristic features and strategies of postmodern writing – such as the preoccupation with the past and historical representation and the reliance on quotation, pastiche, and parody – arise out of the feeling of being late and derivative.[49]

*Wise Children* offers a particularly acute and fearless pastiche of this haunting in its treatment of Shakespeare as "the great popular entertainer of all time",[50] although Thiem's choice of the term "late" in this context carries a particularly poignant echo in relation to this, Carter's last novel. In *Dr Hoffman*, time is the Doctor's favourite plaything, Desiderio informing us that "I often glanced at my watch only to find its hands replaced by a healthy growth of ivy or honeysuckle which, while I looked, writhed impudently all over its face" [*DH*, 21], while Lizzie's own tricks with time in *Nights* have already been noted. In *Wise Children*, for all the "singing and dancing until we drop" [*WC*, 232], the simple fact of the matter is that time *is* running out. Some critics have seen *Wise Children* as Angela Carter's "swansong", a novel in which she took on and brought together a huge tapestry of her concerns succeeding, as Salman Rushdie put it, in giving "death the finger".[51]

But before we are swept away on a tide of sentiment, perhaps we should remember that swans have a fairly hard time of it in Carter's novels, not least *Wise Children*, in which "the entire carcass of [a] swan ... Its feathers so blackened ... it looked more like an upstart crow" is consumed by the obnoxious child Saskia, "crouched, legs akimbo, disarticulating one by one its limbs and chewing off the meat" [*WC*, 102]. If the swan is not a victim it is usually an omen, as in *Dr Hoffman*, in which "Every assumption we [conventionally] make is undermined ... We assume a white swan; it is black. We assume it is yet beautiful; it is ugly. But then we are told that it was both ugly and marvelous" as Carter fills in the details of "Its vapid eyes [being] set too close together ... and express[ing] a kind of mindless evil"[*DH*, 30].[52] Where *Nights at the Circus* momentarily reverses this demonic association, the painting of Leda hanging above Ma Nelson's mantelpiece in the whorehouse permitting Fevvers to switch roles by "swooping down on [Walser] and gleefully smothering him in feathers" towards the end of the narrative,[53] it cannot contend with the most powerful of Carter's iconic swans, for nothing in Carter's career matches that early malevolence embodied by Uncle Philip's puppet-swan in Carter's *The Magic Toyshop*, a novel to which we turn in Chapter 7.

# 7

# Mannequins in the Marketplace: Angela Carter, Pat Barker and Margaret Atwood

> Dolls revive childhood memories. They stir up feelings about our mothers and our relationships with them...In a doll's face, we see ourselves...[1]

The magic of magic realism, discussed in the previous chapter, is conjured up again in the title of Carter second novel, *The Magic Toyshop* (1967). Published earlier in her career than both *The Infernal Desire Machines of Dr Hoffman* (1972) and *Nights at the Circus* (1984), one might expect it to operate as a prototype for ideas developed in greater depth in those two texts. To some extent this is true, not least in the fact that Carter's treatment of this material in *The Magic Toyshop* is, to some extent, more generically enclosed. Structurally the novel utilizes the metaphor of the dream to construct a series of enclosed circular worlds. We begin at the outer circumference of this set of ever-diminishing circles with Melanie and her siblings in their parental home. Fantasy as it exists at this stage of the text is that of the simplest kind in narrative terms: adolescent wish-fulfilment conceptualized from within a largely realist framework. On the death of Melanie's parents, however, we find ourselves moving into the world of the gothic, as we enter the toyshop itself and, along with it, a "*Walpurgisnacht* of carved and severed limbs".[2] It is in this space that worlds subdivide into the shop, the living quarters and, most sinisterly of all, a crypt-like basement which is home to Uncle Philip's puppet-booth and the space of his darkest, most clandestine desires. In itself it forms a replica of a sinister dollhouse, "Occupying a space within an enclosed space...center within center. Within within within. The dollhouse is a materialized secret...."[3]

Most obviously *The Magic Toyshop* is a fictional rendering of Sigmund Freud's "The 'Uncanny'", with its proliferation of mannequins, castration motifs and *unheimlich* domestic scenarios. But Melanie is also a dreamer whose dreams frequently comment on the world of the apparently every-day. This is just one of the many characteristics that link Melanie to Freud's Dora, while the larger family aspects of the text deal directly with Freud's discussion of the horror of incest in *Totem and Taboo*.[4] Most disruptive of all, challenging the symmetrical structure of worlds within worlds are a couple of inexplicable narrative phenomena that *can* only be understood as magically real. One of the most perplexing of these is the depiction of the shadowy character Jonathan, Melanie's younger brother. A natural enthusiast for model-making, Jonathan is the only character to be seen to benefit from the move to the London toyshop. Finn informs Melanie, later on in the text, that "He is of your uncle's flesh. A Flower" [*MT*, 116], an observation of crucial significance to Jonathan's unexplained disappearance in one of Melanie's dreams, a dream that proves to be realized by his parallel disappearance in (fictive) reality.

The second and perhaps the most haunting disruptive moment, is the suddenly discovery, on Melanie's part, of a child's severed hand in the kitchen knife drawer, "all bloody at the roots . . . [but] with pretty, tapering fingers the nails of which were tainted with a faint, pearly lacquer . . . Melanie heard blood fall plop in the drawer" [*MT*, 118]. We will return to this scene later on in the chapter. The third relates to Uncle Philip's dog and its relationship to its own portrait, hung above the kitchen fireplace. As the dog flees the housefire at the end of the text, Melanie believes herself to have seen the painted dog, rather than the real dog running down the stairs, having come to life and supplanted its original, evidenced by the "basket of flowers in its mouth" [*MT*, 198]. The whole toyshop is, we eventually learn, populated with replicas of what Susan Stewart considers to be archetypal examples of eighteenth- and nineteenth-century automata: "jigging Irishmen, whistling birds, clocks with bleating sheep, and growling dogs guarding baskets of fruit". For Stewart these more ancient automata are gradually replaced by a new wave of inanimate models of the kind Jonathan finds especially fascinating: "ships, trains, airplanes, and automobiles, models of the products of mechanized labour".[5] In the light of what happens to Jonathan in the novel this desire to replace the old model with the new should not go unnoticed.

Dora and Scheherazade both make a reappearance in the novels discussed here, Melanie's situation being analogous to that suffered by Freud's patient, and Karen F. Stein reading Offred in *The Handmaid's Tale* (1985) as a "Scheherazade of the future", but one locked into a paradox, simultaneously "telling her story to save her life", yet realizing that "to tell her tale is to risk her life".[6] And yet there is a problem with identifying Offred in these terms, because Scheherazade is an icon of the magical real, a fabulous fabricator. And where *The Magic Toyshop* does flirt with magic realism, even if it remains, on the whole, generically conformist, *The Handmaid's Tale* is straight genre fantasy of the dystopian variety, a mode which bears no relation to the magical real. In itself this would not be an insurmountable obstacle, except for the impact it unavoidably has upon the profound ideological significance of Atwood's text. We have no objections to Scheherazade stringing us along with the Sultan, but we need to believe in the authority of what Offred tells us, otherwise *The Handmaid's Tale* lacks much of its narrative potency. This distinction also accounts for the radically different styles of writing employed in these two novels.

*The Magic Toyshop* can afford to play around with rich and often convoluted symbolism because of its central usage of dream imagery to set up competing fictive worlds and, in the magic realist moments, points of Todorovian hesitancy.[7] Atwood's narrative style is as stark a contrast to Carter's as one could find, being almost clinically articulated. The main section of Offred's narrative is told in the first person, present tense, adding the weight of presentness to what would otherwise be too easily dismissed by the reader as speculative fiction dealing with distanced material. But a coda is appended to the end of that narrative, headed "Historical Notes", and written in a different narrative voice. Set out in the format of an academic conference, this section is told primarily by Professor Piexoto, again in the first person, but here being delivered in the past tense, detailing what he claims to be "his" discovery of Offred's tale, recorded after the events on audio tape. Suddenly, what has been a futurist sense of presentness takes on an archaic, almost quaint sense of obsolescence magnified by Piexoto's treatment of the Handmaid as a flawed, unreliable (hysterical?) narrator.

Stein, despite her reservations about Piexoto ("just as Freud failed to resolve the problems Dora raised, so Piexoto fails to discover who Offred was and what became of her"), allows him to become the voice of authority in the text which overlays Offred's own and, in the process, discredits her narrative altogether, not just for his audience, but also the reader. The Historical Notes section, Stein claims, "renders [Offred's] version suspect. Her use of present tense for recollection of the past suggests fiction, perhaps even trickery, deceit."[8] Stein's reading succeeds, in that it does indeed transform Offred from her relatively mundane role of fictive diarist or documentor into the more creative one of the fabulator

Scheherazade. Stein sees this as the explanation underlying Offred's many conscious references to the textuality of her own tale: "I would like to believe that this is a story I'm telling... If it's a story I'm telling, then I have control over the ending."[9] But David Sisk offers a different reading of Offred's own introjections and it is one I find far more helpful in political terms. For him such introjections reflect Offred's awareness of the workings of political critique: "unlike the Gileadean regime... [Offred] understands that telling cannot silence other stories",[10] of which Piexoto's is one, but not necessarily a verifiable one.

The problem with Stein's reading, as already suggested, is that it has profoundly damaging implications for the political significance of Atwood's text. She tries to recoup this damage by noting that Offred's retrospective recreation of herself in the guise of storyteller demonstrates her determination to reveal herself as a more complex subject than Gilead permits her to be. But if we are no longer sure we can believe her depiction of Gilead this revelation will fall on deaf ears. By falling into the trap of equating truth and authority with the male academic voice, Stein erases the authority of Offred's words in one fell swoop and, in the process, stunts what is always a central concern of the dystopia, namely to effect a reaction in the reader that might help us change the present. The obvious point Stein overlooks is that the discrepancies between Offred's version of events and Piexoto's cast as much doubt upon his words as they do hers, a point actually invited by the text's final words – aimed directly at his presentation, not Offred's account – "Are there any questions?" [*HT*, 324].

What both novels share, despite their differing relationships to fantasy and the fantastic, is their central treatment of women as commodities on a marketplace that is simultaneously economic and libidinal. Eye imagery is central to both texts, being so prevalent in Atwood's novel that even when Offred compares the place in the ceiling of her room where the chandelier used to be with "the place in a face where the eye has been *taken out*" [*HT*, 17], we still suspect the presence of surveillance equipment, watching Offred's every night-time move. Not unconnected with the gaze, desire and its dangers is another key trope shared by both novels. Hence, although *The Handmaid's Tale* manages to divorce sex from desire by treating it solely as a reproductive function, the latter repeatedly surfaces in illicit forms, through Offred's desire for the chauffeur Nick, or the Commander's desire for Offred behind closed doors. In both cases households are the obvious modes of constraint for these women. Both live in households which belong to other people and are aware of being anomalously positioned with regard to what they see as the core household. Both novels operate by focusing upon the nuclear family unit in detail, but in doing so demonstrate its own oppressive and ill-fitting social codes. Both novels also utilize intertextual connections with fairy tales, "Snow White" and "Briar Rose" in the case of *The Magic Toyshop* and "Little Red Riding Hood" in the case of *The Handmaid's Tale*. Finally, and not unconnected with this last point, the primary role for women in both novels is that of the mannequin, performing at the behest of a patriarchy that sees them in no other legitimate role.

## Women on the Market: *Blow Your House Down* (1984)

Before moving on to an in-depth discussion of these two texts, by way of introduction I want to briefly consider the manner in which Pat Barker's *Blow Your House Down* (1984) deals in similar motifs. Though predominantly realist in narrative form, a closer reading of this text reveals the latent presence of certain significant fantasy tropes that operate as a paradigmatic model for the concerns of this chapter. In the process it foregrounds two important issues: the economic basis upon which the phallocentric libidinal economy is structured and the fairy-tale paradigms which contribute to its perpetuation. Based around the Yorkshire Ripper murders, which took place between 1975 and 1981, the novel tells the story of a group of working-class prostitutes based in the Bradford area of West Yorkshire and their relation to clients and with each other. In its treatment of the gaze, the novel documents the gender implications of social invisibility versus literal visibility through the icon of the street-girl soliciting for business. Like Head's *A Question of Power*, or Carter's *Dr Hoffman*, mannequin imagery lies at its core as a crucial signifier of women as sexual merchandise and the violent hatred inflicted upon them by the men to whom they are sold. But whereas the gaze often remains the prerogative of the male predator, here, as the serial killer of the novel discovers, it can be uncomfortably reciprocated:

> When he straightened up again her eyes were open. It shook him a bit because he was pretty certain they'd been closed. He bent over her, but there was no sign of life ... Deliberately then he turned away and started searching the floor for anything he might've left behind ... He could feel her staring at him, though he kept his back turned. He kept thinking. *Why don't her eyes close?*[11]

Kath, the woman in question here, is the iconic figure of the hunted woman as haunting presence, her eyes staring down as fixedly from city bill-boards following her disappearance as they stare back into her murderer's face here. It is in this context that we realise that *Blow Your House Down* exists as a contemporary ghost-story, one in which women are repeatedly killed, but refuse to play dead. As for the puppeteer, this is partly a game and partly a performance. The killer, abandoning Kath's corpse, contemplates how best to exhibit his handiwork: "He didn't want her found too quickly, but on the other hand he did want her found. They still hadn't got the last one and it infuriated him when the newspapers got his total wrong" [*BHD*, 65]. As Nicole Ward Jouve points out, in the case of the actual Yorkshire Ripper murders this performative aspect became a spectator-sport in itself, one in which, like a sick Punch and Judy show, both killer and victims became pawns in a collective Oedipal struggle between what we might aptly refer to here as "the man on the street" and the Law (of the Father?):

> A hoaxer who called himself "Jack" sent a tape to the police. The police had it played on the loudspeakers of Leeds football stadium, hoping it would jolt somebody's memory, but the Leeds fans drowned out the voice with chants of "Eleven-Nil". Eleven was the number of the known victims. Nil was the police score.[12]

The very title of Barker's novel is a crucial signifier, implying the fragility of hearth and home to a social group of women with no economic status. One of the primary reasons for the killer's disgust with Kath is that she takes him to a squalid, derelict house which he quickly ascertains to be a make-shift home:

> The window was boarded up ... There was a smell of candle grease, and something else. Dried urine? ... He flashed the torch round the room. A living carpet of blackclocks scuttled for cover ... Mattress. A packing case pulled up and used as a table. There was even a chair. She was lying when she said she didn't live here. [*BHD*, 61]

This literary fascination with territorial demarcations and their influence on woman's price within the market-place has a far longer literary inheritance than contemporary women's fiction. In a traditional romance like Richardson's *Pamela* (1740), for example, we find just the same market forces as in Barker's novel and a heroine whose "reward" is predominantly economic. Determined to add Pamela to his proprietorial assets, Mr B. enlists the help of homely furnishings to secure a down payment. So he hides within wardrobes, lurks behind screens, cloaked in curtains, waiting to pounce. On one level these exploits are comic and ridiculous, easily laughed off as part of the game. Only once we place texts like this alongside Barker's do we find rather less to laugh about than we might first have thought. Witness the relationship of another of Barker's characters to her own living space, this time Maggie, a worker at the local chicken-factory, attacked from behind on her way home after work, but surviving as the killer is disturbed by a third party. Returning to her house after a stay in hospital, it is not the outdoors that defines her fears:

> Their own bedroom. She knew every mark on the wallpaper, every creak of the floorboards, every bump and sag in the mattress. It ought to've been completely safe, but it wasn't. She found herself listening for Bill's footsteps on the stairs ... As long as she could *see* Bill ... she was alright. But if he was behind her, or in a different part of the house, she started to worry. [*BHD*, 90]

In its choice of title, *Blow Your House Down* carries clear intertextual allusions to genre fantasy, evoking the reference to "The Three Little Pigs". Bruno Bettelheim's reading of this fairy/folktale goes out of its way to ignore the type of discomforting themes Barker's novel represents, but that her characters are also meat, "herded into Northgate, like into a pen" [*BHD*, 123] by other "pigs" (a police-force determined to use them as bait), cannot be lost on any reader. Not satisfied by their slaughter, both parties parade their scores, hanging them up like carcasses in a butcher's shop-window. Compare these dynamics with Bettelheim's cosy reading of "The Three Little Pigs" as a safe but cautionary tale about the work ethic. In his terms, those pigs who are devoured by the wolf are simply "lazy and take things easy". They shun genuine hard graft, and the "oral greed" that is their ultimate downfall simply mirrors their own desires for the "immediate gratification" that houses of straw and sticks provide. These animals deserve their fate for they have wilfully chosen sloth over decent, hard work. Only the third pig, who invests wisely in bricks and mortar, can enjoy the pleasures of his own market garden. After all, he has learnt the "world of difference between eating and devouring" that constitutes the distinction between good and bad ways of obtaining food.[13]

Bettelheim's reading is at best superficial. But there is something more duplicitous in his determination "not to see". What, in fact, he succeeds in reproducing is society's double standard about prostitution. These women do not choose "the game" over work, even if they *are* struggling to maintain a variety of collapsing households. Undoubtedly, in society's eyes, they have chosen bad rather than good ways of putting food on the table, but this is not because of their ignorance over the difference between "eating and devouring". On the contrary, it reflects their all-too-keen awareness that there is a "world of difference" between eating and starving. What may seem oral greed to Bettelheim, is something very different for a prostitute like Brenda: "She went on sucking but then his hands came down, gripping the top of her head and forcing her mouth so far down onto his cock that she gagged. She was afraid, but she went on sucking." [*BHD*, 27]

In "The Three Little Pigs" and *Blow Your House Down* a presiding law of differential payments exists, some paying the ultimate price for going to market, while others live on to face another day. According to Bettelheim, children easily come to terms with the disappearances of the first and second pig of the nursery tale by reading each of the three pigs as mere versions of the child's own younger self, now left behind. The absence of such consolatory strategies in Barker's novel derives in part from the fact that former victims do not disappear, or at least not indefinitely. Instead they *refuse* to go away, their living faces "overlaid by that horror on the slab" [*BHD*, 115], or a collective superimposition takes place in the mind whereby "a whole line of faces...young, old, fat, thin, smiling, serious...fade[s] and [is] replaced by a line of chickens waiting to be killed" [*BHD*, 155–6].

*Blow Your House Down* is a novel about horrific metamorphoses and the transactions involved in evicting sex from the bedroom and throwing it out onto the streets. Repeated stress is placed upon the juxtapositions between inner and outer worlds, and, as in Carter's and Atwood's novels, what emerges through such juxtapositions is the powerful mythology surrounding the gendering of hearth and home and what happens when this mythology is placed under explicit material scrutiny. Psychoanalysis features heavily in this chapter because it shares this preoccupation with the "mysterious" territory which forms the boundary markers of the "transactions between private and public realms", transactions that are equally of material significance.[14] Returning to Freud's story of "Dora", one cannot help but notice the role played by money within it. Initially, much is made of Dora's father's wealth, earned through commercial success rather than inherited. Later Dora informs Freud that Frau K. takes money from her father, "for she spent more than she could possibly have afforded out of her own purse or her husband's".[15] She presumes his wealth to be the chief motivation for the attraction he holds for Frau K., a point reinforced by Dora's father's economic power being set up in direct competition with his sexual impotence.

So far Freud's has been a narrative about patriarchal wealth and its often perceived attractiveness to women wishing to secure an elevated rung of the social hierarchy. But the real point of this narrative for our concerns is that Dora also perceives herself as currency, the price paid to Herr K. by her own father, partly as compensation for his own infidelity with Herr K.'s wife, but also as a reward for turning a blind eye in return (note the castration reference). What Dora does not seem to perceive, but which is clear to the reader beyond the text, is that there is a third, unspoken manner in which Dora is currency between two males and this reveals itself in Freud's dismissively defensive remark, "At other times she was quite well aware that she had been guilty of exaggeration in talking like this. The two men had of course never made a formal agreement in which she was treated as an object for barter". The reason Freud jumps to their defence is because he is also in on the deal. Notice the analogy he employs, later on in his text, to explain the workings of psychoanalysis:

A daytime thought may very well play the part of *entrepreneur* for a dream; but the *entrepreneur*, who, as people say, has the idea ... can do nothing without capital; he needs a *capitalist* who can afford the outlay, and the capitalist who provides the psychical outlay for the dream is invariably and indisputably, whatever may be the thought of the previous day, *a wish from the unconscious*.[16]

As a metaphor for the psychoanalytic process, capitalism is a strange, even an ill-fitting choice, but as a literal description of the set-up between Freud and Dora's father the dynamics are perfect. Freud, the so-called entrepreneur with the "ideas", pairs up with the capitalist, Dora's father. In these terms, whatever Freud's own denials, precisely such a "formal agreement" has been entered into and Dora is the sole currency allowing both men to bond. Freud acknowledges that "it was only her father's authority which induced [Dora] to come to me at all" and refers elsewhere to discussing her case, in her absence, with her father. Once Dora has left Freud's consultations, his disappointment again seems to revolve around considerations of her father and his desire to be seen in a similar light: "...it was clear that I was replacing her father in her imagination ... She was even constantly comparing me with him consciously".[17]

Freud's desire for the father's approval is continual, as is his ongoing fascination with him. Despite the revelation of at least two potentially

incriminating pieces of information about the father, namely his con-
traction of venereal disease through promiscuous sexual encounters in
his younger life and his unwillingness to protect his daughter from the
sexual advances of a friend, Freud consistently speaks of him in the
highest possible terms. He is attributed with "intelligence" and sympa-
thized with over his wife's apparent "psychosis", a term which turns
out to describe an over-zealous attitude towards housework presumably
brought on as a reaction to her husband's infection of her own body –
and hence the body of her house – with his disease. Freud's continually
disparaging remarks about this woman and lack of sympathy for her
plight frequently sounds like pure jealous spite. But as is typical of
Freud he ravels up his own desires in an elaborate labyrinth of counter-
transference, accusing Dora of jealously desiring him, jealously desiring
Frau K. and abandoning her analysis "because of the unknown quantity
in me which reminded Dora of Herr K . . . What this unknown quantity
was I naturally cannot tell. I suspect it had to do with money, or with
jealousy of another patient . . . ."[18] As is so frequently the case with Freud's
dealings with female patients, we have to read his text as if written in
mirror writing. As we saw in Chapter 4, for Irigaray patriarchal economic relations are entirely homosocial in orientation: "Women, signs,
commodities, and currency always pass from one man to another; if it
were otherwise, we are told, the social order would fall back upon incestuous and exclusively endogamous ties that would paralyse all com-
merce."[19] This observation brings us neatly to Carter's *The Magic Toyshop*.

## The Return of (the Repressed) Dora: *The Magic Toyshop* (1967)

Dora's so called hysteria is brought on by a complex set of interfamilial
relations in which taboos are breached by more than one party, but
always from behind a veneer of social respectability. In *The Magic Toyshop* the same paradigms are followed. Three potentially nuclear families interconnect and, in the process, interrupt their respective nuclear
orientations. The first family comprises Melanie, Jonathan, Victoria and
their parents, the second Uncle Philip and Aunt Margaret, and the third
Margaret, Francie and Finn. This structure sets up Uncle Philip as the
totemic father to an extended tribal network, who will be dispatched at
the end of the text to enable Finn and Francie to take possession of the
women they desire. Like Herr K., Uncle Philip makes indecent proposals
towards a surrogate daughter figure, but here he uses his grotesque
puppet-swan as a stand-in:

It was almost as tall as she, an egg-shaped sphere of plywood painted white and coated with glued-on feathers...The wings were constructed on the principle of the wings of model aeroplanes, but curved...It was dumpy and homely and eccentric. [*MT*, 165]

Just as Freud seems unwilling to believe that Dora could be repulsed by the attentions of Herr K., so our response to Melanie's trauma is one of disbelief. How can she be afraid of something so obviously synthetic? The answer lies in its twin scene, in which Finn takes Melanie to the pleasure garden and then extracts his payment for the guided tour in the form of a kiss:

His lips were wet and rough, cracked. It might have been anybody, kissing her...She wondered why he was doing this, putting his mouth on her own undesiring one, softly moving his body against her. What was the need?...
Finn inserted his tongue between her lips, searching tentatively for her own tongue inside her mouth. The moment consumed her. She choked and struggled...convulsed with horror... [*MT*, 105–6]

This scene returns us to Freud's own fantasy reconstruction of events involving Herr K. and Dora and their fateful encounter beside the lake. Already analysed in relation to *Alias Grace*, the passage will withstand a rehearsal in the context of *The Magic Toyshop*:

I believe that during the man's passionate embrace she felt not merely his kiss upon her lips but also the pressure of his erect member against her body. This perception was revolting to her; it was dismissed from her memory, repressed and replaced by the innocent sensation of pressure upon her thorax, which in turn derived an excessive intensity from its repressed source.[20]

Finn is, like Herr K., simultaneously surrogate uncle and favourite of Melanie and, like Dora, she is simultaneously repulsed and fascinated by his figure. She is deeply troubled by the intrusion of the phallus and the feeling of Finn "softly moving his body against her", recognizing desire in this movement, but not being able to give a name to that desire ("What was the need?"); that is until Finn rapidly "articulates" this need through the turgid penetration of his tongue, causing Melanie's resistant choking. Does this also explain the source of the otherwise inexplicable "terrible affliction...like a curse. Her silence" [*MT*, 37] which comes upon Margaret on her wedding-day (or night)? Certainly Margaret falls into line with Freud's observation concerning the unusual fluency of the writing technique in the case of what he terms "hysterical mutism",[21] the necklace Uncle Philip buys Margaret as a sign of her bondage visualizing the "choking" of both women in these terms.

I have said already that Freud's encounter with women frequently brings about a gothic scenario. In this novel gothicism is there from the moment Melanie is locked out of her parental home:

> She almost despaired when she realised she could not go through the door . . . [Now] it was the apple tree or nothing, even though she must walk round to the back of the house, whatever lurked there. Whatever monsters. Whatever huge, still, waiting things with soft, gaping mouths, whose flesh was the same substance as the night. [*MT*, 18–19]

In the second of Dora's two dreams, she describes walking in a strange area, entering "a house where I lived" (not, notice, a *home*), and finding a letter from her mother informing her of her father's death. The rest of the dream concerns her circuitous and uncertain route to the railway station, confused by her lack of knowledge about its whereabouts.[22] These dynamics are shuffled, but still recognizable in the plot structure of Carter's novel. Here, however, the news of not just her father's, but also her mother's death comes in the form of a telegram which Melanie has no need to read, because "she knew what [it] contained, as if the words were printed on [the messenger's] forehead" [*MT*, 24] and it is not until *after* this that Melanie finds herself, firstly at a London railway station and then embarked on a mysterious journey to a house in which she will live, but which will never be home.

The dialogue in the taxi between Finn and Melanie, though terse, is important. Watching the fare mount, shilling by shilling, and already starting to feel her throat and nostrils constrict against the smell of Finn and Francie's unwashed flesh, Melanie asks a seemingly literal question: "'Is it very far, still?' . . . 'Still farther,' said Finn abstractedly . . . 'Still farther,' he repeated. 'It is beginning to get dark,' she said, for the light drained from the streets . . . 'And will get darker,' responded Finn" [*MT*, 36–7]. The first element of the conversation implies that what Melanie reads as a literal journey, Finn knows to be symbolic too. He has, of course, taken this road himself, accompanying Margaret and Francie just as these three children travel together and again, their own orphan status is inferred to be one motivation behind the change. Two inferences cohere in Finn's choice of the words "still farther". The first is that he still has a way to go before his own "journey" with regard to the toyshop is complete and, in these early words, we hear the goal for which he aims: the supplanting of Uncle Philip, "still father" to the household. Reading closely, we realize that once in the toyshop Finn immediately starts to put his plan into action, for it is he, not Philip, who imposes a strict dress code upon Melanie, even though he purportedly does so on behalf of another patriarch: "No, you can't wear them!... He can't abide a woman in trousers... No make-up, mind. And only speak when you're spoken to. He likes, you know, silent women" [*MT*, 62–3]. Nor should we miss the fact that the minute he verifies Melanie's identity at the railway station, the first words he speaks to her are "Let me take the child off you" [*MT*, 35]. Uncle Philip is not the only businessman on the premises, and, despite his squint, Finn has a keen eye for a bargain and a keener one for profligacy: "'A whole pound went on chocolate?' 'And magazines... One called *Sea Breezes* for Jonathan and the *Beano* annual for Victoria...' 'Nevertheless, it is a lot,' he said" [*MT*, 35–6].

Though the toyshop is a far cry from the aristocratic gothic mansion, being "a dark cavern... so dimly lit one did not at first notice it", situated next to "a failed, boarded-up jeweller's" [*MT*, 39] (the probable source of Aunt Margaret's ghastly choker), the interior is gothic in its most conventional sense. Resistant to intruders, including customers (which raises the obvious question of what, exactly, is "for sale" and to whom), Finn has to push hard against the resistance of the door as, in the second important threshold moment of the text, it "momentarily" refuses to open and allow them in. Once across the threshold all will change for Melanie, as her role of interloper in this female gothic text situates her indoors and thus controlled by the presence of a more powerful, sexualized masculine figure.

Melanie remains largely incomprehending about her position within the house, musing to herself "Behind the doors (which doors?) slept, at nights, Aunt and Uncle, Francie, Finn" [*MT*, 83], even allowing the architectural structures of the mansion house to conspire with their master against her, provoking the third threshold moment of the book: "Blocking the head of the stairway on the kitchen landing was the immense, overwhelming figure of a man. The light was behind him and Melanie could not see his face" [*MT*, 69]. Similar uncertainty surrounds Melanie's role in the house. Neither child nor wife (the only two recognizable roles for women in such a set-up), Melanie risks being surplus to requirements unless she "earns her keep". In a household in which women are not permitted to have money of their own, and in which, as Irigaray would put it, "It is out of the question for them to go to 'market' on their own, enjoy their own worth among themselves, [or] speak to each other",[23] their only currency is their own flesh. As in all examples of the female gothic, the protagonist is simultaneously fascinated and afraid, desperately curious about the mystery that lies at the centre of the house, but aware that her curiosity may get her into danger; and that danger, while often violent, is always of a sexual kind.

## Olympia and the Swan-Maiden

We recall, in E.T.A. Hoffmann's story of "The Sandman", that two elements of the story prove of particular interest to Freud: the mannequin Olympia, the ultimate object of Nathaniel's desires and what Freud sees as Hoffmann's own unconscious narrative focus in his text, the connection between a reiterated eye motif and a presiding but latent theme of castration. Both are omnipresent in *The Infernal Desire Machines of Dr Hoffman*, coming together most obviously in the figure of the old man who runs the sordid seaside peepshow:

> A tear trickled out from under his glasses so that I knew he had eyes even if they were sightless ... [Suddenly] he struck me full in the face with his cane so that blood streamed into my eyes from a cut above my forehead and, when I could see again, he was gone.[24]

Simultaneously castrated and castrator, this man prefigures our later introduction to Dr Hoffman himself in the novel, who is shown up to be no more than a mad professor cranking gears as mechanically as a bad puppeteer jerks strings. The obvious question for our purposes now is whether the same proves true of Uncle Philip for, as in *Dr Hoffman* and "The Sandman", *The Magic Toyshop* portrays a libidinal economy in which the most feared character is a tradesman later revealed to be engaged in an Oedipal struggle with another male for sole control over a doll:

> The professor had hold of a female figure by the shoulders, the Italian Coppola had it by the feet, and transformed with rage they were tearing and tugging at it for its possession ... [F]laring into a furious rage, [Nathaniel] went to rescue his beloved, but at that moment Coppola ... wrenched the figure from the professor's hands and dealt

him a fearful blow...Then Coppola threw the figure over his shoulder and, laughing shrilly, ran quickly down the staircase... Nathaniel stood numb with horror. He had seen all too clearly that Olympia's deathly-white face possessed no eyes...she was a lifeless doll!"[25]

With intriguing ambiguity, Alix Strachey's 1925 translation of Freud's "The 'Uncanny'" refers to Olympia's eyes having been *"put in* by Coppola".[26] In the case of windows, "putting in" is something done either by a glazer or a brick. In other words it is not clear from Strachey's translation whether Coppola blinds Olympia or gives her sight. Nor is the ambiguity resolved by the fact that this tug of war between the two men ends up with Olympia's "blood-flecked eyes" lying on the floor, for Coppola could either be her assailant or her saviour, as his flight with her down the stairs also shows. At the end of the story another tug of war ensues, but on this occasion Professor Spalanzani and Coppola are replaced by Nathaniel and Lothario, while the doll Olympia has become Nathaniel's beloved and Lothario's sister, Clara:

> Grasped by the raving Nathaniel, Clara was hanging in the air over the parapet of the gallery...As quick as lightning Lothario seized his sister and drew her back in, and at the same instant dealt the raging madman a blow in the face with his clenched fist so that Nathaniel stumbled backwards and let go his prey.
> Lothario ran down the steps of the tower, his unconscious sister in his arms. She was saved.[27]

As in *The Magic Toyshop*, then, women and mannequins are shown to be interchangeable in the terms of the Law of the Father. So Margaret, Melanie and Melanie's mother are all reduced to the status of puppets while Nathaniel, making love to Olympia as if she were real, accuses Clara of being a "lifeless accursed automaton!".[28] And just as the two instances involving a tug of war in Hoffmann's text revolve around trading and the market-place, so the triangular power dynamics in *The Magic Toyshop* always revolve around the still centre of Uncle Philip as he fights Melanie's father for possession of Melanie's mother, Finn for possession of Melanie, and Francie for possession of Aunt Margaret.

But unlike Coppola/Coppelius, Uncle Philip loses, a point that returns us to the role of the mysterious Francie and his own relationship with the libidinal economy. Just as, at the end of "The Sandman", the final encounter is set at the top of the Town Hall tower, from which Nathaniel throws himself as it casts "a giant shadow over the market-place",[29] so Francie, when Melanie first sees him at the railway station, has a gait which Melanie describes as that of "a tower falling, a frightening, unco-ordinated progression in which he seemed to crash forward uncontrol-lably at each stride, jerking himself stiffly upright and swaying for a moment on his heels before the next toppling step" [*MT*, 34]. Encapsu-lated in the meeting point of these two scenes is a figure who is simultan-eously puppet-like and phallically threatening, a delicate balance Francie maintains throughout the narrative, until the point at which the bal-ance tips and throws his whole weight crashing down upon Uncle Philip's world. As in Hoffmann's "The Sandman", in *The Magic Toyshop* eye imagery is everywhere: in the spectacle of performing mannequins, in the voyeurism of the eye-hole in Finn and Francie's wall, in the keyhole through which Melanie watches "the red people" at play.[30] Although Finn sets himself up as Uncle Philip's main rival, Francie's subversive potential is made clear in this third example of occular intru-sion. Looking through the keyhole in the fourth threshold moment of the text, Melanie spies on Francie and describes him as "a statue of a fiddler with only his hands alive" [*MT*, 50]. But we should not be fooled by this automaton-like pose. Francie is the archetypal example of Freud's uncanny clockwork doll that seems to hover continually on the boundary between animation and inanimation.[31] Just like Uncle Philip, this pose reminds us that Francie is a string-player *par excellence*, and as his fingers are "hover[ing] like butterflies over a *flowerbed*" [*MT*, 51 – my emphasis], we cannot fail to grasp the innuendo. Francie is "playing" with Margaret in and around Philip Flower's bed while Uncle Philip "fiddles" with dolls in his basement.

Underlying what proves to be the revelation of the secret of Francie and Margaret's incestuous relationship is a matching desire that never finds full, uncloseted articulation. This is the latent incestuous fascina-tion felt by Uncle Philip for Melanie's mother, which erupts on several occasions as an example of trans-generational haunting, concretized by the omnipresence of the wedding photograph. Standing "alone" as her mother's "only relative living" [*MT*, 13], Uncle Philip apparently acts as auctioneer at the sale, but is actually forced to give away the only "lot" he wishes to keep, one who will become de-"Flowered" in the process. Thus, not only does Uncle Philip lose his precious Olympia to another, he loses her to a man who, in ironic inversion to Coppola/Lothario, rap-idly ascends, rather than descends the economic ladder/staircase with her, rubbing in Uncle Philip's own inferior role in the masculine libid-inal economy:

Their father liked them all to go to church on Sundays. He read the lesson, sometimes, when he was at home. Born in Salford, it pleased him to play gently at squire now he need never think of Salford again. [*MT*, 7]

Philip's desired revenge takes the form of trying to turn his brother-in-law's "precious kids" into "little Flowers" [*MT*, 144]. In effect he comes to embody the role of the phantom bridegroom Melanie believes she desires for herself at the start of the text, *fantasizing him* into existence in "an extra-dimensional bathroom-of-the-future in honeymoon Cannes. Or Venice. Or Miami Beach" [*MT*, 2], but *realizing herself* in a bathroom with "no hot-water system . . . [no] proper toilet soap . . . a crack in the deep, old-fashioned wash-basin and a long, red hair [which] was fixed in the crack and floated out in the water as the basin filled [*MT*, 55]. Melanie's major point of contiguity with Uncle Philip proves to be this shared fascination with her mother for, as Freud observes, "A daughter usually takes her mother's love-story as her model" and Melanie proves no exception to this rule.[32]

Finn's killing of the swan is often read as a symbolic castration motif, a reading upheld by the earlier stress Carter places upon the sexual nature of the swan's assault upon Melanie. But this does not, in itself, explain the leap between fantasy and realism in the text, for the chopping up of the swan can only be a *fantasized* attack upon Philip. The full significance of the scene becomes clearer once we recognize that Finn's actions, coupled with his desires for Melanie, cut right across what Freud saw as the two most basic laws of totemism, namely "not to kill the totem animal and to avoid sexual intercourse with members of the totem clan of the opposite sex":

> What is a totem? It is as a rule an animal (whether edible and harm-less or dangerous and feared) . . . which stands in a peculiar relation to the whole clan . . . [who] are under a sacred obligation . . . not to kill or destroy their totem and to avoid eating its flesh . . . From time to time festivals are celebrated at which the clansmen represent or imitate the motions and attributes of their totem in ceremonial dances.[33]

That the complex family structure in this household is a clan structure is clear from the fact that, like the primitive tribes upon which Freud bases his survey, non-blood relations share a familial-style structure within the house. The "ceremonial dance", in this context, is obviously the puppet show in which Melanie is devoured by the swan, a connection which helps to explain the privacy surrounding the show, for only the clan can take part in these sacred rituals. That the swan stands in totemic relationship to the "clan" can be the only explanation for the otherwise inexplicable degree of fear and horror both he and Melanie express, following what is otherwise a relatively minor act of vengeance:

> Sick and sorry, [Finn] came creeping to her bed . . .
> "Where have you been?" [Melanie] asked at last.
> "In the pleasure gardens . . . I went to a burying . . . It was the swan."
> "What's this?"
> "The swan. Rest in peace. The swan."
> "You buried," she repeated, to get it clear in her own mind, "the swan . . . Oh, Finn, you never did."
> "I did so." . . .
> "Finn, the enormity of it!" [*MT*, 170–1]

In the middle of this dialogue, immediately following Finn's entry into her bed, "A withered flower fell from the geranium at that moment, with a soft tissue-paper noise. One flower less" [*MT*, 170]. At first glance this appears to be another symbolic "deflowering" matching that of Melanie's mother, a reading that may well take on coherence once we consider that Finn later describes himself as "almost a family man, now" [*MT*, 191]. But the sign is also a portent relating to Uncle Philip (the sole remaining Flower) and, in the process, anticipates the plot against him and the subsequent dismantling of the clan structure.

One further element of the swan as totemic image raises itself. As Freud observes, "totems are hereditary and not changed by marriage";[34] they are also inherited via male or female lines of descent. At this point we remember Melanie's early encounter with both the photograph and the wedding-dress, prior to her parents' death. Looking at the photograph of her mother, Melanie notices that her dress "had scooping sleeves, wide as the wings of swans" [*MT*, 11] and, as she tries on the veil, it seems to take on animation in a manner that prefigures the later assault upon her by the swan, as it: "blew up around her, blinding her eyes and filling her nostrils. She turned this way and that, but only entangled herself still more. She wrestled with it, fought it, and finally overcame it." [*MT*, 15] In part, the full development of this totemic symbol depends upon a return to the fairy lore of chapter 5 and, in particular, mythology relating to swan-maidens. In one Kurdish tale, recounted by Edwin Sidney Hartland, we find a narrative scenario which runs parallel to Melanie's own:

> [A] daughter has been ensnared by a giant [Uncle Philip] when she and three [two?] other birds were out flying [her Mother and Father]; but she is at length rescued by two heroes [Finn and Francie], one of whom she weds. When she becomes homesick she puts on her feather-dress and flies away.[35]

According to Hartland the "feather-dress" can also take other, related forms, such as "the hide of a quadruped, ... wings, a robe, an apron, a veil". All of these occur as disguises or costumes at one time or another. The whole issue of the deflowerment which comes up in Carter's novel is also equated, by implication, with this mythology. Hartland explains that "Capture of the Swan-maiden proper is effected by theft of her robe ... either by main force, or more frequently with her consent ... or by her own initiative".[36] Melanie is a strange mixture of all three perspectives in different parts of the book. Ultimately, then, the swan totem is inherited from that clan shared by Melanie's mother and Uncle Philip and thus manifests itself as a larger narrative involving the mother and trans-generational haunting.

We recall that when Dora's father purchases jewellery for his wife, Frau K. and Dora, he uses the gifts as a means of stringing all three along in the process. Compare, in this context, Melanie's gesture of giving away her confirmation pearls (inherited from her mother) to Aunt Margaret at the end of the text as her dead mother looks on from her photo frame on the mantelpiece. The scene seems to mirror the one at the start of the text when Melanie dresses up as her mother to kill her mother. Here Melanie dresses up Margaret in her own "pretty green frock" [*MT*, 186] and pearls in order, also, to send her to her death. Once again, Melanie looks at the other woman, simultaneously asserting her difference from that other and using her as a reflection upon herself: "'Goodness', she thought, 'Am I as thin as that?' For the dark green dress fitted her aunt perfectly" [*MT*, 189]. According to Paulina Palmer, Melanie's desire to give these personal possessions to Margaret is testimony to "a spontaneous act of generosity" on Melanie's part, but one tinged with melancholy:

> The reference to the framed photo of Melanie's mother in the room draws attention to Melanie's orphaned state ... Attention is also focused on Melanie's sudden recognition of the sensuous attraction

of Margaret's appearance. Elements of the erotic and the maternal unexpectedly surface...With her own mother dead, she unconsciously sees Margaret as a surrogate mother...She hopes that Margaret will, in time, grow so attached to her that she will think of her as her own child.[37]

In her desire to see positive bonding between these women Palmer reads the role of Melanie's mother and her photograph here both too literally and too passively. What is stressed on this occasion is that Melanie's relationship to her mother has shifted considerably. Where her initial response was a complex one intermingling adoration and envy, now she is afraid of the photograph and the image it contains, hence her exclamation that "The house is haunted" when she first sees it in the room [*MT*, 187]. This is also the only feasible explanation for her otherwise inexplicable fear that if Margaret refuses to accept her part in the bargain/exchange, "nothing would go right; *the figures in the photograph might come alive*, Uncle Philip might come home early with a machine-gun" [*MT*, 188 – my emphasis].

The mother is a ghost who will continue to haunt Melanie's future, but she is not the only ghost in the text. Returning to the aforementioned vision of the child's severed hand in the kitchen drawer, an explanation starts to cohere in relation to the parallel treatment of Aunt Margaret in the house. Fainting on the kitchen floor from the shock, Melanie is discovered unconscious by Francie. What almost gives the game away from the start is his own defensive reaction to Melanie's story: "Knife drawer? But she keeps knives there, only. Maggie would only keep knives there. After all, it is the knife drawer." [*MT*, 119] His surprise is not related to *what* Melanie says she has seen, but *where* she has seen it or, in other words, Margaret's inability to keep it hidden. Taking Melanie straight to Margaret, their "wordless communication... too deep and personal for Melanie to comprehend" [*MT*, 122] implies that what Melanie has stumbled across is the ghost of Francie and Margaret's dead child, the blood always freshly flowing because ghosts haunt in their presentness, not in our pasts. Whether this phantom is the literal or metaphorical manifestation of a prohibited desire is never made clear, but it does explain why Victoria must be sacrificed to the flames along with them, rather than escaping with Finn and Melanie, for she is the substitute, another price paid.

As in the Dora story, then, parental relations and their displacement onto other figures are crucial aspects of the incest motif. But what of Melanie's own Oedipal relations? Fleeing with Finn from the burning toyshop, Melanie recalls her own father's playful nursery song:

> Sally go round the stars,
> Sally go round the moon,
> Sally go round the chimney pot
> On a Sunday afternoon.
> Wheeeeeeee! [*MT*, 199]

Again, as in Freud's essay, issues of flight are directly related to a choice between "flying *with*" or "fleeing from" and involve running from one father figure into the arms of another. But, as we said from the start, though psychoanalytic relations are crucial here, so are the social circumstances in which they are situated. Melanie has little choice but to fly with Finn because she does so in order to flee Uncle Philip. As Finn and Melanie face each other in the garden, the "wild surmise" [*MT*, 200] on their faces makes it clear this is no Edenic, utopian escape. All the evidence points towards Melanie's life with Finn following the same pattern as the other transactions we have examined in this chapter. Finn and Philip do not just share a phonetic similarity of names, they also share a fascination with women as spectacular commodity. Hence Finn's "Atlantic-coloured regard" washing over Melanie [*MT*, 34] in chapter 2, just as Philip will later "size her up" with his eyes as he casts her in the role of Leda to his swan. Right from day one, Finn controls Melanie's movements and appearance, practising his puppetry skills with one squinty eye always on his own inheritance.

## The (Market-)Value of Words: *The Handmaid's Tale* (1985)

The compulsive reproductions represented by Uncle Philip's toys are set up in direct contradiction to the lack of biological reproduction behind the scenes of his toyshop. Though women are currency exchanged from man to man, no human "miniatures" are produced to compete with his mechanical ones. In that sense the ethos of production seems different to that of *The Handmaid's Tale*, the libidinal economy of which places biological reproduction at its core. The result, however, is much the same, and not just because such miniatures have the rarity of collectors' items. Once again, women are not allowed to journey to market alone, the protagonist Offred and her partner Ofglen always travelling together like Red Riding Hood twins, two "nondescript women[e]n in red [each] carrying a basket" [*HT*, 28]. As in *The Magic Toyshop*, they are not

permitted to handle money because they *are* money and, in a step further along the line of oppression both reading and writing are prohibited them (a point of direct comparison with nineteenth-century slave
narratives and their late-twentieth-century representations in novels
like Morrison's *Beloved* and Butler's *Kindred*). Where, therefore, Carter
treats marriage as metaphorical slavery (Margaret's collar mimicking the
neck-iron worn by the slave-coffles in *Kindred* or by Sethe's mother in
*Beloved*), in *The Handmaid's Tale* Offred is a literal slave whose worth is
directly tied to her reproductive potential.

In a novel like *Kindred*, we saw that reproduction among slaves is seen
as an economic success for the plantation owner and a necessity for the
slaves' survival, although even those who do reproduce will have their
children taken away and sold to new owners. This is an identical socio-
economic situation to that of *The Handmaid's Tale*, in which those Handmaids who still remain childless after three unsuccessful placements are
shipped off to the Colonies to clear up toxic waste. Those who succeed
in having children are made to hand them over to the Commanders
and their Wives to bring up. These novels share a dystopic identity, but
whereas *Kindred* projects us a century into the past and is based on verifiable socio-historical information, *The Handmaid's Tale* reads like a piece
of futurist speculative fiction, until we are informed in the Historical Notes
section that Gilead is set in a synchronous chronotope to our own
present. The major difference between these two novels in economic
terms, is that while both are about trading bodies and their worth on
the market, in *The Handmaid's Tale* money has disappeared underground. This is so much the case that when Offred observes that "Money
has trickled through this [sitting-] room for years and years, as if through
an underground cavern" [*HT*, 89] we are suddenly surprised by her
words, for money is strikingly absent in the narrative. Desiring "to steal
something from this room" [*HT*, 90], Offred unwittingly finds her
desire to be matched, for standing behind her, his foot clandestinely
making contact with her own, is Nick, whose name is itself synonymous
with theft.

This mercantile analogy is also clear in the "illegitimate" romance chronotope that links Offred with Nick and that is mediated and set up by
the Commander's Wife, Serena Joy. Where the terms of the contract
with the Commander are clear (even in their illicit encounters), this is
far less the case with Serena Joy. It is tempting to read her as a similar
figure to Uncle Philip, a brooding, controlling, resentful presence whose
relationship to the household is one of tyranny and suspicion. This is
even implied by the details of her first encounter with Offred, which

identically reproduces Melanie's first encounter with Uncle Philip, Serena Joy "just [standing] there in the doorway, blocking the entrance" [*MT*, 23], leaving Offred to consider, again in the manner of Carter's Melanie, that "The threshhold [sic] of a new house is a lonely place" [*HT*, 24]. But it is a mistake to attribute too much agency to Serena Joy; she too is a puppet in a patriarchal game, epitomizing the same obsolescence as Carter's Aunt Margaret in her inability to have children of her own. While her initial conversation with Offred is one in which she asserts relative dominance, Serena Joy acknowledges Offred's literacy and intelligence and has the honesty to admit "this is like a business transaction" [*HT*, 25].

Two of the most interesting and imaginative readings of Atwood's novel are Madonne Miner's reading of "the Romance Plot" in the text and Joseph Andriano's attention to its usage of the metaphor of the crossword, as epitomized by the Scrabble game.[38] Miner focuses upon the roles played in the text by the three main male protagonists, Luke, Nick and the Commander. It is not particularly unusual that she sees similarities between the first two of these; after all, the phonetic similarities between Luke and Nick alone, in a text in which Offred admits to fabricating names for her own purposes, obviously implies their innate similarity, despite the fact that their Biblical connections (not insignificant in a novel like this) place them poles apart. Luke, an Apostle, is on the side of the angels, whereas Nick must be related to "Old Nick" himself. But then, being on the side of the "Angels" is not such a positive thing when those same Angels are the secret force of State tyranny and harbingers of death. What is most original about Miner's reading are the ways in which she demonstrates the similarities not only between these two characters, but also between Luke and the Commander, beginning with their shared facility with words. As Miner observes, it is Luke who first explains the origins of the emergency phrase "Mayday" to be "*m'aidez*" and points out that "fraternize" lacks a corresponding female term: "*Sororize*, it would have to be, he said" [*HT*, 15]. Miner's larger point is that Luke's educational background is distinct from Offred's, but matched by the Commander's, whose own proficiency in Classical terminology is sufficient to explain the joke behind the (literally) closeted phrase "*Nolite te bastardes carborundorum*" [*HT*, 62]. More significantly, what Luke and the Commander share is a position of social privilege that enables them to effect "a subtle reaffirmation of classical gender roles and inequalities" based upon this unequal knowledge.[39] Ultimately the Commander betrays Offred, Nick embodies the possibility (hence the power) to save or betray her and, most revealingly of all, Miner indicates that Luke, seemingly idealized in retrospect, also betrays her in an earlier, cumulative sequence of events.

Luke's passive attitude towards the various legislative means by which the protagonist is economically and socially disempowered prior to capture is the first and most obvious point at issue. Less obvious, but more revealing, are the astute observations Miner makes about Luke's role in the apparent escape attempt as they and their daughter try to cross the border to safety. Miner points, on this occasion, to the *narrator's* passive role in the preparation for the escape plan. Luke organizes the paperwork, obtained from a concealed source, and is responsible for the failure of the attempt. All things considered, as Miner observes, "It may very well be that Luke's 'plan' is larger than the narrator realizes". In answer to perceived resistance to this reading (and a number of even feminist critics have been strangely desperate to perceive Atwood's stance on the male characters in this text to be a positive one), Miner reminds us of Luke's former betrayal of his first wife as evidence of his track-record. What Miner does not really offer, however, are clear motivations behind Luke's actions in (possibly) betraying the narrator in this manner, beyond the fact that Luke is shown up as being "a man who betrays women".[40] Instead she focuses upon its implications for what some feminist critics have objected to in this text, namely Offred's apparent fascination with past, present and future romance, rather than political motivation. For Miner, once we recognize that none of the three main male figures are fully trustworthy, the surface romance plot Offred constructs is shown, also, to be a retrospective fabrication. I am largely persuaded by Miner's reading of Luke, but think this casts greater light on the economic basis of the text than it does its treatment of romance. In the process it also offers a more credible set of motivations for Luke's actions. After all, his unreliable attitude towards sexual faithfulness is surely not of the same order of magnitude as selling a woman knowingly into slavery – *unless* it reveals a basic belief in women being no more than merchandise to start with.

Let us first consider a couple of points Miner overlooks. Surely it is not insignificant that the illustrations she picks out to underline Luke's facility with language also cite him as the originary source for terms later connected with the two other members of the triumvirate. "Mayday" is the underground organization in which Nick is involved and his perceived absence of an existence of "sororizing" is surely another way of putting the Commander's claim that women lack a collaborative identity: "For [women], one and one and one and one don't make four ... [they make] one and one and one and one" [*HT*, 195]. Offred knows, full well, that Scrabble is not just a word-game, it is a game of strategy, one which she hopes to be able to use to her advantage beyond the confines of the room. For Miner the game also takes on a further clandestine significance as a shared secret understanding between implied author and implied reader:

> ... in this sequence ... we readers receive instructions in the reading process, lessons in how to construct meaning out of disparate pieces ... just as Offred and the Commander 'bend the rules' ... so too we may find that 'taking up extra letters' and playing with seemingly bizarre connections actually may lead us to some new understandings of the text.[41]

Andriano pays even closer attention to the Scrabble game than does Miner, looking in detail at the "value" of actual words Offred spells out with her Scrabble counters. Noting that she is "a better player than she thinks", he reminds us of the calibre of the words she lays down: "*Prolix, quartz, quandary, sylph,* and *rhythm*". Carefully weighing up her words, Andriano also reminds us that Scrabble is not just a word-game and a strategy-game, it is also, and crucially, a game of economics. Hence "*quandary* is an eight-letter word that would give her a fifty-point bonus" and "Zilch", as she notes herself, is "a convenient one-vowel word with an expensive *z*" [*HT*, 193]. More generally, Andriano notes, "[She] keeps finding herself in the situation of having too few vowels, too many consonants. The latter have greater value in Scrabble".[42]

Again, then, seeking to turn the Commander's own maxim on its head, Offred shows us that one tile plus one tile plus one tile plus one tile do not make four, they make as many points as a good Scrabble player can amass, depending on her positioning of the word on the board. Offred hopes that her very participation in the game will suffice to maximize both her position and her assets. She hopes it will "buy" her loyalty (and, perhaps, time). But of course she is wrong. The Commander is always one step ahead of the game, not least because it is *his* game they are playing, and in more ways than one. Seemingly unsure of whether or not "Zilch" is an "acceptable" word in Scrabble terms, Offred offers to look it up in the dictionary, but the Commander lets her have it anyway. With his customary attention to detail Andriano assures us "(It is an acceptable word.) But sexual politics demand that he have the power to decide, not some extrascriptural text".[43] In other words, just as the Commander lets Offred "let" him win their second game, so here he may even be playing with *her* in doubting the acceptability of the term, just so that he can remind her that he is the ultimate authority. He is in command, holds all the cards, and is determined to demonstrate, as my own father might say, that "a good scorer will beat a good player any day". If Luke and the Commander are in it together, here the Commander toys with Offred in a way that acts out Luke's own bargaining position. He sells her to the authorities in exchange for some unspecified privilege for himself. In a further cruelly ironic twist, her new name even tells her that she has been the price "Off(e)red".

## Mothering and Melancholia

If marriage is an anachronism in Gilead, mothering now proves inseparable from loss: "Each of us holds in her lap a phantom, a ghost baby" [*HT*, 178]. According to Stewart, the concept of longing has a well-established relationship with maternal desire. In part this derives from the term's connection with "the fanciful cravings incident to women during pregnancy"[44] but, in this dystopian society these also cohere around that particular form of nostalgia known as melancholia. As Kristeva claims, "Conscious of being destined to lose our loves, we are perhaps even more bereaved by noticing in our lover the shadow of a loved object, formerly lost".[45] This is never more apparent than in *The Handmaid's Tale*. All the Handmaids are women whose reproductive potential is proven prior to the regime, a proof implying that every Handmaid has at least one child she has lost and, if she is successful in her duties, will lose another. But Offred's daughter reappears constantly, manifesting her presence amid entirely unconnected objects, just part of the clutter that is Offred's distorted reproduction of the past:

> She fades, I can't keep her here with me, she's gone now. Maybe I do think of her as a ghost . . . a little girl who died when she was five. I remember the pictures of us I had once . . . locked in a frame, for safety. [*HT*, 75]

As in *Blow Your House Down*, then, elements of the ghost story surprise us by cohering in this text. The absence portrayed by the presence under glass here is also mirrored on the other side of the looking-glass in which, Offred fears, "I have been obliterated for her. I am only a shadow now . . . You can see it in her eyes: I am not there" [*HT*, 240]. Intriguingly, the metaphor of the body of glass around which Piercy builds her own futurist narrative, becomes a similarly frequent motif in *The Handmaid's Tale*. Offred is, after all, a fragile vessel, "A cradle of life, made of bones; and within, hazards, warped proteins, bad crystals jagged as glass" [*HT*, 122]. By far the most ironic of all illustrations of this fragility occurs when Cora, finding Offred asleep on the floor of her room, drops her breakfast tray, believing her dead:

> The eggs had broken on the floor, there was... shattered glass... [Cora] was kneeling on the floor, picking up the pieces ... she went into the bathroom and flushed the handful of egg, which could not be salvaged, down the toilet ... [*HT*, 159–60]

Like the glass, Offred is shattered (exhausted) and, in the process, reminds us of the glass-like vulnerability of her role and place in this household. Where Melanie was aware of her potentially extraneous position to the Flower household, Offred cannot afford for this household to define her as redundant, for the sole and immediate consequences of such definition would be her own death. Nor should we overlook the fact that it is the eggs which are spoilt, just as her own is, month by month, as the clock ticks away.

Though Handmaids are denied their own mirrors, two household icons, a mirror and a clock, remind Offred continually that her own biological clock is ticking. Even the structure of the narrative reflects this, following the rhythms of diurnal time, but only ever by anchoring themselves at night, the time which Offred believes to be " ... mine, my own time, to do with as I will" [*HT*, 47], despite the omnipresence of a spyglass "round, convex, a pier-glass, like the eye of a fish" [*HT*, 19], set at the centre of the Commander's house. Gazing at the gravestones in a churchyard, Offred notices their ornamentation with "winged hourglasses" [*HT*, 41]. Though relating, in this context, to human mortality, in the context of Gilead we surely also think of the hour-glass figure as the desired form for female fecundity. As the saucy seaside "pier-glasses" in Carter's *Dr Hoffman* demonstrate, such scopophiliac equipment inevitably transforms sexual women into mannequins, automata performing like living dolls. Aunt Lydia warns that the "Eyes" are everywhere: "To be seen ... is to be ... penetrated. What you must be, girls, is impenetrable" [*HT*, 39], but Offred is there to be penetrated, as such lenses make clear. The ultimate irony of this preoccupation with the glass body, however, is reserved for the Historical Notes section, during which the pompously misogynistic Professor Piexoto documents his quest to unearth the "real" name of the Commander. Though not conclusive, he points to the most likely candidate being one Frederick R. Waterford, the importance of this analogy then becoming crystal-clear. Openly defined as a combination of the O that defines Offred's reproductive function and the stamp of his ownership in the form of the Commander's Christian name, now his surname is shown to have encapsulated Offred's vessel-like status, carved in the form of a body of glass.

Glass also frames Offred's relationship to fantasy. Surreptitiously watching Nick from her window, Offred's stance is once again like Melanie's, the latter staring from the toyshop window as "[t]he nights drew in earlier and earlier . . . seeing not the bleak yard . . . but berries reddening on the hedges around home and fields glinting with frost" [*MT*, 93]. Nick similarly represents former pleasures and privileges now "legitimately" closed off. In the dystopian context of Atwood's novel Offred's view, through the window, of the empty garden makes a statement about the futility of collective as well as personal wish-fulfilment. At the beginning of chapter 3, just before she tells us about her first face-to-face encounter with Serena Joy, she describes leaving the house for one of her chaperoned shopping trips and introduces us to a brief layout of this garden. As in *The Magic Toyshop*, then, the garden evokes the possibility of utopia only to mockingly signal its absence: "I once had a garden. I can remember the smell of the turned earth, the plump shapes of bulbs held in the hands, fullness, the dry rustle of seeds through the fingers" [*HT*, 22]. This is the site of Serena Joy's melancholia as Offred's snidely imagined retort demonstrates: "No use for you . . . they're the genital organs of plants" [*HT*, 91]. Detailing the colour of the tulips as "red, a darker crimson towards the stem, as if they had been cut and are beginning to heal there" [*HT*, 22], they somehow evoke an image of severed fallopian tubes. So what seems a space of pleasure and creativity becomes a site of visible humiliation and mockery, a space of non-creativity which Serena Joy pathetically tries to fill by churning out endless spools of scarves which, though purportedly for the military, are transparently motivated by the purposeless desire for reproduction:

> Fir trees march along the ends . . . or eagles, or stiff humanoid figures, boy and girl, boy and girl. They aren't scarves for grown men but for children. Sometimes I think these scarves aren't sent to the Angels at all, but unravelled and turned back into balls of yarn, to be knitted again in their turn. [*HT*, 22–3]

For Stewart, in her full-length study of longing, the garden is often a signifier for maternal loss: "The prevailing motif of nostalgia is the erasure of the gap between nature and culture, and hence a return to the utopia of biology and symbol united within the walled city of the maternal. The nostalgic's utopia is prelapsarian ... ".[46] Consequently, what we should not forget is that Offred and Serena Joy are mirrored in this space by a *shared* sense of redundancy, a recognition realized as Serena Joy "fits the skein of wool over [Offred's] two outstretched hands, starts winding" as she bargains with her, offering her two pieces of forbidden fruit: news of her daughter and the body of Nick the chauffeur. Not unusually, Offred fails to recognize Serena Joy's own victim status, believing herself alone in having been "leashed ... manacled; cobwebbed" [*HT*, 213] by the wool. Nevertheless, we see a shared moment of bondage, although the illusion of greater power lies with Serena Joy. In fact it is inside the living-room, purportedly Serena Joy's domain, that "the stench of her knitting" [*HT*, 109] becomes most unbearable, the smoke from her cigarettes becoming absorbed by the fibres, while rotting flowers stand on the shelf plunged in stagnant water. This household is going rotten and Serena Joy sits at its core.

According to Palmer, Carter is guilty of "an element of distortion" in her early work which, "while presenting a brilliantly accurate analysis of the oppressive effects of patriarchal structures, [runs] the risk of making these structures appear even more closed and impenetrable than, in actual fact, they are".[47] But if Carter stands guilty as charged, then what of *The Handmaid's Tale*? At least in *The Magic Toyshop* it is the uncles who embody patriarchy, while in Atwood's novel the Aunts are part of it too. Despite their respective uses of anti-mimetic forms, the most chilling aspect of these novels resides in their all-pervasive familiarity. Both are situated in everyday households, set in a recognizable everyday world. Rather than their main characters being the larger than life heroines or grotesque monsters of Chapter 1, Melanie and Offred are recognizably ordinary: just like us. Because of this point of identification, despite our frustration at their apparent unwillingness or incapacity to take on the system we simultaneously recognize our own complicity in them. In the Historical Notes section, Piexoto refers to Gilead's system of Aunts as proof positive that "the best and most cost-effective way to control women ... was through women themselves" [*HT*, 320]. This system of control does not need to define women as rivals among themselves. It is sufficient for women to be self-policing, deciding to take the "easy way out" (which is shown, in this chapter, to offer no way out at all).

# Conclusion: The Lost Mother

This book ends as it began in Chapter 1, with Susan Stewart's reading of longing, a melancholic dynamic that pulls together the infinitely drawn out elongation of desire with an intrinsic connection with the mother, not least in the "yearning desire[s]" of pregnancy. But, as Stewart stresses, it is the mother as "an *imagined* location of origin" that is applicable here, not the mother as actual parent.[1] Taking these 23 novels as a corpus, I have been surprised by the consistency with which the spectre of the mother manifests herself in fantastic terms. This is an identification suggesting that women's fantasies remain imprinted by what must always be that "other-space" of the maternal. The point remains, irrespective of whether we cast ourselves in the role of daughter longing for (or fleeing from) the mother, or cloak ourselves in the body of the (good or bad) maternal alter-ego.

Both roles alternate in this book, from Wittig's desire to set us free from the shackles of biological reproduction in Chapter 1 (a call echoed by Donna J. Haraway's work on the feminist implications of reproductive technology in Chapter 2), through to Morrison's horrifying killing of the infant in Chapters 3 and 4, to Eloise's naive bargaining with the fairies in Chapter 5, Nora and Dora's search for the missing mother in Chapter 6, and Offred's dreams in Chapter 7, in which the pronouns "she" and "her" repeatedly pull together the mother, daughter, Moira, Offred's dead predecessor, and so many other "sister" selves cohering into one shared dystopian space of loss. Throughout, while three decades of feminist criticism have accustomed us to reading the mother in increasingly idealized terms as that "first music from the first voice of love which is alive in every woman",[2] this book demonstrates quite clearly that the fantastic source of that bodily connection with the mother can also be one of two-way possessive retribution. As Chapter 3 has demonstrated in its exploration of the mother/child as vampire/ prey analogy, on the one hand we find Meredith Skura's work emphasizing the mother as controlling predator against whom the vampire struggles, and on the other we have Ernest Jones's comment: "Vampires often lie on the breast and induce suffocation".[3] As Julia Kristeva notes, Mother is the root source of all abjection, the first point at which the process of separation from the "not-I" is enforced in a manner which mirrors the dynamics of the gothic world: "As if the fundamental opposition were between I and Other or, in more archaic fashion, between Inside and Outside".[4]

Forming a counter-weight to this insider/outsider debate is our core group of *literary* foremothers, Woolf's Mary Beton (Seton/Carmichael), Tennyson's Lady of Shalott, Freud's Dora and Scheherazade. The first two offer alternative readings of female creativity, Woolf's protagonist being a writer, while Tennyson's is a needlewoman. Though neither is explicitly identified as maternal, both are constrained (even suffocated) by the domestic enclosures which so commonly trap mothers; and yet the nature of that entrapment is different in each case. Where Tennyson's Lady is shut up by "four gray walls and four gray towers", Woolf's protagonist is shut out:

> ...here I was actually at the door which leads into the library itself. I must have opened it, for instantly there issued, like a guardian angel barring the way with a flutter of black gown instead of white wings, a deprecating, silvery, kindly gentleman, who regretted in a low voice as he waved me back that ladies are only admitted to the library if accompanied by a Fellow of the College or furnished with a letter of introduction.[5]

Dora and Scheherazade's creative identity is predominantly narrative and, in both cases, the maternal connection is quite clear. Dora's story is, like the plot Claire Kahane discovers at the root of the female gothic, haunted by the phantom of the silenced mother.[6] Freud is quick to tell us that Dora does not get on with her mother and, though Freud never meets this woman, he is "led to imagine her as an uncultivated woman and above all a foolish one, who had concentrated all her interests upon domestic affairs". Never, of course, is the mother permitted to tell her own story; rather, like Dora herself, she is ultimately erased from view, replaced with a new image of the orally-defined woman, choked off as Freud "tells the stories of the stories told him – which is not the same as retelling the original stories".[7] We have seen that Freud's own gagging of both women is displaced onto what he insists are Dora's own hysterical symptoms, manifest in a variety of oral fears, but deriving from a sexual rather than a textual nature. In the process Freud effects the textual trickery which Patricia Parker identifies as *"Ecrasez la femme*, ways of mastering or controlling the implicitly female, and perhaps hence wayward, body of the text itself".[8] By the end, like the Lady of Shalott, Dora has become "framed" as a mere fantasy of desire.

This is the point at which a distinction between Dora and her "sister" Scheherazade starts to surface, for where Dora is controlled via Freud's ventriloquism, Scheherazade refuses to shut up, carrying out the framing of her own text and its many characters. As *The Thousand and One Nights* lacks any one attributed author, Scheherazade almost exists as her own creator (much as we found Allende's Eva doing in Chapter 6). In refusing to be owned by any one author and, in the process, eschewing his/her authority, she evades what Gilbert and Gubar read as the controlling mechanism of literary paternity.[9] Thus, as critics such as Wendy B. Faris affirm, Scheherazade becomes her own mother. Though bearing the Sultan three children during the course of her narrative, it is not these children who define her status as mother, for "they have no substantial part in the frame of the tales". Instead Scheherazade gives birth to a text in which

> ... generativity operates at all levels ... on the structural plane with stories that grow out of other stories; on the mimetic front with characters who duplicate themselves in miraculous feats of doubling; in the metaphorical register with images that take on lives of their own and engender others beyond themselves, independent of their referential worlds.[10]

But as well as being mother to her own text, Faris projects Scheherazade into the role of mother to a generation of late-twentieth-century magic realist writers which includes, among others, Gabriel García Márquez, Salman Rushdie, Patrick Suskind and Toni Morrison. Strangely, Faris omits to mention Isabel Allende here, for her character Eva Luna is an obvious "child" to Scheherazade in these terms. So we find Eva's mother Consuelo providing Eva with an escape valve from the type of "suffocating" domesticity by which the Lady of Shalott and Dora's mother are both constrained. Instead, like Scheherazade, she brings the wider world of the globe into the house, her legacy to Eva being the ability to do the same:

I gave each room a name ... Katmandu, Palace of the Bears, Merlin's Cave – and it took only the slightest effort of imagination to pass through the door and enter the extraordinary stories unfolding on the other side of the walls.[11]

In summary, our journey through this book has taken us from the grotesque utopia to the gothic, to the ghost story and beyond. We have crossed continents, centuries and chronotopes and, in the process, encountered cyborgs, clowns and clones. The novels under discussion have projected us backwards into the past or forwards into futurism; beyond space and time into ancient folklore or into outer space via science fiction. But underlying all of that territory, it seems, is that first other-place and space, one which we alternately shun and desire: the maternal.

# Notes

## Introduction

1. Louis Marin, "The Frontiers of Utopia", in Krishan Kumar and Stephen Bann (eds), *Utopias and the Millennium* (London: Reaktion Books, 1993), 10.
2. Virginia Woolf, *A Room of One's Own* (London: Grafton, 1977), 7–8, 95, 47, 107–8.
3. Gaston Bachelard, *The Poetics of Space*, trans. Maria Jolas (Boston: Beacon Press, 1994), 53.
4. Mark S. Madoff, "Inside, Outside and the Gothic Locked-Room Mystery", in Kenneth W. Graham (ed.), *Gothic Fictions: Prohibition/Transgression* (New York: AMS Press, 1989), 49.
5. Woolf, *A Room of One's Own*, 6 and 100.
6. *Ibid.*, 6 and 95.
7. Adalaide Morris, "First Persons Plural in Contemporary Feminist Fiction", *Tulsa Studies in Women's Literature* 11 (1992), 12.
8. Lynne Pearce, *Feminism and the Politics of Reading* (London: Arnold, 1997).
9. Terry Castle, *The Apparitional Lesbian: Female Homosexuality and Modern Culture* (New York: Columbia University Press, 1993), 2 and 30–1.
10. Daphne du Maurier, *Rebecca* (London: Arrow Books, 1992). Subsequent quotations are referenced within the main body of the text, accompanied by the abbreviation *R*.
11. Sandra Gilbert and Susan Gubar, *The Madwoman in the Attic: The Woman Writer and the Nineteeth-Century Literary Imagination* (New Haven, CT: Yale University Press, 1984), 38.
12. Donna J. Haraway, *Simians, Cyborgs and Women: The Reinvention of Nature* (London: Free Association Books, 1991), 149 and 180.
13. Cyndy Hendershot, "Vampire and Replicant: The One-Sex Body in a Two-Sex World", *Science Fiction Studies* 22 (1995), 373–98.
14. Donna J. Haraway, *Modest_Witness@Second_Millennium.FemaleMan©_Meets_OncoMouse*™: *Feminism and TechnoScience* (New York: Routledge, 1997), 74.
15. Jenijoy La Belle, *Herself Beheld: The Literature of the Looking Glass* (Ithaca, NY: Cornell University Press, 1988), 104. Anne K. Mellor, *Mary Shelley: Her Life, Her Fiction, Her Monsters* (New York: Routledge, 1989), 128.
16. "*And so far as the organism is concerned, what happens if the mirror provides nothing to see?* ... So it is with the girl ... Whence that 'paranoic alienation, which dates from the deflection of the specular I into the social I'": Luce Irigaray, "The 'Mechanics' of Fluids", in *This Sex Which Is Not One*, trans. Catherine Porter and Carolyn Burke (Ithaca, NY: Cornell University Press, 1985); 117–18. For a fuller discussion of Lacan's original theory, see Jacques Lacan, *Ecrits: A Selection*, trans. A Sheridan (London: Tavistock, 1977).
17. Morris, "First Persons Plural in Contemporary Feminist Fiction", 25. Rosemary Jackson, *Fantasy: The Literature of Subversion* (London: Methuen, 1981), 87–8.

18. Mary Daly, *Gyn/Ecology: The Metaethics of Radical Feminism* (London: The Women's Press, 1979), 3.
19. Gilbert and Gubar, *The Madwoman in the Attic, 617–18*.
20. Marin, "The Frontiers of Utopia", 10.
21. Claire Kahane, *Passions of the Voice: Hysteria, Narrative, and the Figure of the Speaking Woman, 1850–1915* (Baltimore: Johns Hopkins University Press, 1995), 17.
22. Sigmund Freud, *Case Histories I*, Penguin Freud Library, Vol. 8, ed. Angela Richards (Harmondsworth: Penguin, 1990), 29–164.
23. *Ibid.*, 163.
24. E.T.A. Hoffmann, "The Sandman", in *Tales of Hoffmann*, trans. R.J. Hollingdale (Harmondsworth: Penguin, 1982), 85–125.
25. Lynne Pearce, *Reading Dialogics* (London: Edward Arnold, 1994).
26. Lucie Armitt, *Theorising the Fantastic* (London: Arnold, 1996), 183–6.
27. Joanna Russ, *The Female Man* (London: The Women's Press, 1985), 213–14.
28. Tzvetan Todorov, *The Fantastic: A Structural Approach to a Literary Genre*, trans. Richard Howard (Ithaca, NY: Cornell University Press, 1975), 24–5.
29. Any reader wishing for a fuller theoretical discussion of the nature of the interrelationship between all three terms can find one in chs 1 and 2 of *Theorising the Fantastic*.
30. Leslie Fiedler, *Freaks: Myths and Images of the Secret Self* (New York: Simon and Schuster, 1978), 91.

## 1. The Grotesque Utopia

1. Angela Carter, *Nights at the Circus* (London: Picador, 1984), 285. Subsequent quotations are referenced within the main body of the text, accompanied by the abbreviation *NC*.
2. Lucie Armitt, *Theorising the Fantastic* (London: Arnold, 1996), 183.
3. *Ibid.*, 184.
4. Susan Stewart, *On Longing: Narratives of the Miniature, the Gigantic, the Souvenir, the Collection* (Durham: Duke University Press, 1993), ix.
5. Angelika Bammer, *Partial Visions: Feminism and Utopianism in the 1970s* (New York: Routledge, 1991), 2.
6. Mary Russo, *The Female Grotesque: Risk, Excess and Modernity* (New York: Routledge, 1994), vii.
7. Silvia Bovenschen, "Is There a Feminist Aesthetic?", in Gisela Ecker (ed.), *Feminist Aesthetics* (London: The Women's Press, 1985), 47.
8. Joanna Russ, *The Female Man* (London: The Women's Press, 1985), 134. Subsequent quotations are referenced within the main body of the text, accompanied by the abbreviation *FM*.
9. Donna J. Haraway, *Modest_Witness@Second_Millennium.FemaleMan©_Meets_ OncoMouse™: Feminism and TechnoScience* (New York: Routledge, 1997), 70 and 75.
10. Jeanette Winterson, *Sexing the Cherry* (London: Bloomsbury, 1989), 133. Subsequent quotations are referenced within the main body of the text, accompanied by the abbreviation *SC*.
11. Naomi Wolf, *The Beauty Myth* (London: Chatto and Windus, 1990), 153.
12. Lynne Pearce, *Reading Dialogics* (London: Edward Arnold, 1994), 178.

13. Allon White, "Pigs and Pierrots: The Politics of Transgression in Modern Fiction", *Raritan*, 2 (Fall 1981), 67.
14. Note, here, that this scene of "revolting" female display is similar to that involving two young, beautiful French prostitutes who, during the French Revolution, stood at the barricades, taunting the National Guard by raising their dress to the waist, baring their genitalia and challenging the authorities, "Cowards! Fire, if you dare, at the belly of a woman!". In the historical account, both are shot dead, an event analysed in Freudian terms by Neil Hertz in "Medusa's Head: Male Hysteria under Political Pressure", *Representations*, 4 (Fall 1983), 27–54. In *Sexing the Cherry*, identical dynamics are employed, except that here the grotesque Dogwoman succeeds where the beautiful French prostitutes fail.
15. Julia Kristeva, *Powers of Horror: An Essay on Abjection* (New York: Columbia University Press, 1982), 1.
16. *Ibid.*, 2.
17. Ricarda Schmidt, "The Journey of the Subject in Angela Carter's Fiction", *Textual Practice*, 3 (Spring 1989), 56–76. Elaine Showalter, *Sexual Anarchy: Gender and Culture at the* Fin-de-Siècle (London: Bloomsbury, 1991), 39.
18. Anne Fernihough, "'Is She Fact or Is She Fiction?' Angela Carter and the Enigma of Woman", *Textual Practice* 11 (1997), 90.
19. Linda Ruth Williams, *Critical Desire: Psychoanalysis and the Literary Subject* (London: Edward Arnold, 1995), 97.
20. Russo, *The Female Grotesque*, 172.
21. Paulina Palmer, "From 'Coded Mannequin' to Bird Woman: Angela Carter's Magic Flight", in Sue Roe (ed.), *Women Reading Women's Writing* (Brighton: Harvester, 1987), 180.
22. Russo, *The Female Grotesque*, ix.
23. Louis Marin, "The Frontiers of Utopia", in Krishan Kumar and Stephen Bann (eds), *Utopias and the Millennium* (London: Reaktion Books, 1993), 7.
24. Marin, "Frontiers of Utopia", 7 and 15.
25. Stewart, *On Longing*, 23.
26. Hélène Cixous, "L'Approche de Clarice Lispector", extract translated by Toril Moi, in *Sexual/Textual Politics: Feminist Literary Theory* (London: Methuen, 1985), 115.
27. Hélène Cixous, "The Laugh of the Medusa", trans. Keith Cohen and Paula Cohen, in Elaine Marks and Isabelle de Courtivron (eds), *New French Feminisms: An Anthology* (Brighton: Harvester, 1981), 251.
28. Monique Wittig, *Les Guérillères*, trans. David Le Vay (Boston: Beacon Press, 1985), 30–1. Subsequent quotations are referenced within the main body of the text, accompanied by the abbreviation *LG*.
29. These ideas are developed in full in Jacques Lacan, *Ecrits: A Selection*, trans. A. Sheridan (London: Tavistock, 1977).
30. Russo, *The Female Grotesque*, 86 and 127.
31. Cixous, "The Laugh of the Medusa", 256.
32. Monique Wittig, *Across the Acheron*, trans. David Le Vay (London: Peter Owen 1987), 105. Subsequent quotations are referenced within the main body of the text, accompanied by the abbreviation *AA*.
33. Luce Irigaray, "Sexual Difference", in Margaret Whitford, ed., *The Irigaray Reader* (Oxford: Basil Blackwell, 1991), 174–5.

34. Monique Wittig, "One Is Not Born a Woman", *Feminist Issues*, 1 (1981), 47.
35. Kim Chernin, *The Hungry Self: Women, Eating and Identity* (New York: Times Books, 1985), 186.
36. Patricia Parker, *Literary Fat Ladies: Rhetoric, Gender, Property* (London: Methuen, 1987), 33.
37. Jane Palmer, *The Watcher* (London: The Women's Press, 1986), 6. Subsequent quotations are referenced within the main body of the text, accompanied by the abbreviation *TW*.
38. Russo, *The Female Grotesque*, 70.
39. *Ibid.*, 29.
40. For a fuller discussion of this concept see Sandra Gilbert and Susan Gubar, *The Madwoman in the Attic: The Woman Writer and the Nineteenth-Century Literary Imagination* (New Haven: Yale University Press, 1984).
41. See Irigaray, "Sexual Difference", 173.
42. Russo, *The Female Grotesque*, 176.
43. Irigaray, "Sexual Difference", 173. See also Nicola Bown, "'There are Fairies at the Bottom of our Garden': Fairies, Fantasy and Photography", *Textual Practice* 10 (Spring 1996), 73.
44. Patricia Parker, *Literary Fat Ladies*, 106 and 26.
45. *Ibid.*, 26.
46. Chernin, *The Hungry Self*, 184.
47. Cixous, "The Laugh of the Medusa", 245.
48. Nicole Ward Jouve, *Female Genesis: Creativity, Self and Gender* (New York: St Martin's Press, 1998), 2 and 3.
49. Mikhail Bakhtin, *The Dialogic Imagination: Four Essays by M. M. Bakhtin*, ed. Michael Holquist, trans. Caryl Emerson and Michael Holquist (Austin: University of Texas Press, 1981), 98.
50. *Ibid*, 84–5.
51. Pearce, *Reading Dialogics*, 177.
52. Bakhtin, *The Dialogic Imagination*, 150. Pearce, *Reading Dialogics*, 14.
53. Pearce, *Reading Dialogics*, 174, 59 and 194.
54. Pearce, *Reading Dialogics*, 18 and Bakhtin, *The Dialogic Imagination*, 84.

## 2. Chronotopes and Cyborgs

1. Jonathan Friedman, "Global System, Globalization and the Parameters of Modernity", in Mike Featherstone, Scott Lash and Roland Robertson (eds), *Global Modernities* (London: Sage, 1995), 70.
2. Mikhail Bakhtin, *The Dialogic Imagination: Four Essays by M. M. Bakhtin*, ed. Michael Holquist, trans. Caryl Emerson and Michael Holquist (Austin: University of Texas Press, 1981), 84. Cited in Lynne Pearce, *Reading Dialogics* (London: Edward Arnold, 1994), 67.
3. Angela Carter, *The Sadeian Woman: An Exercise in Cultural History* (London: Virago, 1990), 9.
4. K.K. Ruthven, *Feminist Literary Studies: An Introduction* (Cambridge: Cambridge University Press, 1984), 30. Octavia Butler, *Kindred* (London: The Women's Press, 1988), 60. Subsequent quotations are referenced within the main body of the text, accompanied by the abbreviation *K*.
5. Bakhtin, *The Dialogic Imagination*, 153.

6. Pearce, *Reading Dialogics*, 184.
7. *Ibid.*, 185 and 194.
8. *Ibid.*, 184.
9. *Ibid.*
10. Mary O'Connor, "Chronotopes for Women under Capital: An Investigation into the Relation of Women to Objects", *Critical Studies*, 2 (1990), 137–51. Cited in Pearce, *Reading Dialogics*, 110.
11. Marge Piercy, *Body of Glass* (Harmondsworth: Penguin, 1992), 12 and 55. Subsequent quotations are referenced within the main body of the text, accompanied by the abbreviation *BG*.
12. Joanna Russ, *The Female Man* (London: The Women's Press, 1985), 6–7. Subsequent quotations are referenced within the main body of the text, accompanied by the abbreviation *FM*.
13. Pearce, *Reading Dialogics*, 1.
14. *Ibid.*, 185.
15. For a fuller discussion of these ideas see Jacques Lacan, *Ecrits: A Selection*, trans. A. Sheridan (London: Tavistock, 1977).
16. Virginia Woolf, *A Room of One's Own* (London: Grafton, 1977), 95.
17. Fay Weldon, *The Cloning of Joanna May* (London: Flamingo, 1993), 49, 55 and 56. Subsequent quotations are referenced within the main body of the text, accompanied by the abbreviation *CJM*.
18. Donna J. Haraway, *Modest_Witness@Second_Millennium.FemaleMan©_Meets_ OncoMouse™: Feminism and TechnoScience* (New York: Routledge, 1997), 79 and 52.
19. Pearce, *Reading Dialogics*, 180. Haraway, *Modest_Witness@Second_Millennium*, 79 and 80.
20. Haraway, *Modest_Witness@Second_Millennium*, 79.
21. *Ibid.*, 69.
22. *Ibid.*, 70 and 22.
23. *Ibid.*, 70.
24. Mary Russo, *The Female Grotesque: Risk, Excess and Modernity* (New York: Routledge, 1994), 12.
25. M.E. Clynes and N.S. Kline, "Cyborgs and Space", *Astronautics*, Sept. 26–7, 1960. Cited in Haraway, *Modest_Witness@Second_Millennium*, 51.
26. Haraway, *Modest_Witness@Second_Millennium*, 113.
27. *Ibid.*, 31–2.
28. *Ibid.*, 32 and 24–5.
29. *Ibid.*, 267.
30. Devon Hodges, "*Frankenstein* and the Feminine Subversion of the Novel", *Tulsa Studies in Women's Literature* 2 (Fall 1983), 157.
31. Haraway, *Modest_Witness@Second_Millennium*, 21.
32. *Ibid.*, 45.
33. Mary Shelley, *Frankenstein Or, The Modern Prometheus* (Harmondsworth: Penguin, 1985), 60.
34. Marge Piercy, *Woman on the Edge of Time* (London: The Women's Press, 1979), 102.
35. Although it is perhaps worth remembering that Avram is implicitly criticized for preferring to father cyborgs rather than children. [*BG*, 337]
36. Shelley, *Frankenstein*, 189.

37. Franco Moretti, *Signs Taken for Wonders*, trans. Susan Fischer, David Forgacs and David Miller (London: Verso, 1983), 85.
38. Haraway, *Modest_Witness@Second_Millennium*, 208 and 209.
39. Piercy, *Woman on the Edge of Time*, 105.
40. Haraway, *Modest_Witness@Second_Millennium*, 186.
41. Nicole Ward Jouve, *Female Genesis: Creativity, Self and Gender* (New York: St Martin's Press, 1998), 16.
42. Haraway, *Modest_Witness@Second_Millennium*, 45 and 52.
43. *Ibid.*, 119.

## 3. Vampires and the Unconscious

1. Ellie Ragland-Sullivan, "Death Drive (Lacan)", in Elizabeth Wright (ed.), *Feminism and Psychoanalysis: A Critical Dictionary* (Oxford: Basil Blackwell, 1992), 58.
2. James B. Twitchell, *Dreadful Pleasures: An Anatomy of Modern Horror* (New York: Oxford University Press, 1985), 51–2.
3. Donna J. Haraway, *Modest_Witness@Second_Millennium.FemaleMan©_Meets_OncoMouse™: Feminism and TechnoScience* (New York: Routledge, 1997), 79. Ken Gelder, *Reading the Vampire* (London: Routledge, 1994), 20.
4. Nina Auerbach, *Our Vampires, Ourselves* (Chicago: University of Chicago Press, 1995), 63.
5. Auerbach, *Vampires*, 4.
6. Elaine Showalter, *Sexual Anarchy: Gender and Culture at the Fin-de-Siècle* (London: Bloomsbury, 1991), 180.
7. Gelder, *Reading the Vampire*, 13.
8. For Julia Kristeva, this precarious border-territory between the "I" and the "not-I" is the space/place where/through which the process of abjection takes place: "There, I am at the border of my condition as a living being. My body extricates itself, as being alive, from that border. Such wastes drop so that I might live, until, from loss to loss, nothing remains in me and my entire body falls beyond the limit – *cadere*, cadaver." *Powers of Horror: An Essay on Abjection* (New York: Columbia University Press, 1982), 3.
9. Auerbach, *Vampires*, 13.
10. Klaus Theweleit, *Male Fantasies, Vol. 1: Women, Floods, Bodies, History*, trans. Stephen Conway, Erica Carter and Chris Turner (Cambridge: Polity Press, 1987), 191–2. The *Freikorps* were the volunteer armies who, in the years following World War I, fought to restrain the German working-classes in revolt. For Theweleit the motivation behind the Freikorps was entirely gendered and revolved around the hatred of women: "it would not be going too far to say that their perpetual war was undertaken to escape women" (p. xiii). Though Theweleit's project focuses upon a precise period of history, the symbolism and iconography revealed as representing this misogyny transcends that historically precise moment, as is evidenced here.
11. Auerbach, *Vampires*, 182–3.
12. Sherry Lee Linkon, "'A Way of Being Jewish That Is Mine': Gender and Ethnicity in the Jewish Novels of Marge Piercy", *Studies in American Jewish Literature* 13 (1994) 95.
13. Gelder, *Reading the Vampire*, 10.
14. Linkon, "A Way of Being Jewish", 100.

15.  A. Waskow, "Androgyny and Beyond", *Tikkun*, 7 (Nov. 1992), 72–4, cited in Linkon, "A Way of Being Jewish", 102.
16.  Thomas Laqueur, *Making Sex: Body and Gender from the Greeks to Freud* (Cambridge, Mass.: Harvard University Press, 1990). Cited in Cyndy Hendershot, "Vampire and Replicant: The One-Sex Body in a Two-Sex World", *Science Fiction Studies* 22 (1995), 373.
17.  Hendershot, "Vampire and Replicant", 377.
18.  *Ibid.*, 383.
19.  Marge Piercy, *Body of Glass* (Harmondsworth: Penguin, 1992), 331. Subsequent quotations are referenced within the main body of the text, accompanied by the abbreviation *BG*. See also Hendershot, "Vampire and Replicant", 389.
20.  Hendershot, "Vampire and Replicant", 379.
21.  Marge Piercy, "Jewish Identity", *Shmate* Pesach (1984), 25. Cited in Linkon, "A Way of Being Jewish", 93. See also p.102.
22.  Sander Gilman, *The Jew's Body* (New York: Routledge, 1991), 4–5.
23.  *Ibid.*, 76.
24.  Showalter, *Sexual Anarchy*, 180.
25.  Gilman, *The Jew's Body*, 81 and 93–4.
26.  *Ibid.*, 188.
27.  *Ibid.* Earlier on Gilman does the same thing with the genitalia. Citing Freud's notorious assertion that women hold a particularly narcissistic relationship with their own genitalia and therefore respond with particular self-loathing and humiliation to any unsightliness or infection [Freud, *Case Histories I*, 121], Gilman reminds us that this observation is particularly contradictory from a practitioner who spoke repeatedly of the female genitalia as connoting absence rather than presence. Deriving a disappointingly narcissistic conclusion of his own from this astute observation, however, Gilman goes on to claim that what Freud is revealing here is not the inconsistency of his own theories on female sexuality, but that unconsciously he is using "Dora" as a stand-in for the (male) Jew as (feminised) hysteric: "The special quality of seeing the female genitalia . . . points towards the *other* genitalia, the male genitalia, seen by the male which when 'disordered' points towards pathological nature of the male" (Gilman, *The Jew's Body*, 83).
28.  *Ibid.*, 111.
29.  J.N. Isbister, *Freud: An Introduction to His Life and Work* (Cambridge: Polity Press, 1985), 114.
30.  *Ibid.*, 118.
31.  See Neil Hertz, "Medusa's Head: Male Hysteria under Political Pressure", *Representations*, 4 (Fall 1983), 30, and Showalter, *Sexual Anarchy*, 180.
32.  Margaret Atwood, *The Robber Bride* (London: Virago, 1994), 461. Subsequent quotations are referenced within the main body of the text, accompanied by the abbreviation *RB*.
33.  Gilman, *The Jew's Body*, 99.
34.  Toni Morrison, *Beloved* (London: Picador, 1988), 37. Subsequent quotations are referenced within the main body of the text, accompanied by the abbreviation *B*.
35.  See Dennis Giles, "Conditions of Pleasure in Horror Cinema", in Barry Keith Grant (ed.), *Planks of Reason: Essays on the Horror Film* (Metuchen: Scarecrow Press, 1984), 38–52.

36. Meredith Anne Skura, *The Literary Use of the Psychoanalytic Process* (New Haven, CT: Yale University Press, 1981), 104.
37. Pamela Barnett, "Figurations of Rape and the Supernatural in *Beloved*", in Carl Plasa (ed.), *Toni Morrison: Beloved* (Cambridge: Icon Books, 1998), 79.
38. Franco Moretti, *Signs Taken for Wonders*, trans. Susan Fischer, David Forgacs and David Miller (London: Verso, 1983), 101.
39. Auerbach, *Vampires*, 109.
40. Moretti, *Signs Taken for Wonders*, 99.
41. Twitchell, *Dreadful Pleasures*, 134.
42. Barnett, "Figurations of Rape", 80.
43. Skura, *Literary Use of the Psychoanalytic Process*, 104.
44. Barnett, "Figurations of Rape", 74 and 79.
45. Bessie Head, *A Question of Power* (London: Heinemann, 1974), 16. Subsequent quotations are referenced within the main body of the text, accompanied by the abbreviation *QP*.
46. Jacqueline Rose, *States of Fantasy* (Oxford: Clarendon, 1996), 102.
47. Tzvetan Todorov, *The Fantastic: A Structural Approach to a Literary Genre*, trans. Richard Howard (Ithaca, NY: Cornell University Press, 1975), 25.
48. Biodun Iglina, "Black Feminist Critique of Psychoanalysis", in Elizabeth Wright (ed.), *Feminism and Psychoanalysis: A Critical Dictionary* (Oxford: Basil Blackwell, 1992) 32.
49. Letter to Charles Sarvan, 1980, cited in Rose, *States of Fantasy*, 105.
50. Rose, *States of Fantasy*, 106.
51. This is Twitchell's phrase. See *Dreadful Pleasures*, 103.
52. Sigmund Freud, *Case Histories I*, Penguin Freud Library, Vol. 8, ed. Angela Richards (Harmondsworth: Penguin, 1990), 37.
53. Kathleen L. Spencer, "Purity and Danger: *Dracula*, the Urban Gothic, and the Late Victorian Degeneracy Crisis", *ELH* 59 (1992), 216.
54. Rose, *States of Fantasy*, 113.
55. Freud, *Case Histories I*, 151.
56. Theweleit, *Male Fantasies*, 195.
57. Barbara Ehrenreich, "Foreword", in Theweleit, *Male Fantasies*, xiii.
58. Gilman, *The Jew's Body*, 107.
59. Twitchell, *Dreadful Pleasures*, 30.
60. Gilman, *The Jew's Body*, 119.
61. Freud, *Case Histories I*, 59.
62. Rosalind Coward, *Female Desire* (London: Paladin, 1984), 117.
63. Angela Carter, *The Sadeian Woman: An Exercise in Cultural History* (London: Virago, 1990), 4–5.
64. The phrase "dirty squirter" is J.N. Isbister's who, in his summary of the treatment of Irma, speaks of her having contracted a syphilitic infection through having been injected in the mouth with a dirty syringe. The phallic implications of the action cluster, again, around fantasies of fellatio. Isbister, 118–19.
65. Margaret Atwood, *Alias Grace* (London: Bloomsbury, 1996), 466–7. Subsequent quotations are referenced within the main body of the text, accompanied by the abbreviation *AG*.
66. Freud, *Case Histories I*, 45–6.
67. *Ibid.*, 46 and 34.

68. Freud's "Prefatory Remarks" to this case history include a series of defensively apologetic explanations for why he chooses to reveal so much personal information about the patient "Dora" and the extent to which he has attempted to conceal her true identity from the reader. When he notes, however, "I naturally cannot prevent the patient herself from being pained if her own case history should *accidentally* fall into her hands" [Freud, *Case Histories I*, 37 – my emphasis], it is clear that her permission has not been sought prior to publication. That it should have been does not seem to cross Freud's mind, this "oversight" forming another piece of evidence revealing his belief that Dora is not her own property, but his.
69. Freud, *Case Histories I*, 92.
70. Twitchell, *Dreadful Pleasures*, 42.
71. Freud, *Case Histories I*, 60–1, my emphasis.
72. *Ibid.*, 52.
73. Haraway, *Witness*, 233–4.

## 4.  Ghosts and (Narrative) Ghosting

1. Daphne du Maurier, *Rebecca* (London: Arrow Books, 1992), 47. Subsequent quotations are referenced within the main body of the text, accompanied by the abbreviation *R*.
2. Freud, "The 'Uncanny'", *Art and Literature*, Penguin Freud Library, Vol. 14, ed. Albert Dickson (Harmondsworth: Penguin, 1990), 365.
3. *Ibid.*, 368.
4. Jenni Dyman, *Lurking Feminism: The Ghost Stories of Edith Wharton* (New York: Peter Lang, 1996), 5.
5. See Alison Light, *Forever England: Femininity, Literature and Conservatism Between the Wars* (London: Routledge, 1991), 156–207 passim and Avril Horner and Sue Zlosnik, "Daphne du Maurier and Gothic Signatures: Rebecca as Vamp(ire)" unpublished manuscript forthcoming in Avril Horner and Angela Keane (eds), *Body Matters: Feminism, Textuality, Corporeality* (Manchester: Manchester University Press).
6. Luce Irigaray, "This Sex Which Is Not One", in *This Sex Which Is Not One*, trans. Catherine Porter and Carolyn Burke (Ithaca, NY: Cornell University Press, 1985), 23–33.
7. Terry Castle, *The Apparitional Lesbian: Female Homosexuality and Modern Culture* (New York: Columbia University Press, 1993), 2.
8. *Ibid.*, 63.
9. Eve Sedgewick, *Between Men: English Literature and Male Homosocial Desire* (New York: Columbia University Press, 1985). See also Luce Irigaray, "Women on the Market" and "Commodities Among Themselves" in *This Sex Which Is Not One*; 170–91 and 192–7.
10. Castle, *The Apparitional Lesbian*, 72–3.
11. Margaret Atwood, *The Robber Bride* (London: Virago, 1994), 201. Subsequent quotations are referenced within the main body of the text, accompanied by the abbreviation *RB*.
12. Irigaray, "Commodities Among Themselves", 196.
13. Irigaray, "This Sex Which Is Not One", 24.
14. *Collins English Dictionary*, 3rd edn, 1991.

15. Jeanette Winterson, *Written on the Body* (London: Jonathan Cape, 1992), 89. Subsequent quotations are referenced within the main body of the text, accompanied by the abbreviation *WB*.

16. Castle, *The Apparitional Lesbian*, 88.

17. See Castle, *The Apparitional Lesbian*, 104; Lynne Pearce, *Feminism and the Politics of Reading* (London: Arnold, 1997), 159; and Sue Roe, Susan Sellers, Nicole Ward Jouve, with Michèle Roberts, *The Semi-Transparent Envelope: Women Writing – Feminism and Fiction* (London: Marion Boyars, 1994), 29.

18. Irigaray, "This Sex Which Is Not One", 24.

19. Castle, *The Apparitional Lesbian*, 7–8.

20. Pearce perceives, in the work of Winterson in general, "an ambivalence that centres on a tension between the perception of romantic love as a non-gendered, a-historic, a-cultural 'universal', and as an 'ideology' which the specificities of gender and sexual orientation constantly challenge and undermine. By attending to the 'universalising' discourses in Winterson's work the (heterosexual) 'general' reader can, of course, see the texts as transcending the particulars of sexual orientation ... ". Lynne Pearce, "'Written on Tablets of Stone'?: Jeanette Winterson, Roland Barthes, and the Discourse of Romantic Love", in Suzanne Raitt (ed.), *Volcanoes and Pearl Divers: Essays in Lesbian Feminist Studies* (London: Onlywomen Press, 1995) 148. See also Castle, *The Apparitional Lesbian*, 6.

21. Pearce, *Feminism and the Politics of Reading*, 24.

22. *Ibid.*, 18 and 96.

23. *Ibid.*, 117.

24. *Ibid.*, 140.

25. *Ibid.*, 143.

26. *Ibid.*, 157, 113 and 164.

27. *Ibid.*, 165.

28. Castle, *The Apparitional Lesbian*, 46.

29. Paul Gilroy, "Living Memory: A Meeting with Toni Morrison", in Carl Plasa (ed.), *Toni Morrison:* Beloved (Cambridge, Icon Books, 1998), 37–8.

30. Linda Hutcheon, *The Politics of Postmodernism* (London: Routledge, 1989), 81–2; cited in Plasa (ed.), *Toni Morrison*, 41.

31. Plasa, *Toni Morrison*, 58; citing Shlomith Rimmon-Kenan, "Narration, Doubt, Retrieval: Toni Morrison's *Beloved*", *Narrative* 4 (1996), 109–23.

32. Toni Morrison, *Beloved* (London: Picador, 1988), 200, 205, 210 and 214. Subsequent quotations are referenced within the main body of the text, accompanied by the abbreviation *B*.

33. Elizabeth B. House, "Toni Morrison's Ghost: The Beloved Who Is Not Beloved", in Plasa (ed.), *Toni Morrison*, 66 and 71.

34. Plasa, *Toni Morrison*, 43.

35. Linden Peach, *Toni Morrison* (London: Macmillan, 1995), 101.

36. Barbara Hill Rigney, "'A Story to Pass On': Ghosts and the Significance of History in Toni Morrison's *Beloved*", in Lynette Carpenter and Wendy K. Kolmar (eds), *Haunting the House of Fiction: Feminist Perspectives on Ghost Stories by American Women* (Knoxville: Tennessee University Press, 1991), 229.

37. A.S. Byatt, "An American Masterpiece", in Plasa (ed.), *Toni Morrison*, 18.

38. Hélène Cixous, "The Laugh of the Medusa", in Elaine Marks and Isabelle de Courtivron (eds), *New French Feminisms: An Anthology* (Brighton: Harvester, 1981), 250.

39. Pamela Barnett, "Figurations of Rape and the Supernatural in *Beloved*", in Plasa (ed.), *Toni Morrison*, 84 – my emphasis and 77–8.
40. Lynne Pearce, *Reading Dialogics* (London: Edward Arnold, 1994), 193.
41. Irigaray, "The 'Mechanics' of Fluids" in *This Sex Which is Not One*, 112.
42. Deborah Horovitz, "Nameless Ghosts: Possession and Dispossession in *Beloved*", in Plasa (ed.), *Toni Morrison*, 60.
43. Peach, *Toni Morrison*, 94.
44. Plasa, *Toni Morrison*, 86; citing Hazel Carby, "The Multicultural Wars", in Gina Dent (ed.), *Black Popular Culture* (Seattle: Bay Press, 1992), 193.
45. Hélène Cixous and Catherine Clément, *The Newly Born Woman*, trans. Betsy Wing (Manchester: Manchester University Press, 1987), 94.

## 5. Fairies and Feminism

1. Edwin Sidney Hartland, *The Science of Fairy Tales* (London: Walter Scott, 1891), 25.
2. Lewis Spence, *The Fairy Tradition in Britain* (London: Rider and Company, 1948), 114–5.
3. Maureen Duffy, *The Erotic World of Faery* (London: Hodder and Stoughton, 1972), 35 and 219.
4. Hartland, *Science of Fairy Tales*, 11–13.
5. Nicola Bown, "'There Are Fairies at the Bottom of Our Garden': Fairies, Fantasy and Photography", *Textual Practice* 10 (Spring 1996) 57–82. Duffy, *The Erotic World of Faery*.
6. Duffy, *The Erotic World of Faery*, 97.
7. *Ibid.*, 75–6.
8. *Ibid.*, 173.
9. *Ibid.*, 293.
10. *Ibid.*, 77 and 220.
11. Alice Thomas Ellis, *Fairy Tale* (London: Viking, 1996), 31–2 and 28. Subsequent quotations are referenced within the main body of the text, accompanied by the abbreviation *FT*.
12. Note that Hartland claims the names "Good People and Fair Family" to be complimentary euphemisms employed by humans to avoid retribution, *Science of Fairy Tales*, 313.
13. Mary Daly, *Gyn/Ecology: The Metaethics of Radical Feminism* (London: The Women's Press, 1979), 3–4.
14. Nicole Ward Jouve, *The Street Cleaner: The Yorkshire Ripper Case on Trial* (London: Marion Boyars, 1986), 17.
15. W.Y. Evans Wentz, *The Fairy-Faith in Celtic Countries* (London: Oxford University Press, 1911), 135–53 passim.
16. Duffy, *The Erotic World of Faery*, 320.
17. Hartland, *Science of Fairy Tales*, 247.
18. Evans Wentz, *The Fairy-Faith*, 142.
19. Julia Kristeva, *Powers of Horror: An Essay on Abjection* (New York: Columbia University Press, 1982), 77.
20. Evans Wentz, *The Fairy-Faith*, 148.
21. Maria Tatar, *The Hard Facts of the Grimm Fairy Tales* (Princeton: Princeton University Press, 1987) cited in Jacqueline Schectman, *The Stepmother in*

*Fairy Tales: Bereavement and the Feminine Shadow* (Boston: Sigo Press, 1993), 20. See also Schectman, *Stepmother in Fairy Tales*, 27.

22. Sandra Gilbert and Susan Gubar, *The Madwoman in the Attic: The Woman Writer and the Nineteeth-Century Literary Imagination* (New Haven, CT: Yale University Press, 1984), 39.
23. *Ibid.*, 38.
24. Hartland, *Science of Fairy Tales*, 50.
25. *Ibid.*, 69.
26. *Ibid.*, 98.
27. Evans Wentz, *The Fairy-Faith*, 146.
28. Schectman, *The Stepmother in Fairy Tales*, xv.
29. Duffy, *The Erotic World of Faery*, 323–4.
30. Fay Weldon, *The Cloning of Joanna May* (London: Flamingo, 1993), 5. Subsequent quotations are referenced within the main body of the text, accompanied by the abbreviation *CJM*.
31. Elaine Tuttle Hansen, *Mother Without Child: Contemporary Fiction and the Crisis of Motherhood* (Berkeley: University of California Press, 1997), 184 and 223.
32. Klaus Theweleit, *Male Fantasies, Vol. 1: Women, Floods, Bodies, History*, trans. Stephen Conway, Erica Carter and Chris Turner (Cambridge: Polity Press, 1987), 283.
33. Elizabeth Baines, *The Birth Machine* (London: The Women's Press, 1983). Subsequent quotations are referenced within the main body of the text, accompanied by the abbreviation *BM*.
34. Chris Turner and Erica Carter, "Political Somatics: Notes on Klaus Theweleit's *Male Fantasies*", in Victor Burgin, James Donald and Cora Kaplan (eds), *Formations of Fantasy* (London: Routledge, 1986), 203.
35. Kristeva, *Powers of Horror*, 75.
36. Spence, *The Fairy Tradition in Britain*, 314.
37. Kristeva, *Powers of Horror*, 2–3.
38. Schectman, *The Stepmother in Fairy Tales*, 33.
39. *Ibid.*, 73.
40. Roland Barthes, *The Pleasure of the Text*, trans. Richard Miller (Oxford: Basil Blackwell, 1990), 37 – my emphasis, and Susan Rubin Suleiman, "Writing and Motherhood", in Shirley Nelson Garner, Claire Kahane and Madelon Sprengnether (eds), *The (M)other Tongue: Essays in Feminist Psychoanalytic Interpretation* (Ithaca, NY: Cornell University Press, 1985), 356.
41. Jennifer Waelti-Walters, *Fairy Tales and the Female Imagination* (Montreal: Eden Press, 1982), 81.
42. Suleiman, "Writing and Motherhood", 361–2.

## 6. Magic Realism Meets the Contemporary Gothic

1. Alejo Carpentier, "On the Marvelous Real in America", in Lois Parkinson Zamora and Wendy B. Faris (eds), *Magical Realism: Theory, History, Community* (Durham: Duke University Press, 1995), 86.
2. Franz Roh, "Magic Realism: Post-Expressionism", in Parkinson Zamora and Faris (eds), *Magical Realism*, 16.

3. For a fuller discussion of this issue see Simon During, "Postmodernism or Post-Colonialism Today", in Bill Ashcroft, Gareth Griffiths and Helen Tiffin (eds), *The Post-Colonial Studies Reader* (London: Routledge, 1995), 125–9.

4. Lynne Pearce, *Reading Dialogics* (London: Edward Arnold, 1994), 195.

5. William Rowe and Vivian Schelling, *Memory and Modernity: Popular Culture in Latin America* (London: Verso, 1991), 214.

6. See Bill Ashcroft, Gareth Griffiths, and Helen Tiffin (eds), "Introduction", *The Post-Colonial Studies Reader* (London: Routledge, 1995), 117.

7. Isabel Allende, *Eva Luna*, trans. Margaret Sayers Peden (Harmondsworth: Penguin, 1989), 266. Subsequent quotations are referenced within the main body of the text, accompanied by the abbreviation *EL*.

8. Simon Slemon, "Magic Realism as Postcolonial Discourse" in Parkinson Zamora and Faris (eds), *Magical Realism*, 411–12.

9. Wendy B. Faris, "Scheherazade's Children: Magical Realism and Postmodern Fiction", in Parkinson Zamora and Faris (eds), *Magical Realism*, 171–2.

10. Isabel Allende, *The House of the Spirits*, trans. Magda Bogin (London: Black Swan, 1986), 78. Subsequent quotations are referenced within the main body of the text, accompanied by the abbreviation *HS*.

11. Rowe and Schelling, *Memory and Modernity*, 107.

12. Rawdon Wilson, "The Metamorphoses of Fictional Space: Magical Realism", in Parkinson Zamora and Faris (eds), *Magical Realism*, 210. Angela Carter, *The Infernal Desire Machines of Doctor Hoffman* (Harmondsworth: Penguin, 1982), 18. Subsequent quotations are referenced within the main body of the text, accompanied by the abbreviation *DH*.

13. See Wilson, "The Metamorphoses of Fictional Space", in Parkinson Zamora and Faris (eds), *Magical Realism*, 227–8. Also Carpentier, "On the Marvelous Real in America", 81.

14. Angela Carter, *Nights at the Circus* (London: Picador, 1985), 53. Subsequent quotations are referenced within the main body of the text, accompanied by the abbreviation *NC*.

15. A.A. Mendilow, *Time and the Novel* (New York: Humanities Press, 1972), 40.

16. *Ibid.*, 10.

17. For a fuller exploration of "impossibility" in conjunction with *Nights at the Circus* see Derek Littlewood, "Uneasy Readings/Unspeakable Dialogics", in Derek Littlewood and Peter Stockwell (eds), *Impossibility Fiction: Alternativity, Extrapolation, Speculation* (Amsterdam: Rodopi, 1996), 191–207.

18. Carpentier, "On the Marvelous Real in America", 76–7.

19. Freud, "Uncanny", 359–60. This discussion of "The 'Uncanny'" as traveller's tale is further developed in my essay "The Magical Realism of the Contemporary Gothic", in David Punter (ed.), *Companion to the Gothic* (Oxford: Basil Blackwell, forthcoming 1999). See also Alejo Carpentier, "The Baroque and the Marvelous Real", in Parkinson Zamora and Faris (eds), *Magical Realism*, 104.

20. Fred Botting, *Gothic* (London: Routledge, 1996), 83.

21. Lucie Armitt, "The Fragile Frames of *The Bloody Chamber*", in Joseph Bristow and Trev Lynn Broughton (eds), *The Infernal Desires of Angela Carter* (London: Longman, 1997), 90.

22. P. Gabrielle Foreman, "Past-On Stories: History and the Magically Real, Morrison and Allende on Call", and Lois Parkinson Zamora, "Magical

Romance/Magical Realism: Ghosts in US and Latin American Fiction", in Parkinson Zamora and Faris (eds), *Magical Realism*, 285 and 497.

23. Parkinson Zamora, "Magical Romance/Magical Realism", 503.
24. Jan Nederveen Pieterse, "Globalization as Hybridization", in Mike Featherstone, Scott Lash and Roland Robertson (eds), *Global Modernities* (London: Sage, 1995), 51.
25. Sharon Zukin, *Landscapes of Power: From Detroit to Disney World* (Berkeley: University of California Press, 1991), 224.
26. *Ibid.*, 224 and 232.
27. Angela Carter, *The Passion of New Eve* (London; Virago, 1982), discussed in Lucie Armitt, *Theorising the Fantastic* (London: Arnold, 1996), 167–9.
28. Epigram – my emphasis.
29. E.T.A. Hoffmann, "The Sandman" in *Tales of Hoffmann*, trans. R.J. Hollingdale (Harmondsworth: Penguin, 1982), 107, 105 and 96–7.
30. Beate Neumeier, "Postmodern Gothic: Desire and Reality in Angela Carter's Writing", in Victor Sage and Allan Lloyd Smith (eds), *Modern Gothic: A Reader* (Manchester: Manchester University Press, 1996) 142.
31. David Punter, "Angela Carter: Supersessions of the Masculine", *Critique: Studies in Contemporary Fiction* 25 (1984), 211 and 213.
32. Hoffmann, "The Sandman", 109–10.
33. Rowe and Schelling, *Memory and Modernity*, 211.
34. John Stokes (ed.), *Fin de Siècle, Fin du Globe: Fears and Fantasies of the Late Nineteenth Century* (London: Macmillan, 1992). See, in particular, Carolyn Steedman's essay, "New Time: Mignon and her Meanings", 102–16.
35. Sarah Gamble, *Angela Carter: Writing from the Front Line* (Edinburgh: Edinburgh University Press, 1997), 157.
36. Magali Cornier Michael, *Feminism and the Postmodern Impulse: Post-World War II Fiction* (Albany: State University of New York Press, 1996), 173.
37. Susanne Kappeler, *The Pornography of Representation* (Cambridge: Polity Press, 1986), 65.
38. Jon Thiem, "The Textualization of the Reader in Magical Realist Fiction", in Parkinson Zamora and Faris (eds), *Magical Realism*, 237.
39. Faris, "Scheherazade's Children", 172.
40. Linda Ruth Williams, *Critical Desire: Psychoanalysis and the Literary Subject* (London: Edward Arnold, 1995), 92.
41. Angela Carter, *Wise Children* (London: Chatto and Windus, 1991), 1 and 3. Subsequent quotations are referenced within the main body of the text, accompanied by the abbreviation *WC*.
42. Gerardine Meaney, *(Un)Like Subjects: Women, Theory, Fiction* (London: Routledge, 1993), 223.
43. Clare Hanson, "'The Red Dawn Breaking Over Clapham': Carter and the Limits of Artifice", in Joseph Bristow and Trev Lynn Broughton (eds), *The Infernal Desires of Angela Carter* (London: Longman, 1997), 70.
44. Kate Webb, "Seriously Funny: *Wise Children*" in Lorna Sage (ed.), *Flesh and the Mirror: Essays on the Art of Angela Carter* (London: Virago, 1994), 293–4.
45. Parkinson Zamora, "Magical Romance/Magical Realism", 498.
46. Paul Magrs, "Boys Keep Swinging: Angela Carter and the Subject of Men", in Joseph Bristow and Trev Lynn Broughton (eds), *The Infernal Desires of Angela Carter* (London: Longman, 1997), 196.

47. Michael Billington, "The Reinvention of William Shakespeare: In Which All the World is a Pluralist's Stage, *World Press Review* (July 1992), 25.
48. Homi K. Bhabha, "Signs Taken for Wonders", in Bill Ashcroft, Gareth Griffiths and Helen Tiffin (eds), *The Post-Colonial Studies Reader* (London: Routledge, 1995), 32. Rowe and Schelling, *Memory and Modernity*, 205.
49. Thiem, "The Textualization of the Reader", 241.
50. Angela Carter, "Omnibus Profile", BBC 1, screened 15 September, 1992. This phrase is taken from a larger, characteristically mischievous remark about Shakespeare, in which Carter remarks, "We were all subsumed to the huge, overarching, intellectual glory of Shakespeare, a man who was probably very deeply lovable but not, I think, terribly clever, but never mind . . . he was the great popular entertainer of all time".
51. "Death snarled at [Angela Carter] and she gave it the finger, Death tore at her and she stuck out her tongue". Salman Rushdie, tribute to Angela Carter. *The Late Show*, BBC2, 1992.
52. Colin Manlove "'In the Demythologising Business': Angela Carter's *The Infernal Desire Machines of Dr Hoffmann* [sic] (1972)", in Kath Filmer (ed.), *Twentieth-Century Fantasists: Essays on Culture, Society and Belief in Twentieth-Century Mythopoeic Literature* (London: Macmillan, 1992), 153.
53. Anne Fernihough, "'Is She Fact or Is She Fiction?' Angela Carter and the Enigma of Woman", *Textual Practice* 11 (1997), 98.

## 7.  Mannequins in the Marketplace

1. Margaret R. Yocom, "'Awful Real': Dolls and Development in Rangeley, Maine", in Joan Newlon Radner (ed.), *Feminist Messages: Coding in Women's Folk Culture* (Urbana: University of Illinois Press, 1993), 129.
2. Angela Carter, *The Magic Toyshop* (London: Virago, 1981), 66. Subsequent quotations are referenced within the main body of the text, accompanied by the abbreviation *MT*.
3. Susan Stewart, *On Longing: Narratives of the Miniature, the Gigantic, the Souvenir, the Collection* (Durham: Duke University Press, 1993), 61.
4. Sigmund Freud, *Art and Literature*, Penguin Freud Library, Vol. 14, ed. Albert Dickson (Harmondsworth: Penguin, 1990) and *The Origins of Religion,* Penguin Freud Library, Vol. 13, ed. Albert Dickson (Harmondsworth: Penguin, 1990).
5. Stewart, *On Longing*, 57–8.
6. Karen F. Stein, "Margaret Atwood's *The Handmaid's Tale*: Scheherazade in Dystopia", *University of Toronto Quarterly* 61 (Winter 1991–2), 269.
7. See Tzvetan Todorov, *The Fantastic: A Structural Approach to a Literary Genre,* trans. Richard Howard (Ithaca, NY: Cornell University Press, 1975), 25.
8. Stein, "Scheherazade in Dystopia", 274.
9. Margaret Atwood, *The Handmaid's Tale* (London: Virago, 1987), 49. Subsequent quotations are referenced within the main body of the text, accompanied by the abbreviation *HT*.
10. David W. Sisk, *Transformations of Language in Modern Dystopias* (Westport, CT: Greenwood Press, 1997), 118.
11. Pat Barker, *Blow Your House Down* (London: Virago, 1984), 65. Subsequent quotations are referenced within the main body of the text, accompanied by the abbreviation *BHD*.

12. Nicole Ward Jouve, *The Street Cleaner: The Yorkshire Ripper Case on Trial* (London: Marion Boyars, 1986), 31.
13. Bruno Bettelheim, *The Uses of Enchantment: The Meaning and Importance of Fairy Tales* (Harmondsworth: Penguin, 1991), 42–44 passim.
14. Victor Burgin, "Fantasy", in Elizabeth Wright (ed.), *Psychoanalysis: A Critical Dictionary* (Oxford: Basil Blackwell, 1992), 84.
15. Freud, *Case Histories I*, 65.
16. *Ibid.*, 66 and 125.
17. *Ibid.*, 52 and 160.
18. *Ibid.*, 48–9 and 161.
19. Luce Irigaray, "Commodities Among Themselves", *This Sex Which Is Not One*, trans. Catherine Porter and Carolyn Burke (Ithaca, NY: Cornell University Press, 1985) 192.
20. Freud, *Case Histories I*, 60–1.
21. *Ibid.*, 71.
22. *Ibid.*, 135–6.
23. Irigaray, "Commodities Among Themselves", 196.
24. Angela Carter, *The Infernal Desire Machines of Doctor Hoffman* (Harmondsworth: Penguin, 1982), 49.
25. E.T.A. Hoffmann, "The Sandman", *Tales of Hoffmann*, trans. R.J. Hollingdale (Harmondsworth: Penguin, 1982), 119–20.
26. Freud, "The 'Uncanny'", 350 – my emphasis.
27. Hoffmann, "The Sandman", 120 and 124.
28. *Ibid.*, 106.
29. *Ibid.*, 123.
30. In places this eye imagery evokes references to the fairy folk of Chapter 5. Like the fairies, Uncle Philip transforms living people into dead objects and vice versa. As Hartland puts it, "[Fairyland's inhabitants] steal women and sometimes leave in their stead blocks of wood, animated by magical art... They make things seem other than they are... they cast spells over mortals" (Hartland, 335–6).
31. Freud, "The 'Uncanny'", 347.
32. Freud, *Case Histories I*, 149.
33. Freud, *Origins of Religion*, 85 and 55.
34. *Ibid.*, 57.
35. Edwin Sidney Hartland, *The Science of Fairy Tales* (London: Walter Scott, 1891), 262.
36. *Ibid.*, 270 and 331.
37. Paulina Palmer, "From 'Coded Mannequin' to Bird Woman: Angela Carter's Magic Flight", in Sue Roe (ed.), *Women Reading Women's Writing* (Brighton: Harvester, 1987), 191–2.
38. Madonne Miner, "'Trust Me': Reading the Romance Plot in Margaret Atwood's *The Handmaid's Tale*", *Twentieth Century Literature* 37 (1991), 148–68, Joseph Andriano, "*The Handmaid's Tale* as Scrabble Game", *Essays on Canadian Writing* 48 (1992), 89–96.
39. Miner, "Reading the Romance Plot", 154–5.
40. *Ibid.*, 159 and 160.
41. *Ibid.*, 149.
42. Andriano, "Scrabble Game", 94.

43.  *Ibid.*, 95.
44.  Stewart, *On Longing*, ix.
45.  Julia Kristeva, "On the Melancholic Imaginary", in Shlomith Rimmon-Kenan, *Discourse in Psychoanalysis and Literature* (London: Methuen, 1987), 104.
46.  Stewart, *On Longing*, 23.
47.  Palmer, "Coded Mannequin", 180–1.

## Conclusion: The Lost Mother

1.  Susan Stewart, *On Longing: Narratives of the Miniature, the Gigantic, the Souvenir, the Collection* (Durham: Duke University Press, 1993), ix and x.
2.  Hélène Cixous, "The Laugh of the Medusa", trans. Keith Cohen and Paula Cohen, in Elaine Marks and Isabelle de Courtivron (eds), *New French Feminisms: An Anthology* (Brighton: Harvester, 1981), 251.
3.  Ernest Jones, *On the Nightmare* (New York: Liveright Books, 1951), 125.
4.  Julia Kristeva, *Powers of Horror: An Essay on Abjection* (New York: Columbia University Press, 1982), 7.
5.  Virginia Woolf, *A Room of One's Own* (London: Grafton, 1977), 9.
6.  See Claire Kahane, "Gothic Mirrors and Feminine Identity", *The Centennial Review* 24 (1980), 43–64.
7.  Sigmund Freud, *Case Histories I*, Penguin Freud Library, Vol. 8, ed. Angela Richards (Harmondsworth: Penguin, 1990), 49. Charles Bernheimer and Claire Kahane (eds), *In Dora's Case: Freud, Hysteria, Feminism*, 2nd edn (New York: Columbia University Press, 1990), 10–1.
8.  Patricia Parker, *Literary Fat Ladies: Rhetoric, Gender, Property* (London: Methuen, 1987), 11.
9.  See Sandra Gilbert and Susan Gubar, *The Madwoman in the Attic: The Woman Writer and the Nineteenth-Century Literary Imagination* (New Haven, CT: Yale University Press, 1984), 3–44 passim.
10. Wendy B. Faris, "Scheherazade's Children: Magical Realism and Postmodern Fiction", in Lois Parkinson Zamora and Wendy B. Faris (eds), *Magical Realism: Theory, History, Community* (Durham: Duke University Press, 1995), 166 and 164.
11. Isabel Allende, *Eva Luna*, trans. Margaret Sayers Peden (Harmondsworth: Penguin, 1989), 100.

# Bibliography

## Primary Texts

Allende, Isabel, *The House of the Spirits*, trans. Magda Bogin (London: Black Swan, 1986)

Allende, Isabel, *Eva Luna*, trans. Margaret Sayers Peden (Harmondsworth: Penguin, 1989)

Atwood, Margaret, *The Handmaid's Tale* (London: Virago, 1987)

Atwood, Margaret, *The Robber Bride* (London: Virago, 1994)

Atwood, Margaret, *Alias Grace* (London: Bloomsbury, 1996)

Baines, Elizabeth, *The Birth Machine* (London: The Women's Press, 1983)

Barker, Pat, *Blow your House Down* (London: Virago, 1984)

Butler, Octavia, *Kindred* (London: The Women's Press, 1988)

Carter, Angela, *The Magic Toyshop* (London: Virago, 1981)

Carter, Angela, *The Infernal Desire Machines of Doctor Hoffman* (Harmondsworth: Penguin, 1982)

Carter, Angela, *Nights at the Circus* (London: Picador, 1985)

Carter, Angela, *Wise Children* (London: Chatto and Windus, 1991)

Ellis, Alice Thomas, *Fairy Tale* (London: Viking, 1996)

Head, Bessie, *A Question of Power* (London: Heinemann, 1974)

Morrison, Toni, *Beloved* (London: Picador, 1988)

Palmer, Jane, *The Watcher* (London: The Women's Press, 1986)

Piercy, Marge, *Body of Glass* (Harmondsworth: Penguin, 1992)

Russ, Joanna, *The Female Man* (London: The Women's Press, 1985)

Weldon, Fay, *The Cloning of Joanna May* (London: Flamingo, 1993)

Winterson, Jeanette, *Sexing the Cherry* (London: Bloomsbury, 1989)

Winterson, Jeanette, *Written on the Body* (London: Jonathan Cape, 1992)

Wittig, Monique, *Les Guérillères*, trans. David Le Vay (Boston: Beacon Press, 1985)

Wittig, Monique, *Across the Acheron*, trans. David Le Vay in collaboration with Margaret Crosland (London: Peter Owen, 1987)

## Secondary Texts

Alexander, Flora, *Contemporary Women Novelists* (London: Edward Arnold, 1989)

Anderson, Linda (ed.), *Plotting Change: Contemporary Women's Fiction* (London: Edward Arnold, 1990)

Andriano, Joseph " *The Handmaid's Tale* as Scrabble Game", *Essays on Canadian Writing*, 48 (1992), 89–96

Armitt, Lucie (ed.), *Where No Man Has Gone Before: Women and Science Fiction* (London: Routledge, 1991)

Armitt, Lucie, *Theorising the Fantastic* (London: Arnold, 1996)

Armitt, Lucie, "Space, Time and Female Genealogies: A Kristevan Reading of Feminist Science Fiction", in Sarah Sceats and Gail Cunningham (eds), *Image and Power: Women in Fiction in the Twentieth Century* (London: Longman, 1996), 51–61

Armstrong, Isobel (ed.), *New Feminist Discourses: Critical Essays on Theories and Texts* (London: Routledge, 1992)

Ashcroft, Bill, Gareth Griffiths and Helen Tiffin (eds), *The Post-Colonial Studies Reader* (London: New York, 1995)

Auerbach, Nina, *Our Vampires, Ourselves* (Chicago: University of Chicago Press, 1995)

Bachelard, Gaston, *The Poetics of Space*, trans. Maria Jolas (Boston: Beacon Press, 1994)

Bakhtin, Mikhail, *The Dialogic Imagination: Four Essays by M.M. Bakhtin*, ed. Michael Holquist, trans. Caryl Emerson and Michael Holquist (Austin: University of Texas Press, 1981)

Bammer, Angelika, *Partial Visions: Feminism and Utopianism in the 1970s* (New York: Routledge, 1991)

Barnett, Pamela, "Figurations of Rape and the Supernatural in *Beloved*", in Carl Plasa (ed.), *Toni Morrison: Beloved* (Cambridge: Icon Books, 1998), 73–85

Barr, Marleen, *Alien to Femininity: Speculative Fiction and Feminist Theory* (Westport, CT: Greenwood Press, 1987)

Barthes, Roland, *The Pleasure of the Text*, trans. Richard Miller (Oxford: Basil Blackwell, 1990)

Bartkowski, Frances, *Feminist Utopias* (Lincoln: University of Nebraska Press, 1989)

Bayley, John, "Fighting for the Crown", *New York Review*, (23 April 1992), 9–11

Bernheimer, Charles and Claire Kahane (eds), *In Dora's Case: Freud, Hysteria, Feminism*, 2nd edn (New York: Columbia University Press, 1990)

Bettelheim, Bruno, *The Uses of Enchantment: The Meaning and Importance of Fairy Tales* (Harmondsworth: Penguin, 1991)

Bhabha, Homi K., "Signs Taken for Wonders", in Bill Ashcroft, Gareth Griffiths and Helen Tiffin (eds), *The Post-Colonial Studies Reader* (London: New York, 1995), 29–35

Billington, Michael, "The Reinvention of William Shakespeare: In Which All the World is a Pluralist's Stage, *World Press Review* ( July 1992), 24–5

Bjork, Patrick Bryce, *The Novels of Toni Morrison: The Search for Self and Place within the Community* (New York: Peter Lang, 1992)

Bloch, Ernst, *The Utopian Function of Art and Literature: Selected Essays*, trans. Jack Zipes and Frank Mecklenburg (Cambridge, Mass.: MIT Press, 1988)

Botting, Fred, *Gothic* (London: Routledge, 1996)

Bovenschen, Silvia, "Is There a Feminist Aesthetic?", in Gisela Ecker (ed.), *Feminist Aesthetics* (London: The Women's Press, 1985), 35–48

Bown, Nicola, "'There Are Fairies at the Bottom of Our Garden': Fairies, Fantasy and Photography", *Textual Practice*, 10: 1 (Spring 1996), 57–82

Bradfield, Scott, "Remembering Angela Carter", *The Review of Contemporary Fiction*, 4: 3 (Fall 1994), 90–3

Brée, Germaine, "Experimental Novels? Yes, but Perhaps 'Otherwise': Nathalie Sarraute, Monique Wittig", in Ellen G. Friedman and Miriam Fuchs (eds), *Breaking the Sequence: Women's Experimental Fiction* (Princeton: Princeton University Press, 1989); 267–83

Breen, Jennifer, *In Her Own Write: Twentieth-Century Women's Fiction* (London: Macmillan, 1990)

Bristow, Joseph and Trev Lynn Broughton (eds), *The Infernal Desires of Angela Carter* (London: Longman, 1997)

Britzolakis, Christina, "Angela Carter's Fetishism", in Joseph Bristow and Trev Lynn Broughton (eds), *The Infernal Desires of Angela Carter* (London: Longman, 1997), 43–58

Bronfen, Elisabeth, *Over Her Dead Body: Death, Femininity and the Aesthetic* (Manchester: Manchester University Press, 1992)

Burgin, Victor, James Donald and Cora Kaplan (eds), *Formations of Fantasy* (London: Routledge, 1986)

Burns, Christy L., "Powerful Differences: Critique and *Eros*" in Jeanette Winterson and Virginia Woolf, *Modern Fiction Studies*, 44: 2 (1998), 364–92

Byatt, A.S., "An American Masterpiece", in Carl Plasa (ed.), *Toni Morrison: Beloved* (Cambridge: Icon Books, 1998), 15–18

Campbell, June M., "Beyond Duality: A Buddhist Reading of Bessie Head's *A Question of Power*", *Journal of Commonwealth Literature*, 29: 1 (1993), 64–81

Carpenter, Lynette and Wendy K. Kolmar (eds), *Haunting the House of Fiction: Feminist Perspectives on Ghost Stories by American Women* (Knoxville: Tennessee University Press, 1991)

Carpentier, Alejo, "On the Marvelous Real in America", in Lois Parkinson Zamora and Wendy B. Faris (eds), *Magical Realism: Theory, History, Community* (Durham: Duke University Press, 1995), 75–88

Carpentier, Alejo, "The Baroque and the Marvelous Real", in Lois Parkinson Zamora and Wendy B. Faris (eds), *Magical Realism: Theory, History, Community* (Durham: Duke University Press, 1995), 89–108

Carter, Angela, *The Sadeian Woman: An Exercise in Cultural History* (London: Virago, 1990)

Castle, Terry, *The Apparitional Lesbian: Female Homosexuality and Modern Culture* (New York: Columbia University Press, 1993)

Cixous, Hélène, "The Laugh of the Medusa", trans. Keith Cohen and Paula Cohen, in Elaine Marks and Isabelle de Courtivron (eds), *New French Feminisms: An Anthology* (Brighton: Harvester, 1981), 245–64

Clark, Robert, "Angela Carter's Desire Machine", *Women's Studies*, 14 (1987), 147–61

Clayborough, Arthur, *The Grotesque in English Literature* (Oxford: Clarendon Press, 1967)

Coldsmith, Sherry, "He, She, and It", *Foundation*, 58 (1993), 108–15

Coser, Stelamaris, *Bridging the Americas: The Literature of Toni Morrison, Paule Marshall and Gayl Jones* (Philadelphia: Temple University Press, 1994)

Cornwell, Neil, *The Literary Fantastic: From Gothic to Postmodernism* (Hemel Hempstead: Harvester Wheatsheaf, 1990)

Coward, Rosalind, *Female Desire* (London: Paladin, 1984)

Coyle, William (ed.), *Aspects of Fantasy: Selected Essays from the Second International Conference on the Fantastic in Literature and Film* (Westport, CT: Greenwood Press, 1986)

Daly, Mary, *Gyn/Ecology: The Metaethics of Radical Feminism* (London: The Women's Press, 1979)

Debord, Guy, *The Society of the Spectacle* (New York: Zone Books, 1994)

Delbaere-Garant, Jeanne, "Psychic Realism, Mythic Realism, Grotesque Realism: Variations on Magic Realism in Contemporary Literature in English", in Lois

Parkinson Zamora and Wendy B. Faris (eds), *Magical Realism: Theory, History, Community* (Durham: Duke University Press, 1995), 249–63

De Weever, Jacqueline, *Mythmaking and Metaphor in Black Women's Fiction* (New York: St Martin's Press, 1991)

D'haen, Theo. L., "Magic Realism and Postmodernism: Decentering Privileged Centers", in Lois Parkinson Zamora and Wendy B. Faris (eds), *Magical Realism: Theory, History, Community* (Durham: Duke University Press, 1995), 191–208

Donawerth, Jane L. and Carol A. Kolmerten (eds), *Utopian and Science Fiction by Women: Worlds of Difference* (New York: Syracuse University Press, 1994)

Donawerth, Jane, *Frankenstein's Daughters: Women Writing Science Fiction* (New York: Syracuse University Press, 1997)

Duffy, Maureen, *The Erotic World of Faery* (London: Hodder and Stoughton, 1972)

Du Maurier, Daphne, *Rebecca* (London: Arrow Books, 1992)

DuPlessis, Rachel Blau, "The Feminist Apologues of Lessing, Piercy, and Russ", *Frontiers*, 4: 1 (1979), 1–8

During, Simon, "Postmodernism or Post-Colonialism Today", in Bill Ashcroft, Gareth Griffiths and Helen Tiffin (eds), *The Post-Colonial Studies Reader* (London: New York, 1995), 125–9

Dyman, Jenni, *Lurking Feminism: The Ghost Stories of Edith Wharton* (New York: Peter Lang, 1996)

Ecker, Gisela, (ed.), *Feminist Aesthetics* (London: The Women's Press, 1985)

Elliott, Robert C., *The Shape of Utopia: Studies in a Literary Genre* (Chicago: University of Chicago Press, 1970)

Ellis, Kate Ferguson, *The Contested Castle: Gothic Novels and the Subversion of Domestic Ideology* (Urbana: University of Illinois Press, 1989)

Evans Wentz, W.Y., *The Fairy Faith in Celtic Countries* (London: Oxford University Press, 1911)

Falzon, Alex. R "Interview: Angela Carter", *The European English Messenger*, 3: 1 (Spring 1994), 18–22

Faris, Wendy B., "Scheherazade's Children: Magical Realism and Postmodern Fiction", in Lois Parkinson Zamora and Wendy B. Faris (eds), *Magical Realism: Theory, History, Community* (Durham: Duke University Press, 1995), 163–90

Featherstone, Mike, Scott Lash and Roland Robertson (eds), *Global Modernities* (London: Sage, 1995)

Feldstein, Richard and Judith Roof (eds), *Feminism and Psychoanalysis* (Ithaca, NY: Cornell University Press, 1989)

Felski, Rita, *The Gender of Modernity* (Cambridge, Mass: Harvard University Press, 1995)

Ferguson, Rebecca, "History, Memory and Language in Toni Morrison's *Beloved*", in Susan Sellers (ed.), *Feminist Criticism: Theory and Practice* (Hemel Hempstead: Harvester Wheatsheaf, 1991), 109–27

Fernihough, Anne, "Is She Fact or Is She Fiction? Angela Carter and the Enigma of Woman", *Textual Practice*, 11: 1 (1997), 89–107

Ferns, Chris, "The Value/s of Dystopia: *The Handmaid's Tale* and the Anti-Utopian Tradition", *Dalhousie Review*, 69: 3 (1989), 373–82

Feuer, Lois, "The Calculus of Love and Nightmare: *The Handmaid's Tale* and the Dystopian Tradition", *Critique*, 38: 2 (1997), 83–95

Fiedler, Leslie, *Freaks: Myths and Images of the Secret Self* (New York: Simon and Schuster, 1978)

Filmer, Kath (ed.), *Twentieth-Century Fantasists: Essays on Culture, Society and Belief in Twentieth-Century Mythopoeic Literature* (London: Macmillan, 1992)

Foreman, P. Gabrielle, "Past-On Stories: History and the Magically Real, Morrison and Allende on Call", in Lois Parkinson Zamora and Wendy B. Faris (eds), *Magical Realism: Theory, History, Community* (Durham: Duke University Press, 1995), 285–303

Freud, Sigmund, *Case Histories I*, Penguin Freud Library, Vol. 8, ed. Angela Richards (Harmondsworth: Penguin, 1990)

Freud, Sigmund, *The Origins of Religion*, Penguin Freud Library, Vol. 13, ed. Albert Dickson (Harmondsworth: Penguin, 1990)

Freud, Sigmund *Art and Literature*, Penguin Freud Library, Vol. 14, ed. Albert Dickson (Harmondsworth: Penguin, 1990)

Freud, Sigmund and Joseph Breuer, *Studies on Hysteria*, Penguin Freud Library, Vol. 3, ed. Angela Richards (Harmondsworth: Penguin, 1991)

Friedman, Ellen G. and Miriam Fuchs (eds), *Breaking the Sequence: Women's Experimental Fiction* (Princeton: Princeton University Press, 1989)

Friedman, Jonathan, "Global System, Globalization and the Parameters of Modernity", in Mike Featherstone, Scott Lash and Roland Robertson (eds), *Global Modernities* (London: Sage, 1995), 69–85

Gallop, Jane, "The Monster in the Mirror: The Feminist Critic's Psychoanalysis", in Richard Feldstein and Judith Roof (eds), *Feminism and Psychoanalysis* (Ithaca, NY: Cornell University Press, 1989), 13–24

Gamble, Sarah, *Angela Carter: Writing from the Front Line* (Edinburgh: Edinburgh University Press, 1997)

Game, Ann, "Time, Space, Memory, with Reference to Bachelard" in Mike Featherstone, Scott Lash and Roland Robertson (eds), *Global Modernities* (London: Sage, 1995), 192–202

Garlick, Barbara, "*The Handmaid's Tale*: Narrative Voice and the Primacy of the Tale", in Kath Filmer (ed.), *Twentieth-Century Fantasists: Essays on Culture, Society and Belief in Twentieth-Century Mythopoeic Literature* (London: Macmillan, 1992), 161–71

Garner, Shirley Nelson, Claire Kahane and Madelon Sprengnether (eds), *The (M)other Tongue: Essays in Feminist Psychoanalytic Interpretation* (Ithaca, NY: Cornell University Press, 1985)

Gelder, Ken, *Reading the Vampire* (London: Routledge, 1994)

Gilbert, Sandra and Susan Gubar, *The Madwoman in the Attic: The Woman Writer and the Nineteenth-Century Literary Imagination* (New Haven: Yale University Press, 1984)

Giles, Dennis, "Conditions of Pleasure in Horror Cinema", in Barry Keith Grant (ed.), *Planks of Reason: Essays on the Horror Film* (Metuchen: Scarecrow Press, 1984), 38–52

Gilman, Sander, *The Jew's Body* (New York: Routledge, 1991)

Gilroy, Paul, "Living Memory: A Meeting with Toni Morrison", in Carl Plasa (ed.), *Toni Morrison:* Beloved (Cambridge, Icon Books, 1998), 35–8

Graham, Kenneth W. (ed.), *Gothic Fictions: Prohibition/Transgression* (New York: AMS Press, 1989)

Grant, Barry Keith (ed.), *Planks of Reason: Essays on the Horror Film* (Metuchen: Scarecrow Press, 1984)

Green, Michell Erica, "'There Goes the Neighborhood': Octavia Butler's Demand for Diversity in Utopias", in Jane L. Donawerth and Carol A. Kolmerten (eds),

*Utopian and Science Fiction by Women: Worlds of Difference* (New York: Syracuse University Press, 1994), 166–89

Greenwood, Gillian, "Flying Circus", *The Literary Review*, 76 (October 1984), 43

Grixti, Joseph, *Terrors of Uncertainty: The Cultural Contexts of Horror Fiction* (London: Routledge, 1989)

Haffenden, John, *Novelists in Interview* (London: Methuen, 1985)

Hansen, Elaine Tuttle, *Mother Without Child: Contemporary Fiction and the Crisis of Motherhood* (Berkeley: University of California Press, 1997)

Hanson, Clare, "'The Red Dawn Breaking Over Clapham': Carter and the Limits of Artifice", in Joseph Bristow and Trev Lynn Broughton (eds), *The Infernal Desires of Angela Carter* (London: Longman, 1997), 59–72

Haraway, Donna J., *Simians, Cyborgs and Women: The Reinvention of Nature* (London: Free Association Books, 1991)

Haraway, Donna J., *Modest_Witness@Second_Millennium.FemaleMan©_Meets_Onco Mouse*™: *Feminism and TechnoScience* (New York: Routledge, 1997)

Hartland, Edwin Sidney, *The Science of Fairy Tales* (London: Walter Scott, 1891)

Heinze, Denise, *The Dilemma of 'Double Consciousness': Toni Morrison's Novels* (Athens, Georgia: University of Georgia Press, 1993)

Hendershot, Cyndy, "Vampire and Replicant: The One-Sex Body in a Two-Sex World", *Science Fiction Studies*, 22 (1995), 373–98

Hertz, Neil, "Medusa's Head: Male Hysteria Under Political Pressure", *Representations*, 4 Fall (1983), 27–54

Hirsch, Marianne, *The Mother/Daughter Plot: Narrative, Psychoanalysis, Feminism* (Bloomington: Indiana University Press, 1989)

Hodges, Devon, "*Frankenstein* and the Feminine Subversion of the Novel", *Tulsa Studies in Women's Literature*, 2: 2 (Fall 1983), 155–64

Hoffmann, E.T.A., *Tales of Hoffmann*, trans. R.J. Hollingdale (Harmondsworth: Penguin, 1982)

Horner, Avril and Sue Zlosnik, *Daphne du Maurier: Writing, Identity and the Gothic Imagination* (London: Macmillan, 1997)

Horner, Avril and Sue Zlosnik, "Daphne du Maurier and Gothic Signatures: Rebecca as Vamp(ire)", unpublished manuscript forthcoming, in Avril Horner and Angela Keane (eds), *Body Matters: Feminism, Textuality, Corporeality* (Manchester: Manchester University Press)

Horovitz, Deborah, "Nameless Ghosts: Possession and Dispossession in *Beloved*", in Carl Plasa (ed.), *Toni Morrison: Beloved* (Cambridge: Icon Books, 1998), 59–66

House, Elizabeth B., "Toni Morrison's Ghost: The Beloved Who Is Not Beloved", in Carl Plasa (ed.), *Toni Morrison: Beloved* (Cambridge: Icon Books, 1998), 66–71

Hume, Kathryn, *Fantasy and Mimesis: Responses to Reality in Western Literature* (New York: Methuen, 1984)

Humm, Maggie, *Border Traffic: Strategies of Contemporary Women Writers* (Manchester: Manchester University Press, 1991)

Irigaray, Luce, *This Sex Which Is Not One*, trans. Catherine Porter and Carolyn Burke (Ithaca, NY: Cornell University Press, 1985)

Irigaray, Luce, "Sexual Difference", in Margaret Whitford, ed., *The Irigaray Reader* (Oxford: Basil Blackwell, 1991), 165–77

Isbister, J.N., *Freud: An Introduction to His Life and Work* (Cambridge: Polity Press, 1985)

Jackson, Rosemary, *Fantasy: The Literature of Subversion* (London: Methuen, 1981)

Jackson, Rosemary, "Narcissism and Beyond: A Psychoanalytic Reading of *Frankenstein* and Fantasies of the Double", in William Coyle (ed.), *Aspects of Fantasy: Selected Essays from the Second International Conference on the Fantastic in Literature and Film* (Westport, CT: Greenwood Press, 1986), 43–53

Jones, Ernest, *On the Nightmare* (New York: Liveright Books, 1951)

Jordan, Elaine, "Enthralment: Angela Carter's Speculative Fictions", in Linda Anderson (ed.), *Plotting Change: Contemporary Women's Fiction* (London: Edward Arnold, 1990), 18–40

Jordan, Elaine, "The Dangers of Angela Carter", in Isobel Armstrong (ed.), *New Feminist Discourses: Critical Essays on Theories and Texts* (London: Routledge, 1992), 119–31

Jump, Harriet Devine (ed.), *Diverse Voices: Essays on Twentieth-Century Women Writers in English* (Hemel Hempstead: Harvester Wheatsheaf, 1991)

Jump, Harriet Devine, "Margaret Atwood: Taking the Capital W off Woman", in Harriet Devine Jump (ed.), *Diverse Voices: Essays on Twentieth-Century Women Writers in English* (Hemel Hempstead: Harvester Wheatsheaf, 1991), 97–121

Kahane, Claire, "Gothic Mirrors and Feminine Identity", *The Centennial Review*, 24 (1980), 43–64

Kahane, Claire, *Passions of the Voice: Hysteria, Narrative, and the Figure of the Speaking Woman, 1850–1915* (Baltimore: Johns Hopkins University Press, 1995)

Kaler, Anne K., "'A Sister Dipped in Blood': Satiric Inversion of the Formation Techniques of Women Religious in Margaret Atwood's Novel *The Handmaid's Tale*", *Christianity and Literature*, 38: 2 (1989), 43–62

Komar, Kathleen L., "The Communal Self: Re-Membering Female Identity in the Works of Christa Wolf and Monique Wittig", *Comparative Literature*, 44 (1992), 42–58

Kristeva, Julia, *Powers of Horror: An Essay on Abjection* (New York: Columbia University Press, 1982)

Kumar, Krishan and Stephen Bann (eds), *Utopias and the Millennium* (London: Reaktion Books, 1993)

La Belle, Jenijoy, *Herself Beheld: The Literature of the Looking Glass* (Ithaca, NY: Cornell University Press, 1988)

Levitas, Ruth, *The Concept of Utopia* (New York: Syracuse University Press, 1990)

Linkon, Sherry Lee, "'A Way of Being Jewish That Is Mine': Gender and Ethnicity in the Jewish Novels of Marge Piercy", *Studies in American Jewish Literature*, 13 (1994), 93–105

Littlewood, Derek, "Uneasy Readings/Unspeakable Dialogics", in Derek Littlewood and Peter Stockwell (eds), *Impossibility Fiction: Alternativity, Extrapolation, Speculation* (Amsterdam: Rodopi, 1996), 191–207

Littlewood, Derek and Peter Stockwell (eds), *Impossibility Fiction: Alternativity, Extrapolation, Speculation* (Amsterdam: Rodopi, 1996)

Madoff, Mark S., "Inside, Outside and the Gothic Locked-Room Mystery", in Kenneth W. Graham (ed.), *Gothic Fictions: Prohibition/Transgression* (New York: AMS Press, 1989), 49–62

Magrs, Paul, "Boys Keep Swinging: Angela Carter and the Subject of Men", in Joseph Bristow and Trev Lynn Broughton (eds), *The Infernal Desires of Angela Carter* (London: Longman, 1997), 184–97

Mahoney, Elisabeth, "Writing So to Speak: The Feminist Dystopia", in Sarah Sceats and Gail Cunningham (eds), *Image and Power: Women in Fiction in the Twentieth Century* (London: Longman, 1996), 29–40

Manlove, Colin, "'In The Demythologising Business': Angela Carter's *The Infernal Desire Machines of Dr Hoffmann* [sic] (1972)", in Kath Filmer (ed.), *Twentieth-Century Fantasists: Essays on Culture, Society and Belief in Twentieth-Century Mythopoeic Literature* (London: Macmillan, 1992), 148–60

Marin, Louis, "The Frontiers of Utopia", in Kumar, Krishan and Stephen Bann (eds), *Utopias and the Millennium* (London: Reaktion Books, 1993), 7–15

Marks, Elaine and Isabelle de Courtivron (eds), *New French Feminisms: An Anthology* (Brighton: Harvester, 1981)

Meaney, Gerardine, *(Un)Like Subjects: Women, Theory, Fiction* (London: Routledge, 1993)

Mellor, Anne K., *Mary Shelley: Her Life, Her Fiction, Her Monsters* (New York: Routledge, 1989)

Mendilow, A. A., *Time and the Novel* (New York: Humanities Press, 1972)

Michael, Magali Cornier, *Feminism and the Postmodern Impulse: Post-World War II Fiction* (Albany: State University of New York Press, 1996)

Mills, Sara and Lynne Pearce, *Feminist Readings/Feminists Reading*, 2nd edn (Hemel Hempstead: Harvester Wheatsheaf, 1996)

Miner, Madonne, "'Trust Me': Reading the Romance Plot in Margaret Atwood's *The Handmaid's Tale*", *Twentieth-Century Literature*, 37: 2 (1991), 148–68

Moi, Toril, *Sexual/Textual Politics: Feminist Literary Theory* (London: Methuen, 1985)

Moretti, Franco, *Signs Taken for Wonders*, trans. Susan Fischer, David Forgacs and David Miller (London: Verso, 1983)

Morris, Adalaide, "First Persons Plural in Contemporary Feminist Fiction", *Tulsa Studies in Women's Literature*, 11 (1992), 11–29

Mulvey-Roberts, Marie (ed.), *The Handbook to Gothic Literature* (London: Macmillan, 1998)

Neumeier, Beate, "Postmodern Gothic: Desire and Reality in Angela Carter's Writing", in Victor Sage and Allan Lloyd Smith (eds), *Modern Gothic: A Reader* (Manchester: Manchester University Press, 1996), 141–51

O'Connor, Mary, "Chronotopes for Women under Capital: An Investigation into the Relation of Women to Objects", *Critical Studies*, 2: 1–2 (1990), 137–51

Palmer, Paulina, "From 'Coded Mannequin' to Bird Woman: Angela Carter's Magic Flight", in Sue Roe (ed.), *Women Reading Women's Writing* (Brighton: Harvester, 1987), 179–205

Palmer, Paulina, *Contemporary Women's Fiction: Narrative Practice and Feminist Theory* (Hemel Hempstead: Harvester Wheatsheaf, 1989)

Palumbo, Donald (ed.), *Erotic Universe: Sexuality and Fantastic Literature* (Westport, CT: Greenwood Press, 1986)

Parker, Patricia, *Literary Fat Ladies: Rhetoric, Gender, Property* (London: Methuen, 1987)

Peach, Linden, *Toni Morrison* (London: Macmillan, 1995)

Pearce, Lynne, *Reading Dialogics* (London: Edward Arnold, 1994)

Pearce, Lynne, *Feminism and the Politics of Reading* (London: Arnold, 1997)

Pearce, Lynne, "'Written on Tablets of Stone'?: Jeanette Winterson, Roland Barthes, and the Discourse of Romantic Love", in Suzanne Raitt (ed.), *Volcanoes and Pearl Divers: Essays in Lesbian Feminist Studies* (London: Onlywomen Press, 1995), 147–68

Piercy, Marge, *Woman on the Edge of Time* (London: The Women's Press, 1979)

Pieterse, Jan Nederveen, "Globalization as Hybridization", in Mike Featherstone, Scott Lash and Roland Robertson (eds), *Global Modernities* (London: Sage, 1995), 45–63

Plasa, Carl (ed.), *Toni Morrison: Beloved* (Cambridge: Icon Books, 1998)

Punter, David, "Angela Carter: Supersessions of the Masculine", *Critique: Studies in Contemporary Fiction*, 25: 4 (1984), 209–22

Radner, Joan Newlon (ed.), *Feminist Messages: Coding in Women's Folk Culture* (Urbana: University of Illinois Press, 1993)

Raitt, Suzanne (ed.), *Volcanoes and Pearl Divers: Essays in Lesbian Feminist Studies* (London: Onlywomen Press, 1995)

Richardson, Maurice, "The Psychoanalysis of Ghost Stories", *The Twentieth Century*, 166 (1959), 419–31

Rigney, Barbara Hill, *The Voices of Toni Morrison* (Columbus: Ohio State University Press, 1991)

Rigney, Barbara Hill, "'A Story to Pass On': Ghosts and the Significance of History in Toni Morrison's *Beloved*", in Lynette Carpenter and Wendy K. Kolmar (eds), *Haunting the House of Fiction: Feminist Perspectives on Ghost Stories by American Women* (Knoxville: Tennessee University Press, 1991), 229–35

Rimmon-Kenan, Shlomith, *Discourse in Psychoanalysis and Literature* (London: Methuen, 1987)

Roe, Sue (ed.), *Women Reading Women's Writing* (Brighton: Harvester, 1987)

Roe, Sue, Susan Sellers, Nicole Ward Jouve, with Michèle Roberts, *The Semitransparent Envelope: Women Writing – Feminism and Fiction* (London: Marion Boyars, 1994)

Roh, Franz, "Magic Realism: Post-Expressionism" in Lois Parkinson Zamora and Wendy B. Faris (eds), *Magical Realism: Theory, History, Community* (Durham: Duke University Press, 1995), 15–31

Rooney, Caroline, "Are We in the Company of Feminists? A Preface for Bessie Head and Ama Ata Aidoo", in Harriet Devine Jump (ed.), *Diverse Voices: Essays on Twentieth-Century Women Writers in English* (Hemel Hempstead: Harvester Wheatsheaf, 1991), 213–46

Rooney, Caroline, "'Dangerous Knowledge' and the Poetics of Survival: A Reading of *Our Sister Killjoy* and *A Question of Power*", in Susheila Nasta (ed.), *Black Women's Writing from Africa, the Caribbean and South Asia* (London: The Women's Press, 1991), 99–126

Rose, Jacqueline, *States of Fantasy* (Oxford: Clarendon, 1996)

Rowe, William and Vivian Schelling, *Memory and Modernity: Popular Culture in Latin America* (London: Verso, 1991)

Russ, Joanna, *To Write Like a Woman: Essays in Feminism and Science Fiction* (Bloomington: Indiana University Press, 1995)

Russo, Mary, *The Female Grotesque: Risk, Excess and Modernity* (New York: Routledge, 1994)

Ruthven, K.K., *Feminist Literary Studies: An Introduction* (Cambridge: Cambridge University Press, 1984)

Sage, Lorna, *Women in the House of Fiction: Post-War Women Novelists* (London: Macmillan, 1992)

Sage, Lorna, "Angela Carter", Interview, in Malcolm Bradbury and Judy Cooke (eds), *New Writing* (London: Minerva, 1992)

Sage, Lorna, *Angela Carter* (Plymouth: Northcote House, 1994)

Sage, Lorna (ed.), *Flesh and the Mirror: Essays on the Art of Angela Carter* (London: Virago, 1994)

Sage, Victor and Allan Lloyd Smith (eds), *Modern Gothic: A Reader* (Manchester: Manchester University Press, 1996)

Salvaggio, Ruth, "Octavia E. Butler", in Marleen Barr, Ruth Salvaggio, Richard Law, *Suzy McKee Charnas, Octavia Butler, Joan D. Vinge* (Washington: Starmont House, 1986)

Sargisson, Lucy, *Contemporary Feminist Utopianism* (London: Routledge, 1996)

Sceats, Sarah, "The Infernal Appetites of Angela Carter", in Joseph Bristow and Trev Lynn Broughton (eds), *The Infernal Desires of Angela Carter* (London: Longman, 1997), 100–15

Sceats, Sarah and Gail Cunningham (eds), *Image and Power: Women in Fiction in the Twentieth Century* (London: Longman, 1996)

Schectman, Jacqueline, *The Stepmother in Fairy Tales: Bereavement and the Feminine Shadow* (Boston: Sigo Press, 1993)

Schmidt, Ricarda, "The Journey of the Subject in Angela Carter's Fiction", *Textual Practice*, 3: 1 (Spring 1989), 56–76

Sears, John, *Angela Carter's Monstrous Women* (Sheffield: Pavic Publications, 1992)

Sellers, Susan (ed.), *Feminist Criticism: Theory and Practice* (Hemel Hempstead: Harvester Wheatsheaf, 1991)

Shaktini, Namascar, "Displacing the Phallic Subject: Wittig's Lesbian Writing", *Signs*, 8 (1982), 29–44

Shands, Kirstin W., *The Repair of the World: The Novels of Marge Piercy* (Westport, CT: Greenwood Press, 1994)

Shelley, Mary, *Frankenstein Or, The Modern Prometheus* (Harmondsworth: Penguin, 1985)

Showalter, Elaine, *The Female Malady: Women, Madness and English Culture, 1830–1980* (London: Virago, 1987)

Showalter, Elaine, *Sexual Anarchy: Gender and Culture at the* Fin-de-Siècle (London: Bloomsbury, 1991)

Sisk, David W., *Transformations of Language in Modern Dystopias* (Westport, CT: Greenwood Press, 1997)

Skura, Meredith Anne, *The Literary Use of the Psychoanalytic Process* (New Haven: Yale University Press, 1981)

Slemon, Simon, "Magic Realism as Postcolonial Discourse", in Lois Parkinson Zamora and Wendy B. Faris (eds), *Magical Realism: Theory, History, Community* (Durham: Duke University Press, 1995), 407–26

Spector, Judith, "Dr Jekyll and Mrs Hyde: Gender-Related Conflict in the Science Fiction of Joanna Russ", *Extrapolation*, 24 (1983), 370–9

Spence, Lewis, *The Fairy Tradition in Britain* (London: Rider and Company, 1948)

Spencer, Kathleen L., "Purity and Danger: *Dracula*, the Urban Gothic, and the Late Victorian Degeneracy Crisis", *ELH*, 59 (1992), 197–225

Stein, Karen F., "Margaret Atwood's *The Handmaid's Tale*: Scheherazade in Dystopia", *University of Toronto Quarterly*, 61: 2 Winter (1991–2), 269–79

Stein, Karen, "Margaret Atwood's Modest Proposal: *The Handmaid's Tale*", *Canadian Literature: A Quarterly of Criticism and Review*, 148 (Spring 1996), 57–73

Stewart, Susan, *On Longing: Narratives of the Miniature, the Gigantic, the Souvenir, the Collection* (Durham: Duke University Press, 1993)

Stokes, John (ed.), *Fin de Siècle/Fin du Globe: Fears and Fantasies of the Late Nineteenth Century* (London; Macmillan, 1992)

Strathern, Marilyn, *Reproducing the Future: Anthropology, Kinship and the New Reproductive Technologies* (Manchester: Manchester University Press, 1992)

Suleiman, Susan Rubin, "Writing and Motherhood", in Shirley Nelson Garner, Claire Kahane and Madelon Sprengnether (eds), *The (M)other Tongue: Essays in Feminist Psychoanalytic Interpretation* (Ithaca, NY: Cornell University Press, 1985), 352–77

Suleiman, Susan Rubin, "The Fate of the Surrealist Imagination in the Society of the Spectacle", in Lorna Sage (ed.), *Flesh and the Mirror: Essays on the Art of Angela Carter* (London: Virago, 1994), 98–116

Theweleit, Klaus, *Male Fantasies, Vol. 1: Women, Floods, Bodies, History*, trans. Stephen Conway, Erica Carter and Chris Turner (Cambridge: Polity Press, 1987)

Thiem, Jon, "The Textualization of the Reader in Magical Realist Fiction", in Lois Parkinson Zamora and Wendy B. Faris (eds), *Magical Realism: Theory, History, Community* (Durham: Duke University Press, 1995), 235–47

Todorov, Tzvetan, *The Fantastic: A Structural Approach to a Literary Genre*, trans. Richard Howard (Ithaca, NY: Cornell University Press, 1975)

Tomc, Sandra, "'The Missionary Position': Feminism and Nationalism in Margaret Atwood's *The Handmaid's Tale*", *Canadian Literature*, 138–9 (Fall 1993), 73–87

Tucker, Lindsey, *Textual Escap(e)ades: Mobility, Maternity, and Textuality in Contemporary Fiction by Women* (Westport, CT: Greenwood, 1994)

Turner, Chris and Erica Carter, "Political Somatics: Notes on Klaus Theweleit's *Male Fantasies*", in Victor Burgin, James Donald and Cora Kaplan (eds), *Formations of Fantasy* (London: Routledge, 1986) 203

Turner, Rory, "Subjects and Symbols: Transformations of Identity in *Nights at the Circus*", *Folklore Forum*, 20: 1 (1987), 39–60

Twitchell, James B., *Dreadful Pleasures: An Anatomy of Modern Horror* (New York: Oxford University Press, 1985)

Vargas, Virginia, "The Feminist Movement in Latin America: Between Hope and Disenchantment", *Development and Change*, 23: 3 (July 1992), 195–214

Waelti-Walters, Jennifer, *Fairy Tales and the Female Imagination* (Montreal: Eden Press, 1982)

Walker, Nancy A., *Feminist Alternatives: Irony and Fantasy in the Contemporary Novel by Women* (Jackson: University Press of Mississippi, 1990)

Ward Jouve, Nicole, *The Street Cleaner: The Yorkshire Ripper Case on Trial* (London: Marion Boyars, 1986)

Ward Jouve, Nicole, *Female Genesis: Creativity, Self and Gender* (New York: St Martin's Press, 1998)

Webb, Kate, "Seriously Funny: *Wise Children*", in Joseph Bristow and Trev Lynn Broughton (eds), *The Infernal Desires of Angela Carter* (London: Longman, 1997), 279–307

Weissberg, Liliane, "Gothic Spaces: The Political Aesthetics of Toni Morrison's *Beloved*", in Victor Sage and Allan Lloyd Smith (eds), *Modern Gothic: A Reader* (Manchester: Manchester University Press, 1996), 104–20

White, Allon, "Pigs and Pierrots: The Politics of Transgression in Modern Fiction", *Raritan*, 2: 2 (Fall 1981), 51–70

Whitford, Margaret (ed.), *The Irigaray Reader* (Oxford: Basil Blackwell, 1991)

Williams, Linda Ruth, *Critical Desire: Psychoanalysis and the Literary Subject* (London: Edward Arnold, 1995)

Wilson, Rawdon, "The Metamorphoses of Fictional Space: Magical Realism", in Lois Parkinson Zamora and Wendy B. Faris (eds), *Magical Realism: Theory, History, Community* (Durham: Duke University Press, 1995), 209–33

Wittig, Monique, "One Is Not Born a Woman", *Feminist Issues*, 1: 2 (1981), 47–54

Wolf, Naomi, *The Beauty Myth* (London: Chatto and Windus, 1990)

Wolmark, Jenny, *Aliens and Others: Science Fiction, Feminism and Postmodernism* (Hemel Hempstead: Harvester Wheatsheaf, 1993)

Woolf, Virginia, *A Room of One's Own* (London: Grafton, 1977)

Wright, Elizabeth (ed.), *Feminism and Psychoanalysis: A Critical Dictionary* (Oxford: Basil Blackwell, 1992)

Yocom, Margaret R., "'Awful Real': Dolls and Development in Rangeley, Maine", in Joan Newlon Radner (ed.), *Feminist Messages: Coding in Women's Folk Culture* (Urbana: University of Illinois Press, 1993), 126–54

Zamora, Lois Parkinson, "Magical Romance/Magical Realism: Ghosts in US and Latin American Fiction" in Lois Parkinson Zamora and Wendy B. Faris (eds), *Magical Realism: Theory, History, Community* (Durham: Duke University Press, 1995), 497–550

Zamora, Lois Parkinson and Wendy B. Faris (eds), *Magical Realism: Theory, History, Community* (Durham: Duke University Press, 1995)

Zanger, Jules, "A Sympathetic Vibration: Dracula and the Jews", *English Literature in Transition, 1880–1920*, 34 (1991), 33–44

Zukin, Sharon, *Landscapes of Power: From Detroit to Disney World* (Berkeley: University of California Press, 1991)

# Index